INTEREST

on the

River

ALSO BY CLARE CHASE

Murder on the Marshes

Death
on the
River

CLARE CHASE

Bookouture

Published by Bookouture in 2018

An imprint of StoryFire Ltd.
Carmelite House
50 Victoria Embankment
London EC4Y 0DZ

www.bookouture.com

ISBN: 978-1-78681-740-2
eBook ISBN: 978-1-78681-739-6

To Margaret, with thanks for everything; from giving the kids a love of piano to generously sharing your expert knowledge of the Fens. Any mistakes I've made in this book are my own.

PROLOGUE

Agneta Larsson watched an eel slide off the dead man's arm as the police divers removed his body from the car he'd been driving. The classic Alfa Romeo was still partially submerged in the waters of the Forty Foot Drain, dark and swirling where the team worked. Agneta stood at the top of the bank, clothed in her white overalls. She'd observe for now, then move down by the water once the body was pulled clear to give her first impressions. She wouldn't be sorry to get back to the mortuary at Addenbrooke's, though. It might be where she cut up cadavers, but there was something far eerier about the Fens.

The Forty Foot Drain itself was notorious; countless drivers landed themselves in it having come off the raised road that ran along its bank. Problems were more common in winter, when the weather was bad. But last night had been a warm autumn evening. The accident investigators would be working overtime to try to find out what had happened. Of course, the body might provide the answer: a heart attack at the wheel, or too much to drink, leading to a mistake with catastrophic consequences.

Larsson shivered in the morning air and looked out over the landscape. All that black soil, and the endless sky. Flat land, lonely and bleak, as far as the eye could see. Today, the heavens were almost indigo, and rain fell in thick droplets, the weather finally breaking after a two-week Indian summer. The birds were absolutely silent. It was as though everything had paused, holding its breath.

And then, at last, the first hint of thunder came; a low, angry rumble, threatening something more. Above it, she could hear the voice of Detective Sergeant Patrick Wilkins, making light of the scene in front of him. She knew it was a defence mechanism, but there were ways and ways of dealing with death. And now he and Detective Constable Max Dimity seemed to be arguing. She zoned out. Wilkins made her feel argumentative too, but this wasn't the time or the place.

It wasn't long before they were ready for her to take a closer look. She made her way down towards the water, edging forwards, her weight on the balls of her feet to avoid slipping on the wet grass.

The dead man was dressed in a white linen shirt and well-cut casual trousers. The saturation of his clothes meant Agneta could see the shape of his body underneath; the slight thickening of his waist, the lack of firm definition around his ribcage. The smell of the water weeds rose off him.

His head was bruised – probably where it had hit the steering wheel as he'd crashed. But it was his right hand and arm that surprised her. They bore multiple bruises too, and not the sort she'd expect from the impact of his car hitting the water.

She thought for a moment about the road, at the top of the bank. There had been no skid marks – no sign that the driver had made any attempt to avoid his fate. That suggested he might have passed out at the wheel – have fallen asleep perhaps, or simply been too drunk to display the normal reactions.

But the bruises suggested otherwise. They spoke of wild flailing limbs. His left hand and arm wouldn't have connected with much, but his right would have hit against the partially lowered driver's side window and the car's frame.

The drowned man had thrashed around before he died.

If he'd suffered from seizures, that might explain the circumstances, but then why would he have been driving? Unbridled fear up on the road would explain the bruising – and the fact that he hadn't braked. But what could have caused such a reaction?

She sighed. It was pointless speculating. She needed to cut him open and let the physical evidence speak for itself.

CHAPTER ONE

Late November, Cambridge

There was something about the face of the woman at Tara's front door that made her hesitate before opening up. Spyholes always gave a distorted view, and the effect was accentuated in this instance. The woman's face was right up close, as though she thought she could somehow see Tara there on the other side. Tara knew damn well that she couldn't, but still something inside her stomach curdled. She'd had the spyhole installed four years earlier, before she'd left Cambridge to train as a police officer, after she'd received a death threat. Her cottage was isolated; her only neighbours were swans, ducks and cattle.

The woman had wild, dark hair, streaked with strands the colour of storm clouds. It blew sideways across her face in the fierce wind outside on Stourbridge Common. Her eyes were a piercing grey. Whoever she was, she looked pretty damned keen to come in. She battered at the door again as Tara turned the key in its mortise lock and pulled it ajar until it snagged on its chain.

The woman reached a thin arm through the gap, her wrist sinewy, the joints in her hand rather swollen. 'Tara Thorpe?' she said. 'My name is Dr Monica Cairncross. I want to talk to you about the death of my brother.'

Tara accepted her ice-cold hand and shook it, but kept the chain on the door. 'I'm not on duty at the moment. You'd better go to the police station, over on Parkside. They'll be able to help you.' *How the hell has this woman managed to find my house?* But

Tara guessed the answer to that before she'd finished having the thought. Her return to Cambridge as a detective constable had been covered in the press.

'It's you I wanted to speak to,' the woman said, almost shouting against the gale. 'There was an article about you in *Not Now* magazine. I found a copy in the lounge of the hotel where I'm staying.'

It was as she'd thought. Once again, Tara cursed Giles, the editor of *Not Now*. The headline he'd used had been '*Victim joins the Force that saved her*'. Victim. He knew she'd hate that label. But there was no love lost between her and Giles. The piece had even included a photograph of her house, leaving her wide open to any weirdo who felt like tracking her down. Her place was easy to spot – an isolated cottage on a bit of no-man's land in the centre of the common.

'The article said you used to be one of *Not Now*'s journalists,' Monica Cairncross said, 'and that you'd trained to be a police officer after you were almost killed.'

Tara didn't need to be reminded; she knew the piece almost word for word. It had implied that her cavalier attitude whilst researching a story about a murder victim, Samantha Seabrook, had led her into danger. Anyone reading the piece would believe she'd caused the police who rescued her a whole lot of bother because of her own arrogance. It had also raked over her past; something she'd rather not have highlighted – particularly to any of her new colleagues who didn't yet know the story.

'If you're thinking I'm judging you on what I read, you're right,' Monica Cairncross said, leaning forward, hard up against the door, her grey eyes intense. 'It's those details that made me single you out. It was clear to me that you were determined to get to the truth, even if it meant bypassing the official channels. And using unorthodox methods. And yet now you've joined the police force yourself. It made me think you'd understand my concerns and see the matter from both sides. You're not one to take things at face value.'

'Concerns?'

The woman nodded. 'My brother – the author, Ralph Cairncross – was found drowned in the Forty Foot Drain in September.' She pronounced his name 'Rafe'. 'His vehicle had come off the road. As far as anyone knows, he was alone. I don't believe it was an accident.'

For a second the name distracted Tara. She knew it – and had heard of the man's death too – without remembering the precise circumstances. But within a moment she was back in the here and now. The freezing winter air rushed round the door; Tara's house was badly insulated, as she knew, now that she was finally occupying the place in winter. It would take hours to get it warm again.

'The best thing would be to go to the investigating officer who worked on your brother's case.'

'I contacted the man at the time.' Her dry lips were pursed. 'It was a Detective Sergeant Wilkins. He didn't take me seriously. I met with him when I flew back to the UK for Ralph's funeral. I had to return to New Zealand almost immediately to complete my visiting scholarship there but I've been doing my best to make headway with him ever since. As he wasn't helpful when I stood opposite him at the police station, you can imagine he was even less so when I tried to get a response remotely.'

Patrick Wilkins. Tara's new boss and a patronising idiot. She'd been trying to give him a chance; it hadn't worked.

'Contacting me behind DS Wilkins' back isn't likely to help your cause,' Tara said. She was leaning forwards too now, so that the woman could hear her above the wind. The whole thing was getting faintly ridiculous. 'You'd be best off approaching him again now that you're around to do that in person. If you don't get anywhere, you could take your complaint to his superior, Detective Inspector Blake.'

Blake. The man who'd helped save her life. And who at one point she'd thought was going to ask her out… but who was now back with his wife and their young daughter. The dynamics of her new working environment promised to be complicated. When she'd moved away from Cambridge to train as a police officer, she'd never imagined having to work directly with him or Wilkins. But personal reasons had brought her back. Bea, her mother's cousin, who'd all but brought her up, had just lost her husband. Now she was struggling to run their boarding house on her own. Bea had been there for Tara when she'd needed her. It was more than time to return the favour.

Monica Cairncross's tone didn't change. 'I've no desire to speak to DS Wilkins again.'

In fairness, that was relatable.

The woman met Tara's gaze once more. Her stare was reptilian. 'Ralph's "accident" wasn't the first. Please can I come in and talk to you?'

DS Wilkins was in hot pursuit of promotion to detective inspector. Digging her nose into a case that he'd already investigated to his satisfaction would go down about as well as pâté de foie gras at a vegan picnic. It made the prospect more appealing, but all the same, Tara wasn't sure about Monica Cairncross.

The woman seemed to sense her scepticism. 'When I read more about your background I saw you'd been let down by the police when you were a teenager, too,' she said. 'You gave them evidence when you were stalked, and they ignored it. They missed catching the person who'd been tormenting you, and they're still out there.' For a second she looked over her shoulder, out towards the dark common. When she turned back again her face was just inches from Tara's. 'You know first-hand how much can slip through the net because officers have closed their minds or taken shortcuts.'

Tara rubbed her fingers together to try to keep some feeling in them. 'All right,' she said, and took the chain off the door, letting Dr Cairncross in as quickly as possible now, so that she could shut out the bitter winter night.

She took the woman through to her kitchen. She didn't want to extend her visit, but she needed a drink to warm herself up. 'Can I get you a coffee or a hot chocolate?'

'Something stronger, if you have it,' Dr Cairncross said, pulling out a chair at the table.

'I haven't.' It was a lie, but there were limits. She might be a public servant, but this wasn't a bar.

'In that case nothing. Thank you.'

Tara made herself a hot chocolate and sat down opposite the woman. 'You'd better tell me everything.' It would be the quickest way of getting her house back, but in truth, there was something compelling about Monica Cairncross too.

'The week before he drove off the road, on a clear, calm, September night,' she paused, presumably to make sure Tara had got the point, 'he was nearly killed by electrocution.'

Tara found herself pulling a notebook and pen from her jeans pocket. She'd got changed the moment she'd come in from work. She'd enjoyed being able to wear more stylish clothes since she'd moved into CID, but at home her outfits were restricted by the temperatures in her cottage. It was back to an unvaried uniform: this time of jeans 'teamed' with an assortment of warm jumpers. 'What happened?'

'He put on a lamp in his garage – an old one, but one that he used quite regularly – and got an almighty shock from it. Jolted him across the room, apparently. I believe it had been tampered with. Why hadn't he had any trouble with it before, otherwise? He mentioned it to me in an email and I told him to watch out. He took no notice, and by the end of the following week he was dead. He was an assured driver, and he knew the road well. Some of the banks out in the Fens are far narrower than the Forty Foot.'

'What makes you think someone would have wanted to harm him?'

'He created waves, Constable Thorpe. He lived an unconventional life; the sort that would make him a target. But although he was a public figure, my mind always ran closer to home when I thought of those most likely to do him harm. My sister-in-law, or their daughter.'

Their family parties must be fun. 'Do you have any evidence for that?'

'I heard my niece say she wished he were dead.'

That wasn't what Tara would call evidence. She'd heard plenty of other kids shout similar abuse at their parents. It didn't mean they were about to act on the matter. 'I presume you mentioned the lamp incident to DS Wilkins?'

She nodded. 'Of course.'

'And what did he say?'

'He mumbled about faulty wiring and said that it wasn't uncommon for "the bereaved" to look for someone to blame.' Her mouth was tight. 'It's the first I've heard of a detective being qualified to psychoanalyse people. I didn't appreciate his efforts. And I had the impression his point about the wiring was based on supposition rather than fact. He wouldn't confirm that he'd checked.'

Tara could imagine that. He probably hadn't. 'And did you ever contact Patrick Wilkins' boss, DI Blake?'

Monica Cairncross shook her head. 'I decided you'd be the best person to talk to next. I'm staying locally until everything is sorted out to my satisfaction.'

Tara could have done without the favour. She just wanted to go out in the morning, do her job, and then retreat inside her cottage. And for everyone else to back off. All the same, it was a novelty to find someone who wanted to talk to her in preference to an older – or more male – colleague.

She sighed. 'Where was your brother travelling, the night he died?'

The woman nodded, as though Tara had given in, and her cooperation had never seriously been in doubt. 'He was on his way back from a social gathering made up of a group of young academics and free-thinkers,' she said. 'They were all his fans – his entourage, if you like. He called them the "Acolytes". They'd gathered at a house Ralph owned, out in the Fens. He'd travelled there earlier on – in the late afternoon – from his place on Madingley Road.' A moneyed, leafy main route into Cambridge, full of large detached houses, set well back from the street. 'He left my sister-in-law and niece at home.'

It was time to bring the woman back to reality again. 'And how do you think someone could have engineered the accident?' Tara asked.

'Perhaps they tampered with the car, just as they did with the lamp.' She held up a hand. 'I know the authorities checked for mechanical faults after the accident, but they might have missed something. People do make mistakes. And if not that, then maybe someone put something in the road, to distract Ralph.'

Except this unknown person couldn't have banked on Ralph being the first person to happen upon the 'distraction' – not unless they'd been very precise with their timing. And then they'd have had to come and take whatever it was away again afterwards. As murder methods went, it would probably score two out of ten for reliability, and a lot higher when it came to the probability of getting found out.

Monica Cairncross ignored her silence. 'Or someone could have called him and distracted him deliberately.'

'His mobile records would have shown that. It would have been cited as a possible reason for the accident. Even if it hadn't been deliberate, calls are often associated with people losing concentration. Did you ask DS Wilkins if your brother's phone records had been checked?'

After a moment, Dr Cairncross nodded. 'He said nothing showed up for the time he was driving. But all the same…'

Tara was loath to agree, even tentatively, with DS Wilkins, but it was possible that in this case he was right about Monica Cairncross's theories.

'Whatever your initial reactions are, I would like you to prove yourself better than your colleagues by casting your eyes over the records for the case,' the woman said. 'See if anything strikes you as off. It won't take a moment. You can reach me at the University Arms Hotel with your conclusions.'

Easy for her to say. Tara got up from her seat. 'I can't promise anything,' she said, standing over her visitor. 'But if I hear of something that makes me feel there's more to discover, I will let you know.' She paused. 'Your brother's car accident following on so closely from the incident with the lamp might have been a genuine coincidence. They're not as uncommon as you'd think.'

Monica Cairncross gave her that cold-eyed stare again. 'It wasn't,' she said.

The woman was still sitting down, looking up at her. Tara was on the point of spelling out that it was time to leave when she got to her feet.

They walked through to the square hallway. Just before she left, Dr Cairncross's eyes lit on a supply of Tara's business cards, sitting on the hall table.

'I'll take one of those, if I may.'

There wasn't much Tara could do about it.

It was raining now, as well as dark. Across the common, the lights that ran along the path by the River Cam gave a pale glow, made more diffuse by the icy drizzle. Tara's own porch light lit the tiny front garden but no further. Between the two was the floodplain: an expanse of dark space, dotted with patches where the shadows intensified. Leafless willows and London plane trees thrashed in the wind. The rough, narrow path that would lead Monica Cairncross back towards civilisation was unlit. Tara had been relying on a bike light or her phone to illuminate her journeys.

'It's an unusual place to live,' Dr Cairncross said, stepping half out of the doorway and fumbling with a black umbrella she'd pulled from her bag. For a second she paused. 'I'll wait to hear from you, then.'

Tara watched for a moment as the woman started out, struggling with her brolly as the wind threatened to turn it inside out. She doubted there'd be much to tell, but she couldn't bring herself to reiterate the fact before the woman left. It was well and truly time for a vodka and tonic, not for prolonged efforts to manage expectations.

She shut her door against the blast, but the wind whistled round the jamb and the keyhole cover rattled.

Ten minutes later, she was the right side of her drink, finishing a packet of pistachios and cooking a bolognaise. She felt almost human. There were so many maintenance jobs she needed to do around the house, but they'd have to wait. The place had been standing for 150 years, she was sure it could cope on its own for a few more months. When she'd got the money, the doors and windows would be the first priority; the al fresco atmosphere was a bit much in midwinter. And then maybe some insulation. In one corner of the kitchen, condensation ran down the wall thanks to its icy inner surface.

She put a bottle of red wine in some hot water in the sink to warm it up, then added some tomato purée to her bolognaise sauce.

She was just about to put the pasta on when her work mobile rang. The number calling wasn't familiar and for a second she thought about shunting whoever it was through to voicemail. But the pasta wasn't actually cooking yet…

She picked up. 'Tara Thorpe.'

'It's Monica Cairncross.' She sounded breathless, and spoke quickly. The contrast to the cool, insistent tone of earlier made Tara put down the wooden spoon she'd been about to use to stir the bolognaise.

'What can I do for you, Dr Cairncross?'

'I've only just got back to the hotel,' she said. *'I didn't want to call you until I was inside. Something's happened that confirms my feelings about Ralph's death.'*

Tara waited.

'Someone was watching me.'

'Watching you when?'

'As I left your house. I was halfway back towards Riverside when I saw a shadow in the distance, near the base of that narrow bridge that goes across the river.'

The Green Dragon Bridge. Tara made a noise but Dr Cairncross cut across her.

'The moment I turned in their direction they dodged out of sight. They didn't want to be identified. I'm not imagining it. Someone knows what I'm up to – and they want to ensure I don't make any headway.'

Whether Monica Cairncross was mistaken or not, Tara knew fear when she heard it. And she was quite sure it wasn't something that the woman was used to experiencing.

After they'd finished talking she went to switch off the kitchen light, then walked over to the room's side window. It looked out towards the river. Drawing back the thin, checked curtains, she could see the bridge straight ahead, and to her right the route towards Fen Ditton.

The base of the bridge was shrouded in shadow, but everything looked still. Tara closed the curtain again, switched the light back on and shivered as she put the pasta on to boil.

Had there really been someone out there?

Over her supper she decided to google Monica Cairncross. And maybe download one of her brother's books, too. She needed to know more about who she was dealing with.

Wednesday 28 November

I watched Monica today. She doesn't know anything, of course. I'm not even sure why she's so convinced there's something amiss. Inbuilt arrogance, I suppose, in relation to herself and her dead brother. She can't imagine he could ever have been at fault, therefore his death can't have been an accident. Oh, but it was, Monica – it was. My making it all possible doesn't alter that. I was just testing him, to see if he was ready to embrace death. From the reports of his injuries, I think I can safely say that he wasn't. There was no calm acceptance. So satisfying to know. The pathologist spoke of flailing limbs – put down to some kind of fit. Very convenient. But if Ralph had been as invincible as he thought, he could easily have survived. I just twisted the dial of fate.

And as for him being faultless, there never was a more flawed man. He was a sexual predator and a hypocrite, responsible for so much misery, and for spreading a taint that must be stopped.

When it comes to Monica, she makes me laugh. Genuinely. She looks so frightening – shockingly witch-like – and the more bombastic and unreasonable she is, the more she plays into my hands. She's meant to be clever, but clearly her emotional quotient is down through the floor. She's been sniffing around everyone who was involved with Ralph, and it seems she's put the authorities' backs up, which is perfect. And now, I see she's resorted to pestering a new recruit to the local CID – a former journalist according to my research. And she hunted this woman down in her own home. I can't imagine that will go down well if the officer who first investigated the death finds out.

What about that ex-journalist though? Will curiosity get the better of her? I'm sure it will. But even journalists need facts, unless they work for the gutter press. This one's reputation was dodgy when it came to method, but sound when it came to quality. She'll want facts.

And that's the beauty of it, Tara Thorpe – they will be very hard to come by. Hints, yes. What the police might call 'circumstantial evidence', and oh-so-flimsy at that. Because I'm many steps ahead of you, Tara.

But if you get too close, I know what to do.

I can't say I'm worried.

CHAPTER TWO

'Do I remember her?' DS Wilkins rolled his eyes. 'She's pretty hard to forget and it was only a couple of months or so back. She was ranting. I took her to be completely unhinged and she looked the part too – all that wild hair.'

Tara took a deep breath. Did her boss seriously believe you could tell whether a person was talking sense by the conventionality – or otherwise – of their hairstyle?

'If she's been on at you too, I imagine you'll have made the same assessment.' Wilkins stretched in his seat. It was something he did a lot after he'd taken off his jacket. Tara was convinced the move was deliberate: engineered to show off the muscles he'd been honing at the gym. Did he also buy shirts that were ever so slightly too small to increase the effect?

'Was she after me?' he asked. 'Is that why you ended up having to deal with her?'

'I think she'd shifted her attention to me because she'd already tried you.' Tara wasn't going to tell him that she'd seen Monica Cairncross outside work. And she especially wasn't going to admit she'd met her in her own home. 'I realise she's probably annoyed you by being so persistent, but I assume there was nothing that struck you as off-key about Ralph Cairncross's death?'

Wilkins looked at her. 'You think I'd have left it uninvestigated if there were?'

It all depended on how big a thing they were talking about. Tara was willing to believe he'd ignore a reasonable-sized detail if the balance of probabilities told him it wasn't relevant. He wasn't a man to question his own judgement. 'No, of course not.' She met his eye as she lied. 'But given that she's come asking again, I promised I'd check. I need to be able to tell her that I have.'

'And you think that'll shut her up? Well, good luck with that. She's obsessed.' He closed his eyes for a moment. 'God, I hate dealing with that sort of woman.'

Tara gritted her teeth. She wanted to tell DS Wilkins that women were all individuals, not grouped into stereotypes. She'd never met anyone like Dr Cairncross before, yet her boss had immediately pigeonholed her. She could imagine what he'd filed the dead man's sister under. Wilkins had a particular way of dealing with women. If they accepted him in the role of teacher, protector and advisor, he was perfectly happy. Step outside that dynamic – dare to start asking questions – and you were in trouble. Tara had asked several during her first week. She hadn't been criticising him; just wondering why he'd handled certain things the way he had. And rather than explaining so she understood, he'd taken offence. Not openly – that would have been fine. Tara was quite capable of dealing with confrontation. But with Wilkins, you could just see the resentment, simmering beneath the surface.

Every so often, she caught DI Blake watching them both with his dark, brooding eyes. He was probably wondering how long it would take for one of them to blow.

Tara had had to be self-controlled as a journalist – willing to hide whatever she felt about her subjects in order to get the maximum out of them. She could make the most despicable person feel she was on their side if it served her purposes. But it was different with Wilkins. With her interviewees, she'd only had to keep up the pretence for an hour or so. After one week with the DS, she realised just how much harder it was going to be to hide her real feelings towards him.

'But to satisfy your needs,' Wilkins went on, 'you can take it from me, there was nothing to indicate that the death was anything more than an accident.' He turned away and started sifting through some papers on his desk.

He wasn't planning to share the details, clearly, but Tara stayed where she was, standing close to his workstation.

'Dr Cairncross mentioned the close call her brother had the week before he died, when he got a shock off a lamp in the family's garage.'

Wilkins let out a sharp sigh. 'Yes. By all accounts the lamp was something of an antique. It had belonged to Ralph Cairncross's father and had been sitting there getting knocked around in the garage for years. His wife had already suggested he get rid of it – she was worried about the wiring – but she told us her husband didn't like people fussing. Suggesting he did something sensible pretty much ensured he wouldn't, I understand. All the same, he gave in after he got the electric shock. By the time we enquired, the item had been junked. Cambridge is full of people with hand-me-downs like that.'

Which was a fair point; and especially true of those who lived in large houses and had enough space to simply add to their belongings without having to throw stuff out. Things could hang around for generations.

Suddenly DS Wilkins stood up, forcing her to move back, away from his desk. He laughed. 'You can so tell you used to be a journalist. You're scenting a story, not a case to be answered. We need more than a whiff of scandal and intrigue here. We're spending taxpayers' money, don't forget, and there's precious little of it to go round. So, I'd appreciate it if you turned that gossip-hungry mind of yours back towards what you actually should be working on: the Hunter case. I want you to check his phone records against those for the five pay-as-you-go mobiles Davies had. If we find any numbers in common, we might be in business. Get to it. The DI wants our full attention on this.'

Tara had only been there for four weeks, and she'd never given anything less than that, as Wilkins must be well aware. With effort, she resisted the impulse to give him what he wanted: a sharp retort he could complain about later.

She conjured up an innocent look instead, coupled with an earnest nod as she stepped back towards her desk. 'Understood.' *And up yours, Wilkins. Up yours.* She slid into her chair and opened the relevant file on her computer. For a second, he stood staring at her, but then seemed to abandon trying to work out if she was being sarcastic. He turned back to his own desk and appeared to forget all about her. *Happy days.*

Later on, when Wilkins went to lunch, Tara carried out her plan to raid the files on Ralph Cairncross. She was entitled to a break too, and if her boss wasn't going to give her the proper background she'd use her free time to satisfy her curiosity. That and fulfil her duty to Monica Cairncross. The woman wanted a second eye on the evidence, not just to hear Wilkins' initial findings repeated back to her.

Tara was halfway down one witness statement, frowning and absorbed, when something – a small noise? – pulled her out of what she was reading. Looking behind her, she realised that Wilkins had re-entered the room and was staring at her computer screen. His jaw was jutting, his eyes dark. If she'd met him in a pub when she'd been in uniform she'd have singled him out as the person most likely to start a fight...

'It's my lunch hour,' she said.

It was a moment before Wilkins spoke. She guessed he was trying to contain himself. 'And yet you're working. Very commendable. However, if you don't want to take a break I suggest you continue with the tasks you're being paid to do. Other than that, go and buy a sandwich. You're displaying a lack of trust and a poor sense of priorities. Not what DCI Fleming wants in her team. You're new here, don't forget.'

And then he actually sat back down at his desk. Tara had been convinced he'd intended to go out. Was he seriously going to sit there and watch her? Like a toddler who didn't want someone else playing with their toys when they were absent? She'd never found it so hard to control herself. At last, she stood up and walked out of the door. She didn't want to eat lunch – she was too angry. Instead she exited the building, turned right and walked unseeingly up Parkside, waiting for the chill winter air to calm her. Eventually, she became conscious of her surroundings again: the tall townhouses to her right and the queueing traffic to her left.

Bloody Wilkins. She couldn't believe he'd threatened her. *You're new here, don't forget.* She'd got every reason to complain about *him* to DCI Fleming, in fact. But that wasn't the way she did things. Not like her snivelling boss…

As for the Ralph Cairncross files, she hadn't read much, but what she had seen had made her almost as angry as Wilkins' behaviour.

At home that evening, she called the dead man's sister.

'You didn't tell me your brother was over the drink-drive limit when he crashed,' she said, without preamble. The man had had enough alcohol to flatten most people, if the witness statement she'd half read was anything to go by. 'I presume you knew?'

Monica Cairncross's tone was clipped. *'Of course I did. What difference does that make?'*

Tara made a sound but Dr Cairncross cut across her.

'I know the law, of course, but that's just as a safeguard, surely? Because not everyone can drink and still drive safely. But Ralph could. He was excellent behind the wheel. He was rarely sober, but he'd never had an accident before.'

The woman really was delusional. And as for her brother, he'd certainly been lucky up until that point – as had anyone who'd crossed his path on the highways. 'It would definitely be reason enough for what happened,' Tara said.

'*There's still the matter of the lamp,*' Dr Cairncross persisted.

'The *antique* lamp, handed down by his father.'

'*Which Sadie, his wife, now says she told him to throw away, months ago. And she no doubt saw to it that it was finally discarded. It's very convenient that no one can check that wiring.*'

'Dr Cairncross, what would you have done, if you'd got a shock from an old bit of electrical equipment that had been in your family for decades? Wouldn't you have assumed it was past its prime and taken it to the dump, just as Mrs Cairncross says?'

'*What I would have done is neither here nor there.*'

'I'm sorry for your loss, but I really don't think there's anything more I can do for you.'

She gave a sharp sigh. '*Very well, I understand. Thank you for your time. And goodbye.*'

Tara hadn't expected her to give up so easily. She had a strange sense of anticlimax as she went around the house, drawing the cottage's threadbare curtains closed against the night.

Later that evening Tara lay in the bath. She'd made the water almost scalding hot, but the enamel of the tub itself was still cold on her back. She sank lower into the water, wishing she could get her knees and shoulders underneath at the same time. Outside, she could hear an owl hooting, and the wind battering at her windows again. She wondered about the figure Monica Cairncross thought she'd seen by the Green Dragon Bridge. But there were all sorts of people out on the common. Workers travelling back out of town to villages north of Cambridge; drinkers on their way to the

Green Dragon pub; drug dealers; and down-and-outs, looking for somewhere sheltered to rest. She pitied them if they were out in this weather. It was dry now, after the rain of the previous day, but the temperature was plummeting, and the flat landscape would give no protection against the bitter wind.

She'd been stalked on the common before; she knew that fear. But most likely the figure Dr Cairncross had seen was completely innocent. It was easy to see menace where there was none in such a lonely place.

She got out, dried herself in double-quick time, and pulled on the super-thick fleece pyjamas she'd bought two days after arriving back at the cottage. And then she dragged on two jumpers as well, and some bed socks.

Bed socks. Hardly the height of glamour – but they did work. For a second, she thought of Blake. He wore some of the best-cut suits she'd ever seen, and he wore them well. For some reason his otherwise scruffy appearance made them all the more appealing.

And then she thought of her actor mother, Lydia. She bet the mansion she lived in, out in the Fens, was warmer than Tara's place now, even though none of the family was in residence. Lydia was in Madeira filming whilst Tara's stepfather closed a property deal in China and her half-brother, Harry, was at boarding school. Tara had imagined she might be living comfortably by the time she was in her thirties. But she'd wanted to do it on her own terms, and she still did.

She fetched two hot water bottles for her bed and then decided to have a last look at her emails on her phone, before settling down with her Kindle.

There now. A message from Monica Cairncross, sent half an hour previously, to her work account. If only she hadn't left her business cards out on the hall table… There was always the option to delete the message unread, of course. The subject line was: *One last thought.*

Inbuilt overriding curiosity was an excellent trait for a journalist. It was less good for a detective constable who needed her sleep. She gave in to the inevitable and tapped on the email to open it.

I appreciate that you have finished looking into this matter as a police officer, but I am sending this email in case you might want to research my brother's death in your off-time, to satisfy your journalistic instincts.

Tara rolled her eyes. *Seriously?*

The woman had thoughtfully included the names of her sister-in-law, Sadie, and niece, Philippa, both of whom had been at her brother's house the evening he'd died. She'd failed to provide the names of the pals he'd driven to see, out in the Fens, Tara noted. She put down her phone without replying.

She'd bought Ralph Cairncross's last novel for her Kindle, but she'd had just about enough of the family for the time being. Instead, she turned to the thriller she had on the go. After that she lay down with her light off, and everything but her nose under the duvet.

Sleep was hard to come by. The fierce wind rattled her windows, making her wonder how strong the frames were. And Monica Cairncross's email went round and round in her mind. Crazy. There was nothing in it. Why was Tara even letting it occupy her headspace? It would have helped if she could have looked at the rest of the case notes. Wilkins blocking her like that had made her feel she'd left the job half done.

Why was Dr Cairncross so obsessed with her brother's wife and daughter? How had such a strong resentment built up? If Tara had believed there'd been any wrongdoing in this case, she'd have looked just as hard at the friends Ralph Cairncross had gone to visit, the night he'd died. After all, they'd have been more aware of his movements – better placed to intervene on his journey home.

She thought back to the witness statement she'd been trying to read when Wilkins had interrupted her. It had been made by one of Ralph Cairncross's 'Acolytes', as his sister had said he called them, Lucas Everett. It had sounded as though they'd been having quite a party that night, out in the Fens. She remembered Lucas had said Ralph had appeared to be in good spirits, and that it was possible he'd seemed drunker than usual, but not so much that Lucas was worried about him setting off home in his car. Tara imagined Lucas had probably been quite far gone himself.

His statement had mentioned that one of the group – a man named Stephen Ross, if she remembered rightly – had tried to dissuade Ralph Cairncross from leaving. But Lucas had told his interviewer that the author hated anyone fussing over him. It mirrored what Ralph's wife had apparently told Wilkins. Stephen's concern had made Ralph all the more determined to go. Lucas had said none of them had thought of calling the police to warn them he was on the road. It was just too normal a circumstance.

Tara remembered Lucas's details. They'd stuck in her head because he was a postdoctoral researcher in the English faculty at the University of Cambridge. She'd wondered if he wanted to write books too, like Ralph Cairncross. Perhaps he'd hero-worshipped him and seen his behaviour as exotic rather than dangerous.

Enough. She tried to switch off again, ready for sleep, but twenty minutes later it hadn't come. At last she sat up, reached for her Kindle and opened Ralph Cairncross's last published book, *Out of the Blue*. She knew enough of the writer by reputation to guess she'd find his work challenging, but the reality wasn't what she'd expected. The opening scene was richly written. A man was swimming in a lagoon off the coast of northern Australia. Tara could smell the salt water, feel her body slide through it, appreciate its warmth. The body of the swimmer was sensuously described: the power of his muscles, the supple movement of his limbs, the weight of his dark wet hair. And then came his physical reactions to fear when he saw a creature in the water: an ornate reef snake, one of the most poisonous species in the world. The build-up made the resolution of the scene all the more shocking. The swimmer turned in the water, taking strong strokes away from the reptile, but as he ploughed through the waves, his mind turned to the life he'd had, and to his fading youth, and he stopped. He turned back in the direction of the sea snake again, dipping under water, his eyes open, scanning for the foe he'd been fleeing until a moment before. And at last he saw it. And it saw him.

They swam towards each other, until the swimmer was close enough to the snake to grasp it and bring it up to his neck, where it struck him. And then he lay on his back, looking at the blue sky above, and waited to die.

The act seemed all the more horrifying because the descriptions were so beautiful and vivid, and because his decision was so unnatural. Tara shivered. She read enough of the next chapter to guess that the rest of novel must be in the form of a flashback, telling the story of the swimmer's life up until they'd entered the lagoon on that last day.

What kind of person wrote such a book?

She thought again of Lucas Everett. Had he studied Ralph Cairncross's work? What did he make of it? Hunched over her phone, swaddled in bedding in her cold room, she googled the postdoctoral researcher.

And caught her breath, a gasp of ice-cold air that went deep into her lungs.

CHAPTER THREE

Blake had been ambushed by Patrick Wilkins on his way into the station, before he'd even had the chance to raid the coffee machine. Now, he was sitting in Detective Chief Inspector Fleming's office, feeling at odds with the world at large, and his DS in particular.

Karen Fleming didn't look happy either. She was intent on running a tight ship and Patrick's complaints about their newest detective constable were creating bothersome ripples. If he'd come to Blake first, he'd have told Patrick that Fleming would be short on patience.

'This isn't primary school.' Fleming looked at Blake, of course. 'And even there, I don't suppose they call the headmistress in every time one of the class misbehaves.'

Blake could defend himself if he chose; he hadn't even realised Patrick and Tara were spoiling for a full-blown fight – though knowing them both, he might have guessed. But although it wasn't fair to lay the blame at his door, he couldn't bring himself to whine about it. It would be giving Fleming's criticism more weight than it was due. He'd save his energy. He looked pointedly at Patrick instead.

'I wanted to air the problem with someone who's less directly involved,' his DS said, catching Blake's gaze for a moment before sliding his eyes to meet Fleming's. Blake didn't like what he seemed to be insinuating. Or his tone.

'Well,' Fleming said, 'now that we're all gathered here, perhaps you'd like to explain what's wrong.' She'd got herself a cup of coffee and wrapped her hands around it. The smell almost made Blake weep.

Patrick expounded on his gripe. It seemed that Tara had been approached by the sister of a road traffic accident victim, with far-fetched claims that someone had helped him on his way. Blake remembered the case – and letting Patrick handle it. Patrick said he'd told Tara there was nothing to the sister's claims, and 'encouraged' her to get on with her work. Blake could imagine how well that would have gone down. But Tara wouldn't have allowed her anger to show; she'd have made up her mind to circumvent Patrick's wishes privately.

'You didn't think it was proper to share more of the background with her, even briefly?' Blake said.

'You know how busy we all are with the Hunter case. I told her what she needed to know. That should have been enough. But later, when she thought I'd gone out to lunch, I found her digging into the files about Ralph Cairncross's accident anyway.'

'And was she taking time out from the work you'd asked her to complete to do her research?' the DCI asked.

Blake noticed her eyelids twitch. Never a good sign.

Patrick frowned.

'You mentioned you were on your way to lunch when you returned unexpectedly and discovered her,' Fleming said. 'So perhaps she was taking her break then too, and decided she could spend the time following up on the enquiry she'd received. Did she finish the task you'd given her in a reasonable timeframe?'

The DS's tone was grudging. 'It was acceptable. But it was the lack of trust I objected to. She should have taken my word for it that there were no suspicious circumstances surrounding the Cairncross death.'

Fleming put her coffee down and her shoulders back. 'I don't want to discourage enquiring minds. I don't think what she did implies a lack of trust, necessarily.'

Blake agreed, though he was quite sure Tara's level of trust in Patrick Wilkins would be low. She didn't suffer fools gladly.

'If she'd been dealing with a grieving relative, it wouldn't be unnatural to want to see the records first-hand. It would be sensible to talk to her about her worries.'

'Grieving relative.' Patrick shook his head. 'The woman's a tyrant.'

Fleming frowned. 'Going back to Tara, I wonder if the issues you have go beyond the Cairncross incident, Patrick. If so, it's best that we tackle them openly, now. I'm aware, of course, that you know a lot about her background, thanks to the Seabrook murder case.'

Patrick shook his head. 'I'm sorry, ma'am, but I still can't believe we've got someone on the team who committed an assault as a civilian. And who was carrying an offensive weapon when she was abducted by Samantha Seabrook's killer.'

'Patrick, you know how strict the rules are about eligibility for police work. The higher-ups considered her past and accepted that there were extenuating circumstances. And she was never convicted of anything. Furthermore, she comes to us with an excellent training record and no disciplinary issues. I want us to make full use of her skills and help her develop her career. If you have any genuine cause for complaint you can of course raise it with DI Blake who will escalate it, *if necessary*. Do I make myself clear, both of you?'

Patrick's angry look was directed at him as much as at the DCI, Blake noticed. 'Crystal clear,' his DS said.

'Ma'am,' Blake said, when Fleming looked in his direction.

'And Blake, perhaps you could have a quiet word with Tara? Make sure she's transparent about what she's up to. The more open we all are, the fewer the chances for these time-consuming misunderstandings.'

He nodded. He still wished he could erase the drink he and Tara had had together in the Champion of the Thames, at the end of the Seabrook case. It was weird. Nothing had happened, but the atmosphere had been charged. Somehow, that occasion had opened a door onto something that could never be, but which was still on both their minds. He'd seen it in her eyes the first day she'd joined his team, and he knew she'd have seen it in his, too.

Five minutes later, coffee in hand, Blake was on his way back to his office when he heard Tara and Patrick talking. Their voices weren't raised by much, but he could tell tempers were frayed. Patrick was probably taking Fleming's advice and talking to Tara about her worries over the Cairncross death. But not in the tactful way the detective chief inspector had meant. For a second, he wondered whether to let them battle it out for themselves, but it might be a good moment to have the word that Fleming had recommended. He put his head round the door of the open-plan room his team occupied.

'A quick word in my office, please.' He could cope with the politics, now he'd got his caffeine supply.

Tara's red-gold hair was piled high on her head. Her style hadn't changed much since he'd first met her. Today she was wearing a classy-looking trouser suit his fashion designer sister would have appreciated: a warm brown with a subtle pattern, the jacket nipped in at the waist and the trousers fitted. He caught a glimpse of her green eyes, but she didn't try to catch his look. Wilkins did though. His expression told him he was challenging Blake to take his side.

Tara brought her laptop in with her. She sat down in front of his desk.

'Sit please, Patrick,' Blake had to say. He tried not to sound tired. As soon as he'd got them both settled, he asked what they'd been talking about. 'The conversation sounded strained,' he added. 'Were you asking Tara about the Cairncross case, Patrick?'

Tara's eyes widened a fraction. It seemed she hadn't known that Wilkins had been discussing her behind her back. And the DS wore a telltale frown, like a schoolboy who'd been caught misbehaving.

'I'll take that as a yes,' Blake said. He looked at Tara. 'It might be an idea to tell a lead officer if you're planning to dig for more information on their case,' he said. 'If everyone's clear about what they're up to then there's no room for misunderstandings.' He would tell Patrick to be more receptive to questions, too. And not to be an arse. But not in front of Tara. And perhaps not quite in those words.

'Understood,' she said. 'I was just looking during my break for my own satisfaction, so I didn't think anyone would mind.' That smile. She was treating him like all the others, managing his impression of her. Before they'd been colleagues she'd always been brutally honest. He didn't like the change.

'And was it useful, to know more?'

She shrugged. 'I didn't get very far, but there was some fundamental information that supported the fact that Ralph Cairncross had died by accident rather than design. He'd been drinking very heavily the night he died. Knowing that coloured the way I reported back to his sister.'

So that was one of the small details Patrick Wilkins had decided not to share.

'Because I didn't get much information from the records here,' Tara went on, her eyes sliding towards Patrick for a moment, 'I did a small amount of internet research last night instead. I wanted to make sure my background knowledge was secure.'

He doubted the 'small amount' description was accurate. 'Is that why you've got your laptop with you now?'

Patrick Wilkins sat forward in his chair. 'What DC Thorpe's found doesn't make any difference to the fundamentals of the original—'

Blake cut across him. 'All right, Patrick. I'd like Tara to answer my question, please.'

'That is why I've brought it in,' she said, tucking a tendril of hair behind her ear and flipping open the lid. 'I looked up one of the group of people Ralph Cairncross was going to visit, the night he died. They were his inner circle, if you like, his "Acolytes", as he and his sister called them.'

Wilkins' jaw was taut.

'And what did you find?'

Tara put her laptop on his desk and turned the screen to face him, so that he could see the news article. She glanced sideways at Wilkins. 'This information on one of the group, Lucas Everett. It was his witness statement I'd started to read when DS Wilkins asked me not to continue.' Her green eyes were on his. 'I appreciate it could be a coincidence. But given that Monica Cairncross has been pushing for more information I wondered if it was worth spending a short time making enquiries, to satisfy ourselves that her worries are groundless?'

It was the headline that hit Blake first: about a young man drowning off the Suffolk coast. He'd swum out too far. Lucas Everett. The date of the article was 4 October – shortly after Cairncross had drowned, if he remembered correctly.

Blake frowned. 'Could this be a suicide, as a result of his mentor's death?' He indicated the computer screen. 'Maybe Everett and Cairncross were especially close?' He hadn't read the full story.

But Tara shook her head. 'I don't think so. I found a more recent article, which reported the coroner's findings. They recorded misadventure, just as they did for Ralph Cairncross. There aren't many details in either of the newspaper reports, but if I went over to Suffolk I could find out more by talking to Lucas Everett's mother.'

'We *are* in the middle of the Hunter case.' He could hear the anger in Patrick's voice. Blake guessed a lot of the emotion derived from Tara 'interfering' with a case he'd shelved. For a moment his mind went to his former DS, Emma Marshall, who'd got her promotion to DI two months earlier and left him with Patrick. At times like this, he missed her cool-headedness and good humour more than he could say. The higher-ups were still deciding whether to replace her role or recruit another DC. *More upheaval...*

He sighed. Things weren't that stretched at the moment. He could sub someone in for the rest of the day to give Wilkins the manpower he needed, and let Tara go. But was it justified? That was the question. Two drownings of two interconnected men within a short time period was certainly striking, but it didn't shout 'foul play' to him.

'Leave it with me,' Blake said, waiting for his DS and DC to vacate the room. It was time for him to have a look at the case notes. That would decide matters.

Fifteen minutes later, he was staring unseeingly at his screen, having read Agneta Larsson's report. Somewhere deep inside him the first twinge of doubt stirred. He called Tara into his office.

'All right,' he said. 'Get over to Suffolk for the day, then report back to me. I'll make sure Patrick has the support he needs in your absence. Use kid gloves. There's probably nothing to it, but I'd rather be sure.'

CHAPTER FOUR

Tara was glad to get out of the office, even though the alternative was driving through the snow, which had just started to fall, towards Suffolk on the A14. As Blake had said, there was probably nothing in it. Unless she found something concrete by the end of the day she could look forward to Patrick Wilkins' sneering face – but not until Monday, at least. The weekend lay ahead – before her return to more paperwork relating to the Hunter drugs case. As she'd made her preparations for the day, she'd heard Blake sorting out someone to cover for her. He'd assigned DC Max Dimity to do the leg work she'd normally have undertaken.

Wilkins wouldn't be pleased with the arrangements. He called Max Dimity 'Max Dim' behind his back. Never in front of Blake though – he wasn't quite *that* stupid. Tara had first met Max four years earlier when she'd been caught up in the Samantha Seabrook investigation. She had a feeling still waters might run deep as far as he was concerned, and it would be a while before she knew him well. Blake seemed to rate him.

The snow was coming down faster now, and thicker. She wondered whether she should have brought more gear with her: warmer clothes, a bottle of water and food in case she got stuck. She'd got her long coat at least: a knee-length woollen number that was smart enough for work. Ahead of her she could see a multitude of brake lights coming on, and from somewhere behind came the sound of sirens. A moment later an ambulance wove its way past.

She was heading for a seaside town called Kellness, where Lucas Everett's mother lived. He'd been staying with her in early October when he'd drowned – taking a few days out from the research project he'd been working on in Cambridge's English faculty. She planned to visit the local coroner's office before she returned home too. How had the authorities decided on a verdict of misadventure rather than accidental death? They must have had reason to believe a deliberate action by Lucas had been a deciding factor in his demise.

She'd called ahead to talk to Lucas's mother, Jackie Everett. Tara was going to meet her at the family home in – she glanced at the time on the car's dashboard – one hour. Then she looked at the snow. Hell. When you'd called someone out of the blue to ask to discuss an emotionally harrowing family death, the last thing you wanted was to keep them waiting. She wasn't second-guessing what she'd find, but the two deaths in quick succession made her wonder. And then there was Monica Cairncross's attitude towards her sister-in-law and niece and the relationship Ralph had had with his group of young friends. All the dynamics gave her an uneasy feeling in her gut.

And then, finally, there was the mere fact that Blake had decided to send her off to Suffolk. What had he been doing in those fifteen minutes after he'd dismissed her and Wilkins from his office? If he'd been reading the files she'd been denied, they must have triggered his decision. Was there something odd about the case? Something that ought to have made Wilkins look more closely?

If so, it would explain why he was dead against her finding out more. And it meant she owed it to Monica Cairncross to investigate further – even if booze had been the deciding factor in her brother's death.

The car's heater was going full blast, but it didn't stop the chill she felt inside.

*

At three, Tara drew up outside a large, well-proportioned, red-brick Victorian villa overlooking the sea. Jessop House, the home of Lucas's mother. The woman had explained on the phone that his father had died five years earlier, and that Lucas was an only child. It had been just the two of them, when he'd been at home. The house was right on the edge of Kellness, a good hundred metres from its nearest neighbour. Just a narrow lane separated it from the town's stony beach. Snow fell over the grey, turbulent water. Standing outside her car, Tara watched the waves for a moment; heard the relentless repeated crash as they smacked up onto the shingle, then the sound of the water dragging at the stones as it receded again. Gulls called as though in distress, and the smell of saltwater was carried on the wind.

It was hard to imagine someone choosing to swim out into the sea there. It was so exposed. Wind and the icy flakes whipped into her face, chilling her nose and cheeks. She tried and failed to visualise the beach in summer, crowded with children carrying rubber rings and beach towels. In October, when Lucas had drowned, it had been mild, but the North Sea would still have been freezing.

After a second, she turned back towards the house. It had gates guarding the drive, but she'd decided to park in the lane, rather than opening and closing them behind her. She used a smaller side gate to enter the property and made her way up to the red front door. The windows looked dark, as though the life had gone out of the place. It was a couple of minutes after she'd knocked before she heard movement inside. At last she saw a shadow through the glass in the front door, slowly getting nearer. The woman who opened up was around sixty, Tara guessed. She had grey hair, cropped short, and was dressed in a blue denim fisherman's smock and navy slacks, with a green knotted scarf around her neck.

She stood back once Tara had introduced herself and shown her ID. Inside, the hall was cold and almost dark, but there was light at the rear of the house.

'It's warmer in the kitchen,' Jackie Everett said. 'I pretty much live there in winter, because of the Aga. You must be cold after your journey. Can I get you some tea?'

Tara accepted and followed the woman through.

'I didn't expect to hear anything more about Lucas's death,' Mrs Everett said. 'And you mentioned this visit relates to Ralph Cairncross. I thought that was all tied up now.' She was busying herself with an old-fashioned kettle that was already sitting on one of the Aga's hotplates, but Tara didn't miss her change in demeanour as she mentioned Cairncross's name. Her jaw tightened, and there was a constrained quality to her voice, as though she was trying to master her feelings.

'We thought so too,' Tara said. 'And it's still likely that that's the case. But questions have been raised over the manner of his death.' She was glad the woman hadn't witnessed Monica Cairncross's accusations or Wilkins' scepticism. 'As a result of some background checks we found the press reports about your son's death. As far as we know, no one was officially aware that two people who were so closely connected had died in quick succession. We're just making a couple of routine enquiries, to ensure we've covered everything properly.' She took the tea Mrs Everett had poured for her and added milk from the bottle the woman had put on the kitchen countertop and pushed towards her. 'I'm sorry. The last thing we want is to force you to have more painful conversations about your son. I shouldn't take up much of your time.'

Jackie Everett motioned Tara to take a seat at a vast, solid wooden table. 'I like speaking about my son, DC Thorpe, but talking about his connection with Ralph Cairncross brings back bad memories. And I can't see how there can be any question over how he died. Lucas told me that Ralph had been drinking heavily the night he drove his car into the river.'

Tara took the seat Mrs Everett had indicated and loosened her coat. 'You didn't like Mr Cairncross?'

Jackie Everett sank down onto a ladder-backed chair next to the Aga and let the steam from her tea warm her face. 'Lucas changed when he took up with him. He used to come back here quite frequently, and that tailed off. It wasn't a problem. He was twenty-seven; he'd probably been spending too much time at home. He was overdue a life of his own – but not with someone like Ralph Cairncross. I wanted him to have healthy relationships with people his own age.'

'I had the impression the other members of Mr Cairncross's inner circle were around Lucas's age too,' Tara said, sipping her drink. She remembered Monica Cairncross saying they were young. As she set her mug back down on the table she realised it wasn't altogether clean and closed her eyes for a moment, wishing she could un-see the lipstick mark she hadn't made.

'Oh yes!' Mrs Everett's laugh was mirthless. 'Ralph Cairncross liked to gather youthful people around him, evidently. But they weren't a group of interconnected friends. They all related to each other through him. He was the common link, if you like. And he was in charge of who came and went – who was part of the gang, and who wasn't. He reminded me of some of the girls I used to know when I was a child.'

Tara knew what she meant. They'd had that sort at her school too. 'And you said your son changed, when he joined Ralph Cairncross's group?' she said. 'Beyond just coming home less frequently?'

Jackie Everett nodded. 'He started to look down on anyone who didn't share Ralph Cairncross's outlook on life,' she said.

Tara raised a questioning eyebrow.

'That youth is everything. That we should burn bright, then embrace death and burn out.'

Tara thought of Ralph Cairncross's last book for a second: of the swimmer who'd decided to meet death and accept it. She had to quell a shudder.

Mrs Everett's eyes were far away for a moment. 'I wondered if Ralph Cairncross had got drunk that night and been reckless because living into old age would have gone against his whole policy on life. Perhaps he liked the idea of going out suddenly like that, on what he would have thought of as a high, rather than fading away gradually.' She looked down into her drink. 'He was fifty-seven when he died, you know. Younger than me.'

Tara guessed others might have wondered the same thing, if that had been Cairncross's creed. Would he have done that? His sister clearly didn't buy it.

'But Lucas believed Ralph Cairncross's drowning was the result of a straightforward accident,' Jackie Everett added. 'He said Ralph measured age – in himself at least – by behaviour and attitude rather than actual years. That was why he kept his group of young ones close. And if he carried on behaving like a foolish teenager, then he was being true to his principles.' Suddenly there were tears in her eyes. 'But he'd already had a good life, and he was old enough to make his own decisions. If he wanted to live like that, careless of his own future, then fine. But he had no right to infect Lucas with his warped ideals.' Her damp eyes met Tara's. 'My son would never have risked such a swim before they'd met – of that I'm certain.'

Tara leant towards the woman. 'I'm so sorry.' She paused for a moment to give her time to recover. 'Did you speak to Lucas in the immediate aftermath of Ralph Cairncross's death? Was he very upset?'

'You're wondering if that might have made him more careless of his own safety, because he was grieving?'

'It happens sometimes.'

Jackie Everett nodded. 'I must admit, I was worried that he'd be devastated.' She looked away for a moment. 'My son was gay, you see, and I wondered if Ralph Cairncross's influence on him was so great because Lucas had fallen in love.' Her eyes met Tara's. 'But yes, I did speak to him – the day after the accident, as a matter of fact – and I knew then that I'd been wrong. Lucas was upset. Of course he was. And shocked too. But not broken. Not like I was when his father died. And' – she took a deep breath – 'he was more his old self than he'd been in a while.'

'And how was he when he returned here that final time?' It would only have been a couple of weeks after his mentor's death.

The tears were back in her eyes. 'He'd pulled himself together. The shock had dulled, and he was talking about how the rest of Ralph Cairncross's circle were determined to carry on their association in his memory. And to live by his rules. I could have wept when he said that. They were cruel rules. And they were destructive. And now Lucas is dead.'

'Forgive me,' Tara said, 'the coroner found death by misadventure, but the details weren't given. I can get the records from their office, but I wondered if you'd mind sharing the circumstances with me?'

Tears pooled in Jackie Everett's eyes. 'He went out for a late-evening swim,' she said. 'I'd gone to visit my sister in Ipswich overnight, so I had no idea what he was up to. It was some neighbours who found his clothes on the beach early the next morning, when they were out walking their dog. He'd left a note, too. It said: "An adventure in memory of Ralph. And if I die, then death is not the end."' Without warning, she took her mug and threw it down on the hard kitchen tiles. The remainder of her coffee spattered over the white wall next to the Aga, and bits of china flew in all directions. She clenched her fists and pushed them into her eyes. 'Stupid, stupid boy,' she said. 'Because death is the end. It's the end for me.'

Tara had tried to help Jackie Everett tidy up the broken china before she went, but the woman had made it clear she just wanted to be left in peace. Tara could understand that well enough. What would happen to her now? How well did she know the neighbours who'd found her son's clothes? Was there anyone around to break up the hours of her day?

The snow had stopped, but slushy piles of it lay on the ground. She walked back down the driveway of Jessop House and let herself out again by the side gate, tightening the belt of her coat. The sky was still thick with pinkish-brown cloud. How long would it be before the weather closed in again?

She went around the corner to buy a sandwich and a Coke from a small Co-op supermarket before starting her journey home, via the local coroner's office. She wanted to double-check the full details; she sure as hell couldn't ask Mrs Everett for more information.

Three hours later, Tara walked back home across Stourbridge Common, the snow wetting her boots. There was no vehicular access to her place, and she hadn't bothered with her bike that morning.

Her head was full of the information she'd got from the coroner. It wouldn't be enough to convince Blake to extend her enquiries into the case on Monday, but everything she'd learned made her uneasy. She was glad she'd got the weekend in which to find out more about Ralph Cairncross and his family. She had one daunting appointment on Saturday – with Bea; it made her stomach clench – but after that, she'd devote herself to the task.

She glanced ahead to her cottage, sitting in darkness and isolation. She was the first person to tread that particular route since the snowfall. Everything was very quiet and still.

Her mind ran back to the summer, four years earlier, when she'd been followed – and when there'd been a murder right outside her door. You never really knew how safe you were.

Had the deaths of Ralph Cairncross and Lucas Everett really been simple misadventure? She could see Lucas might have thrown caution to the winds in some kind of delayed reaction to his friend's death, even if he hadn't set out to end his life.

Instinctively, she looked over her shoulder at the white world. The sky was mainly covered by cloud, but moonlight shone through a gap, making the snow sparkle and the common look less dark than usual. She could see further than she would normally. And she knew anyone watching her – perhaps carefully hidden – would be able to, too. But though she strained her eyes, she couldn't detect any movement, or anything out of the ordinary. Except perhaps that the whole place was more deserted than usual.

Hardly surprising, given the temperature.

At last, key in hand, she reached the low brick wall that marked the border to her tiny front garden. She opened the gate to walk the short tiled path leading to her front door, and stepped forwards.

Within a second, she was out of control. Her right foot slid from under her, and as she brought her left foot up to try to steady herself it met with the same ice-rink surface beneath the snow, spanning the width of the tiles, giving no grip. She fell hard, hitting her lower back and then her left elbow. Her right foot slammed into the stone step up to the front door itself. Her laptop bag was flung off to one side, and her handbag, which had been open, had landed upside down, losing half its contents.

As Tara tried to scramble up again she glanced over her shoulder once more – not to check for spectres in the dark, but for anyone who might have seen her make such an idiot of herself. But everything was quiet. The damn tiles were as slippery as hell. In the end she had to slide off them, onto one of the small patches of gravel that lay either side of the path, inside the brick wall boundary of her so-called garden. At last she was able to right herself and reach for her scattered belongings.

When she'd finally gathered everything together, she leant across to unlock her front door and stepped diagonally into the house, avoiding the snowy tiles this time.

She was cold after the fall and desperate for a change of clothes. She went straight to her bathroom, undressed and stood in a hot shower, where she pointed the jets at her back, hip and elbow, hoping to ease the pain. Already she could see that the large red area where she'd smacked onto the ice was turning purple.

As soon as she was out she changed into jeans and layered up tops and jumpers – thin, thicker, thicker still – to try to keep herself warm. The most figure-hugging one was cashmere – a present from her mother, of course, who didn't really believe in other sorts of sweaters. Tara grudgingly admitted that it was effective at keeping out the cold.

After that she boiled the kettle and made hot chocolate to drink and a hot water bottle to sit on her lap. She rounded the arrangement off with a vodka chaser, two ibuprofen and the softest cushion she could find to perch on at her seat at the kitchen table. She needed to email Blake. He'd sent her a message asking for a full update and making it clear he knew she'd been keeping some of the details back from him. But he hadn't bawled her out for meeting Monica Cairncross unofficially.

The act of starting to type her notes made images of the day flit through her head. She remembered how cross Wilkins had looked when he realised Blake was seriously going to commandeer her for what her boss regarded as a wild goose chase. And the relief of escaping the station and heading out on her journey.

And then suddenly, she stopped, and stared into space as she thought back further, to when she'd left her house earlier that day.

It had rained the previous night, but by the morning it had cleared. Her path had been dry when she'd left home. Then, as forecast, the temperature had plummeted. As she'd left for Suffolk in the early afternoon it had started to snow.

The temperature had been below freezing since then. There'd been no chance for any of the snow to thaw and refreeze. There would be well-trodden areas in Cambridge where the snow had compacted into ice. But her front path wasn't one of them.

So why—

Within a second, she was back outside again, crouching down in her front garden. She swept the snow from the tiles in front of her house, feeling the pain as the intense cold worked its way into her fingers.

Underneath the snowfall was sheet ice. A thick layer – the sort you got when someone had unthinkingly thrown a bucket of water over a car windscreen to clear it, leaving a skiddy death trap to form on the road for the next poor sod who was passing.

Except this ice was deeper than that. And no one would ever spill water over her front tiles by accident.

Someone had done this deliberately. It was the only possible answer. She caught her breath in the frigid air and felt her heart rate increase.

At one point – after her death threat – she'd had cameras installed at her house. They'd been police property – interlinked with the station – and had long since been removed. She wished now that she could see who'd visited her place earlier that day – before the snow had started. She pulled her phone from her jeans pocket and photographed the scene. If whoever had stopped by had left any other evidence behind, she'd only see it once the snow had melted.

She stood again slowly, feeling the pain in her back as she straightened up. She was getting stiff now.

Her accident was meant to happen, she was sure of it. All the perpetrator had needed was her address, the weather forecast and a few bottles of water.

Why had they done it? To warn her off? To make her scared? Or maybe to make her colleagues think she was paranoid if she was determined enough to report it.

The evidence was destined to melt away, and she was willing to bet Wilkins would call her 'accident' misadventure…

CHAPTER FIVE

Tara had grown seriously cold as she investigated the situation outside her cottage. She guessed most of the shaking her body was doing was down to that. Most, but not all. She put the chain on the front door, kicked off her snowy boots and then walked around the house quickly, closing all the curtains – something that hadn't seemed like a priority when all she'd wanted was a hot shower. Still she shook. She went to check the elderly boiler but it was firing away; the heating was on all right – the insulation just wasn't good enough.

Resolutely, she refilled her hot water bottle and microwaved her chocolate (nothing stayed warm in her house for more than a few minutes). After removing the revolting skin that had now formed on top of her drink she returned to her task of emailing Blake, half her mind still on the sheet ice outside.

After she'd given the DI all the salient points from both Lucas Everett's mum and the coroner's office near Kellness, she pressed send.

She hadn't yet told him about the situation outside her front door. It seemed ridiculous. Who the hell would do something like that? He'd think she was being paranoid, and that was nothing to what Wilkins would say if he ever found out. At last she abandoned the idea of mentioning it. It probably wasn't important, anyway.

For a moment she felt too tired to move. She needed food, but the cooker – though only four feet away – felt distant. She found herself staring into space, and thinking of Blake, wondering what he'd think of the information she'd gathered that day. Though of course he probably wouldn't be sitting there reading non-urgent work emails on a Friday night. It must be family time.

Every so often she'd heard snippets of gossip about his wife at the station. People often said how gorgeous Babette was, and how enchanting their daughter Kitty was proving to be. Kitty was six, apparently, so she must have been a toddler when Blake and his wife had had their trial separation. Years had gone by, but there were still hints that they weren't happy. She'd heard Wilkins question how anyone could complain about being hitched to someone like Babette. And wonder why on earth she'd chosen a scruff like Blake. Hardly surprising – Wilkins saw all other blokes as rivals, and spent his time working out how he measured up against them.

For a second, the thought of having Blake there with her flitted across Tara's consciousness. The image of him came unbidden: sharing theories on Ralph Cairncross, opening up a bottle of red, each mucking in with the cooking. She pushed the idea out as soon as it arrived. She was happy on her own. It was just that it had been unexpectedly satisfying, pooling ideas with him when they'd been caught up in the same murder investigation.

She'd shared thoughts on multiple police cases since then, of course – though not with Blake. Her mind ran over the connections she'd made over the last four years, during her time in uniform and after she'd joined CID. There were a few colleagues who'd been hard to take – sexist, defensive or patronising – but several that she'd really valued. She'd got as far as joining them for evenings at the pub, and with one guy things had gone further. Her thoughts lingered on Toby for a moment. She'd liked him, but there'd been something missing; she still wasn't sure what.

It was ironic, really. There were very few people Tara could be herself with. In fact, she could count them on the fingers of one hand. Literally the fingers: she didn't even need the thumb. There was Bea, who'd looked after her as a child; Kemp, the ex-cop who'd taught her self-defence when she was stalked as a teenager; Matt, her old colleague at *Not Now* magazine – and, well, that was about it really. With most other people she put on an act of some kind or another: to get information as a professional, or to save face or because of her pride. And the one other person she could see herself adding to that very short list was Blake. That had become obvious to her oddly quickly. They'd emailed briefly, after the court case where Samantha Seabrook's killer had been convicted, but as Blake had settled back into his marriage the messages had become stilted. She guessed he hadn't wanted to share anything personal. In the end, the correspondence had tailed off. She had a feeling it had been she who'd failed to respond to Blake's last message, but she guessed he'd been relieved that the exchange had petered out.

It really was time to cook, but she couldn't settle to it straight away. Before she started, she walked into her darkened sitting room and stood by the window, tweaking the curtain very slightly so that she could see out onto the common, towards the river. The moon was behind a cloud now, but still the scene seemed to glow. She felt as though she was illuminated, even though she was standing well back from the glass and to one side. In an instant, she let the curtain fall back into place. If there was anyone out there now she didn't want to be seen. But the view she'd glimpsed had looked like a perfect, empty stage set. Whoever was playing games, they'd have long since gone home.

She went back to the kitchen and poured herself a second vodka and tonic, then set some leftover pasta sauce to heat up whilst she boiled the kettle for some spaghetti water. She swigged her drink and wandered back over to the table again.

An email from Kemp had come in.

How's life back at the old homestead? And what about work? Coping all right with DS Wilkins? The guy sounds like a prick.

Tara smiled. She'd met Kemp when she was seventeen, but right from the start he'd treated her as an equal – never talked down to her, never doubted her word. Over the long years they'd known each other their relationship had developed and by her mid-twenties they were sometimes more than just friends. Despite that, he never expected anything of her and their association was as relaxed and balanced as it had always been. That didn't mean he wasn't frank with his opinions though. It had taken him about two years to get over the fact that she'd decided to train as a police officer, but these days he was keen to hear her gossip. His own opinion of the force was low. He'd left under a cloud, following a complaint about his attitude and professional conduct. He'd always been cagey about the exact circumstances of his departure and she didn't care. The important thing from her point of view was that he'd been there for her when no one else would listen. He'd seen her in tears on her way into the station where he worked, just as he was on his way out for the final time. He'd taken her in hand and taught her self-defence, including some low tricks to ensure she no longer felt like a victim.

She composed a reply.

Homestead is slightly less warm than an igloo, but I'll work on it. Wilkins is causing all the problems I anticipated, but I'll work on that too.

If her DS imagined he was going to get the better of her she would delight in disappointing him. All the same, when she'd seen the opening for her job, she'd never imagined quite how hard it would be to work as his subordinate. For a second she wondered if she'd have still applied if she'd known – but she'd been waiting for an opportunity to come up in Cambridge so she could be close to Bea. She sighed and added:

How's life in the world of security? Decked any villains recently? X

And clicked 'send'.

Over her pasta she reviewed everything she'd come up with that day.

The visit to the coroner's office had thrown up some new information. Lucas Everett had been drinking heavily the night he died, just as Ralph Cairncross had. It fitted with the risky behaviour he'd indulged in. Would he have gone ahead with his swim if he'd been sober? Tara could imagine him getting fired up about his plan as he consumed more booze. All the same, his head must have cleared pretty quickly when he'd waded out into the North Sea. Even on a mild autumn evening the water would have been intensely cold. Yet he went ahead.

According to the police reports that had been submitted, no one had seen Lucas go out onto the beach, but that wasn't surprising. His clothes had been found further out of town from where his mother lived. She was guessing that bit of the seafront would be pretty reliably deserted in the late evening. He'd last been seen at 9 p.m. on the night he'd died, in the same Co-op where she'd bought her sandwich that lunchtime. He'd purchased a bottle of Adnams East Coast vodka. It had been found – very much depleted – amongst his clothes. The only clear prints on it had been his and those of the person who'd served him. The cashier said he'd been cheerful. 'As though he'd had a good day and was looking forward to the rest of his evening.' Apparently he'd even joked with the staff as he left the store. There'd been a twinkle in his eye. One of the colleagues of the woman who'd served him had wondered if he'd already had a drink or two, but it might have just been high spirits. He hadn't smelt of alcohol and he hadn't talked about his plans for later.

It sounded to Tara as though he'd been excited. If he'd already decided to undertake his late-night swim by that stage, she was guessing he was anticipating it and feeling confident.

The handwriting on the note he'd left on the beach had been identified as his by his mother.

Tara had been so absorbed she was forgetting her pasta. She took a forkful and found it was already lukewarm. Microwave time again…

As she walked stiffly over to reheat her food, her mind turned to the last item on the reports the coroner had passed on to her. It related to the paper Lucas Everett had used to write his note.

An adventure in memory of Ralph. And if I die, then death is not the end.

It said that the paper had been ripped from a pad. There were small bits of glue along one edge, where it had been bound in amongst other pages.

Lucas hadn't had the rest of the pad on him, and no one had managed to locate it. It hadn't seemed important at the time.

All the same, that bit of paper had to have been ripped from somewhere – a point she'd made to Blake in her email. But as she'd typed the words she'd privately acknowledged that the case she was trying to build looked shaky at best.

CHAPTER SIX

Blake was sitting at the kitchen table at his home in Fen Ditton, enjoying a moment of peace and quiet. He glanced out of the French windows into his back garden. The leafless trees were heavy with snow. The shrouded shrubs loomed out of the shadows, glowing shapes in a shaft of moonlight that had slipped between the clouds. He wondered how Tara had got on in Suffolk – and if she was safely home. There was a thaw forecast overnight, with more rain, but conditions now weren't great for driving.

On glancing back at his laptop he saw an email had come in from her; it was as though he'd conjured her up by allowing her into his thoughts.

He'd just opened the message when the sound of his wife, Babette, at the doorway made him start. He'd thought she was still upstairs. She'd dozed off whilst he was reading Kitty's bedtime story and he hadn't disturbed her. She stretched, elongating her petite stature slightly, and yawned. She was graceful and cat-like in her movements.

'I'm sorry,' she said. 'I hadn't realised how tired I was.' She walked over to the table and he felt his shoulders tense. 'What's that?' She was standing behind him, peering at his inbox. 'Work?' And then she laughed. 'Silly question, of course it is!'

He nodded and resisted the urge to shut the laptop lid. The email wouldn't be private, of course, but he wished Babette didn't feel she had carte blanche to read his messages over his shoulder. *He* hadn't even had the chance to look at it yet. For a second, he wondered what would have happened, when Kitty had been a toddler, if he'd taken the same approach with his wife's emails. Would he have known she'd been planning to walk out on him, instead of it coming as an ice-cold shock, taking his breath away?

For the hundredth time he questioned his decision to accept her back into his life. He'd done it because he couldn't bear to be apart from Kitty, but then he'd let the child down. For the first year after Babette had moved back in, he hadn't been able to treat either of them as he had before. The burning anger he'd felt towards his wife made a resurgence, and every interaction with Kitty felt staged.

In the end, Babette had had it out with him. The knife-edge atmosphere was more damaging for Kitty than them being apart. She'd told him he needed to conquer his feelings if he really wanted to make a go of it. He knew she was right, but it didn't make it any easier. The fact that she'd been planning to remove Kitty from his life for good meant forgiveness was hard to summon. Babette had explained repeatedly how wrong she'd been, though. And spent months begging him to take her back. For a time, he'd managed to transfer the anger he'd felt towards her to the man who'd persuaded her to leave him.

It was complicated, and he knew he needed to make an effort. He turned to look up at Babette, reaching out to take her hand. 'Yes, it's work. Something unexpected came up earlier today.'

Babette met his eyes for a moment before dropping her gaze. 'I was going to suggest an early night.'

After they'd got past the early days, when Blake had barely been able to hide his feelings, they'd begun to have sex again. And now, Babette had started to talk about wanting a baby brother or sister for Kitty. It was something he'd been refusing to tackle head on. He baulked at the idea. He wasn't even sure it was right to stay in the marriage – it sure as hell couldn't be right to have another child.

He waited for her to look at him again. 'I'm afraid I've got a lot more to get through here.'

'Ah. Okay then.' Her voice sounded worn. 'I might go on up. I'm shattered.'

After she'd left the room he spent a few minutes doing battle with guilt before he managed to settle back to work. He hadn't started the mess with Babette, but he knew he was perpetuating it.

At last he shelved the thoughts that had been causing his stomach to tense and focused on Tara's email. He shifted in his seat, frowning. The report on her interview with Jackie Everett made uncomfortable reading. Ralph Cairncross's little band felt like a cult. It seemed as though Lucas Everett had followed the man so unquestioningly, even after his death, that he'd lost his own life. Cairncross had certainly wielded considerable power. But although the circumstances made Blake's skin crawl, none of it added up to anything criminal, or even hinted that there was more to uncover.

He shivered and went to draw the curtains on the dark winter world outside before returning to his seat. Misadventure. Two men who'd drowned in tragic circumstances, but circumstances where their demises were sadly predictable. Too much to drink, too far a swim – too much bravado. Maybe each had been careless of their safety for different reasons: Cairncross from a desire to live as he had when he was young, and Everett because he was influenced by his dead mentor.

What had Tara got apart from that? A page torn from a notebook that couldn't be found; a wild-sounding accusation of foul play from one of Cairncross's relations; and a claim by that same woman that she'd been followed. It was tissue-paper thin.

Except… except for what he'd read in Agneta Larsson's post-mortem report. It was probably nothing; the coroner had obviously decided on balance that it wasn't significant. The guy had been so damned drunk when he'd drowned – that had to have been the overriding factor. Blake made up his mind to have coffee with Agneta sometime soon – just to get her take on things.

CHAPTER SEVEN

Patrick Wilkins sat in his Rondo leather armchair with a whisky on the side table next to him. Instead of relaxing and drinking it, he was staring at the corner of his flat's open-plan living room, frowning. When his girlfriend, Shona, came into the room and spoke, he jumped.

'What?'

'I said you're miles away. I was just telling you about the story I'm working on. Shall I start again?' She rolled her eyes and he wished she wouldn't. She worked for *Not Now* magazine, the same publication that had employed Tara Thorpe when he'd first met her. Patrick and Shona had hooked up over a missing child case a year back, but he'd been eyeing her up for a lot longer than that. They kept their relationship under wraps. It avoided the entire station coming down on him each time there was a leak to the press. And Shona liked her colleagues to think every little snippet of information she acquired was down to her hard work and diligence – not because of who she was shagging.

She was a glamorous woman, and they had some laughs, but her constant need to share her enthusiasm for her job wore him down. He wasn't enjoying life at the station at the moment, and hearing her talk up her own career was the last thing he felt like. He just wanted to switch off.

Still, it wouldn't do to say so. 'Yeah, sure.' He picked up his drink. 'Sorry. Start again.'

She told him about the artist the magazine was featuring, and how she was cohabiting with her own nephew by marriage. *Not Now* liked that kind of thing.

At last Shona stopped and perched on the arm of the chair he occupied, her clingy dress riding halfway up her thigh. 'What's eating you?' she said. 'You've been positively sullen since last week.'

He didn't normally share stuff about work. He gave Shona the most positive spin on everything that he did. He had his pride. And besides, you could never be sure with journalists. If their relationship went sour he didn't want to give her anything damaging she could quote in some future story. But Shona had worked with Tara Thorpe. It was tempting to confide. *Not Now* had run a story about her appointment with the Cambridgeshire Constabulary. They'd used all their inside knowledge about her and shown no loyalty. He knew she hadn't been well-liked whilst she'd been with them, either.

'It's my new detective constable,' he said.

'Ah yes. My erstwhile colleague Tara. Don't tell me she's giving you trouble already?' Shona put her head on one side and stroked his neck with her right hand. She had long, elegant fingers.

'I feel as though she's walking all over everyone at the station. And she's only been with us a matter of weeks.'

Shona sighed. 'I can't say I'm surprised. It was the same when she worked at *Not Now*.' She gave him a look. 'You do know the circumstances around her leaving, right?'

Patrick shrugged. 'I heard she resigned.'

Shona laughed. 'Yeah, right before she was pushed. Giles' – Giles was Shona's editor at the magazine – 'well, he gave her an ultimatum. He found out she'd been holding back a whole lot of information about the Samantha Seabrook murder case that would have led to a massive spike in readers for us. She hadn't even told him she'd been threatened by Samantha Seabrook's murderer. When he found out, he told her she'd got to display some loyalty and behave like a proper journalist. He wanted the full, personal story from her as an exclusive, or else she could pack her bags. Rather than help him out, she resigned.' She got up from the chair arm and went to fetch the glass of white wine she'd left on the sideboard. 'She's got no sense of loyalty, whatsoever. She's only out for herself.'

She brought her drink back and settled down again.

Patrick hadn't heard about the circumstances before. It all figured. 'I'd love to know what made her decide to apply for police training after that,' he said.

Shona smiled. 'Well, I think her journalism career was scuppered. You know she once decked another reporter, when they came after the same story she was onto?'

'She'd been stalked, hadn't she? And she thought the guy might be him?'

Shona opened her eyes wide. 'Well, yes, I think that's what she *said*. But the incident with the fellow journalist was years after her stalker gave up. Besides,' she sipped her drink slowly, 'she didn't do things by halves. The journalist she hit ended up with a black eye and a broken finger.'

Patrick nodded. 'That much I'd heard.'

'She's lucky he dropped the charges. I'm amazed the police allowed her in.'

'I was too. Exceptional circumstances, apparently.'

'And you think that was enough?'

He looked at Shona. 'What do you mean?'

She glanced sideways at him, her ice-blue eyes on his. 'I remember seeing Tara having a drink with your DI Blake once, during the Seabrook murder investigation.' She paused. 'My colleague Gav was there too. We both thought they looked pretty chummy. It wouldn't surprise me if he'd put in a good word for her. Maybe he even suggested the police as a career.'

Patrick felt his heart rate increase and his jaw tense. He still remembered the look of horror on Blake's face when he'd arrived just in time to see Tara's apparently lifeless body, underwater, out in the Fens. He'd been in after her in seconds, even though another officer was already on the scene, and in the process of hauling her out. Then he'd waited whilst she'd been resuscitated. He'd been completely still, his face pale, his eyes concentrated on hers, waiting for them to open. Patrick had known then that Tara Thorpe had some kind of hold on his boss's feelings. But *then* it hadn't mattered. And she'd gone off for four years. Even when she came back he hadn't anticipated her being quite such a thorn in his side. After all, Garstin Blake had got back together with his wife. He presumed Tara Thorpe had just been a distraction whilst they'd been on a break. Patrick had only found out his boss's marriage had been foundering at all thanks to some overheard gossip.

'What are you thinking?' Shona said.

'That you might be right about DI Blake putting a word in.' Though if he had, he bet Tara Thorpe didn't know anything about it. She was the kind of person who'd resent any good turns as patronising. 'And I reckon he still favours her now. I think her presence is colouring his judgement and damaging my standing, too.'

'In what way?' Shona shifted her body closer to his and he could feel her warmth.

'Tara started to secretly investigate an old incident behind my back. It's nothing – less than nothing – a complete waste of time. But she's sweet-talked Blake into letting her spend more hours on it.'

'She went over your head?' Shona sounded shocked and Patrick felt a bit better.

He nodded. 'And then, without consulting me, the DI took her off the Hunter case and gave me Max *Dim*-ity in her place.' He didn't mention that Blake had only given Tara the day to look into the Cairncross business, and the fact that the arrangements were only temporary. One way or another, he wouldn't be surprised if Tara Thorpe managed to wangle an extension.

He glanced at Shona, whose own eyes were now on the middle distance. He watched as she slowly turned to face him again. 'Well,' she said. 'I imagine it would cause quite a scandal if your DI and our Tara took things further. What with him being married, and it affecting his judgement at work too, maybe.'

Patrick gave a hollow laugh. 'You're right there.'

'So,' she sipped at the last of her wine, 'if there's ever any shred of evidence that DI Blake and Tara Thorpe are having an affair, you can slip the information to me. Anonymously of course. Giles is a great one for holding a grudge. If there's anything that might bring Tara down, he'd be delighted to give it the oxygen of publicity.'

Friday 30 November

I didn't stay to watch you come home, Tara. Why would I waste my time, out in the cold? As before, I just sowed a seed and stood back to let events take their course.

Did you fall? And are you lying awake in bed now, wondering? Trying to think of another logical explanation for the sheet of ice outside your door? A leaky pipe, perhaps? Old houses like yours often have problems with plumbing and electrics. I bet that's what your colleagues will assume, if you tell them. But will you even share the information? People will only think you a fool.

Are you worried about what might happen next?

I'm sorry – but I wanted to get at you – if only in a small way. It makes me angry that the police are spending any time on such worthless men as Ralph and Lucas. But you're safe for now. I've no need to twist fate again unless you get too close to the truth.

No – it's others you should worry about. Because I haven't finished, yet.

If two deaths by misadventure is frustrating, how will you feel when there are three?

CHAPTER EIGHT

Tara found it hard to relax that Friday night. She ached from her fall and couldn't help listening for sounds out on the common. The ice sheet outside her door preyed on her mind. She simply couldn't think of any logical explanation for its presence. It was a matter of physics. But anyone could have been responsible, of course – it might have been Wilkins for all she knew.

At last she must have managed to drop off, but the night felt short, and she wasn't refreshed when she woke. Now there she was, at six on Saturday morning, worrying about her appointment with Bea later. But the whole reason she'd come back to Cambridge was to help her mother's cousin through her grief at losing her husband. Today would be part of that process.

She lay curled up in the cool bed, knowing she wouldn't get back to sleep, but refusing to give in to it. It would be colder still when she got out from under the covers. At last, at six twenty, she got up, dragged on her clothes and settled down to coffee and toast, her laptop booted up at her side.

After her second slice, she turned to her computer and opened her email. She found herself rereading Monica Cairncross's message first. She sat back, closed her eyes for a moment and cursed Wilkins. If he hadn't blocked her attempts to read up on the Cairncross case at work Tara might have been satisfied by now – content to let the matter rest. As it was, her decision to double check for anything that looked off had been thwarted.

At last, against her better judgement, she replied to Dr Cairncross, saying she'd do a small amount of extra digging in her free time. She'd have to use unofficial means to extend what she knew. Her first move was to ask the dead man's sister for the details of the rest of the group he'd gone to visit the night he'd drowned.

It would be a challenge, but she'd secretly enjoy it. And it would be good to have something of her own to pursue. She thought of Kemp. His intervention when she'd been stalked had pretty much saved her sanity, and she valued his opinion. Consequently, she'd been disgruntled when he'd laughed at her decision to join the police. He'd told her she'd be rubbish. She wasn't a team player, hated taking orders from anyone else, and was far too impatient. In short, he'd told her she was just like him. He was a lone wolf now, taking on security and investigative work. His doubts had made her determined to prove him wrong. She could keep herself in check when she needed to, and four years working closely with colleagues had almost turned her into a team player. In particular, her first two years – spent in uniform – had introduced her to a feeling of camaraderie she hadn't known before, and hadn't thought she could be a part of. But from time to time, she did miss being autonomous. Until Giles at *Not Now* had forced her to resign, he'd at least given her plenty of freedom.

Four hours later, Tara was outside Bea's house. They'd just finished clearing away and washing up after her paying guests. Tara had spent the previous half hour with her hands submerged in scalding-hot soapy water. The contrast outside was startling. It was dry for now, after the rain that had fallen in the early hours, but the temperature was bitter and patches of the pavement under their feet were still slippery, where yesterday's snow had been compacted into ice that was too thick to have thawed. Despite the weather and their walk, Tara hadn't worn jeans and jumpers. It hadn't felt formal enough somehow. She'd opted for a knee-length woollen dress and boots, with her coat over the top.

She looked down at Bea – tiny, her eyes slightly red and her cheeks pink from the cold. She was carrying the china urn containing her husband Greg's ashes.

Her mother's cousin let out a small giggle that cracked partway through, and gulped back what might have turned into a sob. 'I hope to God I don't drop him here. Ditton Meadows, he said in his will, by the river. Not just off Chesterton High Street.'

Tara leant down, put her arm round Bea's shoulders and gave her a squeeze. She had to pause a moment before she spoke. Greg hadn't been around when Bea had looked after her as a child; she'd only met him later. Tara could still remember the sparkle she'd seen in Bea's eye when she'd relayed the story of the new 'friend' she'd made.

When they'd married and bought the boarding house she'd never seen Bea happier. It was as though things had finally fallen into place. And Tara felt almost as relaxed with Greg as she did with her mother's cousin. Bea had spent years putting everyone else first, and it had seemed she'd finally got her happy ever after. But it wasn't to be. They'd had seven laughter-filled years together before his aneurism. It had all been over so quickly. Tara wished she'd been on the spot for Bea when it had happened.

'We'd better watch out at the bottom of the Green Dragon Bridge,' Tara said. 'That's the spot that'll get us if anywhere does. There's a patch that still hasn't thawed. I almost went flat on my backside there on my way over to your place.' She hadn't mentioned that it would have been the second time in twenty-four hours. Her own ice patch hadn't finished melting yet either.

They didn't talk much on the walk to Ditton Meadows. As they traversed the slippery boardwalk next to the river, under the railway, Tara saw a few flakes of snow fall. *Again?* She'd already had enough of it.

She felt Bea tense next to her. 'I want to put him straight down on the bare ground,' she said suddenly. 'I want to see where he goes; not leave him to be carried away by melting snow.'

A woman walking a dog, going in the other direction, glanced at them curiously, then darted her eyes away.

'Don't worry.' Tara hugged Bea again. 'I don't think the snow's going to lie.'

They carried on walking up the river, crossing the wooden bridge that spanned the small stream coming off the Cam, then trudging along the Reach. At last they passed through the gateway that gave on to the meadow nearest Fen Ditton. Ahead, Tara could see the edge of the village and the church.

'I thought maybe we should scatter him round here,' Bea said, her gloved hands tight on the urn. 'It'll be peaceful if I want to come and feel near to him, but within sight of the village, so it's not too lonely. And when the Bumps are on he'll get a visit from all the spectators. I think he would have liked that.'

The Bumps. Rowing races where either college boats or those from the town clubs raced to try to catch each other up. Fast and furious affairs, watched from the meadows by picnickers when the weather was better. Tara nodded and pictured Greg's laughing face. His image made her throat feel tight. 'I think you're right. And if you visit, and you feel like company, you can knock on my cottage door on your way.'

Bea nodded, swallowed and took off her right glove, putting it in her pocket. And then, without looking at Tara, she removed the lid of the urn and reached inside it, taking a handful of the ashes. She walked forward and let the dust run through her fingers as she went. After a moment she took another handful and another, walking here and there across the cold, hard ground. At last she turned. 'Would you like to scatter a handful? Greg liked you so much.'

Tara went forward and put her hand into the urn, feeling the dust, like sand between her fingers. She copied Bea, whilst trying to focus hard on tiny details: the shape of the grass at her feet, the sound of a swan landing on the river. Allowing her mind to dwell on the enormity of what Bea had lost would undo her. As she watched the remains rain down, flakes of snow stung her cheeks, but the ground was still bare.

At that moment, she looked up in the direction of Fen Ditton and caught her breath. Blake. What the hell was he doing there? She could see him across the meadow, outside a house that was out on the edge of things, just like hers, side on to the plain. He had a young girl in his arms and was lifting her high into the air and then swinging her down again. The girl threw her head back and laughed – a look of glee on her face. And in that second a petite woman appeared at the house's door, slamming it shut behind her. Tara watched the woman for a moment, observing Blake and the child. There was an odd stillness about her. Then Blake realised he had company and brought the girl down one final time, took her hand and walked towards a car, where the woman joined them. Suddenly he turned in the direction of the meadows and she was afraid he'd see her.

Not that it would matter. It wasn't as though she was spying on him. She'd had no idea he lived in Fen Ditton. It was weird that his house was almost a pair for hers – except that hers was further out on a limb. That had to be a metaphor for her life. How ironic.

But she didn't want to be seen. The picture of his family life she'd just witnessed seemed so intimate somehow. She tried to ignore the weight that she suddenly felt in her chest. In a second she'd tugged up the collar of her coat and turned quickly towards Bea, her head down.

Her relative's face looked more relaxed than she'd seen it in a while. 'I'm sorry,' she said.

'What for?'

'For saving this up until you were back. But I can't tell you how much it's helped, tackling it together.'

'I'm glad. And I'm glad to be here.'

She nodded. 'Shall we go home now?'

'Yes. I can make you hot chocolate at my place before you go back to the fray.'

Bea rubbed her hands and pulled her right-hand glove back on. 'That sounds like a plan.'

Back at the cottage, Tara had to warn Bea about the ice on the tiles, but she didn't explain her suspicions about how it had come to be there. Unlike Tara's colleagues, Bea would take it seriously, and the last thing she needed was more worry.

Instead, she ushered her inside, put the kettle on and went to drag a fan heater out of the under-stairs cupboard. 'Sit down,' she said, 'and I'll point this at your feet.'

Bea rolled her eyes. 'I still can't believe you've moved back here.'

But Tara guessed it wasn't just the lack of creature comforts that made Bea wonder. People tended to imagine that having been stalked in her teens, and targeted by a killer, she'd want to avoid such a secluded location. Who would hear her if she screamed? But Tara saw it the other way round. Out where she was, in the open, it was easier to spot anyone who'd singled her out. In the centre of the city, the malignant stranger that meant you harm could be the person who'd just rented the flat one floor down. But there were other advantages to being away from the hubbub too. When she'd moved to Suffolk to do her police training she'd had to rent the bottom half of a semi-detached house in suburban Ipswich – the income she'd got from letting out her Cambridge cottage had barely covered her mortgage, so upgrading hadn't been an option. The person upstairs had been a web designer who preferred working at night. To loud music. She'd missed the tranquillity of her home on the common. She valued her own space. She couldn't say that to Bea, though. Not now. Not when she was suddenly in the same position against her will: all alone except for her paying guests.

'I'm fond of this place,' she said instead. 'It's like living in the countryside, being out here by the river and the meadows. And I can play my music as loudly as I like if I'm feeling cross. I'm definitely doing any potential neighbour a favour.'

She put chocolate powder into their mugs, ignoring the stingy instructions advising three heaped teaspoons per serving, and added the boiling water.

'I'm not looking forward to Christmas,' Bea said suddenly, her eyes fixed determinedly on a knot in the table's wood.

'That's hardly surprising. Mum will want you to go to them, of course.' She was due back from Madeira the week before, and she'd get someone in to help with the preparations, anyway. ('Fiona from the village is very willing, and she's fine really, so long as I give her plenty of clear instructions and something decent to wear when she arrives. I call it a uniform to avoid offence.')

Bea nodded, her head still down. 'She's asked me. But I've got guests booked in. I don't want to lose them. I'm doing them a champagne breakfast and a Christmas lunch. But I'll have the evening to myself.'

Tara could hear the wobble in her voice. 'I'll come and help you,' she said. 'And then we can watch films and get squiffy.'

She put the mugs down on the table and sat opposite Bea, who looked up at last. Her eyes were red and her cheeks blotchy, but she smiled. 'Thanks, darling, but your mother will definitely want you there.'

'Officially yes, but in all honesty, no. She'll be relieved if I say I can't come.' Her mother wouldn't acknowledge it, even to herself, but Tara knew her shoulders would relax just a little if her awkward elder child wouldn't be at the dinner table, saying all the wrong things. 'You're my perfect excuse, so please don't let me down.'

Bea put her head on one side.

'You of all people know I mean it,' Tara said. And she did. Her stepfather Benedict's put-on heartiness, together with stilted conversations with her half-brother, Harry – the wanted child – weren't something she felt she ought to have to deal with over the festive season. What's more, her mother had told her that Harry had applied to study at Cambridge the following year. If he got in she'd have to deal with him at closer quarters, running the risk of bumping into him in town. She ought to keep her distance whilst she still could.

It was time to move the conversation on, before Bea could argue the point further. Tara distracted her with news of her visit from Monica Cairncross, and what she'd found out since. Officially, she shouldn't discuss work, but thanks to Wilkins, some of what she'd found out had been through her own private efforts anyway. As for the rest – well – she trusted Bea; she was family, and there was no way she'd pass on the details to anyone.

'Dr Cairncross is very determined,' Tara said, when she'd summed up what the woman had said.

'Might be guilt.' Bea sipped her chocolate. 'Maybe she feels responsible for her brother's death in some way. People don't always think rationally when they've lost someone.'

'True.' Tara paused for a moment. 'But she didn't seem overwhelmed with grief. It's something else that's driving her. It's as though she's on a mission. She's furious and she's out for justice.' She pulled a face. 'She clearly hates her sister-in-law and her niece. They're prime suspects as far as she's concerned. Only there's no hard evidence of a crime. But – I don't know – I feel as though there's something odd going on.

'As for Ralph Cairncross, I can't help wondering what he was like as an individual.' She told Bea about the opening of his final novel: the fit man in the warm seas swimming towards the snake that would kill him.

Bea shivered. 'That sounds rather warped to me. I remember reading about his death in the papers, of course. The coverage was hard to avoid, what with him having been well-known.'

'Have you read any of his books?'

Bea gave her a look. 'No – to be honest. From the reviews, I always suspected I'd find them difficult to appreciate, and what you've just told me confirms my opinion.'

Tara smiled for a moment. 'I can understand that.' But although she'd got no desire to acquire any more of Cairncross's work, the passage she'd read had stayed with her. Why had it been so powerful? The intensity of the language? Its sensuality? Or simply her shock at the man's actions? She wished she could banish the image from her head. 'We can have an online snoop at Ralph Cairncross and his family, if you like. And I'm researching what remains of the group he was partying with the night he died too. Monica Cairncross says Ralph called them "the Acolytes".'

'Odd.' Bea looked up from her drink and met Tara's gaze. 'Aren't they the people who help in church?'

Tara nodded. 'Or at least, that's one of the meanings. I had to look it up. The primary definition was "someone who helps an important person and supports their ideas, often without ever criticising them".'

'Doesn't sound all that healthy.'

'No, that's what I thought. And given the high esteem Monica held her brother in, I get the impression that's the meaning she meant. And that she doesn't think there's anything odd about him having had that sort of following.'

She saw the ghost of a smile cross Bea's lips. 'You're getting me intrigued now.'

That was all to the good. Any kind of diversion at a time like this was worth grasping. Tara fetched her laptop from the cupboard where she kept it and set it down on the kitchen table.

She moved round so that she was next to Bea, and they huddled together to see the information Tara brought up. Ralph Cairncross's page on his publisher's site included a potted biography, with photographs of him as a young man and then one that had been taken just a year before. His face had been hauntingly beautiful in his twenties, though dissolute-looking by his fifties.

'He looks like a drinker by the later picture, doesn't he?' Bea said. 'There's still some sort of magnetism about him there, though.' She sighed. 'It's so odd, seeing how someone changes over time like that. All that youth and promise – that sort of freshness someone has – and then seeing things start to crumble.' She looked down at her own hands. 'I wonder what he'd have looked like if he'd lived until he was ninety.'

'From the sound of his lifestyle, I guess that wasn't on the cards.'

'No.' She frowned, her eyes scanning the text. 'Just as well, looking at his views on aging.'

Ralph Cairncross had courted controversy, something the publishers had made even more of than the awards he'd received. He'd declared publicly (around ten years earlier) that people past a certain age lost their usefulness and elasticity of mind. It had caused a media storm, and was pretty ironic given he'd been approaching that age himself when he'd died. What would he have done at that point? Announced that he'd changed his mind? Or just withdrawn from public life to enjoy the mountains of cash he'd amassed by being such a notorious figure?

'I don't think much of him, based on this,' Bea said. 'Having just lost someone who would have valued his later years – and been rightly valued by others during them – I find his views repellent.'

'Agreed.'

When Tara explored the other search results Google had come up with, she could see that his notoriety had brought a lot of attention with it. He'd been followed by the press and lauded by several critics, despite his abhorrent opinions. It looked as though he'd lived a rock-and-roll lifestyle. Perhaps it went some way to explaining the loyalty of the group of young Acolytes who'd been prepared to trail round in his wake. They'd probably enjoyed seeing their photographs in the papers and being plied with free champagne at the glamorous receptions their mentor had taken them to. She could see they'd been in evidence a lot of the time.

Tara tried to imagine being prepared to suck up to someone like Ralph Cairncross in return for reflected glory and free booze, but failed. His followers would have to have been gullible, shallow or cynical, she reckoned. Or maybe just too young to have seen the man for what he was. She returned to the Google homepage, where she entered his wife's name instead. Monica Cairncross had said she was called Sadie. They read the results in companionable silence. She turned out to have quite a web presence too. Apparently, she'd been a professional flautist when she was younger, but her career seemed to have stopped abruptly when she'd hit thirty-five. What had happened? There were still recordings of her work on sale on Amazon, and photographs of her in the Albert Hall during the Proms.

Tara glanced to one side. Bea was just as absorbed by the text as she had been.

'Odd, isn't it?' Tara said, when her mother's cousin glanced up. 'It looks as though she was riding high, until that cut-off point. And now she doesn't even have a Facebook page.'

'What about the daughter?'

Twenty-year-old Philippa. Tara performed the search. She had a Facebook page all right, but she'd taken care of her privacy settings. They could only see her profile and cover photos, and she'd been circumspect with those. Just the side of her face complete with sunglasses for the former, and a fenland landscape for the latter. But when Tara looked more closely she was almost certain it was the Forty Foot Drain. The picture had been updated two months previously. She glanced sideways at Bea. 'That's where her father died. What kind of daughter would choose to update her cover photo to an image like that, given the associations it must have?'

'What kind indeed?' Bea frowned, then sighed. 'This is interesting. Let me know what you come up with, would you? But I'd better be getting on now. I'm going to slow-cook boeuf bourguignon for the hungry hordes tonight.' She caught Tara's look. 'No. I know what you're going to say, but I don't want help. You need to have a weekend, and I – well – I need to get used to the new status quo. And if I can't manage then I need to form a plan of campaign.'

Bea stood up and fetched her coat from the hall and Tara hovered, waiting to hug her goodbye. The snow started again as her mother's cousin exited the house. Tara watched the person who'd been a tiny tower of strength during her childhood make her way resolutely back towards the Green Dragon Bridge.

After she'd gone, Tara reached for her Kindle and opened up Ralph Cairncross's book again. It gave her an eerie feeling, as though just by looking at the dead man's words she was opening up a link between them that made her uncomfortable.

She shook off the response. She wanted to know more about the man the author had been. What better way than to examine the very last book he'd written? She scrolled back from where the file opened, so that she could look at his dedication. It might show who he'd been closest to at the time.

But the words just raised more questions.

To T, who managed to escape unscathed. You are blessed indeed.

What the hell did that mean?

CHAPTER NINE

Tara got up early on Monday morning and headed to Addenbrooke's before going into the station. It was one more bit of official digging she could do before Blake told her to stop – possibly on the sneaky side, but worth it.

Now she was sitting in the hospital branch of Costa opposite Agneta Larsson, the pathologist who'd been in charge of looking into the circumstances of Ralph Cairncross's death. They hadn't met properly before, but Tara had seen her in court. She'd been the pathologist on the Samantha Seabrook murder case too.

All around them vignettes played out: a woman pulling clothes for a newborn baby from a Mothercare bag, ready to show to her companion; an elderly man and a middle-aged woman, each clutching tissues, their eyes red; a nurse sipping hastily at his steaming cup of coffee between regular glances at the clock on the wall.

Agneta Larsson looked tired, but her eyes had that slightly startled appearance that came from already being well-stoked with caffeine. She was nodding, sending her blonde hair over one eye. 'Yes, I remember it all very clearly, as a matter of fact.' She sighed. 'Just such a waste, you know? So unnecessary.' She took a sip of her drink. 'So, what can I tell you? The blood alcohol was very high. If his sister says he regularly went out and drove in that state then I am honestly surprised he lasted as long as he did.'

'You think she might be wrong?'

Agneta shrugged. 'Others said it too – he regularly drove when he'd been drinking.'

That was true; the part of the statement Tara had read backed that up. The Acolytes had been so used to it that only one of them had tried to discourage him from setting off.

'But,' Agneta said, 'I would be surprised if he regularly drank so very much and then took the wheel.'

'I see.' If he'd had more than usual that night, Tara wondered why.

'It was certainly enough to explain his accident and for the coroner to record misadventure. But I don't believe it was the only factor, as I said in my report.'

The report Wilkins had prevented her from reading. 'Could you explain?'

Agneta nodded. 'Ralph Cairncross was covered in bruises, of course. Some were consistent with his crash. For instance, I believe he knocked his head on the steering wheel. He might have been unconscious as his car sank. It was summer and he had his windows down. The water would have rushed in very quickly.'

For a second Tara's mind ran back to when she'd thought she was going to drown. She remembered the feeling of unbridled panic, the struggle and the burning sensation in her lungs as she ran out of air. The clutch of her would-be killer's hand on her ankle, dragging her further down. She looked up and realised the pathologist was watching her with recognition in her eyes.

'I'm sorry,' she said. 'Flashback? I should have thought.' She knew the story, of course. Tara had only just escaped ending up on her slab.

Tara shook her head. She wanted to move the conversation on. 'You were telling me about the bruising on Ralph Cairncross's body?'

'Sure.' The pathologist took a sip of her coffee. 'So as I said, some were consistent with the impact he'd have received from the crash. But several were not. The odd ones out made me think he'd thrashed around in the car in a very uncontrolled way – I'd guess just before his car left the road.'

Wilkins had prevented Tara's access to significant information. What the hell was he playing at? Was it really just him being territorial? 'What would explain that?'

Agneta sighed. 'That's the trouble. Pathology cannot crack every puzzle. The most likely conclusion – in the absence of any other evidence – is that he had a sudden seizure of some kind. Unfortunately, as there were no witnesses and of course' – she gave a brief smile – 'his brain activity at the time is unknowable, I cannot say for sure. But for me there were question marks over that as the most likely answer.'

Tara raised an eyebrow.

'He had no medical history of fits. In addition, I might have expected other circumstantial evidence – loss of bladder or stool control, for instance. That sometimes happens even just as a result of the fear induced by a crash. There was nothing in this case, but that doesn't prove no seizure took place. And if one did, it would tie in with the lack of tyre marks on the road. He wouldn't have been in a position to brake. As alcohol poisoning can result in a seizure, the package of evidence led to the misadventure conclusion. His own actions had likely been a deciding factor in his death.'

Tara's eyes were on Agneta Larsson's. 'You're not completely convinced?'

'Seizures due to alcohol poisoning are brought on by lowered blood sugar levels. Ralph Cairncross's weren't as low as I would have expected. But when a man has drunk that much, such technicalities come across as minor details. The coroner had to decide between misadventure and accidental death and on balance he came down in favour of the former. If he'd been satisfied that the fit hadn't been alcohol related then he might not have.'

Tara nodded. It was interesting, but it didn't point to the foul play Monica Cairncross suspected. She ought to let the pathologist get on. 'Just before I go, I wondered if there were any incidental things about the case that struck you. You visited the scene of the accident?'

She nodded. 'It was a horrible day. The night before had been calm and warm, but when we went to recover the body the weather suddenly broke. Thunder, lightning, the whole show. It didn't make the job any easier.'

Agneta closed her eyes for a moment. 'The only other thing I remember from that bit of the day was seeing an eel in the water, slithering off the body when it was moved.' Her shoulders quivered. 'That and hearing Patrick Wilkins and Max Dimity arguing.'

Tara raised an eyebrow. 'What about? Do you know?'

She shook her head. 'DS Wilkins was trying to show how at ease he was, seeing death at close quarters. It's a way of coping, of course, but the way he expressed himself was inappropriate. So I focused on my own thoughts.'

Always a better option than listening to Wilkins. She caught Agneta's eye and a look of understanding passed between them.

The pathologist drained her coffee. 'I looked Ralph Cairncross up afterwards. I knew he was a famous author, but not much more than that – I had never read his books. I said to you what a waste it was, him dying when he did, but given his views on aging he got what he wanted in some ways.' She pulled a face. 'Not much comfort for those left behind.'

'Were you there when his wife came to identify his body?'

She nodded, looking down at the table. 'She was in a terrible state. Of course, that's what you'd imagine, but the sound of her crying was so raw, so abandoned.' She shook her head, like a cat trying to get water out of its ears. 'I can still hear it, you know?'

'Was anyone with her?'

Agneta nodded. 'Her daughter. And she looked angry. Those eyes will stay with me too. Not that I am surprised. Ralph Cairncross had been careless of his own safety and the results were affecting her and her mother.' She put her hands on the table as though readying herself to stand up. She must need to get on. 'Anger was not an unnatural reaction.'

Tara thought again of the image of the Forty Foot Drain that Philippa Cairncross had put up on Facebook.

Back at Parkside, Tara greeted those of her colleagues who were in the office, earning her a grunt from Wilkins, who didn't ask her for an update. No surprises there. She was back on research for the Hunter drugs case. She was beginning to think there'd be nothing to find on Ralph Cairncross and Lucas Everett's deaths anyway. The only odd circumstance she'd managed to identify was the note that Lucas had left with his clothes, torn from a notebook that couldn't be found. He could have slung it into a bin on his way to the beach for all she knew. Other than that it was just Monica's accusations, and they didn't hold water. The only feeling of doubt came from the ice on her own doorstep… but that had been nothing more than a nasty prank, and she could think of several people who might have been responsible.

She glanced up at Wilkins. He was busy looking busy and frowning to show just how very focused he was. To be fair, the Hunter case was important; no argument there. She wasn't going to have the DS complaining she wasn't patient enough to complete her routine work.

By mid-morning, she was ready for a coffee and walked out of the open-plan room and down the corridor to the machine. There were two people in the queue ahead of her – one of them being Max Dimity. After he'd got his drink he paused next to her.

'Sorry you had to cover for me on Friday,' Tara said. 'I probably did have a wasted trip in the end.'

Max's brown eyes were friendly. 'Don't worry. What were you after anyway, over in Suffolk? The DI said something about the death of a man connected to Ralph Cairncross?'

Tara put her mug underneath the coffee dispenser. 'That's right. The visit was to this other man's mother, just to check some of the details. Although the deaths might be interrelated, it doesn't look as though there's anything untoward about them.'

Max nodded. 'I see. Still, you can't know unless you check.'

So much better than Wilkins' attitude. Tara smiled. 'True. You attended the scene of Ralph Cairncross's accident, didn't you?'

Max nodded.

Tara took her full mug from the machine and raised it to her lips. It was too hot for her to do anything more than taste the coffee. 'I just wondered, was there anything that stuck in your mind from that day?'

Max raised his eyebrows. 'You're still wondering about the death?'

She held her mug to her chest, enjoying its warmth through the polo-necked sweater she was wearing. 'No, not really. It's just a compulsion, you know – to know everything there is about something.'

Max nodded. 'I recognise that feeling.'

'I've spoken to Agneta over at Addenbrooke's. I gather the weather was stormy?'

His eyes were far away now and looked darker still. 'That's right,' he said. 'It was.'

'And did you and DS Wilkins discuss the accident much: the way the car appeared, the position of the body? Anything like that?' She was hoping Max might mention the argument Agneta had overheard. She couldn't help wondering about it.

'We talked about the fact that there were no tyre marks on the road,' Max said. 'And no sign of potholes or anything like that.' He sighed. 'To be honest, I found the scene a bit hard to take. My wife' – she saw his Adam's apple move quickly as he swallowed – 'my wife was killed in a car accident four and half years ago. The DS did a lot of joking, to try to take away from the awfulness of what we could see, I suppose. That's what he told DCI Fleming later, anyway – someone mentioned it to her. But it was too near the knuckle for me.'

Tara had had no idea about Max's wife. She'd assumed he was simply young, free and single. She caught her breath. 'I'm so sorry for your loss,' she said. 'Attending the scene of Ralph Cairncross's accident must have been horrendous.' Wilkins' behaviour would explain the argument Agneta had overheard. 'Did you tell DS Wilkins what you felt at the time?' *How could he have been so unfeeling?*

But Max shook his head. 'I should have, of course. I focused in on the job instead – or tried to. But it meant I was short-tempered with the DS, and he's not my biggest fan, even at the best of times.'

Tara wondered if Max knew about the cruel nickname her boss had given him. 'You argued?'

Max nodded. 'Over trifles – that's the stupid thing. But I had local knowledge to contribute and I thought I might as well give it, even if it wasn't important.'

'What was it?'

A sad smile crossed Max's lips. 'The DS made some kind of joke about an "eel" that slid off the dead man's body as it was moved. London boy, the DS is. You get eels in the Fens of course – that's even how the city of Ely gets its name. But you get grass snakes there too. They're swimmers. And that was most definitely a grass snake.' He gave Tara a look. 'Doesn't make any difference, I realise that. But I'm a country boy and I know this area. That's one thing DS Wilkins can't take away from me.'

Back at her desk, Tara thought about what Max Dimity had said. She was a local too; she understood his frustration. She'd seen a grass snake once, swimming in water close to her mother's house, out in the Fens. It had been longer than an eel – over a metre, she guessed. And their bodies weren't the same shape – not when you looked properly, anyway. Eels had a fin along their backs. But she couldn't blame Agneta for misidentifying the creature at a distance. And even closer to, with the rain coming down, dark skies and swirling, muddy waters, one might have passed for another. Wilkins ought to have listened to Max when he'd explained though. If he'd been a decent guy Tara would have put his lack of attention down to being preoccupied with the victim, but she knew better. It sounded as though he'd taken time out to rubbish Max's assertion, given that Agneta had heard them arguing.

She battled on with the work on Hunter – cross-checking phone numbers on a series of account records – until lunchtime. Every so often she was conscious of a fresh wave of fruitless frustration at Wilkins' behaviour towards Max but she tried to shelve it. She wouldn't allow herself to lose concentration.

All the same, at 1 p.m., over a sandwich, her mind was back on Ralph Cairncross's death and the scene that had played out on the morning that his body had been recovered. She found herself idly googling grass snakes in a childish desire to prove to herself how ignorant Wilkins was.

Two minutes later she was caught up in an article she'd found. The room around her faded until anyone could have come up to her without her noticing. She sat there at her desk for a moment, gooseflesh creeping over the skin of her forearms, the hairs rising on her scalp.

No, this is crazy…

She dug for more information, scanning multiple web pages, and even watched a YouTube clip with her headphones on. She was sitting back in her chair as she started the video – in denial – but by time she'd finished she was full of doubt.

She waited for a moment, irresolute, before crossing the room to Max Dimity's desk. She was glad Wilkins was on the phone.

'Max, do you remember who it was that actually pulled Ralph Cairncross's body out of his car?'

He looked surprised, but nodded. 'Young guy called Tony Griggs. You'll find him on the system.'

Back at her desk she looked up Griggs's number, keyed it into her mobile and left the room. Just outside the front entrance she called him. She didn't want Wilkins to know what she was on to until she did.

Two minutes later she had her answer. But it was ten more minutes before she made her way to Blake's office. Even by her own judgement her idea sounded like something someone would dream after eating too much cheese. But she couldn't let it go, even if it meant ridicule. The more she thought about it, the more she knew it was her responsibility to say something. Yes, her idea sounded mad, but so mad she could write it off? Ignore it with a clear conscience? The answer to that was no – rather to her regret. Why the hell couldn't the first meaty case she had to deal with in her new job be something straightforward?

CHAPTER TEN

Blake's eyes met Tara's across his desk. It was ten minutes since she'd entered his office and started to explain her theory. It seemed ludicrous on the face of it, and yet… it could explain the odd injuries on Cairncross's right arm and hand. And the lack of braking before his car went into the water… It would account for the reservations he'd noted in Agneta's report too. She hadn't been satisfied with the seizure theory. But all the same…

'I know it's as weird as hell,' Tara said, giving him a look. 'But I felt I had to share it with you once the idea had come to me. It seemed important enough to risk being thought of as delusional.'

At last he nodded. He could see where she was coming from. 'You're not going to like this, but I want to get Patrick in here, so you can relay it all to him too.' He could see she'd known it was coming.

'He won't take it seriously.'

They shared a look. It was doubtful his DS would take anything Tara said seriously, which was a problem he needed to address. However, this particular theory was going to be an especially hard sell. 'Granted. But Ralph Cairncross was his case to begin with, and if anything comes out of all this, he'll need to know the facts so far.' And if Blake was about to appropriate Tara again, it was best that Patrick knew why, though he wished the judgement call he'd have to make could be based on something more solid. After a moment, Tara nodded. There was a second's silence. 'We can't have him – or anyone – thinking some members of the team go off and cook things up in isolation.' Patrick was just the sort to jump to that conclusion. Blake sat back in his chair. 'Fleming's right about that. Once the whispering starts, things become unworkable.' And he wasn't sure what form the whispering might take. He had a feeling it would revolve around matters that were a lot more personal than Ralph Cairncross's death.

He picked up his phone and called Patrick in. The man took a minute to appear at the door and made his journey to his seat as slow as possible, Blake noticed.

'Go ahead, Tara,' he said, once his DS was finally settled.

'I've got information and a theory I need to share regarding Ralph Cairncross's death,' Tara said, looking at Patrick. 'It's in relation to the possible involvement of a third party.'

Blake watched Wilkins' face as surprise turned to irritation and then to disbelief. As soon as he heard the details he'd start pulling her theory to pieces. But then her ideas wanted testing. Blake knew he ought to feel more enthusiastic. And less irritated by the way Patrick picked an invisible speck of dust off his suit trousers as he waited.

'I spoke to Tony Griggs a short time ago,' Tara said, directing her words to Patrick again. 'He was one of the guys who retrieved Ralph Cairncross's body from the Forty Foot Drain, though obviously you, Agneta Larsson and Max Dimity were watching too, amongst others.' Patrick had been looking out of the window and Tara paused until his eyes were back on the room. 'Both you and Dr Larsson noticed there was a creature you thought was an eel, entwined with Ralph Cairncross's body as it was pulled free. But Max Dimity told me it was actually a grass snake, and that caught my attention. They're both common in the fenland waterways, but given the different stories, I asked Tony Griggs for more information. He's local, like Max, and he saw it right up close. He says it was definitely a grass snake. And that it was dead.'

'This is starting to sound like something out of Sherlock Holmes,' Wilkins murmured. Tara's expression remained neutral, which Blake thought was impressive, under the circumstances. Having said that, he could grudgingly see where Wilkins was coming from on this one occasion...

'I looked up grass snakes,' she went on, 'and they swim along the surface of the water. They can stay under for an hour if something frightens them, but not longer than that. So, the question is, did this grass snake dive underwater because it was disturbed, swim in through Ralph Cairncross's submerged car window and fail to find its way out again? Or did someone slip it into his car whilst he was parked outside the house where he and the Acolytes met, and then wait for it to give him the shock of his life when he got in to drive home, full of booze and travelling by moonlight?'

Blake noted the deliberate smirk that Patrick allowed to play around his lips. He was on the edge of his seat now, as though he was impatient to get going.

'It's a fascinating theory,' his DS said, 'but we are only talking about a grass snake, Tara. They're not the most threatening of creatures.'

'I can understand your thinking,' she said. 'And if they think they're in danger they sometimes even play dead. But females can grow to well over a metre long, and if they're trapped in a confined space. Well, I'll show you.' Blake watched as she opened the laptop she'd brought in with her. She angled it so that he and Patrick could both see. She had her web browser open on a YouTube page, and clicked the video there, making it full screen.

The film showed a grass snake stuck in a large, plastic tub. It looked substantial – certainly as long as Tara had said, and solid too. The creature raised its head high in the tub and hissed. Its body movements were sudden, fast and aggressive. Each time it drew itself up you got an idea of just how big it was. It made repeated, violent striking movements. The people making the video had identified it as a grass snake. They knew it couldn't reach them and that it wasn't poisonous. And yet he heard the way the pitch of their voices rose, each time the snake suddenly stretched itself towards them and struck out. It was gut instinct, and he felt their nervousness.

'I think if it had been me,' Tara said, looking at them each in turn, 'and I'd been driving along the Forty Foot Bank, drunk, in the dark, and a creature that big had slid out from under my seat, hissing and striking, it would have been enough to send me off the road.' Her eyes were quite calm, but she must have seen that the video had done its work. 'It would account for the bruises Agneta Larsson said were on Cairncross's body when he was discovered. I suspect I might have flailed around in terror. What do *you* think?'

Blake knew Tara was aware of how extraordinary her theory sounded. He took his hat off to her. Her speech had been an impressive performance. She might be willing to acknowledge the fallibility of her thoughts to him, but she sure as hell wasn't going to be that unguarded with Wilkins.

As for Blake, he needed to take a step back. It was a moment before he spoke. 'I agree. Though we can't know for certain that the snake was in the car when it went into the water.'

'Which is a bit of a major sticking point,' Patrick drawled. There ought to be a rule against any member of his team drawling.

'True,' Blake said. 'But for what it's worth, this scenario would fit with the lack of tyre marks on the road, too. He'd have been weaving around to try to avoid the creature; braking wouldn't have been his reflex reaction.'

Wilkins shrugged. 'One thing's certain, if you wanted to kill someone, it wouldn't be the most reliable way to do it.'

'Perfectly true,' Tara said. Once again, her tone was well controlled. Blake felt a moment of amusement. He'd heard recordings of her interviewing her subjects when she'd been a journalist. It was frightening, the way she could deceive her interlocutors into thinking she found their input useful. The look of puzzlement on Patrick's face when she remained so amiable was enjoyable. 'But what if we're dealing with someone who's playing games?' Tara went on. 'If, instead of a perpetrator who was dead set on making sure Cairncross died on a particular date, at a particular time, we have someone who treats their objective as a longer-term goal. Maybe they even get a buzz out of throwing a spanner into the works – not knowing if it will get knocked harmlessly to one side, or jam the machine in a catastrophic way. What if that person tampered with Ralph Cairncross's garage lamp the week before he died, but didn't get anywhere? The lamp incident's written off as an unfortunate accident. Old thing – not well maintained. Our perpetrator's a gambler. From their point of view, they failed first time round, but it doesn't matter. They're free to try again, using another method that at worst will be viewed as an unpleasant prank if Cairncross arrives home, safe but shaken. But at best – from their perspective – Cairncross goes down into the water with his Indian summer windows wide open, and if anyone finds a grass snake near his body, no one thinks anything of it.'

There was silence for a moment.

'And maybe symbolism was important to the perpetrator too – if we believe there really was one,' Tara added.

'Symbolism?' Patrick practically spat the word out.

'In Ralph Cairncross's final book, his main character chooses death by snake bite, whilst he's out swimming in the water.' She explained the passage she'd described to Blake before Wilkins' arrival. 'What if someone decided they'd try to make the final scene in Ralph Cairncross's life mirror the death in his last book? He portrayed the hero's fate as something beautiful and serene. Perhaps the perpetrator wanted to show him what dying's really like.'

'The next thing you'll be telling me is that someone engineered Lucas Everett's drowning, too,' Patrick said.

Tara paused for a second. 'It's not impossible.'

His DS snorted. 'It would be pretty hard to explain. I read your report on your findings in Kellness.' Blake wasn't entirely surprised by this sudden show of diligence. He'd be looking for as much information as possible, so he could hold his own when they reviewed the case. Nothing meant more to Patrick than saving face. 'A third party would have to have persuaded Everett to swim out too far, I presume? He couldn't have been rushing to rescue someone who was pretending to be in trouble – not with that ridiculous bravado-filled note he left on the beach. So, if we say someone was there with Everett, egging him on to take risks, wouldn't they have shared the bottle of vodka that was found on the beach? And yet the only clear prints on it were Everett's and the shop assistant's.'

'A third party could have brought their own booze,' Tara said.

'The idea's even more far-fetched than your theory about the snake.' There was a sneer on Patrick's face.

'Of course, if there is a connection between the two deaths, it might not be that a third party plotted to kill them both,' Blake said. 'What if, at some point, Lucas Everett had been smitten by the older man? Perhaps Cairncross rejected him, and Everett planted the snake in his car to get his own back. He might not have thought through the full consequences of what he was doing. Then when Cairncross wound up dead, maybe Lucas Everett planned his swim whilst he was consumed with guilt.'

'But Mrs Everett dismissed the idea of her son being in love with Ralph,' Tara said. 'And she talked about him being energised, too. He was enthusing about continuing to live according to the ideals Ralph Cairncross had held.'

'I remember you mentioned that.' Blake thought back to the email she'd sent on Friday. 'But mothers aren't always the best at reading their children's emotions' – his certainly wasn't – 'and people who're going through extreme stress can have mood swings.'

'True… but there's the testimony of the woman who served Everett in the Co-op, too. She mentioned how upbeat Lucas was.'

'That could have been because he'd made up his mind to do something to combat his guilt and honour Cairncross's memory,' Blake said. He understood where Tara was coming from but he couldn't help noticing that her the desire to fight her corner overrode her judgement sometimes.

'There are other incidents that make me think this is a wider plot.' Tara hesitated and glanced at Wilkins. At last she turned back to Blake. 'As you know, when she came to see me, Monica Cairncross thought she was being followed.'

He could understand why she'd paused before committing herself. Patrick was just the sort to assume Tara would be seeing stalkers around every corner, given that she'd been menaced as a teenager, and again just four years ago. He'd think she was more likely to believe what he'd view as a cock and bull story, because of her background. But Tara wasn't the fanciful sort.

'And' – there was a longer pause this time – 'someone left a booby trap for me to find when I got home on Friday night.'

Blake leant forward. 'What's that? Why didn't you report it?'

But as Tara relayed the detail, he could see why she hadn't. It sounded like a kid's prank on the face of it, and he saw Patrick raise his eyes to heaven.

'Sure you haven't had a burst pipe or something?' the DS said, with a light laugh. 'It's very easy for that type of problem to occur in winter and if you don't understand about plumbing…' Tara opened her mouth, but Patrick ploughed on. 'And of course, even if it was a deliberate act, I imagine there are a number of people who could have been responsible.' There was a look in his DS's eyes that Blake didn't like. 'There's your old stalker from when you were a teenager,

Tara. Oh, and then there's the journalist you attacked a few years ago. Or maybe an ex-colleague with a grudge? Is there any reason to suppose it's to do with Ralph Cairncross and Lucas Everett?'

'That's enough, Patrick,' said Blake firmly. The guy was way out of line. 'I need some time to digest all this. You can both carry on.'

After they'd left the room, he sat back in his chair. Could Tara be right? Were they dealing with some maniac who was playing God? And what about the ice on her front path? It was very easy to write it off as a joke, or as having an innocent explanation they hadn't identified. But what if someone was trying to make Tara look or feel paranoid? And what if that same person really had been responsible for one death already?

He rang Agneta and left a message, asking for her to contact him; he only had to wait twenty minutes before she called him back. He relayed Tara's theory and waited for her reaction. He heard her whistle down the phone.

It's the weirdest idea I ever heard, Blake, but it would fit every detail. I always was in doubt about the theory of seizure due to alcohol poisoning. I didn't make a secret of it. Hell,' she paused for a moment, *'that creature was big, Blake. If it really was in the car with Ralph Cairncross I can't imagine how frightened he must have been when he saw it. And if Tara's right then the choice the coroner had to make between accidental death and misadventure ought to have been one between misadventure and murder…'*

It was enough. He'd have to square the use of Tara's time with Fleming, who wasn't a fan of outlandish theories, but having spoken to Agneta he knew it was the right thing to do. A minute later he had Tara and Patrick back in his office.

'In light of the developments to date, I want Tara to do some limited additional digging.' He saw Patrick's grim expression and it made him feel better. Who the hell did he think he was, anyway? He'd have it out with him separately about his behaviour; his references to Tara's past earlier were totally unprofessional. 'I want to be sure. We've got capacity and Max can carry on helping out on the Hunter case for a couple of days.' He turned to Tara. 'I want to discuss what your plans are before you put them into action, and to have regular updates. Concentrate on Cairncross's death. After that, I'll take a view as to what we do next. It's a sensible use of a detective constable's time, and there are enough question marks to warrant this.'

Patrick shook his head as he made to exit the room, his fists bunched.

After the door was closed, Blake wondered if Tara would say something about the man's attitude. He realised he wanted her to.

But she just nodded at him. 'So I'll keep digging then,' she said. 'Until your deadline. A couple of days, you said?'

He realised he didn't appreciate her self-control so much when it extended to him, even though he ought to be applauding it. But he nodded. 'Yes. Two days, today being day one.' It was going to be tight, but he had to get the balance right. 'Let me know what you find. Start with talking to Cairncross's wife. And don't write off the theory of Lucas Everett planting the snake.'

'I won't.' She caught his look. 'And I know. Kid gloves, obviously. I'll go carefully.'

She'd read his mind. Just like old times.

She was at his office door, ready to open it, before he cracked. 'You did well with Patrick earlier. Keeping your cool, I mean. Can't have been easy.'

And suddenly she turned towards him and a smile flickered across her lips. 'I've got a secret weapon,' she said, and there was a look in her eye that he remembered.

'What's that?'

She put her head on one side. 'Wilkins-shaped voodoo doll at home. Hand-crafted – for some inexplicable reason, they're not on the market yet.'

He laughed before he could stop himself and hoped no one outside had heard. It was probably the most unprofessional he'd been since he'd entered CID. 'But joking apart, Tara,' he said, 'we have to make this work. And if you find anything concrete, Patrick will be right there with you, investigating.'

Tara gave him a look. 'And if I fail then he'll be convinced he's right and that I'm susceptible to fairy tales. Talk about a double-edged sword.'

CHAPTER ELEVEN

Ralph Cairncross's wife, Sadie, had agreed to see Tara that afternoon. She'd sounded slightly dazed when she'd answered the phone. Then again, Tara's call would have come out of the blue; it wasn't unnatural that the woman had been slow to get to grips with what she was saying.

Tara stood on Madingley Road, where Sadie Cairncross lived, the chill, foggy air catching at her throat. It tasted metallic. The early afternoon traffic was free-flowing on the wide road, and the pavement was deserted. She'd parked in a side street. She wanted to approach on foot to get an idea of the surroundings of the Cairncross home before her presence became obvious.

To her right, long driveways stretched off from the road, leading to vast houses on spacious plots. It wasn't the sort of street where you'd regularly bump into your neighbours. The tall evergreen hedgerow which marked the border of the Cairncross property increased its feeling of isolation. Tara wrapped her coat more tightly round herself and stepped onto the gravel driveway. As she walked further into the grounds, the noise of the cars and park-and-ride buses faded. She could hear a robin singing somewhere nearby, but then it too went quiet.

Ahead of her and to the right there was some sort of square red-brick outhouse, and beyond that the main building itself, a substantial 1920s villa covered in thick, dark ivy, with leaded glass windows.

The outhouse turned out to be a garage-cum-workshop with integral spaces for the storage of gardening equipment. She could see that much by peering through one of the small doors that opened onto the driveway. It had been left ajar. Inside, the compact, box-like section of the building was full of hoes, spades, edge trimmers, trowels and the like. It was all traditional stuff, smelling of oil and earth. There was nothing that you'd plug in.

Round the side of the building she looked in through a window and saw an elderly navy Volvo. There was space for another car, and Tara thought of Ralph Cairncross's Alfa Romeo that had been written off when he'd driven into the Forty Foot Drain.

To the right of the double garage doors, inside, she could see there was plenty of workspace. Tara glanced up at the house for a moment. It all looked quiet, and she was still a couple of minutes early. Cautiously, she moved round to a side door that led to the garage and tried it. Unlocked. To be fair, nothing inside looked nickable, so there'd be no real reason to bother. The arrangements certainly didn't narrow the field when it came to judging who might have tampered with the lamp that gave Ralph the electric shock. If anyone had.

Tara made her way back to the main driveway and continued her walk up to the house. All around her the grounds faded into the fog but the villa was crystal clear now. It looked dark, sombre and uninviting.

She walked up to the varnished wooden door with its leaded glass panel and made use of the art deco knocker. After a moment she saw a change in the lighting levels inside as someone opened an inner door to a lit room. A shadow approached and the front door was pulled slowly open.

Tara found it easy to recognise Sadie Cairncross from the old photos she'd found on the internet. She knew the former flautist was around fifty, but she didn't look it. Her rich chestnut hair reached past her shoulders and she'd avoided middle-aged spread. She had good skin too, and few lines on her face. Her bone structure struck

Tara as elegant. She was wearing a high-necked black sweater, a tartan miniskirt and long black boots.

Tara introduced herself and showed her ID. She knew she was expected, but Mrs Cairncross's eyes still widened just a fraction as she read her name. Tara had got used to it. Even though she was only a junior rank people still tended to expect someone older. Some of them even seemed to feel slighted at being landed with what they thought of as a whippersnapper. For a second she wished she'd worn a suit. Her brown polo neck and herringbone weave trousers were formal enough, but she could use some extra gravitas.

'Come in,' Sadie Cairncross said. She sounded tired and wary rather than curious. Her eyes told Tara this had already been a terrible year. She probably wanted to put the whole thing behind her; whatever the truth behind her husband's death.

And she'd had to battle with something else too. It was only when she spoke that Tara noticed it. She'd lost some mobility in the bottom half of her face. She went through the formality of smiling, and her mouth was beautiful, but lopsided. Could she have had a stroke at a young age? Or maybe she was suffering from Bell's palsy? A family friend had had that; they'd been given steroids and got their mobility back after five months.

'Thank you,' Tara said, as Sadie Cairncross stood back and held open an inner door to a spacious living room. It was lit by a number of table lamps, but the space was big and the windows less so. The overall effect was still of a dark room with the odd patch of illumination. Already the north-facing garden outside seemed to be dimming; the murky day sliding towards an early dusk.

'I'm confused about why you need to see me again at this stage,' Mrs Cairncross said.

Tara nodded. 'I understand, and I'm sorry to intrude. We're making a few additional enquiries, following what's probably a coincidence.'

Mrs Cairncross raised a well-shaped eyebrow.

'Your sister-in-law, Dr Monica Cairncross, came to see us. We understand she was out of the country in New Zealand when your husband had his accident, even though she managed to fly back for the funeral. You're no doubt aware that she's back in the UK permanently now. It seems she has a few more questions about the circumstances of Mr Cairncross's death.'

The woman's eyes flashed. 'She thinks someone else was involved,' she said. 'She emailed me at the time to say she didn't believe it was as simple as everyone was "making out".'

'That's pretty much what she told us.' She smiled at Sadie to show she was on her side. 'Just to get Dr Cairncross's thoughts on her brother's death out of the way immediately, are you aware of anyone who would have wanted to harm your husband? I'm so sorry to ask.' It seemed best to pass the topic off as a matter of pure routine, to be recorded, filed and not raised again… probably.

Sadie Cairncross looked hollow. 'His outlook on life invited strong reactions, Constable. Some people expressed their anger at his views quite openly. Critics and the like.'

'That must have been hard.' Though richly deserved, in Tara's opinion.

Mrs Cairncross shrugged. 'He was used to it.'

'What about closer to home? Was anyone in your husband's immediate circle ever seriously antagonistic towards him?'

'No.' But she said it too quickly, and suddenly, her eyes flitted away from Tara's. Tara couldn't help thinking of how angry Agneta Larsson said Philippa Cairncross had been when she'd come to jointly identify her father's body. What if that anger wasn't at the careless way in which Ralph had lost his life, causing her mother so much grief, but for other reasons? Tara thought again of the photograph she'd put up on Facebook of the scene of her father's death.

'And what about his relations with the Acolytes?' Tara asked, remembering Blake's instruction not to discount Lucas Everett as a possible perpetrator. 'Did he ever talk to you about them?'

Sadie's expression was tired. 'Constable, he rarely talked to me about anything else. Not that we spent an awful lot of time together towards the end.' She put her head on one side. 'He never mentioned any trouble with them, though. He seemed to view them as a collector might view a menagerie of exotic and amusing pets.'

Tara wondered if the Acolytes had been aware of that. 'Did he ever mention any of them pestering him? Or taking up more of his time than he wanted? Calling him at odd hours – that kind of thing?' If Lucas Everett *had* been obsessed enough with Ralph to kill him, she'd have thought he'd have given himself away somehow. She watched as Sadie frowned.

'He never mentioned anything like that,' she said at last. 'He did describe the artist, Thom King, as needy once or twice.' She glanced at Tara as though trying to read her expression and see if that meant anything.

But Tara didn't know if it did or not.

'What exactly did Monica say to you?' Sadie Cairncross asked.

'She claimed it was common for her brother to drink alcohol when he was driving and that it wouldn't have affected his performance.' Tara watched Sadie Cairncross's eyes. From her expression she imagined the woman had had quite enough of her sister-in-law's interference. Tara could play to that. She sat forward in her chair to narrow the gap between them. 'Hard facts don't support what she's saying, to be honest,' she said. And that was true enough. 'I'm sorry, because I'm sure other officers will have said this before and it's an upsetting truth. People often imagine they're just as capable at the wheel if they've had a drink – especially if they're used to alcohol – but it's an illusion. Dr Cairncross feels her brother was a good driver and wouldn't have gone off the road because of it, but that's not why I'm here.'

Sadie Cairncross nodded, and Tara noticed her face relax a little.

'Nonetheless, it would be useful to ask about that. It means I'll have all the information I need when I'm responding to her points.' She grimaced. 'If you don't mind helping me out.'

Sadie Cairncross nodded. 'Okay, I understand. And if it can settle Monica down then it will help us all.' She gave Tara a look. 'She's been round here since she got back too.'

Tara met her gaze. 'I can imagine. Right, so I just wondered for a start, is what Monica said true? Was it usual for your husband to drink and drive?'

Sadie Cairncross's gaze was fixed on the carpet; it took her several moments to answer. 'I doubt there was an hour of any day when he was stone-cold sober. So if ever he got into a car he was probably over the limit. And it's true that he was used to drink; he could take more than most people without it having an obvious effect. He was a large man.' She was clutching and unclutching her hands, which were in her lap.

Tara nodded. 'I see. So you assumed he'd been drinking before he set off home back in September?'

'I didn't think about it one way or the other,' she said. 'It was commonplace.'

'Could you tell me,' Tara asked, 'was your husband in the habit of locking his car when he left it?'

Sadie Cairncross frowned and her hands, which she'd been twisting together, went still as she raised her eyes to Tara's. For a second she looked as though she was going to query the question but at last she sighed and her shoulders slumped. 'No, he wasn't.'

It figured. Tara couldn't see a man who'd been that careless of his own personal safety worrying about car alarms and central locking. Not that his classic model would have had those facilities, anyway.

'What happened when he didn't arrive back when you expected?' she asked.

'I was asleep,' Sadie said. There was a pause. 'I've taken sleeping tablets for years now. My daughter, Philippa, was in the house that night too. She's at university – here in Cambridge – but she only lives in college accommodation during term time.'

'Was your daughter up until late? She didn't worry?'

The woman shook her head. 'A man who wants to live as he did when he was twenty doesn't tell anyone what time he'll be back. And he makes sure all his friends and family know to expect the unexpected. In any case, Philippa was occupied all evening. She nipped out to see a boyfriend in town.' She shrugged. 'It was only when we reconvened for breakfast that I started to worry. And before we'd got as far as calling the police, they called us.' Her face shut down.

'I'm sorry,' Tara said.

Sadie Cairncross nodded. After a moment she took a deep breath. 'But you said you didn't come here based on Monica's comments about my husband's ability to drink and drive.'

'That's correct. I came because, on the back of her worries, we made some very basic enquiries and found that one of the friends your husband visited the night he died is now also dead. He drowned, swimming out too far in the North Sea.' As she explained she saw the woman's expression – there was no trace of shock. 'You were aware of that?'

Sadie Cairncross nodded and put a hand over her eyes for a moment. 'The house where Ralph went that night to meet his group – the Acolytes, as you know he called them – belongs to them now. It was a family house, handed down by Ralph's grandfather. He used it as a sort of bolthole and invited them to do the same. They all had keys to come and go whenever they wanted. And when he died, it turned out he'd left it to them in his will, on condition that they carried on championing his philosophy on life.'

Quite a present. 'And what philosophy was that?'

Sadie Cairncross sighed. 'To live fast and – if it came to it – die young. His outlook meant he despised anyone who gave in to old age, who took it lying down. By drinking too much and living life just as he had in his twenties, he was shaking his fist at age and challenging it to take him if it could.' She closed her eyes for a moment. 'From his point of view, dying in the river would have robbed age of claiming him as a victim. It would have been him embracing death before his life went downhill. I think that's why he drove into the Forty Foot Drain.'

'You believe it was a deliberate act?'

She nodded. 'Monica won't accept it because Ralph was still living life to the full, right up until he died. She doesn't think he was ready to go, and a lot of people have said his ideals were just bluster. But his death proves them wrong. He always lived by the principles he championed.' There was a crack in her voice as she uttered the last sentence, and passion in her tone too.

Did she really believe it? Or was she just trying to find something positive to say about the husband she had been married to for so long? Her argument – that despite the guy's repellent views, he hadn't been a hypocrite – was hardly the most ringing endorsement. You could say the same of many dictators.

'I understood there was bruising on his body consistent with him having had some kind of fit,' Tara said.

The woman's eyes were cold now. 'Due to alcohol poising? I don't believe that. Surely a person who crashes in such a dramatic way would be covered in bruises anyway. Ralph could certainly take his drink. He'd never reacted badly before.'

Agneta must find it frustrating when lay people dismissed her findings like that. 'I'm sorry,' she said, 'we got off track. You were telling me how you heard about Lucas Everett's death?'

'Probate's still going through,' Mrs Cairncross said, 'but I know the contents of Ralph's will, of course, and the executors made each of the Acolytes aware too. We were all informed when Lucas died, and it turned out he wouldn't be around to enjoy his part of the inheritance.'

'What happens to Lucas's share?'

'It's split equally between the remaining members of the group,' Sadie said.

'Do you know the Acolytes well yourself?' she asked.

'A little.' She was looking down at her lap, one finger tracing a line in the tartan on her skirt.

'It must feel odd, to see a family home go to people who're just acquaintances.'

'They were much more than that to Ralph.' The woman sat up straighter in her chair. 'And I certainly wouldn't want the place. Too many bad associations now.'

Tara nodded. 'Of course.' Sadie hadn't mentioned the amount of money involved, she noticed. And judging by the house they were now sitting in, it probably wasn't an issue. Places like this on Madingley Road were worth upwards of two million.

'So, you're looking into a possible connection between my husband's death and Lucas Everett's?' Sadie Cairncross said.

Tara nodded. 'But it's very much a belt-and-braces thing. A routine enquiry to make sure we haven't missed anything.'

'Lucas Everett's mother thinks his recklessness might have been sparked by Ralph's doctrines. She wrote to me.'

That couldn't have been an easy letter to read. Did Lucas's mum blame Sadie in some way, by extension?

The woman must have read her expression. 'Lucas would have known Ralph wouldn't have wanted him to take such a risk. He was still young. Whatever happened, it can't be laid at Ralph's door. My husband's intentions were pure.'

Pure what, was another matter. But Sadie broke down now.

'You must miss him terribly.' Tara could see that she did. It was hard to watch the woman's reaction, even though the man she was mourning sounded abhorrent. She couldn't help wondering how they'd met, and why Sadie seemed to have loved him until the bitter end.

'The day I went to identify his body was like a final letting go, Constable Thorpe,' she said. 'A separation that couldn't be bridged.' She glanced up. Her hands were clasped tightly in her lap now. 'I don't believe in God or reuniting on the other side. The day he was found was the end of a long road.'

Tara raised her eyes.

'When we got together we made a pact. We were both dedicated to our careers. I used to be a flautist so for me it was my music and for him, of course, his writing. We held our artistic pursuits above everything else in our lives. But we each wanted a constant too – someone to act as an anchor and make us feel grounded. In fact, we felt it was necessary, to enable us to give our best. What we had was special. It was me he chose to mother his child when he matured, and wanted to create something new and fresh. But we always agreed we wouldn't tie each other down; we'd each dance to our own tune.'

She glanced at Tara, her eyes damp. 'I genuinely thought I was happy with that arrangement, but when Ralph sought the young people he needed to feed his creativity, I was weak. I gave in to jealousy.' She hung her head. 'I found my mind was on him, rather than my music.' Her hand went to her mouth for a moment. 'We reached our crisis point – a point of my making – and he told me then that his feelings for me hadn't changed. His love for me was unique, and it was the only attachment he had that had lasted – for so many years.'

How did the abrupt end to her career fit in with all this? And if Ralph had hurt her so badly over the years, might she be hiding the effects of the way she'd been treated? Just because she'd loved him, didn't mean she hadn't felt violent rage towards him too...

As Tara made her way back down the drive towards Madingley Road she replayed Sadie Cairncross's words and the woman's reactions to her questions. It only increased her impression that Cairncross's effect on his family and friends had been dangerous, his relationships unhealthy. She could certainly imagine someone wanting to kill him, but that was a far cry from proving that they had. She'd put herself out there, her reputation on the line, for something that might be utter bullshit.

She hoped to goodness she could find some hard evidence.

Blake was standing in his office doorway when Tara arrived back at the station. It had taken her a while; the traffic was already building up as rush-hour proper approached. The DI raised his eyebrows and she met his questioning look.

'Nothing concrete, but it was interesting,' she said. The resignation in his eyes made her heart sink. He'd decided to back her, but it had been a stretch, she guessed. He wasn't expecting her to succeed. 'If I was still a journalist I could write a whole book.' But she wasn't and time was short.

Blake nodded and stood back in his office doorway, nodding her through rather than letting her carry on to her desk. She wondered what was up. He closed the door behind her.

'Patrick has had Philippa Cairncross on the phone.'

'Ralph Cairncross's daughter?' She knew it was; she was just processing the information.

'That's right,' Blake said. 'Her mother must have called her to tell her about your interview as soon as you left. Then Philippa called us.'

'Quick off the mark. What did she want?'

'A very precise explanation about why we're bothering her family again and opening wounds that have barely scabbed over.'

'I did give Mrs Cairncross the background; she seemed all right with it.'

Blake nodded. 'I get the impression the daughter's very protective; I understand she didn't claim to be phoning on her mother's behalf. And apparently she wants to talk to you.'

From his tone, Tara gathered she'd need to indulge in some intensive diplomacy if she wanted to get anything useful out of her.

'Patrick wants to come along to observe. As it was his case originally I've given him the go-ahead.' Blake's look told her he sympathised, even if his words didn't. 'He'll let you lead the questioning.'

Great. Suddenly Wilkins had the spare time and was interested – now there might be a chance to watch Tara struggle, and to report back on her failings. And she knew full well her theory about the grass snake might be wrong. It fitted several aspects of Ralph Cairncross's death, but that could be coincidental. She didn't regret sharing it though – whatever the result. It had been the right thing to do – something Wilkins knew little about. And whatever happened she wasn't going to show any weakness in front of him. He hadn't seen her in action at an interview yet. It was about time she showed him what she could do. 'Do we already have an appointment agreed?'

Blake nodded. 'Ten tomorrow morning, at Philippa Cairncross's college. It's St Audrey's. On the upside, I was going to suggest you talk to her next anyway.'

As Tara walked back to her desk, ready to file her notes on the interview with Sadie Cairncross, she saw a smile spread across Wilkins' face.

CHAPTER TWELVE

The sky had turned clear overnight and there was a heavy frost when Tara made her way to St Audrey's the following day. The grass in front of the stone-built college was etched in sharp, white crystals of ice that glinted in the cool morning light. She walked under an ornate archway, decorated with a crest at its top, and found Wilkins in the Porters' Lodge through a door to her left. He was laughing with the man behind the counter but they both stopped abruptly and looked in her direction when she entered. She wondered what her boss had been saying about their mission – and in particular about her.

'I'll direct you to Philippa Cairncross's room now you're both here,' the porter said, coming out from behind the front desk. His shirtsleeves had been rolled up under his black waistcoat, but he pulled them down hastily when they left the warmth of the lodge. He took them along a short walkway, with a square, grass-covered court to the left, and pointed the way to a staircase entrance opposite them. 'Just through that door, then third floor up.'

He nodded in response to their thanks.

'Something about your attitude with Sadie Cairncross seems to have upset Philippa,' Wilkins said. 'I thought I'd better keep an eye on things this time.'

Tara felt her jaw tense and took a deep breath as she focused on the way ahead. 'It's unexpected. The conversation I had with Mrs Cairncross was perfectly amicable.' It made her wonder what Philippa's real reason was for not wanting her speaking to her mother. But maybe Tara was just clutching at straws…

Wilkins' tone was clipped. 'Please try to remember that's there's no evidence whatsoever that there was anything odd about Ralph Cairncross's death. Rather the opposite, in fact. It was a classic example of the results of drink-driving. If Philippa feels we've upset her mother needlessly, I'm inclined to agree.'

'Whatever you say,' Tara said lightly. She'd come to realise Wilkins found it far more annoying if she kept her cool. It took away his excuse to attack her, but he still knew what she was thinking.

They walked up the spiral stone staircase to the correct floor. Philippa Cairncross had her name on a card slotted into a small brass frame outside her room. Wilkins knocked.

Tara caught her breath when the heavy door swung slowly open. She'd looked at Philippa's Facebook profile picture, but it hadn't been very telling. Only part of her face had been showing, and she'd been wearing sunglasses. Now, here in front of her, it was a shock to find a female version of her father. Her features matched those of Ralph Cairncross in his younger days so closely it was like seeing a ghost. She was gamine, with a neat, slender figure, huge eyes, clear skin and hair cut into a pixie crop.

'Miss Cairncross?' Wilkins said.

'Ms.' Her tone was sharp.

Tara enjoyed the look on Wilkins' face as he took out his ID. She presented hers too, and introduced herself.

Philippa hadn't even closed the door behind them before she started on Tara. 'I'm glad you've come. I want an explanation for why you went to see my mother. And you'd better have a bloody good excuse. I couldn't believe it when she told me you're still bothering her, eight weeks on. It's been an appalling year for her and I bitterly resent you prolonging it.'

Tara could see Wilkins had cheered up. For her part, the onslaught gave her an immediate chance to face what was coming head on and control the situation.

Philippa motioned them to take seats in a sort of anteroom. It was home to three armchairs, a coffee table and a work station. Through an open door she could glimpse a bed. Another inner door was shut. Tara guessed it was to an en suite.

'You get allocated your room according to your exam scores the previous year,' Philippa said. She must have been following Tara's eyes. 'But when you've finished sizing up my accommodation and consequently my intellect, I'd like an explanation.'

Tara started to recount the visit she'd had from Monica Cairncross.

Philippa's features contorted the moment her aunt's name was mentioned and she cut Tara short. 'Monica has always hated my mother,' she said. 'I gather she was horrified when Ralph "tied himself down", as she put it. Not that he did. In no way did he feel shackled to my mother. He used her to have me and then distanced himself.' She'd dispensed with the titles of dad and aunt, Tara noted. That spoke volumes. 'As far as she was concerned, committing to a family was as good as having a millstone around his neck. And my mum was never special enough for her.'

Tara was surprised about that. 'I read that your mother was a professional flautist – and a highly regarded one too. That seems pretty special to me.'

Wilkins frowned. Tara suspected he hadn't known that.

Philippa's features softened a fraction. She nodded. 'I agree.'

Tara thought of the signs of paralysis around Sadie Cairncross's mouth. Was that why her career had ended? 'It must have been awful when she had to give it up,' she said.

'You didn't ask her about that, did you?' Philippa's eyes flashed again.

'No, of course not.'

'It was devastating when it happened. I was only five, but I still remember.'

'What did happen?'

Wilkins cut in. 'That's hardly—'

But Philippa answered quickly, over the top of him. 'Car crash. It damaged her mouth.'

'Oh, I see. I'm sorry.' Another life-changing event resulting from an accident.

'But going back to Monica, I still don't see why anything she said should lead to more questions.' Philippa's eyes were intense.

'I can understand that – and ordinarily it wouldn't have. But some very basic enquiries on paper highlighted a second death in your father's circle, shortly after his own. A man called Lucas Everett.'

Philippa nodded. 'I heard.'

'But it wasn't a connection that had been made before, officially,' Tara went on, 'and given the extra questions your aunt was posing, we wanted to make sure we'd covered all the angles we should have.'

Wilkins leant forward in his seat. 'It's really nothing for you or your mother to worry about. I don't think we need to bother you any further.' His tone was deliberately soothing and entirely wrong for someone like the woman they were dealing with.

And he'd said he was going to observe, not take over. Tara caught Philippa's eye. 'Though in fact, there were a couple of queries I had, when going through the records from September. I certainly don't want to waste your time, but now that we're here, we could tackle them if you don't object? It would mean there's less chance of having to disturb you again.'

'In that case get on with it, for God's sake,' Philippa said, crossing one slim, skinny-jean clad leg over the other. 'Term's just ended. I'd far rather talk to you here than have you tracking me down at home, where my mother will be faced with it all again.'

'That makes sense.' Tara didn't look at Wilkins. She'd got permission from Blake to conduct some enquiries, and if her immediate boss wanted to clip her wings he could square it with his DI.

'Firstly, can you please take me back to the night your father died?' Tara took out her notebook. 'I understand you were with your mother at the family home on Madingley Road when he set out for the Fens.'

'That's right.' Philippa's expressive eyes transmitted her impatience.

'And how did the evening play out after that?'

The girl put her head on one side and sighed deliberately. 'Let's see. We had supper together, chicken if I remember rightly, and then my mother went up to bed early. She tends to anyway, and that night she had a headache. And then I went out at around eight.' She met Tara's eye and clearly realised more was needed. 'To see my boyfriend. He's a PhD student so he was in Cambridge for most of the summer. I went to his rooms. We had sex. Jesus, what more do you want?'

'So you were back latish?'

She nodded, fixing Tara with her stare. 'Around one, I guess.'

'And you walked into town, and back again?'

Philippa shook her head. 'Bike. I knew Ralph wasn't back when I got in, but there was nothing remarkable about that. I didn't even think about it before I went to bed. But when he still wasn't around in the morning, we tried calling his band of Acolytes at the house on the Forty Foot Bank. It was Stephen who answered. He took a while and I guess the others were sleeping it off. He confirmed that Ralph had left in the small hours. We were about to call you lot, but you beat us to it.'

'Thank you for confirming everything.' Tara paused. 'And how well do you know the Acolytes? Do you ever socialise with them?'

Philippa tossed back her head and laughed. 'Not if I can avoid it. Ralph held them up as the crème de la crème of the next generation and they were all too ready to believe him. I wasn't so convinced, myself.' She started to count them off on her fingers. 'Lucas Everett, doing some completely pointless research into an obscure writer I'd never heard of. Getting himself published in some top journals, picked by editors just as deluded as he was.'

She clearly wasn't troubled by speaking ill of the dead.

The woman moved on to her index finger. 'Verity Hipkiss – an over-hyped novelist, from what I hear, researching her PhD; Christian Beatty, a model, for God's sake – he certainly isn't bright. He breaks the mould really, but my father appreciated physical excellence. Then there's Thom King, fancies himself as an artist, and finally Stephen Ross – a little-known poet and currently a part-time tutor to some rich kid. He's the runt of the pack, I think. I wasn't surprised he was the one who was up to answer the phone the day after Ralph died. I got the impression my father only kept him in the group because he enjoyed having someone to belittle.'

Tara remembered that Stephen was the one who'd tried to persuade Ralph Cairncross not to set off home when he was drunk, too.

'There was another girl that used to be part of the merry gang as well,' Philippa said, carelessly, 'a child prodigy who came up to Cambridge two years early or something. But she died at the end of July.'

Wilkins looked up.

Philippa pulled a face. 'Calm down. No question of anyone else's involvement there. It was cancer.'

The lack of feeling in her tone got to Tara, though she didn't let it show. 'They took up a lot of your dad's time, I expect,' she said.

Philippa folded her arms across her chest. 'If you imagine I was jealous then please think again. The one good thing they did do was keep Ralph occupied.'

Tara leant forward. 'Were you ever aware of any of them monopolising him more than the others? Wanting to be in constant contact, calling him at odd times at home – that kind of thing?'

Philippa's eyes narrowed and Tara couldn't work out what she was thinking. 'What I can tell you is that if any of them got involved with him sexually, it would have been through self-interest and what they could get out of the relationship – not because they were caught up in some kind of grand passion. I never got the impression that any of them were bothered about him for his own sake.' She glanced deliberately at her watch. 'Was there anything else?'

Wilkins was busy saying no, but in for a penny, in for a pound. 'I wondered about your cover photo on Facebook,' Tara said. 'I noticed you'd updated it to a picture of the Forty Foot Drain.'

A ray of low winter sunshine filtered in through Philippa Cairncross's mullioned window. The woman smiled, and half closed her eyes. 'I would have thought the reason behind that was obvious. It was a tribute to my darling father.'

She stood up, and Tara followed suit. She couldn't help but be aware that for someone who claimed she had very little contact with the Acolytes, she knew an awful lot about them. And she clearly spent emotional energy on resenting them too.

As Tara followed her boss out into the stairwell, she wondered what mileage he would get from the way she'd conducted the interview. She certainly hadn't got Philippa to love her, but instinct told her the woman respected her more than she did Wilkins. And he knew it too. It wouldn't improve their working relationship.

CHAPTER THIRTEEN

Tara was running out of time to make something of her investigation. Two days, Blake had said, and today was the second. Wilkins was going to love rubbing her nose in her failure. She'd managed to block all thoughts of him whilst she spoke to Philippa Cairncross, but the prospect of being beaten was nagging at her again now.

Between interviews and discussions the day before, she'd tried to work out how to maximise her time, and who to focus on next. She was more than curious about the Acolytes, but at five the previous evening, she'd found a contact that might be able to tell her a lot in a short space of time. She'd consulted Blake about seeing him, and he'd given his approval.

She went straight from St Audrey's to Newnham, to meet Dr Adam Richardson, an expert on Ralph Cairncross's work. It meant she had to leave Wilkins to return to the station alone. He'd enjoy pulling her to pieces to Blake or Fleming whilst she was absent. He'd been smiling to himself as they'd left Philippa Cairncross's college, which was probably down to anticipation. Unless he was plotting something else…

She parked her car in a wide side road lined with a mix of shiny, upmarket vehicles and some venerable old classic cars. They must have been of such sterling quality when they were new that they'd lasted through. The 1960s-built house she was after had a front garden with one stark, leafless willow in it. The water in the bird bath was frozen and the path glinted dully with ice crystals. She knocked at the front door – painted smartly in red – and waited for less than a minute before it was answered. Dr Richardson had curly, dark-grey hair and lively brown eyes.

He stuck out a hand and took hers firmly. 'Delighted to meet you,' he said, standing back. 'Come on in.'

It made a refreshing change to Philippa's welcome, or lack of it.

'Thanks for coming to see me at home,' he said, ushering her down a hall that smelled of wax polish and dried flowers. 'I work much better here when I'm not lecturing. Fewer distractions.' He caught Tara's eye. 'I don't mean you, of course. You're a distraction too, but a worthwhile one. But academics who hang around in their faculty offices are sitting ducks for anyone who wants to ask them about who should be the next head of department, or to whinge about a colleague who's not pulling their weight.' He shook his head abruptly. 'I can't abide politics. Anyway, enough of that. Coffee?'

He walked through to a compact kitchen where he'd got some ready.

'That would be great. Thank you.'

He poured it for her. 'Help yourself to any of the trimmings.' These included milk, brown sugar and tiny mince pies, coated in icing sugar which reminded her of the frost outside. The house itself was wonderfully warm.

He took up the plate of pies, then they gathered their cups and Tara followed him through to a book-lined study which was home to his desk and chair, and a spare one to its left too, for visitors. She put her drink down on a side table.

'So how can I help?' he said, seating himself at his desk and swivelling the brown padded office chair to face her.

'I was approached by Ralph Cairncross's sister, Monica, when she returned from a stint working in New Zealand. It's common for relatives who weren't on the spot when a loved one died to come and ask questions.'

Dr Richardson nodded. 'I'm sure I'd do the same.'

'Firstly, I was curious to know whether there's been speculation about Ralph Cairncross's death amongst the scholars who study his work.'

He smiled, his eyes dancing. 'You'll be aware of Ralph's well-reported views on old age, of course, and the way he glorified people who died young?'

'Yes.'

'Given that, several of us wondered briefly if he'd never intended to return home that night. The police reports said there were no tyre marks on the tarmac. Could he simply have driven off the bank of his own accord, at speed, thinking he probably wouldn't make it?'

'You don't think so, though.'

He nodded. 'You're right, I don't. I met Ralph on frequent occasions and for all his notorious views, he wasn't committed to them on a personal level. I'd say he was loving life. And even if he'd seemed determined to cut his time short, it wouldn't have been the most reliable way to do it.'

That was true.

'And then, of course, the medics decided he'd probably had some kind of fit at the wheel, so the speculation about his possible suicide ended.'

Tara nodded and took a sip of her coffee. 'Looking into matters for Dr Cairncross revealed that one of the men Ralph had been to see, the night of the accident, has also died since. He drowned too.'

'Lucas Everett,' Dr Richardson said, surprising her. 'Oh yes, I know about that.'

But then Tara remembered. 'Of course – Lucas was a researcher. At your department?'

Richardson nodded. 'That's right.'

'I hear that several of Ralph Cairncross's books focus on life and death. I presume none of them feature a young man swimming out to sea and not managing to make his way back again?' She hoped he wouldn't question her reasons for asking. She didn't want to mention the ways in which Ralph's own death echoed his final book; it would be giving too much away.

Dr Richardson's eyes widened and there was a tiny pause before he replied. 'Whatever made you wonder that? As a matter of fact, *The First and Last Day* features a drowning in precisely the same circumstances. A young man swims out from the shore, further and further, knowing and accepting that he's using his entire strength on his outward journey.' His eyes were on hers. 'I imagine you're thinking just what I was when I heard of Lucas's death. Coincidence?'

Tara felt a shiver run over her. Dr Richardson picked up one of the tiny mince pies from the white bone-china saucer and put it into his mouth, whole. After he'd finished it, he said: 'If Lucas Everett was going to do something daring and stupid in honour of Ralph's memory, he might have been influenced by that book. I assume he didn't mean his adventure to end in such a final way though. I saw him in the department before he went home to Suffolk. He didn't seem depressed.'

Had the escapade really been Lucas's tribute to Ralph? Would he have done something so risky off his own bat?

'Don't quote me on this,' Dr Richardson said, 'but I can't say I'm sorry that Ralph's gone. He enjoyed life to the full, but it seems to me that he damaged the people he got close to.'

Tara was surprised. 'Sorry,' she said after a moment. 'I somehow assumed you'd be an admirer.'

'Because I spend so much of my time researching and writing about him?' Richardson shook his head. 'That was all triggered by my trying to understand what the hell made him tick.'

'Did you ever work it out?'

He rubbed his chin with the fingers of his right hand. 'I'm not sure I did. People put forward ideas, of course. Sadie, Ralph's wife, suggested his obsession with youth might be to do with his maternal grandparents. They'd both been very ill in old age. And then, when Ralph's mother died young, apparently people kept saying "at least she never had to contend with the sort of suffering that her parents did".'

'But you don't buy that?'

Dr Richardson's eyes met hers. 'I think Sadie knew in her heart of hearts that his attitudes were unhealthy, and that she was looking for ways to excuse his behaviour. Whether that was because she was still – against the odds – very much in love with him, or whether she wanted to convince herself that she'd been right in supporting him for so long, I'm not sure.' He swallowed some more coffee. 'His views were a mystery to me. If you love your youthful companions you ought to want them to grow into something. Part of the beauty of youth is the promise of what it will deliver later. And the beauty doesn't dwindle with age, it changes in colour and depth. People who've lived a long life have the world in their eyes and certainty in their step. There's nothing more compelling than that. A young person is like the opening chapters of a story – fresh and exciting – but it's only with age that you get the whole book.' He smiled. 'I haven't given up, when it comes to unravelling Ralph's psychological make-up. I want to do more research on his parents. And he's got a wealth of other material I'd like to study too.'

'Really?'

Richardson nodded. 'A whole archive of papers: works and memorabilia from other writers and artists who held similar views to his. I'm planning to contact Sadie about the collection he put together to see if she'll let me have access.'

Tara would be more than curious to see what theories he came up with. She ate one of his mini mince pies herself. It was still faintly warm and tasted of brandy and peel. 'What about the dedication in Ralph Cairncross's last book?' she said. 'Do you know who that message was for?'

Richardson's eyes were twinkling again. 'Ah. Another hot topic. "To T, who managed to escape unscathed. You are blessed indeed."' He leant forward, his elbows on his desk. 'A favourite theory is that T is Tess Curtis, who was Ralph's PA for around twenty years.' He gave Tara a look. 'Impressive staying power, some might say. It's rumoured that she had a reasonably extended affair with him in the early days of their working relationship. It had been over for a number of years though, if the gossip is correct, yet she'd stayed single. And then – around the time that Ralph would have submitted his last novel to his publisher – she took up, rather publicly, with another well-known writer she'd met through Ralph.'

'If it's true – that the dedication was to Tess Curtis – does that imply that Ralph had a lot of affairs, and that he was aware his partners were usually left damaged afterwards?'

Richardson nodded. 'That would be my reading of it. And it fits. He enjoyed the idea of being a rogue and a heartbreaker.'

If that was the case, Tara could hardly believe the way Cairncross had openly advertised his cruelty and arrogance in print. She felt her pulse rate soar as her mind filled with all the things she would have liked to have said to the man.

'Unfortunately, Tess Curtis's affair with the other guy didn't last,' Dr Richardson went on. 'Their break-up was just as well publicised as the original hook-up was.'

'Was Tess still working for Ralph Cairncross when he died?'

Richardson nodded. 'With him to the last. I should imagine she felt completely rudderless when he drowned. Though an academic from my faculty offered her a job within two weeks of her finding herself unemployed.' He sighed. 'I hope Professor Trent-Purvis proves to be a better boss than Ralph was, but his previous PA only lasted six months…'

Poor Tess Curtis. 'You mentioned the dedication in Mr Cairncross's final book was a hot topic. So there are other theories then, as well as the one about Tess?'

'Yes.' The man smiled again now. 'There's a second, less likely one.'

'What's that?'

'One of Ralph's Acolytes – you know he called them that? – Thom, claims he had a close shave with a vehicle – his theory is that the dedication relates to him for that reason. His near miss was just this last August, but although the book would have been well through the editorial process by then, Ralph *could* have requested a rewritten dedication at that point. Thom told me Ralph had shared some advance copies of the book with him and the other Acolytes. He noticed the dedication and wondered if it was meant for him. Apparently he managed to ask Ralph – he made a joke of it, hoping to coax the information out of him – but he wouldn't comment, one way or the other. That figured. He loved to create an air of mystery.'

'What kind of close shave did Thom have?'

Richardson gave her a look. 'He *said* he was almost knocked down by a car driving at speed. He leapt out of the way; otherwise it would have hit him. The driver didn't stop.'

'You think he made it up?'

Richardson laughed. 'Well, I wouldn't go so far as to say that, but I think it's quite possible he was exaggerating the incident for attention. I happened to mention it to one of the others in the group and there was a bit of eye rolling going on. And he said himself that he didn't bother reporting it to the police.'

But it was interesting, all the same.

'I think the idea of being the object of one of Ralph's dedications, even if it was insulting or tongue-in-cheek, was probably quite attractive. And now he's gone, anyone can lay claim to being "the one" and no one will be able to prove them wrong.'

Tara hesitated for a moment. 'I presume no one was killed in a hit-and-run in Ralph Cairncross's novels?' she said at last.

Richardson's brow furrowed. He'd be wondering about her train of thought, but she couldn't help that. She needed his input – she sure as hell hadn't got time to read all of Cairncross's books herself.

'Not a hit-and-run exactly,' he said slowly. 'But in one novel, *Interlude*, the hero meets his end by walking calmly in front of an SUV on Route 66.' His eyes met hers and she could see the wariness there now. 'The vehicle drives on into the distance.' There was a moment's silence. Tara guessed Richardson was waiting to see if she'd explain herself. When she didn't, he sighed. 'To give you more background, every book Ralph wrote follows the same format. They all focus on a hero who's lived their life in an extraordinary way – taking risks and making waves. And they each start at the close of the protagonist's story. The hero spots their own particular "door" out of this world and embraces it, rather than choosing to live on into old age. The rest of the books are told in flashback, revealing the many death-defying adventures each hero undertook before that final decision to bow out whilst in their prime.'

The thought made Tara feel queasy. She could still taste the mince pie she'd eaten. 'I read a little way into his final book,' she said. 'I found the way the death in the lagoon was described shocking; the combination of beauty and tranquillity, with such an unexpected decision to leave it all behind for no reason. I can't get it out of my head.'

Dr Richardson nodded. 'It's a common reaction. However objectionable Ralph's views were, his power to illicit emotion and create a searing image was second to none.'

'What other types of deaths did his heroes embrace? Or heroines?'

'Heroes only in Ralph's novels.' Dr Richardson frowned. 'Let's see.' He swivelled his chair to face some shelves and pulled out a bit of stapled paper from a box file. 'Going through his bibliography, there are plenty of them and all in different circumstances.' He ran his eyes down the page. 'In *All But Over*, the hero's final moments are on an island. He finds an old storm shelter, standing on top of a windswept hill. It's tiny and the door has no handle on the inside. He notes that it's missing, nods and steps inside, where he sits down to read, knowing that it's blowing a gale outside and that every minute he stays put he risks the wind blowing the door shut and trapping him. When it does just that he smiles and carries on reading.'

'He dies of starvation?' Tara said. It was horrific.

But Dr Cairncross shook his head. 'He runs out of air. I presume Ralph thought that would be more aesthetically suitable.'

Right.

'Then,' he ran his finger down the list of books, 'in *On High*, the protagonist steps straight off the top of a high-rise building and falls to his death. The setting's New York at night, and the death there knocks you sideways all the more because of the beautiful descriptions of the lights of Manhattan. Whilst in *The Fine Line*, the death is by electrocution.'

Ralph's 'faulty' lamp… Tara caught her breath. Could it be a coincidence? The feeling of deep unease in her stomach grew. 'How did the hero receive his fatal shock in that book?'

'The scene to start with is pastoral. The hero's been lounging in a meadow, reading with the sun on his back whilst butterflies dance around the wildflowers he's lying amongst. It's an idyllic situation. In a moment of youthful exuberance he climbs a tree, but on the way up, he slips slightly and notices he's not quite as nimble as he once was. Then at the top he looks through the branches – which are thick with leaves – and sees how close he is to an overhead power cable. He reaches out and the scene cuts just as he makes contact.'

He'd conveniently neglected to describe the full horror that would have ensued. His work was one big lie…

'Then there's *Life Blood*, where the protagonist rescues a dog from a burning house before making the decision to go back inside, even though the building is otherwise empty. There's a description of the man walking further and further into the interior, just visible through the flames.'

Tara closed her eyes for a moment.

'And then, of course, there's the death in Ralph's final book, *Out of the Blue*, which is caused by the bite of the sea snake.'

After she'd finished talking to Dr Richardson, Tara sat in her car to take stock of what she'd learned that day. Things had changed since she'd gone into his Newnham home. The constant knowledge, sitting on her shoulder, that her snake theory might be wrong seemed to have lifted and taken flight. Now, her journalist's antennae told her she was definitely on to something. She had a new thrill of anxiety – at not having enough time to see the job through.

Only hours of the official investigation left…

What did she have? Four deaths – or near deaths – which each echoed one of Ralph Cairncross's books. That was just too much of a coincidence. What if the author had made a deadly enemy, setting something in motion that was only just starting to play out? But she couldn't begin to imagine how such a person could have convinced Lucas Everett to do what he'd done.

Added to the way the deaths resonated with the books, she had Agneta's doubts about the seizure that was supposed to have sent Ralph Cairncross off the road. He'd had no history of fits and she'd reckoned his blood results meant convulsions due to alcohol poisoning were unlikely.

And then there was the dead snake that had been found with Ralph's body.

Finally, at the forefront of Tara's mind was his dysfunctional family and the potentially unhealthy dynamic between Cairncross and his Acolytes – not to mention the long-suffering PA Dr Richardson had mentioned.

There were plenty of suspects… and, of course, still no hard evidence whatsoever.

What should she do? She'd discounted Blake's idea now – that Lucas Everett could have put the snake in Ralph's car and then taken his risky swim whilst he was consumed with guilt. She hadn't bought that theory right from the start, but she'd done her bit. No one she'd spoken to had seen any sign that Lucas had been fixated on the author and the people who'd talked to him the night he'd died said he'd been in high spirits.

That left two options: either she was seeing a plot where there was none – *I don't think so* – or some third party had already caused two deaths and had probably tried for a third – that of Thom King. It was interesting that the attempt on him – if it had been one – had been made before Ralph Cairncross died.

Dammit. She was just sitting there, theorising, when she needed to make use of every minute she had. She took a deep breath; she needed to think straight.

If a third party *had* been involved in Lucas Everett's death, surely that person would have been seen at some point, even if the local police had drawn a blank at the time? It was an hour-and-a-half's drive back to the coast, but a trip to Kellness offered the faint hope of picking up on some hard evidence. Without that she was definitely sunk.

So she made her decision. She was already belting along the A14 to Suffolk when she called Blake to update him and get his approval for her return trip. It was just as well that he happened to agree with her approach.

But by ten that night she'd started her drive home, knowing her luck had run out. She'd got no useful information; just a long journey to a shut-up seaside town, where most of the locals she spoke to had been tucked up in bed when Lucas Everett had taken that last swim, out from the shore beyond his mother's house.

She parked her car on Riverside and then checked her emails on her phone as she walked across the common, briefly removing one glove to do so. She saw that Wilkins had booked in a feedback session with himself and Blake to discuss her 'performance' at Philippa Cairncross's interview. She could hardly wait. And he'd also set out her tasks for the following day, now she was back on the Hunter case. She'd be with Max Dimity, doing a door-to-door, close to a fight that had taken place the day before. Max would fill her in and 'bring her up to speed'. He could give her some much-needed direction, according to her boss.

She assumed that was supposed to sting. Wilkins clearly didn't realise what a welcome thought it was, not having to spend the following day working with him. Tara liked what she'd seen of Max. They both shared a healthy scepticism about Wilkins, anyway.

But it didn't alter her frustration over the deaths of Ralph Cairncross and Lucas. She felt so powerless. Her emails also included one from Monica Cairncross, asking about her progress. She hadn't explained the official work she'd been allowed to carry out on her brother's case. She'd wanted to see how things panned out, and now she was glad. She'd been flying up until now on her journalist's instinct and the trip was over. Officially. But that day's discussions with Dr Richardson had switched her mojo back on.

She allowed herself to focus on the unknown enemy she was now sure she was up against. They'd been clever. She shivered. The truth was, sometimes people did get away with murder – quite literally. Not all killers were caught. She glanced up from her phone towards her house, dark and deserted, surrounded by the shadowy common.

She was dog tired, but she wanted to think how to phrase her reply to Ralph Cairncross's sister before she allowed herself to unwind.

Possible words were playing round in her head, forming and reforming.

It left her completely unprepared when a hand came down on her shoulder, gripping her tight…

CHAPTER FOURTEEN

Her training came back to her instantly. She didn't consciously process the thoughts that led to her reaction. Thumb innermost on her right shoulder blade, strong fingers on her collarbone. He was right behind her, not off to one side. The information came to her altogether, along with the correct reaction. Her right forearm smacked down and behind her to where her attacker's groin ought to be.

'Bloody hellfire.' The words came out on the back of a deep groan, and she felt the grip loosen. 'I taught you too well, that's for sure.'

She didn't have to turn around to know who was there.

Instead of smacking Kemp a second time where it would hurt him most – which was sorely tempting – she made do with a violent stream of curses and abuse instead. After a minute or so she finally stopped and fought to get her breath back.

'I don't know why you're so cross,' Kemp said. He looked injured, both physically and emotionally. 'You came out of that just fine. And I can't make sure you're still on form if you know what's coming.' He managed to straighten up and then laughed.

Tara gritted her teeth. 'Not funny, you bastard,' she said. 'I'm aware I'm in good shape. I don't need you to prove it to me.' He of all people knew the sort of fears she'd had to contend with as a teenager. But this sort of trick was entirely in line with his MO. He'd constantly kept her on her toes when he'd taught her self-defence, back when she'd met him at the tender age of seventeen.

Kemp laughed again. 'Yeah, right. Everyone doubts themselves. I can confirm that you're still a danger to all those around you. So, next time you're on a case that puts you in harm's way, you'll have that bit of extra confidence.'

She gave him a look, her head on one side.

'You can thank me later,' he said. He was lifting up a suitcase now. He must have dumped it on the ground nearby, just before he'd grabbed her.

'And you're thinking I'm going to express my gratitude by offering you a bed for the night?'

'I haven't shared *yours* for a bit,' he said. She could hear the smile in his voice.

'And you can't share it now.' It came out immediately – a reflex response. But she was exhausted.

'You are such a killjoy sometimes.' But the smile was still present. 'Either way, I could murder a beer. I thought you were never coming home.'

'You haven't been waiting out here? Why the hell didn't you call me?'

'I was just wondering whether to.' He nodded over his shoulder, back towards Riverside. 'I only got here half an hour ago, to be honest, but it feels like forever. I've been waiting in the pickup. Fancied giving you a surprise if I could.' He laughed. 'I knew it would be more fun. So, why the late return? Is it a new beau, or work?'

She sighed. She was so bloody exhausted. It was well past eleven now and she'd been up since five. 'A case – and a weird one at that. Come on then. I'll tell you all about it inside.'

Half an hour later, after swearing him to secrecy, she'd relayed what had been going on, including Wilkins' scepticism and general obnoxiousness.

Kemp sat back in his chair, the remains of his beer next to him on a side table. 'Interesting.' He drew the word out.

She'd been fighting sleep, but now she sat up straighter again. 'Kemp, if you're at a loose end, you can't come sniffing round this case. I shouldn't even have told you as much as I have.' She glanced pointedly at his suitcase. '*Are* you at a loose end? I thought you were working on that job in Glasgow.' The last time he'd shared his news, he'd been investigating a protection racket.

He gave her a look. 'I got bored. Thought I'd come and see how you're doing.'

'It went pear-shaped, you mean? And you had to get out of town fast?'

He grinned. 'You know me too well. I'm due in London again after Christmas, but as I was passing…'

'Kemp,' she summoned up as much firmness as she could muster, 'don't meddle in this. It's as thin as hell as it is, and I really want to crack it. Officially my time's run out, but I want to angle for another go. Wilkins will do almost anything to make me look stupid. I don't need you to help him.'

'I'm hurt by your lack of confidence.' He swigged down the last of his drink. He was still grinning and she carried on fixing him with her gaze. At last he sighed. 'All right. Understood, mate.'

'As for somewhere to stay, why don't you try Bea? I think she's got space. And she's had you before, hasn't she, whilst I was away? She'll give you friends' rates.'

Kemp nodded. 'She did last time.' He glanced at Tara. 'She's a gem. And I haven't seen her since her old man died.' He went to get himself another beer from the fridge without asking and opened it before Tara could protest. 'Is she all right?'

'She's being brave.' If Kemp booked in with her, Tara would have a spy on the inside, to tell her how Bea was really coping. He could be a handful, but Bea had liked him, the last time he'd stayed.

And she still hero-worshipped him too, for showing Tara there was light at the end of the tunnel when she'd been stalked in her teens.

'It would be good to see her,' Kemp said. Tara knew he was too matter-of-fact to feel awkward about her bereavement. His temperament meant he put his foot in it occasionally, but equally you could relax with him. He wasn't oversensitive.

'All the same,' Kemp said, 'I don't reckon I can go knocking on her door at this hour.'

Tara glanced at her watch. Midnight now. Hell. 'I guess you're right. And I don't have a spare bed yet' – she watched Kemp raise an eyebrow – 'so it's the sofa for you, friend. Sorry – I've been up for twenty hours or something, and tomorrow will be another heavy day. Wilkins will want to make sure of that as part of his revenge.' She knew Kemp wouldn't take her rejection amiss. Sure enough, he was still smiling.

'Understood.' He launched himself out of his seat. 'Just tell me where I can find a duvet or something.'

'Top of the stairs in the airing cupboard.'

'Cheers, mate.'

Suddenly she gave him a smile back. There'd been a delay with it, thanks to her tiredness and the element of surprise he'd employed. 'No trouble. It's good to see you.'

He grinned. 'And you.'

In spite of her exhaustion, it took Tara a while to sleep. Downstairs she could hear Kemp snoring on the sofa. She pictured his hairy bulk, sprawled over the inadequate make-do bed. The old attraction she felt for him was still there and, just for a second, sadness washed over her as she remembered the feeling of his arms around her and the gravelly sound of his laugh as he held her close. Their friendship was special, but they'd never be each other's one and only. There was something missing. Yet there he was, in her house, brilliant company, a whole lot of fun. It would make so much sense to be in love with him, and he her. Shame life wasn't like that. A short while later she heard his snoring stop, and then the kitchen tap running. *Shouldn't have drunk so much beer, Kemp…* But he was probably pretty uncomfortable on the sofa too, all six foot two of him. She felt a moment of guilt. But he could have given her some warning.

Whatever happened, she didn't want anyone to get the wrong impression about their current relationship. There was no love lost between Kemp and the police force, even though he'd left of his own accord. She was pretty sure he'd resigned before they could sack him. Just like her, when she'd left *Not Now* magazine. She knew that could happen through no fault of your own. But the fact remained, being associated with Kemp was a complication she didn't need right now. She guessed Karen Fleming was still assessing her, trying to work out if she was an asset or a liability to the team.

And Tara was twitchy about Blake finding out too – which was ridiculous. It felt as though she was keeping a secret, and one that might be misinterpreted. Now that she knew he lived just up the river she worried he might spot any comings and goings at her place. Kemp had worked locally; Blake might even know him by sight, though he'd bailed out of the police force long ago.

She sighed. Maybe she'd explain the situation to Blake if she got the chance. Given her role in his team and Kemp's iffy reputation, she'd rather make sure he understood just what was going on – and what wasn't. Other than that, of course, it was none of his business.

Saturday 15 December

It's been two and a half weeks since Monica visited the ex-journalist and I think it's fair to say I've won. From the start, it was only Tara Thorpe who seemed to look more deeply.

And now even she is off on some other job, as far as I can make out. Poor Tara. There was never anything you could get any leverage on, was there? How frustrating for you! I suspect you, at least, believed there was a decent mind at work, behind the two oh-so-unfortunate deaths.

But after you turned your back on Ralph and Lucas, even you might be suffering doubts. After all, you've had nothing concrete to make you keep the faith.

But that was the point, of course. You won't get anything concrete from me. Not unless I choose to give it to you.

But I'm looking forward to putting you back into the icy grip of suspicion; perhaps even of fear.

Tonight – I believe – I will give you something fresh to think about. Wait and see.

CHAPTER FIFTEEN

He felt on top of the world. The night was freezing and the going tricky, but most of the rooftop was clear. The rain that had turned to ice, making the streets and pavements so hazardous, must have drained off up here. Suddenly, he was in no doubt at all that he could do this. He stood up tall – stretching to his full height – put his shoulders back and laughed. He didn't feel cold. He felt lit up inside.

Dimly, he remembered the words and the cautions. *Are you sure? Is it wise?* He could hear the awe: fear mixed with admiration.

It was the jump everyone talked about. Several people wanted to try it – talked about trying it – but didn't have the guts. And some people had managed it, of course – people like him: the brave, the winners of this world.

He *could* bloody do it. He knew he could and any doubt he might have felt had left him.

He looked ahead, his eyes focused not on the gap between him and the next jutting bit of roof he wanted to reach, but on his destination.

He leapt.

CHAPTER SIXTEEN

It was Saturday night when Blake's old friend Agneta Larsson called him. She wanted to know if he and Babette would like to join her and her husband, Frans, for dinner on Monday. Babette was soaking in the bath, Kitty in bed already, so they weren't around to overhear the call. Monday was the perfect night to get together, in theory. Kitty already had a play date. It would be a simple matter to ask if that could be extended to a sleepover. They wouldn't even need a babysitter. But suddenly he longed for the chance of a relaxed chat with Agneta, without the pressure of Babette being there. And it would avoid a flashpoint too. Agneta and Frans had a nine-month-old baby. Being in the house with all the attendant paraphernalia would increase Babette's focus on getting pregnant again. And it certainly didn't need increasing. It was already at the forefront of her mind and, consequently, of his too.

'Blake? You are very quiet,' Agneta said. *'You've gone off us, right? And you just need time to think of a polite excuse.'*

He laughed. Agneta still called him Blake – a throw-back to the fact that they'd met through work – but they'd gone out together once upon a time. It had ended in that rare way, with no awkwardness between them. He valued their easy friendship. He liked Frans too. He was informal with an appealing sense of the ironic. Plus, at six-five with blond hair and a chiselled jaw, he was never going to feel threatened by an inveterate scruff like Blake, even if he was an ex. 'No.' He walked to the side of the house furthest from the bathroom. 'It's just – oh, I don't know how to put this without sounding either weird or like a shit.'

She laughed. *That's quite a build-up. You have to say it anyway now. I'm very curious.*

'I wondered if you'd mind me coming on my own?'

It was only a moment before she replied, and her had tone changed. *Sure. Of course, if that's what you want. Are you okay?* But before he could reply she added. *Not the right moment to ask. I understand. But tell me on Monday, if you want to talk.*

'Thanks.' He hadn't meant to be dramatic about it. She'd be expecting something momentous now, and he couldn't imagine telling her the whole truth about him and Babette. He'd kept it entirely to himself so far. No one would understand why he'd patched things up with her if they knew the full story. Even he had to remind himself of the reasons he'd done that – on an almost daily basis currently.

CHAPTER SEVENTEEN

Shona was in Patrick's king-sized bed, her eyes half closed, her fingers stretched out across his chest. The white sheet was pulled up as far as her waist but above that she was uncovered and naked. The colour of the thickly woven, pristine cotton offset her tan nicely. Patrick looked at the deep red of the flawless varnish on her long nails. He wondered how she managed to type the copy she filed for *Not Now* magazine.

'So, what's happening in your world?' she said, sleepily. It was the first time since she'd walked through his door that evening that either of them had introduced a subject unrelated to sex. 'Well done on Hunter. That must be a great feeling.'

'It's got to go to court yet. I'm not counting my chickens.'

'Seems to me it's a safe bet. And most of it was your work. You've done brilliantly.'

He smiled. Fleming had said much the same thing to him. It was nice to have a bit of praise for once.

'And how's it going with our Tara?' She gave him a look. 'Though I'm very glad she's not ours any more. Has she decked any suspects? Started a fling with your DI?'

Wilkins was keen on the idea of dropping Tara in it – she didn't deserve the position she'd managed to claw her way into – but the mention of her name still killed the mood as far as he was concerned. 'If she does anything newsworthy, you'll be the first to know.'

'Great. I promised Giles I'd remind you.'

God, if her editor was actively asking Shona to push for information he must really hate Tara Thorpe. One day, perhaps he'd ask

Shona to arrange a drink with him and Giles. He'd be curious to find out if the journo knew more about his new DC than he did.

'It was so nice of you, giving me those little extra details about Hunter,' Shona said, reaching up a hand to touch his cheek.

'Just don't tell anyone they came from me. They won't prejudice the case, but Fleming would *not* approve, and that's a fact.'

She laughed, got up onto one elbow and then slunk across him, sitting astride him and looking down into his face, her long hair just skimming over his chest. 'What's it worth then?'

He laughed too, seized hold of her and flipped her over. 'Let me show you!'

Patrick jumped when his phone rang in the small hours. He swore. It took him several seconds – including a moment to ease apart from Shona, who was asleep, her arm over his chest – before he found the instrument. He jabbed twice at the button to answer before the call connected.

'Wilkins.'

'Dimity, sir. I've had a call from uniform – Sue – she's out on Amforth Street with Barry.'

'Yes?'

'Someone's jumped from one of the buildings, looks like. Body's a youngish guy – mid-twenties maybe. I'm on my way there directly.'

'Right.' Patrick was sitting up properly now, and Shona was stirring, rubbing her eyes. 'I'll be right there.'

Shona sat up as he dragged on his boxers and trousers.

'Body,' he said. 'Suicide maybe? Jumped off a building in town. Feel free to stay. Help yourself to breakfast.'

She shook her head. 'You're kidding, right? I'm coming too.' She laughed. 'Don't worry. I'll follow on at a discreet distance. No one will know I was with you when the call came through.'

*

They'd already got the area around the body cordoned off when Patrick arrived, and the CSIs were on the scene. He put on the white overalls he was handed and spotted Dim Dimity. He might have a face mask on, but Patrick would know those judging eyes anywhere.

'What have you got?' he said, striding over. He glanced at the body. The guy had been tall and slender. On impact, his head had been forced to an awkward angle and his limbs splayed unnaturally. Other than the blood seeping from his nose and eyes there was very little mess.

'No one saw him jump as far as we know,' Dimity said. 'He was found by a couple on their way back from a club in town.' He nodded behind him to a pair of civilians outside the cordon. They stood close together, huddled and shivering, and were talking to a uniformed officer. The shaking was probably down to shock, but the night was so cold it wouldn't be helping. Wilkins was stamping his feet to keep warm himself and felt a wave of resentment towards the guy who'd jumped.

'Okay,' he said to Dimity. 'I'll talk to the couple in a moment. Do we know who the jumper was?'

Dimity nodded. 'The CSIs have found all his documents in a wallet he had in his pocket. He's—'

'What the hell's she doing here?' At that moment Patrick had spotted someone else at the cordon, pulling on white overalls like his. Tara Thorpe was not required. How did she even know what had happened?

'I called her, sir.' Dimity's eyes were impassive. 'It was just after I called you that the CSIs found the man's ID. The guy who jumped is Christian Beatty.'

The name rang a bell. Patrick felt his heart rate ramp up as he made the connection.

'He was one of the "Acolytes" Ralph Cairncross associated with, sir,' Dimity said. Was it Patrick's imagination or could he see a glimmer of triumph in the detective constable's eyes? 'If I remember rightly from DC Thorpe's notes, he was a professional model. Given her involvement investigating the possible interconnectedness of the previous two deaths, I thought I should call her too.'

And Patrick could hardly reprimand him for that without looking completely unprofessional. His mind spun.

On the face of it, here was one more fatality where no one else was involved. Maybe suicide, maybe misadventure. But with the others, it was bound to renew the interest in the whole Cairncross nonsense. It would make his new DC's theories look more credible – and dilute his power over what she did on a day-to-day basis. She'd be the centre of attention all over again.

He watched as Tara pulled up her hood over her mask. But just as she was ready to duck under the cordon, another figure appeared behind her.

Shona.

Tara must have heard her approaching. She hesitated, one hand on the police tape, and looked round. There was a very long pause.

'Shona,' Patrick heard Tara say. 'My, you managed to get here quickly.'

Shona's smile was cat-like. 'You know us, Tara darling. Always with one ear to the ground and *Not Now*'s interests at heart. I'd never let a story like this go by. It's my duty to pick up on *anything* newsworthy.'

Patrick remembered Shona saying that Tara had withheld information from Giles just before she'd left the magazine. His lover clearly wasn't going to let her forget it. He smiled for a second, but he was uneasy too. Here were two parts of his life that were entangled in ways that could be unpredictable.

He made up his mind to look all the more carefully for damaging information on Tara that he could reasonably leak to *Not Now* – without getting found out.

CHAPTER EIGHTEEN

Conflicting feelings fought for space in Tara's head as she set off to investigate Christian Beatty's death later that morning. By the end of her previous official investigation she'd been convinced a third party had been involved in both Cairncross and Everett's deaths, but there had been nothing she could grab hold of. What had she missed? Could she have saved Christian Beatty's life? The image of his body in its unnatural, disjointed position on the pavement filled her mind each time she dropped her guard. But the gnawing feeling of guilt was mixed with a rush of adrenaline and powerful sense of urgency. The deaths *had* to be linked. Just as with the others, the circumstances of this one mirrored one of the Cairncross books Dr Richardson had mentioned – *On High*. It was too much of a pattern. She needed to find the evidence to prove she was right before anyone else died. Her stomach fluttered with nerves. What if no one had seen anything? What if, once again, she was certain there'd been foul play but had no way of proving it? Why should this time be any different?

How long had she got before another Cairncross connection died? And how would they meet their end?

By fire? Suffocation?

She needed to think, and think fast.

Wilkins had gone off with Blake to view Beatty's apartment and interview his family. Later in the morning they'd also look up his booker at the modelling agency he was signed to, if they could track him down on a Sunday. At least they'd get decent results, now

Blake had finished with Hunter and was free to make sure of it. But given no one was saying murder yet, that would only be a temporary state of affairs. He was likely to get called off to something more pressing at any moment, giving Wilkins free rein again.

She and Max were on door-to-door. Amforth Street – where Beatty had jumped – proved to be a washout. It was full of retail units, as well as pubs, which had all been closed by the time Beatty took his dive. There were a couple of first-floor flats opposite the building he'd climbed, but they had bathrooms at the rear, with opaque glass. Given the weather, it wasn't surprising that the residents they spoke to had had their windows shut and curtains drawn. Neither of them had seen anything. It was lucky that it was the weekend; without that, she and Max probably wouldn't have found anyone to talk to at all.

They moved on to Christian Beatty's smart apartment block, complete with gym, roof terrace and courtyard gardens. There were CSIs present there, just as there had been at the scene of the jump. As they neared the flat that Beatty had occupied, Tara listened for Wilkins' annoying drawl and Blake's low rumble but couldn't hear anything. Perhaps they'd already moved on. She wished she'd been able to look inside, and that she could be a fly on the wall at the interviews too. But there were compensations for going door-to-door. Family and work contacts might know a lot, but bystanders who glimpsed a victim's day-to-day habits were valuable too. Outsiders sometimes saw things more clearly than close contacts with preconceived ideas.

She and Max spoke to Christian Beatty's immediate neighbours first. They were already expecting disturbing news; the presence of CSIs tended to achieve that. The woman in the flat to the left was no help. She'd had a dinner party the night before and admitted her crowd had been rather noisy. As a result of considerable quantities of prosecco (borne out by the overflowing recycling crate in her kitchen), she'd gone to sleep soundly at around midnight. She said she used to pass the time of day with Christian, but she didn't know him well enough to say if he'd been depressed, or troubled about anything. ('Bloody good-looking guy. Can't believe he's gone, just like that. So weird.')

The man on the other side worked long hours for a big accountancy firm in London and had rarely crossed paths with Christian. He said the flat's modern soundproofing meant he couldn't even tell them what music the dead man had liked.

The rest of his floor gave similar results. How had these people lived so close together without finding out more about each other? But then Tara had more reason than most to monitor the people around her; it helped keep you safe.

'Let's go to the apartment directly underneath Christian Beatty's,' she said. 'You never know.'

Max nodded. 'Good idea.'

They walked along the plush carpet, past gilt-framed mirrors. At the end of the corridor ahead of them was an arched window, looking out towards Coe Fen, its grassland dotted with evergreen trees and crossed with paths. It was only a short walk from here to the river, as well as Sheep's Green – where lambs would graze in the spring – and the Paradise Nature Reserve. It would be idyllic in summer.

'Reckon I'm in the wrong job,' Max said.

Tara smiled. 'You and me both. I can't imagine what this lot would think if they saw *my* house. Their hair would probably fall out from shock.'

They knocked on the door of the apartment below Christian Beatty's. The woman who answered was clothed in a dressing gown. Her blonde hair was tousled and her eyes surprised and bleary.

Tara sympathised. Catch her unexpectedly on a weekend morning and she'd be much the same – except wearing more layers, of course. She and Max took out their warrant cards. 'We're speaking to several people in the building about Christian Beatty, whose apartment is just upstairs. Would it be possible to come in, Ms…? I'm sorry, I don't have your name.'

'Cammie Clifford,' the woman said. She retreated into her flat's hallway to allow them to come in, closing the door after them. 'What's this about?'

Tara stepped forward. 'You knew him?'

The woman nodded and Tara explained what had happened, waiting for the news to sink in. 'I'm sorry,' she said at last. 'It must be an awful shock.'

Cammie Clifford nodded again, this time in slow motion.

'Would you like me to make you a drink – a coffee or something?' Max said quietly.

'There's some on the side,' she said. 'I was just about to have my first cup of the day when you arrived.'

'I'll get it for you.' Max turned away.

Cammie sank down onto a yellow leather sofa whilst Dimity crossed the open-plan room to the kitchen area. A space-age-looking coffee machine gleamed on the worktop, an espresso cup already in place and full to the brim.

He brought it over to her.

'So did you socialise with Christian?' Tara asked, as the woman sipped her drink.

'Not exactly, but we'd bumped into each other a few times in the gym. We chatted, and we'd got as far as working out that my flat was directly below his. And then one day I was catching the train to King's Cross for a meeting and found myself sitting opposite him.' Her eyes were still round with the shock of the news and she stared into space as she spoke, rather than looking at Tara.

'I see.'

Tara had taken a seat opposite Cammie Clifford on an armchair, and Max joined them now, perching on the edge of a second.

'Had you chatted to him recently?' Max said.

· The woman frowned. 'Fairly. I last saw him in the gym a week or so ago. And the train journey I mentioned was back in November.'

'How did he seem to you?' Tara asked.

'His usual self,' Cammie said. 'On the train he was off on some modelling job. It was going to keep him in Paris for several days and he sounded pretty pleased about that. He went off to catch the Eurostar when we got to London.'

It sounded glamorous, but Tara couldn't imagine enjoying the work. Presumably it involved long hours standing around whilst other people told you what to do. And you must have to watch your weight and keep working out. Tara kept fit herself, but she ate and drank what she liked. Even if she'd had the looks, there were some sacrifices she wouldn't be prepared to make.

'And more recently, at the gym?' Max said.

Cammie Clifford's face fell. 'He was even more buoyed up then. He'd heard he was up for a new contract. It was with Armani. It wasn't confirmed, but he was pretty confident; already excited and telling people.'

Tara couldn't let go of the idea that this death was part of the larger conspiracy she felt sure she was on to, but she made the effort to pull back. Wilkins was the one who was blinkered, not her. So, had Christian Beatty heard back about the contract, and if so, what had the results been? It was possible he'd had high hopes, puffed himself up in front of his friends and then had a knock-back. It would have been humiliating, but surely not enough to make him give up on everything? Unless there'd been other factors involved too. She made a note to find out. If Blake and Wilkins were talking to his agent, they'd probably already know the answer.

'And after that last time in the gym, you didn't have any more recent contact with him?' Tara said.

Cammie Clifford's eyes met hers at last. 'No, but I did hear him.' She gave a dry laugh. 'These apartments cost an arm and a leg, yet they do have a downside. The soundproofing's great between adjacent flats, but not so good from floor to floor. So I'd sometimes be aware of him playing music, or moving around.' She blushed. 'And occasionally I'd notice if he had a woman round.'

'Anything last night at all?' Max's voice was soft, and Tara held her breath.

'Not late,' Cammie said, 'but maybe eightish or thereabouts, just after I'd finished my supper, he was talking to someone.'

'On the phone?'

But Cammie shook her head. 'No. There were two voices.' Suddenly she looked at them more intently, as though reading their minds. 'But it was all quiet later on. And I couldn't even tell you if it was a man or a woman he had with him. You just get this sort of background murmuring effect down here. I tend to filter it out once I've noticed it; it's a useful tactic if you want to avoid getting irritated.'

'You didn't happen to notice what time they stopped talking, did you?' Tara said.

The woman frowned. 'I'm not absolutely sure, but I went to have a bath at around ten, and it was certainly quiet by that point. I remember lounging there in the bubbles and appreciating it.'

They'd finished the interview, and Cammie Clifford was just showing them out, when the woman paused. 'Have you been to the ground floor yet?'

Tara shook her head.

'Try apartment four,' the woman said. 'Ellie Wagner lives there. I used to see her with Christian occasionally. I think maybe they had a thing going at one point.'

As the door closed, Tara said, 'Wilkins ought to be pleased with all of this information we're adding to his original work on Cairncross.'

Max gave a wry smile. 'Ought to be, yes. And I'll bet he still won't believe it's all one case.'

'I'm sure you're right.' She wondered what Blake's latest thoughts would be. 'Let's go to security next and ask them to send last night's CCTV files to the station.'

As Tara talked to the apartment block's security guard, Max called the station to let them know what to expect, and about the timings of the voices Cammie Clifford had heard. Then they went to the ground floor as the woman had suggested. There was no reply at number four, but the person next door appeared when they tried for a second time, his hair wet, as though he'd just dressed after a shower.

They showed their IDs and asked if the guy had a number for her.

He shook his head. 'Afraid not, but she usually goes to Aromi on Bene't Street for breakfast on a Sunday. A gang of us went once.'

They thanked him and turned towards the exit to the block.

'Sounds like the best excuse we'll get for a coffee all morning,' Tara said, holding the main door open for Max. She was feeling the early start.

Max had googled Ellie Wagner en route to the café. She'd been easy enough to find. It turned out she was a member of the residents' committee for Christian Beatty's apartment block and had been quoted in the local paper in an article about street noise. She was a striking-looking woman, with gold-blonde hair, angular features and a wide mouth which Tara guessed Wilkins would call 'sensual'. She and Beatty must have made an impressive couple if Cammie Clifford had been right about their relationship.

Aromi was crowded, its warm glowing interior humming with chat, its windows misted with condensation. The smell of baked goods and coffee made Tara's stomach rumble, in spite of their mission.

Almost as soon as they entered, Max nudged her. 'Over on the far side there?'

Tara nodded. 'I think you're right.' Ellie Wagner was alone, a newspaper spread out on the table in front of her, a coffee and a croissant at her elbow. She had the air of someone who might linger over her food for some time to come.

She and Max exchanged a glance and then she walked forward to the woman's table. 'Excuse me,' Tara said, approaching her. 'Ellie Wagner?'

Five minutes later, Tara and Max had coffees too: she an Americano, he a mocha. Tara was sitting opposite Ms Wagner at her table for two. Max had managed to secure a space on the next table along when a couple had left. The place was cosy, so the distance was comfortable for a quiet chat without crowding her. They'd broken the news as gently as they could. Shock still registered on the woman's face and her eyes watered slightly.

'We understand you were good friends – at least at one time,' Max said.

He had a comforting voice, Tara thought. Of course, he knew all too well what it was like to receive the worst possible news. It must be harrowing, reliving the day he'd heard of his wife's death each time he had to inform someone of a fatality.

Ellie Wagner swallowed and nodded. 'We met at a residents' drinks party on the roof terrace,' she said, 'around eighteen months ago now.' She shook her head. 'I've hardly seen him recently. Time's gone past so quickly. I guess I've bumped into him a couple of times in the last six months. It was just a nod and a smile by then.' She sighed. 'He was planning to come to the Christmas drinks do. We hold that in the atrium downstairs.'

'Did you get any impression of how he was doing these days?' Tara asked.

'Not really. I'd see his photo in a magazine occasionally, though, so I knew he was flourishing work-wise.' She bit her lip. 'It always brought me up short, seeing his face like that, without warning. I never quite got over my feelings for him, I suppose.' She met Tara's gaze. 'We were sleeping together – only for a few months – but it meant a lot to me.'

Tara paused. 'Do you mind me asking why you broke up?' she said. It was weird being a police officer. Even if Ellie Wagner did mind she'd be likely to answer without protesting. And yet it probably had no bearing whatsoever on Christian Beatty's death. The latitude she had was a far cry from when Tara had been a journalist.

The woman's face was strained. 'He joined a new circle of friends, around about a year ago now.'

'The group that used to hang around with Ralph Cairncross?'

She nodded. 'That's right. He met Ralph at some celebrity party in London, organised by one of the magazines he'd modelled for. Ralph sort of scooped him up – pulled him along, into his orbit.' She looked from Tara to Max. 'That's what it was like. As though if you got too close you couldn't pull free again.' She took a sip of her coffee – it must be cold by now – and sat back in her chair for a moment, closing her eyes. 'I still remember him telling me about their first meeting. Christian hadn't read any of Ralph's books, but he picked one up from Waterstones after they'd been introduced. He seemed really absorbed by it.' She shook her head. 'I dipped into it too, but I hated it – sort of boring and unpleasant at the same time. But I didn't say so to Christian. I could tell he would have belittled my thoughts. He was already a convert.'

'Did you ever meet Ralph and the group, whilst you were in the relationship with Christian?' Max asked.

She nodded slowly. 'Just once. Ralph Cairncross kept saying "any friend of Christian's is a friend of mine", but by the time he'd said it to a third guest at his party, it was obvious what he meant. He wasn't being inclusive. He was making it clear that he was only putting up with me because I was Christian's girlfriend. As though he'd hate anyone to imagine that I was there at his invitation. And suddenly, I realised – or, well, thought I realised – that each new person he repeated it to was laughing at me as well, just as much as he was.

'And when I turned to Christian, looking for support, I saw how uncomfortable he was. He'd become embarrassed by me.' She held her coffee cup tightly in her right hand. Her knuckles were white. 'I knew. And he could see that I knew.'

She sighed. Her eyes were definitely damp now. 'That was it for me and Christian. By Christmas of last year I'd lost him to them.'

CHAPTER NINETEEN

Blake was sitting in a chilly meeting room with Wilkins, DC Megan Maloney and a mug of coffee when Tara and Max dashed in, sliding into seats round the table.

Blake had called them all together for a briefing on Christian Beatty's death. In an ideal world he'd want a much more hands-on role in this investigation, but Fleming had made it clear he needed to hold back. It was Patrick who'd dealt with Ralph Cairncross's accident in the first place, and given Beatty's death looked like misadventure – yet again – it didn't warrant a DI's involvement. Whereas – according to Fleming – it was the perfect investigation through which Patrick could extend his experience. 'He can't learn if you never give him his head' was how she'd put it. And of course, you couldn't make an omelette without breaking eggs. *Give him enough rope and he might even—* He pushed the thought out of his mind. It was all very well, but instinct told him that there was a lot at stake here. Three deaths. And, as Tara had pointed out, two near misses. Was there really an innocent explanation? But innocent was the wrong word. Nothing that was connected with Ralph Cairncross could be described that way. Blake had a feeling in the pit of his stomach that Christian Beatty's death wouldn't be the last. With that in mind – and only paperwork left to do on the Hunter case – he'd taken time out to view the dead man's apartment, and talk to his closest contacts. He thought he'd been remarkably restrained in letting his DS lead the questioning.

'Patrick,' he said, looking at the man he thought wholly unsuitable for promotion, 'do you want to begin?'

His DS nodded, the familiar cocksure look in his eye. Despite the man's early start, he'd somehow found time to take care of his personal grooming. His hair gleamed in the light from the fluorescent tubes overhead. As far as Blake was concerned, that spoke of a man with the wrong priorities. 'Deceased is Christian Fairbrother Beatty, of Gifford House – an apartment block off Fen Grove. I've arranged to attend the post-mortem tomorrow morning, so we might get more then. In the meantime, Agneta Larsson noted at the scene that she could smell alcohol on the deceased, so we assume he'd drunk quite heavily before he jumped. We don't yet know if he deliberately leapt to his death, or if he was climbing and jumping from roof to roof on Amforth Street as a dare or a personal challenge. However, there was a gap he could have been trying to breach, judging by where he fell.'

Megan Maloney put up a hand and Wilkins nodded at her. 'I've had a look online. A few people who are associated with the Cambridge night-climbing community have mentioned the gap you're referring to. It's one people talk about as a challenge. People do attempt it successfully every couple of years, but another guy died, falling there, back in 2012. In his case, it seems he was inexperienced and should never have gone for it. It's notoriously tricky, apparently.'

'Thanks, Megan.' Wilkins nodded. 'Useful to have the background.' He looked around the room. 'You're all familiar with the night climbers, of course? They're usually student crazies who endanger themselves and others by scrambling over various high-level bits of the city.'

Blake noticed Max Dimity give a slight eye roll and mutter something to Tara. They were all already well aware of the night climbers.

Wilkins must have heard the muttering too. 'You had a question?' His gaze fixed on Max.

'We've spoken to a neighbour of Christian Beatty's, sir, who heard voices in his flat from about eight in the evening until sometime before ten. I remembered DC Maloney was looking at the CCTV footage of the approach to the apartments, after I spoke to her on the phone earlier. I was just wondering what she'd seen.'

Wilkins gave him a look. 'I was coming to that next, as a matter of fact. Megan?'

The DC turned her curly, dark-haired head round to face the room. 'I scanned all the footage from six in the evening onwards. There was a fair amount of coming and going at that point. Then there was a quieter patch between six forty-five and seven fifty, and then' – she looked at Tara and Max – 'just after that, which would tie in with the information DCs Thorpe and Dimity phoned in earlier, there was a figure entering the apartment block, dressed in a hooded coat. Whoever they were, they were muffled up against the cold. The hood's fur-lined and they're looking down, but still.' She turned to the table next to her and used a mouse and keyboard to bring up the video on the screen at the front of the room.

Blake watched as the person – a woman? – approached the apartment along the pavement and pressed a button on the entry phone. The camera had been mounted on the front of the building, so it faced the figure from above, but as Megan had said, it didn't give much away.

'Anyone else go in around that time?' Wilkins asked.

Megan shook her curls. 'No one else who needed to use the entry phone, rather than letting themselves in. All the same, I checked the image of a guy who arrived a couple of minutes later and entered independently, just in case. The security people recognised him as a resident. So it seems as though this hooded figure was the person visiting Christian Beatty – unless he met with someone who was already inside the apartment block, of course.'

Wilkins nodded. 'And what about later in the evening?'

Megan clicked on the video again and skipped forward. 'I found what looks like the same person in the hood, leaving at nine twenty,' she said. And although the footage was even less good this time, as the camera only caught the person's rear view, the coat and their gait looked the same.

'A woman,' Wilkins said. 'Or a man wearing a woman's coat?'

Megan nodded. 'Then there are a couple of others that also left in the run-up to ten o'clock, when Tara and Max's witness says things went quiet in Beatty's flat.' She showed them the footage. 'Of course, it's not conclusive. He could have been chatting to another resident from the apartment block, in which case the comings and goings outside won't mean anything. The residents' committee has email addresses for everyone who lives in the building. We're contacting them all with the images and times to see if anyone can confirm the identities of the people who were recorded, and what they were doing there. And we're asking each of them if they visited Beatty too.'

'Good work, Megan,' Blake said, leaping in before he could stop himself. 'And what about Beatty's own movements?'

She nodded. 'He left the block, unaccompanied, at twenty past one.' She found the footage. Beatty had been walking with a spring in his step, hands in his pockets. He wore a jacket and scarf but no hat, and he wasn't obviously drunk. The line he took was straight, and purposeful.

'We should remember,' Wilkins said, 'that this is more than likely a tragic accident. A young man who had a few drinks and decided to go a bit wild. Beatty was a student here in Cambridge. Perhaps something he'd seen or talked about last night reminded him of that particular jump. Maybe it was something he'd always wanted to do himself.'

'Though his family weren't aware that he had any interest in night climbing, or that he'd tried it before,' Blake said.

Wilkins' look was derisive. 'No, but what self-respecting student would tell his parents about something like that?'

'Fair point.' But there was more work to do, whether his DS liked it or not. 'All the same, it would be worth talking to his old college to see if he was ever caught climbing. And checking his name against any related news stories and blogs too, rather than making assumptions.'

He'd tried to put it tactfully – well, a bit, anyway. Wilkins looked as though he'd taken the comment as a rebuke. It took a moment for his DS to turn to Megan and raise a 'you'll do that, won't you?' eyebrow. He hadn't bothered to convey 'please'.

'Will do,' she said.

'Anything from Beatty's mobile yet, Megan?' Blake asked.

The woman shook her head. 'Nothing significant that I can see in the last few days. He called his mum, and he'd been in touch with his agency before the weekend. Whoever was with him last night must have turned up unexpectedly, made their plans some other way, or longer ago. I'll keep going back in time, just in case.'

'Thank you.'

'Had Beatty's parents or his agent noticed him acting depressed or worried recently? Or out of character?' Tara asked. The look in her green eyes was intense.

Wilkins shook his head. 'His work was going well – he'd just been awarded a new contract with Armani – and he seemed to be enjoying life. It would point to misadventure rather than suicide.'

Blake looked over at her and Max. 'Anything useful from the apartment block residents – apart from what you passed on to Megan about the visitor?'

'Nothing that indicates he was depressed,' Tara said. 'But we spoke to an ex-girlfriend of his who lives downstairs. She noticed a change in him a while back, when he started hanging out with Ralph Cairncross and his crowd.'

Blake saw Wilkins raise his eyes to heaven.

'She says he pretty much disowned her at that point.' Tara's voice was firm and clear in the quiet room. 'It sounds as though his social circle got smaller. But the people we spoke to also thought he seemed happy with the way his life was panning out.'

'Thanks.'

'Nothing much of note in Beatty's flat,' Wilkins said. 'There were two coffee cups though, which ties in with the witness downstairs who said she heard voices.' His tone was grudging. 'No sign that he'd been drinking anything strong inside the flat. Just a couple of empty beer cans in the recycling, and a glass that was still wet with beer in the dishwasher. Everything will be analysed, of course.'

Tara put up a hand.

'Yes?' Wilkins said, after a moment.

'I just wondered if there were any similarities at all between the circumstances of Christian Beatty's death and those of Lucas Everett or Ralph Cairncross?'

Wilkins' lips went thin. 'No,' he said.

There was silence. But the subject needed airing. Megan Maloney didn't know about the digging Tara had been doing into the previous two deaths and it looked as though Wilkins hadn't been planning to bring it up. 'There's the fact that they were both associates of Ralph Cairncross, present at the gathering he attended the night he died,' Blake said.

'But there was no note left this time,' Wilkins countered.

Blake's patience was wearing thin. He took a deep breath. 'True, but what about the bottle you mentioned to me, Patrick?'

Wilkins let out a sharp sigh. 'The CSIs found an empty vodka bottle at the foot of the building which Christian Beatty had climbed. No clear prints on it, just smudges. It could have been anyone's.'

'Nonetheless, there was also a vodka bottle found with Lucas Everett's clothes. And the lack of anything discernible might mean the bottle was wiped.'

'Mr Beatty was wearing gloves when he jumped, wasn't he?' Tara said. 'So the lack of his prints would make sense. What brand was the vodka?'

'Something unusual.' Wilkins looked down at his notes. 'The kind of thing he probably drank to make himself feel superior to everyone else.'

Put the guy under the tiniest amount of pressure and his true colours showed. His prejudice against the dead man was already clear.

'Adnams East Coast,' Wilkins said, looking up again. 'Suffolk company. At least he was supporting local business.'

'Same brand,' Tara said.

Her eyes met Blake's for a second.

'Lucas Everett bought his himself, didn't he?' Blake said. 'At the Co-op in Kellness?'

Tara nodded.

And dead men told no tales, so if this was more than coincidence, then whoever had been present when Everett died must have decided to buy the same booze on this occasion. Was someone taunting them? Giving them tiny bits of evidence, knowing it wasn't enough? He felt anger heat him, coursing through his veins. He was increasingly sure this was someone on a mission, who delighted in their own cleverness. Someone who couldn't resist showing off. But that might be their downfall…

Blake turned to Tara, ignoring the look on his DS's face. 'I think you'd better give a run-down of everything you've got on Cairncross and Everett before we carry on,' he said. 'It's my feeling that this is a coordinated series of well-disguised attacks. We can't prove it, but it's certainly time to bring Megan up to speed.'

CHAPTER TWENTY

Tara went through everything they knew about the deaths of Ralph Cairncross and Lucas Everett – and also outlined her theories. As before, Wilkins leapt in to challenge her thinking, but she could take it. She wasn't expecting anyone to accept her words on trust.

Once she'd finished, Blake stood up. He was dressed in a suit that made him look like a million dollars, despite the rough stubble and dark rings under his eyes. When she'd commented on his wardrobe the week before, to Max, he'd told her Blake's sister was a fashion designer, so that little mystery was solved. He certainly didn't seem the sort to set much store by material goods. The way he could still look unkempt in his bespoke suits caused raised eyebrows with DCI Fleming, but as Blake had been just the same four years earlier when Tara had first met him, she guessed he wasn't intending to change. She was glad.

'We need more time to think this through, but not on empty stomachs.' Blake looked from Tara and Max to Wilkins. 'What time were you all up?'

'Round about four,' Max said. 'I like my early mornings, though.'

Blake grinned. 'Just as well. But you can't run on empty. Let's reconvene at the Tram Depot. I'll get the pizzas in.'

Ten minutes later they were huddled inside the pub, crowded round two slatted tables pushed together. The glowing lights and red walls next to them were cosy. Under different circumstances it might almost have made Tara relax, but today she was on edge. She had a Coke in front of her, and was sitting between Blake and Max. Wilkins was directly opposite her. Too close for comfort. Each time she glanced up, his eyes were on hers. She tried to look at Megan Maloney next to him instead; it was much less annoying. The pizza orders were in, and now she could tell Wilkins was just waiting for his chance to carry on rubbishing her theories. The place was packed – they'd be able to talk freely without being overheard.

Blake took a swig of his coffee and looked up. 'I don't believe these deaths are a coincidence. Despite that, they might not be the result of foul play – but I'm increasingly worried it's a possibility. As Tara explained, her theory revolves around a perpetrator who gambles. They might have tampered with Ralph Cairncross's work lamp the week before he was killed, but we have no proof of that. If they did, they'd have needed access to the family's garage, but that doesn't narrow the field of suspects.'

He glanced sideways at Tara and she tried not to react to those dark eyes in the wrong way. Sheesh. He was asking for information on a potential murder case; she ought to be able to edit out the warming effect his gaze had on her. It wasn't as though she was on the vodka.

'That's right.' She visualised the Cairncross's property. 'The garage is part of a large outbuilding, set apart from the house, quite close to the road. The gardens are overgrown, and the garage wasn't locked when I visited.'

Wilkins put down the lemonade he'd been drinking and winced. 'I hope they didn't see you entering their property without permission.'

Tara smiled. 'I didn't enter – I just tried the handle. But the point is, anyone from the house or coming up the driveway could easily have got inside without being seen.'

'All right,' said Blake, as Tara watched Wilkins open his mouth again. 'Then – once more all we have is guesses and circumstantial evidence – but someone could have put a grass snake in Ralph Cairncross's car a week later. This would also indicate a chancer. Someone who gets a kick out of setting certain wheels in motion, then standing back to see what happens. If the snake *was* put in the car, it seems likely that it was placed there whilst Cairncross attended the gathering at the house on the Forty Foot Bank. If it had been put in earlier – when he was at home on Madingley Road – he would probably have seen it before he left the city and either crashed there, or pulled up and halted his journey.'

Two members of the pub's staff appeared, each carrying two pizzas. Tara could smell the chorizo and felt her stomach rumble, in spite of everything.

'Thanks.' Blake paused as they set the platters down and went back for one more. Once they'd all been served he ripped a piece off the pizza he'd ordered. 'We know from Sadie Cairncross that her husband wasn't the sort to lock his car, any more than he was to wear a seatbelt, or stay sober at the wheel.'

Tara had just swallowed a piece of the chorizo pizza practically whole. She swigged some Coke. 'I guess we'll need to talk to the other partygoers next,' she said.

'But we—' Wilkins began.

'Yes,' Blake said to Tara. He turned to his DS. 'We'll have to talk to them, Patrick. I know what you're going to say, and I agree with you. This is far from conclusive. But whilst we're asking them about how recently they each saw Christian Beatty – which is simply following routine procedure – I want to alert them to the possibility that someone's going round, deliberately putting them in harm's way. Or encouraging them to do the job themselves. I couldn't live with my conscience if I stood back and another one of them ended up dead.'

Wilkins gave a series of sharp, annoying sighs. He'd probably start shaking his head in a minute. He hadn't even started on his food yet, which was unusual.

'So, let's say just for a moment that the snake was put into Cairncross's car out in the Fens,' Blake said. 'How could that have been achieved?'

Max leant forward, putting down the bit of Cajun chicken-laden dough he'd been about to eat. 'The perpetrator would have to have caught the snake and kept it somewhere, unless it was completely impromptu. And if they'd been keeping it in Cambridge they must have taken it to the Fens in a vehicle at some point. That could have been done on the night in question or in advance, of course.'

Wilkins had 'give that man a medal' sarcasm written all over his face. He didn't try to interrupt this time though; his mouth was finally full.

Blake nodded. 'Agreed. And if they'd brought it over ahead of time, they'd have to have found a place to keep it locally – somewhere close to the house, probably – but where no one else would spot it. Or, if they brought it to the house on the night of the party, they must somehow have done it without attracting attention. They might have managed it if they'd had a legitimate reason for being there anyway.'

'We should find out what the layout of the place is like,' Tara said, 'including the grounds and parking.' She swigged some more of her Coke and reached for the next slice of pizza, pulling on it until the mozzarella snapped.

'The house overlooks the entrance and the driveway,' Wilkins said. 'I went there, remember. I interviewed the party-goers the day Cairncross was fished out of the drain.'

'So, if someone brought the snake that evening by car or motorbike they would probably have been seen or heard,' Megan said. 'Though if it was after dark they might have managed it. But it would have been a risk. Alternatively, they could have dropped it off in advance and hid it in some kind of container nearby, or—'

'Or someone slung it over their shoulder and strode up the driveway hoping it would be mistaken for an unusual new fashion item,' Wilkins said. He dabbed at the corner of his mouth with a paper napkin.

'You might scoff,' Blake said lightly, 'but you should see some of the designs my sister comes up with. Grass snake couture could be the next big thing.' Megan and Max smiled. Wilkins didn't.

'Let's move on to the next two deaths,' Blake said, leaning back on the wooden bench seat they occupied. 'One young, fit man drinks too much, leaves a note seemingly acknowledging he might not return, and then swims so far out to sea that he can't make it back again. Then a second, similarly healthy, young man makes a dangerous jump on a high building in icy weather – again, drink may be involved. Both seemed to be displaying the sort of daring Ralph Cairncross would have encouraged, from what I've read about him.'

Tara nodded. 'I think you're right. I've been reading his novels over the last week and a half. He believes people should fill their lives with exciting experiences, even if they're dangerous – because a long life isn't worth striving for, if it's a tame one. And then, when people reach a certain point, they should actively seek death rather than running from it.' Tara could see the pain in Max's eyes as she spoke and wished he didn't have to hear views that must strike him at his heart. Having lost his wife so young the twisted nature of Cairncross's doctrines were personal for him, just as they'd been for Bea when she'd sat next to Tara, reading about the man.

'Do the books tell us anything else?' Blake said.

'The deaths so far each resonate with the way one of Cairncross's fictional characters dies.' Tara met his questioning look. 'His novels feature a man who swims too far out to sea, one that steps off a high-rise building and one where a man dies in water from a snake bite.' And then she told him about the other causes of death their conspirator had at their disposal: fire, suffocation and electrocution.

As she finished their group fell silent, and she was conscious of the noise around them: laughter, someone exclaiming over a text they'd just opened, and music playing in the background.

'So how does someone get a man to write a note about the daring act they're planning to perform, and then to swim so far that they can't get back?' Wilkins said. 'I seem to remember asking that before. And not getting a reasonable answer.'

Tara remembered too. Lucas Everett couldn't have gone to help someone pretending to be in trouble. It wouldn't fit with the note he'd left. *An adventure in memory of Ralph. And if I die, then death is not the end.* Hardly the act of a man rushing to someone's rescue. That left someone somehow encouraging him to do what he'd done. 'Someone he admired or felt indebted to might have planted the idea,' Tara said. She could hear herself how weak it sounded. 'If that "someone" was actually there with him, either watching, or even accompanying him, I can believe it happened that way.' No one looked convinced. She ripped off another bit of her pizza and hoped its spicy goodness might trigger some inspiration. She had a nasty feeling chorizo didn't count as 'brain food', however delicious it was.

Wilkins shook his head, slowly. 'You already know my answer to that. If he'd had someone with him you'd expect that person to have shared the vodka he was drinking, but there's no forensic evidence to support that. And not one of the people interviewed had seen him with anyone else.'

Tara's head was starting to ache. 'The perpetrator might have brought their own favourite liquor and taken the bottle away when they left. If they were acting maliciously they'd hardly leave their prints for us to find. And the place where Lucas Everett swam out from was remote. I wasn't surprised there were no witnesses. And then there's the missing notebook – Lucas Everett wrote his message on a page that was ripped from one, but not one that was in his possession.' Talk about clutching at straws…

Wilkins was smiling. 'Oh, well – case proven then! Look, just suppose for one moment we imagine you're right, and this ghost-like person exists. What then? That same person was also admired by Christian Beatty, and similarly encouraged him to go and leap around on top of a tall building in the middle of the night?'

Max and Megan looked all the more doubtful, and Tara couldn't blame them.

But Blake's look was steady. 'I get everything you're saying, Patrick,' he said. 'And yet, we do have three connected people who've died in quick succession in odd circumstances. Their deaths seem to tie in with those used in Cairncross's books and the same unusual brand of vodka was found near two of the bodies.' He raised an eyebrow. 'It's possible both Everett and Beatty liked that sort best, and it's a complete coincidence. But it's also possible someone was there the night Lucas Everett died and decided to buy Beatty exactly the same brand yesterday. And if they did that, I think it was to send us a message. They're laughing at us. They know we've got nothing, but they want to make sure we're wondering. Wondering and aware that there's something going on that's just beyond our reach.' He glanced sideways at Tara. 'And if it was them that iced your front path, they might have got you – or indeed any of us – in their sights. It could escalate. I know I'm not telling you anything you don't know.'

Each of them nodded. Blake was right, though personally, Tara had been trying not to focus on the danger she might be in. Anyone could have set that booby trap…

Watching Megan and Max's faces, Tara could see fresh uncertainly. She wondered what Fleming would think of it all, and if Blake was planning to share his thoughts with his boss.

'What about motive?' Blake said, taking up the final slice of his pizza.

Tara leant forward. 'Christian Beatty's ex said he'd cut her out when he took up with Cairncross. And Sadie Cairncross also seemed to feel she'd been abandoned by her husband. It's clear she still loved him but her feelings seemed a bit obsessive and unbalanced to me. She might have been angry with him, and with the Acolytes, who seemed to hold so much fascination for Ralph. Maybe something he or they did finally drove her over the edge. We've only got her word for it that she took pills and went to bed the night he died.'

'A bit OTT, don't you think?' her DS said, leaning back in his chair, his cool eyes on hers.

Tara shrugged. 'Maybe.' *You're not getting to me, Wilkins. Watch me stay cool whilst you get all wound up…*

'If any of this is true – which I seriously doubt – then I'd have the daughter down for it,' Wilkins added. 'She's a firebrand.'

Tara remembered Philippa Cairncross objecting to Wilkins addressing her as 'Miss' rather than 'Ms'. That would be enough for him to come to that conclusion. *Prat.*

'And although I can't for a minute believe someone could have engineered Everett or Beatty's deaths,' Wilkins went on, 'she could have been admired by them. She's got a certain something about her.' His tone was grudging. 'And she's the image of her father. Even Everett, who was gay, might have been swayed by her looking so much like the leader of their cult.'

And it did seem like a cult. 'Well, she's certainly still angry with her dad and protective of her mother,' Tara said. 'But she was with her boyfriend the night her father died, according to the files. So she couldn't have been out in the Fens, putting the snake in the car.' She bet Wilkins was cursing her for paying attention. 'It's a long shot, but I understand Cairncross bequeathed the house on the Forty Foot Bank to the Acolytes collectively. Each time one of them dies the share the others get increases. And any of them could easily have slipped out of the party and put the snake in the car.' But realistically, she doubted the house out in the Fens was worth that much, and the Acolytes all seemed to come from wealthy backgrounds, so they probably weren't in need. She shook her head. 'I agree with what you're no doubt all thinking: it would be a crazy way to try to make money. But Cairncross's PA might be someone to keep in mind.'

'Who's she?' Blake said.

Tara dragged the memory back without needing her notes. 'Someone called Tess Curtis. The Cairncross academic expert I spoke to says it's strongly rumoured she had a long-term affair with her boss, but that it was over some time before he died. Still, she might have held a grudge against him if he'd treated her badly. And against the Acolytes too, if they seemed to have a greater hold on his affections than she did.'

It was thin; she knew it was.

Suddenly, something Jackie Everett – Lucas's mum – had said, came back to Tara. 'One last idea. Mrs Everett said Lucas seemed more invigorated just before he died. He was talking about the Acolytes banding together and staying strong, so they could keep Cairncross's ideals alive. What if one of them has become so obsessed with Ralph's philosophy that they're wiping the group out, one by one, before they leave their youth behind?' She was sure they all thought she was the one who was crazy, not some unidentified plotter.

But Blake only paused for a moment, before he looked at Wilkins and spoke. 'I want the remaining members of Cairncross's group interviewed and warned, just as I said. And the same for Cairncross's family too. We don't know what we're dealing with, and I'm not happy about that.'

Wilkins turned to Tara. 'I'll take Thom King. You might as well visit Stephen Ross. I know how much you love being involved with this "case" and I'd like to get to bed before midnight.'

Before he could continue, Blake said: 'That makes sense – it'll save time, as you say. Max and Megan – you should go home and enjoy what's left of your Sunday. Tomorrow will do for contacting Christian Beatty's old college to see if he was a known night climber. You can gather additional information from his neighbours then too. I'd like you both to divide your time between that and tying up the last of the Hunter paperwork.'

He looked from Tara to Wilkins. 'You two prioritise this case for now. After Thom King and Stephen Ross, I want you to go together to see Verity Hipkiss. She's the last of the Acolytes you need to tick off, and whatever your opposing views on this, I need you to work as a team. And I want to hear everything that happens.'

CHAPTER TWENTY-ONE

Tara went back to her desk to call Stephen Ross – she wanted peace and quiet for her first talk with him. For a start, she didn't know if she'd be breaking the news of his friend's death. If he'd been out for the day he might not have heard. And she wanted to concentrate on what he sounded like at his least guarded. The idea of him intrigued her. Stephen seemed to be the responsible member of the group. He'd been the one to try to stop Ralph Cairncross from driving home when he was drunk, and the one who'd made it to the phone, the morning after the boozy party, when Philippa had called the house on the bank to try to track her father down. Philippa had implied that Stephen's more conventional outlook on life had meant he'd been seen as a lesser person by the rest of the group. Had he been aware of that, and resented it?

Taking a deep breath and holding all her thoughts together, she dialled.

When she gave him her name and explained who she was, his voice became more definite.

'You're calling about Christian?' he said. *'I already know all about it. It was on the news by early morning. That's part of the reason I came out here.'*

'Out where?'

'I'm at the house on the Forty Foot Bank. Ralph Cairncross – the writer – left it to me and the rest of the Acolytes for us to use after he died. I'm a poet and it's the perfect place to come for peace and quiet.' There was a pause. *'Verity Hipkiss, one of our group, wanted us all to*

meet up in town to "talk about our feelings". I'm not into that sharing stuff. I wanted to work, so I came here instead. What happened to Christian is shocking, but although we admired and respected one another, we weren't close. It was Ralph that linked us all.'

Tara wished she could see Stephen face to face as he spoke, but even without her background knowledge, he didn't sound sincere when he spoke about their mutual admiration. The words he'd trotted out were formulaic; easily said. A poet and a model. It might just be that they had nothing in common. And they sounded as though they were at opposite ends of the spectrum when it came to attitudes to adventure and risk taking. Whatever had happened on Christian's last evening, he must have been happy enough to scale the building he'd fallen from.

'I understand,' Tara said. 'I wasn't just ringing to arrange to break the news in person, though – I'd like to come and talk to you.'

'About what happened to Christian?' He sighed, but it was with irritation, not emotion. He wanted to carry on working, Tara guessed, and she was going to come and interrupt him.

'Yes.' She'd rather give him the full explanation when they were in the same place. She wanted to see his physical reactions.

'All right,' Stephen Ross said at last. *'I haven't managed to get stuck into my writing yet anyway.'*

Would he have said no if he'd been on a roll? Nice sense of priorities…

'Thanks.' She made her voice as warm as cocoa, but mainly because she wanted to make him feel guilty. 'How about if I come straight over now? Then I can get out of your hair and let you carry on.'

As she hung up, she realised Blake was standing just behind her. 'Stephen Ross?' he said.

She nodded.

'He's at home?'

'No. He's out at that house they've all been left, on the Forty Foot Bank.' She gave Blake a look. 'He's gone off there to write poetry and avoid social interaction with the other remaining Acolytes. He knew all about Christian Beatty's death by this morning, apparently. Probably read it on *Not Now*'s bloody website, given how quickly my erstwhile colleague Shona turned up at the scene.'

Blake looked thoughtful, his dark eyes on hers. 'Yes, I heard she materialised as if by magic.'

'I visualise her as a vampire, out at all hours of the night, scenting blood and then seizing on her prey.'

Blake gave her a half smile. 'She's always put me on high alert, when our paths have crossed.'

'A healthy reaction, I'd say.'

He nodded. He had a coffee in his hand – as usual – and was swigging the dregs out of the bottom. 'So you're off into the Fens?'

'Yes.' She really wanted to see both Stephen Ross and the bolthole the Acolytes occupied. What's more, she was glad to go without Wilkins. She reckoned she could pick up on much more when he wasn't wading in. But all the same, darkness would fall before she could make it home again, which wasn't her idea of fun – not that she'd ever admit it. Her mother lived in that direction and she tried to avoid it in winter, when the roads were icy. She knew how treacherous they could be. Ralph Cairncross was witness to that. Still, she wouldn't give up the interview on account of the location.

Blake slapped his empty cup down on a random desk. 'Just a moment,' he said, turning back towards the corridor that led to his office. 'I'm coming with you.'

Automatically, she glanced round the room, but there was no one left to hear his announcement. In particular, no Wilkins; he'd already gone off to mishandle the interview with Thom King. Just as well. She could imagine what he'd have said.

She followed Blake out into the corridor. 'What do you mean you're coming with me? I'm quite all right on my own.' She stood in his office doorway. 'I know I let the side down and required backup when that murderer tried to kill me in the Fens, but I don't intend to make a habit of it.' She'd thought she'd been streetwise back then, when she'd made her living as a hack – but she knew a lot more, now that she'd retrained.

Blake was dragging on a black woollen coat. Although he was looking down she could see there was a twinkle in his eye. 'I know.' Having fastened his buttons, he lifted his head to meet her look. 'If you were in a stand-off with our mystery conspirator it's them I'd be worried about.'

'That's all right then. So, what's going on?'

'I want to see the house. I wasn't there in the summer, don't forget, when Ralph went into the drain. I want to understand more about the set-up, and how things might have played out if someone did plant that snake in his car.'

'Wilkins will *love* this.' *Hell.* She shouldn't have let that worry slip out.

Blake strode out ahead of her towards the car park. 'Lucky it's not his call then. Besides, I'm letting him take the lead. I just want to absorb a few of the background details. Shall we take my car?'

She wondered if he was thinking back to when she'd been forced to drive across the Fens at knifepoint. Her would-be killer had used the weapon she'd been carrying. All in all, not a good memory. But not one that should rule her, either. 'No, I'll drive.'

'All right.'

Great, now she'd got ice, treacherous banks, deep drains and sitting within a hair's breadth of Blake to deal with.

The first five miles were awkward. Or, they were in her head at least. Blake seemed totally relaxed. Thank God the traffic was light, so they covered the ground quickly. They had plenty to discuss, of course. Tara explained about Stephen's apparent standing within the group, and everything she knew about him. But as she talked, she could still feel their past hanging in the air between them. Back in the pub four years ago, she'd been drawn to Blake. At the time she'd been pretty sure the feeling was mutual, but now she wasn't so convinced. The urge to kiss Blake had been pulling *her* like a magnet; maybe she'd just imagined the rest.

As she waited at a junction she snatched a sidelong glance at him. It was inconvenient that she still felt the same way; the fact wasn't easy to hide, for all her acting skills. She suspected he felt only comradeship now. He'd been back with his wife for four years, and they had a daughter, anyway. Tara's parents had been pretty cavalier about her when she was small. She didn't want to see any other child treated that way – or to be responsible for that.

She focused on the road ahead. 'Does Karen Fleming know what we're all up to?' she asked.

'In general terms.'

Tara could hear the smile in Blake's voice, even though she was staring determinedly at some tail lights.

'I had to get her approval for the overtime, for the extra staff doing the door-to-doors and for you and Patrick too. I'll be required to give a convincing explanation of my thinking tomorrow, when she's back in the office.' He didn't sound worried.

'You're pretty sure something's off?'

'I am. Monica Cairncross thinking she was followed... well, maybe. The ice on your path, the matching vodka bottles and the missing notebook... perhaps. But all of that with the link between the books and the way each of them died... it's too much. I'll have to work out what spin to put on it though, when I update Fleming.'

'You're starting to sound like a journalist.'

'Listening to your interviews during the Samantha Seabrook case gave me plenty of tips on how to get the right message across.'

Discussing the case carried them through the rest of the journey. As Tara drove along the Forty Foot Bank, she focused on the road ahead and the fields to her right, scanning for the remote house they needed. But to her left she could also see the channel of cold, dark water, running straight as a rod, below the level of the road.

At last, she saw the turn. The sign for the house was swaying in the wind. As she pulled the car round she saw it up ahead – a large, red-brick building she guessed might be Georgian, set well back from the road. Behind it the sky was stormy and already darkening to a heavy grey that promised snow.

The driveway was a dirt track and Tara wondered about the undercarriage of the car as she bumped along. After a moment she pulled up to one side and parked. Once Blake was out, she made sure the doors were locked. She wasn't taking any chances.

As she walked closer to the house, she realised it hadn't been well maintained. The paintwork was peeling in places and stained in others. It probably needed regular upkeep to cope with the exposed conditions out there, but she was betting Cairncross hadn't been the sort of man to spend time dealing with decorators and getting quotes. As for the Acolytes… She thought of Stephen Ross's voice – his irritability at her interruption. Would he lift his head up from his poems to take care of the place? Would any of the others? Or would the Cairncross family's home fall to wrack and ruin now it had passed out of their hands?

Blake was at the door. He raised an eyebrow. 'Ready?'

She nodded and he knocked.

CHAPTER TWENTY-TWO

Blake heard the sound of a text come in on Tara's phone as they waited for Stephen Ross to answer the door.

'Anything interesting?'

She nodded, her eyes still on the mobile's screen. 'Looks as though Max has carried on working, despite your advice to go home.'

It didn't surprise Blake – the DC had always been dedicated, but he suspected the long hours he'd put in since his wife died saved him from returning to an empty house that still echoed with her memory. He couldn't imagine what it must be like.

'He says the two people who left Christian Beatty's apartment block at around the same time as the hooded figure are accounted for now,' Tara said, strands of her red-gold hair falling over her face. 'One was a resident who has come forward, the second was a visitor who's now been recognised. But no one has been able to identify the visitor in the hood.'

He was about to reply but at that moment he heard the house door open and turned towards Stephen Ross. The man was around five eight, slight and elegant in a cream cashmere polo-necked jumper and jeans. Blake guessed he might be in his mid-twenties. His hair was very fair and his features were angular.

Blake saw the look of recognition in his eyes as they lit on Tara, and then Ross met his gaze.

'No need to bother with your IDs. I know DC Thorpe's face.' He held out a hand to Blake. 'She was featured in an article recently, I believe. In *Not Now* magazine.'

Blake saw Tara's eyes darken. Giles, her former editor, had done his best to make her look unprofessional in the publication's account of her work on the Samantha Seabrook murder case. He could see how much it got to her underneath, even though she was good at hiding her feelings.

'If you read that, please know that it was full of exaggeration,' she said.

Stephen Ross shrugged. 'It's what I'd expect from that sort of publication.' They were all in the hall now, and he closed the front door behind them.

'Quite a remote location,' Blake said.

'One of the reasons Ralph wanted us to have the place,' Ross replied. 'The idea was for it to be a sort of retreat – where we could escape the world and be creative. Or at least, that was the plan.'

The look he gave them both told Blake he didn't appreciate them barging their way into what was supposed to be his haven.

'What about for Christian Beatty?' Tara asked. 'His work was quite different from the rest of the group.'

'You're right,' Stephen said. 'He wasn't a creative. He used this place to recharge his batteries after he'd been running around, posing for the cameras.' He managed to keep his tone almost neutral but his words suggested he didn't think much of modelling as a career. It matched Blake's view, though his sister was always telling him what a tough job it was. She talked up the people who worked for her.

'It's interesting, in a way, that he was part of the group,' Tara said.

Blake guessed she'd noticed his prejudice too, and was playing to it, to soften the guy up. It was very much her style.

'Yes, in many ways he was the odd one out.' He put a slight emphasis on the word 'he', Blake noticed. It made him think of what Tara had said on the way over. Philippa Cairncross had implied that it was Stephen Ross who was on the periphery of the group.

It almost sounded as though he'd been kept in the gang to make the rest feel more loud and outrageous by comparison.

Ross was leading them down a long corridor, with doors coming off it. 'But Ralph was inspired by his appearance. He had a weakness for physical beauty. Christian's appeal was skin deep. I don't mean that in a belittling way.'

Blake couldn't imagine how else he'd meant it…

'Christian used to sit for Thom, too – Thom King, that is, the artist and another one of the gang.' Blake could hear the inverted commas he put around that last word. Ross shook his head. 'Thom was always saying he must paint Christian as often as possible, whilst he was still in his prime. Those paintings will be part of a small but valuable collection now.'

Blake caught Tara's eye for just a moment. The man sounded so cold and analytical. In fairness, you couldn't expect anyone who'd hung around Ralph Cairncross to be an appealing character. Ross was living up to expectations.

'Drinks?' he asked.

Blake eyed the array on a nearby side table. Just about every spirit you could imagine; though no Adnams-branded vodka. There was already a glass in use – containing something dark – whisky or brandy? Next to the table was a Sainsbury's carrier bag.

Stephen Ross followed his eyes. 'Oh, don't worry,' he said. 'We do have coffee in the kitchen if you'd like it.'

'I'm all right, thanks,' Blake said. Tara shook her head too.

Ross sat down and stretched back on a large, slouchy leather sofa. 'You police! I can see the way you're looking at me. I'm not planning on drinking and driving if that's what you think. I'm going to stay here tonight.'

'I'm glad to hear it,' Blake said. The man was irritating him. He took a seat on a chair opposite Ross and Tara chose a second, smaller sofa at right angles to them both.

Blake caught her eye. He'd remembered Fleming's warnings about not being a control freak, and this was Tara's party.

'I understand you live on Grange Road?' she said, turning to their host.

Stephen Ross looked surprised at the sound of Tara's voice. For a second he continued to glance at Blake, as though waiting for him to step in. Blake suddenly felt guilty for being there at all. If he'd let Tara come alone Ross wouldn't have expected him to take charge. Tara must suffer prejudice all the time as a young female officer. Things were better than they had been, but the problems were still there – often a completely unconscious bias. But for all his protestations earlier, he hadn't wanted Tara to come out to this place alone. Even if it had been Wilkins he'd have felt the same. The house was so remote – it wasn't like interviewing someone in town – and his gut told Blake that one of Ralph Cairncross's friends or family was a murderer.

At last, Stephen Ross turned towards Tara and nodded.

'Were you in town last night at all?'

'I was, as a matter of fact, having dinner with an acquaintance in the Eagle from around seven until ten or thereabouts.' He folded his arms. 'Nowhere near where Christian was found. I didn't see him whilst I was out.' His tone was short.

Unlike Blake, Tara always managed to hide her feelings well. 'Not to worry,' her voice was polite; deferential. Ross would no doubt appreciate it. 'It was a long shot. And you went home after that?'

'That's correct.' Blake watched the man's unfriendly eyes meet Tara's over the rim of his glass of spirits. 'I'm having a productive patch at the moment, creatively. I wanted to return to get my ideas down on paper. I made my evening out as short as possible.'

'We're just making sure we know where everyone was, for the record, and asking for alibis. It's routine, given that three closely connected people have died in unusual circumstances, within a few months of each other.'

'Is it really?' Ross said. 'Well, I can give you my dinner companion's number. Other than that I can't help. I live alone so no one can vouch for me later on.' He frowned. 'What's going on? The police think someone else is involved in all this?'

He pulled out a silver pen and a notepad from his pocket and began to write down the details they needed in tight, almost illegible handwriting.

'It's an outside possibility,' Tara said, her tone calm. 'But there are a few similarities between the ways Christian Beatty and Lucas Everett died.'

Blake held his breath, whilst telling himself he was being ridiculous; she wouldn't say what they were. She knew the importance of withholding details. There was always a chance one of their interviewees might mention them independently and give themselves away.

'There's even some crossover with Ralph Cairncross's death too,' Tara added.

Blake watched the man's eyes. No one knew the about the grass snake except the police and – if there was one – the murderer.

Ross was frowning, and it was a long moment before he spoke. 'Really?' His manner was casual. 'What's that? I'd picked up on the way in which Lucas and Christian's deaths mirror Ralph's books, of course. But Ralph's death doesn't fit that pattern.'

'You've read all of his novels, I suppose?' Tara said.

The man nodded, his pale blond fringe flopping over one eye. He put his hand over his mouth for a second and rubbed his chin. 'I wondered if there was a link between *The First and Last Day* and Lucas's death as soon as I heard what had happened. There was that note he left on the beach… I thought he might have been inspired to commit an act of bravado that mirrored a passage in one of Ralph's works. However, it was interesting that he chose to copy one of the death scenes. The characters in the books take

part in many death-defying adventures *before* they die, you see.
It's only when they're past their prime that they choose to walk
towards death and embrace it. Lucas wouldn't have thought he was
past his prime, I'm sure. But he might have swum out to sea as
some sort of test. And now there's Christian's jump. For a moment
I wondered whether a subset of our group could have formed a
pact of some kind – to each take a deadly risk, based on Ralph's
writing and in his honour.'

Blake watched Ross's features as he seemed to turn the idea
over in his head.

'So no one's mentioned such a pact to you?' Tara asked.

Ross shook his head. 'But it wouldn't surprise me if they'd
organised something without me knowing. Christian and Lucas
tended to go in for drunken escapades much more than I do.'

That figured, given what they knew of Stephen Ross. And from his
tone, it didn't sound as though he felt there was any shame in following
a safer way of life. Even if Ralph Cairncross had patronised him in the
way Cairncross's daughter had told Tara – treating him as the runt
of the group – Blake got the impression the poet didn't feel inferior.

'Did you find it affected your relations with the group?' Blake
asked. 'That fact that you didn't enjoy the same wild activities that
they did, I mean?'

'Not at all.' Ross rolled his eyes. 'I'm aware that some of the
others thought my standing with Ralph was less high then theirs,
but it was me he came to first over intellectual things.'

'Such as?'

'I was the first to read the manuscript for his final book. He
handed round copies to the others afterwards, but he gauged
my reaction first. It was just before he died; the book was nearly
through the production process and we had a private discussion
about the contents. He wanted to know if I'd understood some of
the allusions he'd made. And I had.'

Blake wasn't sure if Ross was just keeping his end up. He sounded as though he was remembering the occasion but there was something in his eye that told him his feelings towards Cairncross had been more complex than he was letting on. Was that a spark of anger behind the man's cool façade?

As for the poet's theory about a risk-taking pact amongst the other group members, it would have been a good one, if it hadn't been for the snake in Ralph Cairncross's car. It looked as though Ross hadn't considered the possibility of a third party being involved, assuming he wasn't bluffing. And yet there were so many possible permutations. What if Christian Beatty had been present when Lucas Everett had swum out to sea, and had been or had felt responsible? He could have chosen the same vodka Everett had bought to have a final drink the previous night, before he'd jumped to his death.

Except the CCTV footage outside Beatty's flat showed a sober man with a spring in his step leaving the apartment block. He hadn't looked like a guy who was consumed with guilt and ready to meet his maker.

Tara spoke again. 'It's useful to get your thoughts, Mr Ross.'

'Oh, don't bother with the faux formality.' The young man was lounging back on the sofa again now. 'Stephen will do.'

Tara nodded. She was still managing to smile. *How does she do that?*

'As I mentioned, Stephen, this information-gathering is purely a precaution. We'll be asking the other Acolytes and Ralph Cairncross's family exactly the same questions, just for the record. The other date we're interested in is Saturday 6 October, when Lucas died.'

'I went camping in the Peak District to make the most of the mild weather. I remember reading the news of his death on my phone, lounging on the grass outside my tent. The site's called

Sanderson Farm if you want to check. It's in Wolderam.' He gave Tara a look. 'It won't be much help though. I'm sure they'll remember me, but I was there alone. I wanted to go somewhere remote so I could write.'

'That's understandable.' Tara smiled again and sat back in her chair.

Blake knew she liked solitude too but he suspected her empathetic tone was entirely put on. For his own part, he'd found the house had echoed round him in the time after Babette had walked out, taking Kitty with her.

'I'll make sure this is all typed up,' Tara said. 'Then you can read through the statement and sign it off. It's always good to get the red tape out of the way. But I'd like to pick your brains about the rest of the group too – just in case it helps us understand what happened to your friends. Was it Ralph who christened you the Acolytes?'

Stephen Ross looked resigned to more precious minutes spent away from his poems. He picked up his glass, sipped from it, then shook his head. 'No. That was Tess Curtis, Ralph's PA. She was being sarcastic – mocking us for our loyalty – but Ralph liked it. He kept using it, with a laugh each time, and it stuck.'

'Were you a founding member, so to speak?'

'I was,' Stephen said. 'Along with Letty, who died of cancer earlier this year. She was the youngest of the group – I think she caught Ralph's eye first – she was very bright and beautiful too, like the subject of a Pre-Raphaelite painting.' His eyes were far away, as though he'd conjured up her image. 'Then there was Lucas, Verity Hipkiss and Thom King. Christian came along a bit later.' He shook his head. 'So odd to think that there are only three of us left.'

'And he found you all individually? But in quick succession?'

Blake imagined Cairncross casting his net for the most bright and beautiful young things he could find, like a magpie hoarding specimens that sparkled.

'That's right. Well, almost. Letty and I were at a summer garden party last year, held at the English faculty at the university. She'd come up to Cambridge early; she was still an undergraduate at the time – eighteen years old and about to start her second year. We'd known each other back home, and then by coincidence we ended up sharing the same tutor – though I'd long since graduated by then. Lucas was a researcher at the department and he was at the same party. Verity Hipkiss joined the Acolytes a short while after that – Ralph met her at an awards ceremony – and then Thom. He was working on a commission for Verity's parents. And Christian was the last. I think Ralph found him at some celebrity do around a year ago.'

Tara nodded. 'Have you all met up much, since Ralph Cairncross died?'

'We were destined to, every so often – because we'd inherited this place, apart from anything else.'

She nodded.

Blake watched as he polished off his drink and reached to pour himself another.

'Can you imagine anyone who'd have had enough influence on Lucas and Christian to encourage them to take the sort of risks that led to their deaths?' Tara said. 'Apart from Ralph before he died, that is?'

Stephen Ross put down the bottle he'd been pouring from. 'You think that's a possibility? It seems such a fantastical idea.'

'Nonetheless, it's something we can't discount. And we want the rest of you to be wary if you're approached by anyone with similarly dangerous suggestions. Though I guess that goes without saying at this stage.'

He shrugged. 'I'd be wary in that circumstance, whether you'd warned me or not. But how do you think a person might exercise that sort of influence?'

Blake saw Tara hesitate. 'Someone who Lucas and Christian admired might have encouraged them to show off. Or convinced them to do something extreme, in Ralph's memory.'

Ross shrugged. 'I suppose they were both full of bravado. But in terms of who they might admire, Verity Hipkiss is the obvious answer. She's stunning, and with the best will in the world she likes to make people dance to her tune. She enjoys being the only female Acolyte left.' Blake watched him stare calmly back at Tara, unblinking. 'You can't blame her, I suppose – she's discovered her power over the opposite sex and she enjoys using it.'

'Would Lucas have wanted to impress her in the same way that Christian might have?' Blake put in. He wondered if Ross knew Everett had been gay.

'He liked women as well as men,' Stephen said. 'So in that sense, yes. But I'm getting carried away with my argument. Verity wouldn't want them dead, though a few people might have felt like killing her from time to time.'

'Who do you mean, specifically?' Tara asked.

But Ross waved away her question. 'Surely you didn't take me seriously? She loves an adoring crowd around her; she certainly lapped up Christian's compliments eagerly enough. And Lucas's too. And if she makes people jealous I suspect she finds it entertaining.'

'Was she ever in a relationship with any of you?' Tara asked, lightly.

Ross raised an eyebrow. 'It wouldn't surprise me, but I don't know.'

Blake presumed Ross himself wasn't in Verity Hipkiss's thrall, given he'd come over to the house on the bank to avoid her that day. Of course, there was no reason to suppose he liked women rather than men.

'What about someone from Ralph's family?' Tara smiled. 'Would any of them have known Lucas or Christian well enough to influence them, do you think?'

Ross took another large swig of his drink. 'I wouldn't have thought so. Though I think Ralph's wife and daughter might have felt a certain antagonism towards us. They could have been motivated to cause trouble.'

'What makes you think that?' Blake asked. 'Did you meet them often?'

'Rarely. At the occasional official party, given by Ralph's publishers – that kind of thing. All the same, on those occasions, the expression on Ralph's daughter's face spoke volumes. She used to pass comment too, in stage whispers.' Blake watched as Ross's grip on his glass tightened. The man had managed to keep his tone casual, but Philippa must have got to him with her barbed words. That was interesting. 'Ralph called his daughter "the Dragon",' he added. 'He said she took after his sister, and he was disappointed. When he'd decided to procreate he was hoping for a carbon copy of himself.'

Blake remembered Tara's description of Philippa. She might not have seen eye to eye with her father but she looked just like him, apparently.

'Can you take us back to the night Ralph's car came off the road?' Tara said. 'Who arrived at the party first?'

Ross frowned. 'I think it must have been Verity. I remember she was bustling about when I got here. She'd bought a whole lot of booze and snacks. After that came Christian, then Lucas and then Ralph himself. Thom was last, if I recall rightly.'

'And you all drove, I suppose, given this place is so remote?'

He nodded. 'There's plenty of space to park, as you'll have seen. Out at the front and round the side too. The rest of us always stay over at the house if we're partying, but Ralph never did.'

'Are there places to sleep comfortably here?' Blake asked.

Ross smiled. 'A couple of doubles. We'd usually argue the toss over who would claim them. If Ralph had stayed he would have automatically got one – it was his house.'

'But he liked to get home?'

'I think he liked to stay a little aloof. It wasn't a brotherhood, don't forget. We were the Acolytes.'

That figured. From what Blake knew of Cairncross, he guessed he'd want to maintain a certain distance – amongst them but not of them. The more he heard, the more antagonism he felt towards the dead man.

'I think it was you who tried to persuade Ralph not to drive home the night he died?' Tara said.

Ross nodded, his face grim. 'He could hold his drink, but he'd had more than usual that night. Or he seemed drunker, anyway. I had to try to make him see sense. But it was no good; he was determined to leave. He got cross with me in the end, so the last exchange I had with him was an angry one.' Ross looked irritable himself, rather than sad. Then suddenly his expression cleared. 'I've just thought,' he said, 'the very last person to show up at the house that night was actually Tess Curtis.'

'Tess? What, Ralph Cairncross's PA, you mean?' Tara said, sitting forward in her seat.

'Yes – I'd completely forgotten. Of course, she wasn't there for the party; she just came in, dropped off some papers or something and left again. I remember Ralph rolling his eyes, and we all joked about how dedicated she was. It was ironic that she teased us about our loyalty, really.'

'You must have seen her quite regularly, I suppose?' Tara said.

'Certainly,' Ross replied. 'Ralph had got to the point where he was pretty much reliant on her. She'd keep track of all his business arrangements, chase his agent, prompt him when he forgot appointments and deadlines. And there was a rumour their relationship had been more personal at one stage, too. I got the impression Ralph still enjoyed having her dashing round after him. Why wouldn't he?'

'I'm surprised no one's mentioned her being here on the night of the accident up until now,' Blake said.

Ross shrugged. 'She was in and out in five minutes. And with the shock of what happened I shouldn't think anyone gave it a second thought. She was present so often. And it didn't have any impact on what happened later, of course.'

Probably. Darkness had descended and through the sitting room window, Blake could see snowflakes falling.

Stephen Ross looked at his watch and then at them. He got up to draw the curtains.

After the Acolyte had shown them out, Blake turned to Tara, raising his eyebrows. 'Tess Curtis just became that bit more interesting.'

Tara nodded. 'She did, didn't she?'

He spoke softly. 'Shall we take a quick look round outside? I'd like to see if there's a place where someone could have hidden that snake.'

Tara glanced over her shoulder. The sitting room curtains were shut, and the rest of the house was in darkness. 'Good idea.'

Round the back of the house, they found a cavernous outbuilding. Blake could see its doors were ajar. He strode over to look inside, using the torch on his phone.

Tara was close behind him. 'Seems like a likely spot,' she said. 'A bit risky if anyone decided to go exploring, but it doesn't look as though it's in regular use. I'm guessing the junk in here's been left to rot for a while.'

Blake nodded. Tara was standing so close to him he could feel her warmth. For just one moment his mind ran back four years – to when he'd wanted to ask her out, but had made the decision to try to rebuild his marriage instead.

'True,' he said, firmly turning his mind back to the job. 'Everything here looks abandoned.' He walked over to where there were stacks of large, empty wooden crates. Maybe they'd been used to transport quantities of vegetable crops to wholesalers at one time. 'And if you put some kind of container behind here no one would see it from the door.'

As well as the crates, the building was home to a lot of other junk. There was a long, metal thing that looked like abandoned agricultural equipment – something for spraying crops maybe – and other rusty bits and pieces that were unidentifiable as far as Blake was concerned. Alongside the machinery there were battered old bits of furniture – including a large sofa with a torn leather cover – as well as piles of worn-out tractor tyres. There was nothing that would mean any of the Acolytes or Ralph would have regular cause to visit the place.

Back outside, they looked out over the flat landscape. The snow was coming down faster now; white moonlit flakes falling on black, frost-hardened soil.

'And of course someone could have put a container outside, behind this building too,' Tara said.

They went to look, and round the back of the outbuilding there *was* another crate. It was like the ones inside, but in better condition, and with a lid. Although it was slatted, like the others, the gaps between the wood were narrow – not more than the width of Blake's finger. He used his gloved hands to open it.

Tara was absolutely quiet, as though she was holding her breath.

The inside of the box was pretty much bare but by the light of his torch Blake could see several yellowed strands of grass. There was something about them that reminded him of pet bedding. And given their colour, they couldn't have been there for that long, surely? Might they date back to September, when Ralph Cairncross had died?

'Right,' he said. 'I want this tested. If we find a trace of grass snake DNA, or the DNA of anything they eat, then at least we'll have evidence to back up your theory.'

Tara was still silent but when he looked round at her she nodded at last and he saw her swallow. She'd pushed this case a long way on little more than gut instinct, and Blake had backed her up based on trust and his own hunch. He'd be just as glad as she would of some concrete evidence. The thought of them not being written off as fools was quite appealing…

'Right,' he said. 'Better get back inside and let the charming Stephen Ross know what we're up to…'

CHAPTER TWENTY-THREE

Tara was still trying to suppress a smile as she walked into the bar on Quayside where she and Wilkins were due to meet Verity Hipkiss. The woman had agreed to get there twenty minutes early – before the friend she was due to meet turned up.

What with getting the crate removed from the house on the Forty Foot Bank, then typing up the information Stephen Ross had given them at interview, so it could be printed out, ready for him to sign, it was now seven in the evening. Her smile was due to Wilkins' reaction to the news about the crate.

Okay, so she wasn't home and dry yet. It might not have been where the snake was kept, but it was a hell of lot more promising than anything else they'd found so far. She stuck her hand inside her coat pocket and crossed her fingers as Wilkins pushed open the swing doors to the bar. *Please let there be something to prove I'm not the idiot my DS wants me to be.*

As they walked inside, Tara welcomed the rush of warm air that hit them from an overhead heater. Outside, the cold was intense, and her hands and toes had started to hurt. She stamped the snow from her boots onto the doormat.

Wilkins had made no secret of the fact that he bitterly resented spending his Sunday warning a collection of over-confident, self-satisfied nobodies (his words) that they might be in danger from a figment of her imagination. But interestingly, his tone and body language changed the moment they found Verity Hipkiss. Was it the figure-hugging strappy black dress and vertiginous heels that had made the difference? Or her high cheekbones and long, blonde hair perhaps? But *of course*, Tara was just being cynical. The guy had probably recalled his duty as a police officer and decided to put his back into his work.

Tara watched as he stepped forward between her and the woman they both recognised from her publicity photos. Her debut novel had got her a lot of attention. Her smile mirrored his: radiant and full of shiny white teeth. Tara could imagine why Stephen Ross had cited her as someone who might hold sway with the other Acolytes – and indeed anyone else in the vicinity. She was stunning, all right. And after she'd greeted Wilkins she immediately looked over his shoulder and included Tara in the conversation. It might just be good people-skills, rather than genuine warmth, but it was effective, all the same.

'I rang Stephen a short time ago,' she said, her large grey eyes wide. 'He told me you'd taken a crate from behind the outbuilding on the Forty Foot Bank.' Her look was worried now. 'What's going on?'

Tara was interested that she'd called the poet again. Had she still been pestering him to meet up to talk through his feelings? Was she frustrated that he didn't come running when she called?

'Stephen and I were surprised,' Verity went on. 'I knew there was a load of junk out there, of course. And it'll be our responsibility to deal with it, now that Ralph's dead.' She breathed out his name like a sigh. 'But none of us have had the will to tackle it yet. And probate's still going through, so the place isn't officially ours. In fact, I was surprised when we got the letter from Ralph's solicitors, saying we're welcome to carry on using it in advance of the formal handover.' She looked down for a moment. 'But I don't think the family wants to see it again, after what happened.'

'They've not been round since Ralph's accident, as far as you know?' Tara said.

Verity shook her head.

Wilkins leapt in at that point, to put the woman on her guard against anyone who might wish her and her group harm. Tara listened as he did a lot of laughing and reassuring. ('It's really so unlikely that someone deliberately targeted Ralph, Lucas and Christian that I feel almost foolish even mentioning it to you' – a sidelong glance at Tara – 'but at the same time, it's better to be safe than sorry.') Verity kept nodding, her expression serious. And she didn't raise any objections when Wilkins also asked where she'd been when Lucas and Christian had died. Her answers weren't much help though. She'd been working on edits for her second book back in October when Lucas had drowned; looking at her calendar she couldn't find any evidence that she'd seen anyone who would remember seeing her the night he took his last swim. And the previous evening, when Christian had leapt off the building, she'd been out for a meal with friends, but only until eleven or so. After that she'd gone home to her flat, where she lived alone. She and Stephen Ross were both young to have their own places; Tara was guessing they had family money. Though, of course, Verity's first book was selling well, too.

'Does that give you what you need to know?' she asked, smiling hesitantly.

It was just the sort of smile Wilkins liked. He hastened to tell her that it did. More detail really wasn't necessary, given how tenuous their reasons were for asking. But the take-home message for Tara was 'no alibi'. Though she couldn't imagine why Verity would want to lead her fellow Acolytes to their deaths – or Ralph for that matter. She'd looked wistful when she'd mentioned his name.

'It would be useful to know more about the group Ralph established,' Tara said. 'Are you all close?'

Verity gave an elegant shrug. She was as loose-limbed as a dancer. 'Even though we all came together by chance really –

under Ralph's direction, rather than through choice – I'd say we've bonded quite strongly.'

She might well feel that, if she'd got most of the group swooning at her feet. It was pretty much what Stephen Ross had implied. Tara nodded. 'Did you see the others much, before Ralph died, apart from when he got you all together?'

Verity nodded. 'Reasonably often. Thom would invite me out for coffee occasionally. And Christian and I went for a few drinks together.' She caught Tara's eye. 'Oh, but nothing like that. Just friends. Of course, Christian was very good-looking; it went with his job.' There was a slight colour to her cheeks, Tara noticed, which made her wonder how honest she was being. 'And Thom... ah, well, Thom's a sweetie. I never really see Stephen separately but Lucas and I had a few pleasant times.' She sighed. 'It was intermittent though. They all worked so hard. Letty was charming.' Her words were complimentary but the smile she gave didn't reach her eyes. 'She was several years younger than me, of course. We didn't have much in common. And then she got so ill, poor thing. She and Stephen had known each other longest. They and Lucas joined the Acolytes after attending the same party. Of course, everything changed after Ralph's death. We arranged to meet up at the house on the bank, to talk and come to terms with what had happened.'

'And what about Ralph's family?' Tara asked, ignoring Wilkins' repressive look. 'Did you ever see them?'

'Not so much,' Verity said, tucking her silvery-gold hair behind her ears. She wasn't meeting Tara's eye.

'Stephen said he only really saw them at formal gatherings.'

She nodded. 'It was the same for me.'

'And how were things with them, on those occasions?'

At last Verity's eyes met hers – and they were wary. 'What makes you ask?'

Her tone made Tara wonder. 'I just got the impression there might have been tensions there.'

Verity put her shoulders back and gave a slightly strained smile. 'Nothing I really noticed,' she said.

'That's reassuring,' Wilkins replied, all bonhomie.

'Ah.' Verity's expression cleared. 'Here's Magda now. I'm sorry, but we'd better end our chat there. I appreciate your concern though, and I'll be careful. It was the most awful shock to hear about Christian this morning. I wasn't going to come out this evening but Magda thought it would do me good to talk.'

Tara sensed she felt the need to justify herself.

'I'm sure your friend's right.' Wilkins slithered off the stool he'd been posing on.

To be fair, Tara thought so too. 'One last thing,' she said. 'Stephen mentioned Tess Curtis, Ralph's PA, dropped in briefly, the night he died?'

Tara was quite sure she hadn't imagined the change in Verity's colour. Interestingly, it wasn't instant. Tara guessed she must have been thinking back and then drawing conclusions. She went pale. 'That's right,' she said slowly. 'So she did.' And now the colour in her cheeks rose again. 'She always wanted to be in on whatever was happening. She was so nearly part of the gang, but not quite. And she had serious FOMO.'

'FOMO?' said Wilkins.

Verity suddenly smiled that charming smile of hers again, giving Tara's boss full beam. 'Fear of Missing Out, Sergeant.'

CHAPTER TWENTY-FOUR

Kemp was sitting in the kitchen of Bea's boarding house, his chair pulled up to her scrubbed oak table. Bea herself was opposite him, and they were both tucking into the best sausage casserole he'd ever tasted. It was rich with sage, Bordeaux wine and mushroom ketchup; he knew – he'd helped prepare it, under his host's watchful and expert eye.

'Never tastes like this when I make it,' he said, picking up his glass to swig some of the wine that hadn't gone into the cooking.

'No reason why it shouldn't,' Bea said. 'You're a dab hand at cooking as far as I can see.'

'After two weeks' training.' He grinned. 'You want any help dishing up the boarders' pudding?'

Bea had already prepared the chocolate mousses she was going to serve – they were all lined up ready in the fridge.

She shook her head, tucking a strand of her mid-brown hair behind her ear. 'You've done more than enough today already.'

Kemp didn't have another job lined up until after Christmas, so he'd been making himself useful. He'd talked Bea into letting him muck in, in return for the friends' rates she was charging him for board – which were next to nothing. They'd spent the day refitting one of the guest bedrooms. Kemp hated constructing self-assembly furniture – it was too fiddly and irritating – so he'd decorated whilst Bea had built a chest of drawers in the en suite, ready to move through to the main room once the paint was dry.

Bea was watching him now across the table, whilst she sipped her own wine. She had a shrewd look in her eye that reminded

Kemp forcibly of Tara. 'So, you're off out again this evening, are you?' she said. A half smile played around her lips.

'That's right.' He grinned but didn't elaborate. Instead, he swallowed the last of his casserole and went to wash up his plate. Bea didn't have a dishwasher. She said it ruined the glasses – and besides, the amounts of crockery she had to do never quite fitted in. Strangely, he quite liked washing-up himself. It was a mindless task that helped him think.

He was just about to leave the kitchen to fetch his coat when Bea spoke again.

'Incidentally, will you be seeing Tara tonight, by any chance?'

He could tell she was fishing. 'No, sorry.'

She shook her head. 'Not to worry. I just had a message for her, that's all. It'll keep.'

Kemp smiled to himself as he went through to the hall.

An hour and a half later, he was sitting outside a pub called the Dog and Gun. It was well outside Cambridge – just the sort of place for a meet-up if you didn't want to be seen. He'd only come to be there himself by watching, waiting and then tailing his quarry.

He had his camera at the ready and recorded developments as the man he'd been following left his car and entered the building. Kemp got out of his own vehicle and strolled across the front car park, lighting a cigarette as an excuse to remain outside. Not that he wasn't enjoying it for its own sake, too. He'd been meaning to give up… for around twenty-five years.

He found a position where he could stand in the shadow of a snow-covered cedar tree and see through one of the pub's sash windows towards the bar. After a moment he picked out the guy he'd been tailing again – but he wasn't alone now. He'd been joined by a woman – and they looked pretty damned friendly.

By the time he decided to enter the pub, having taken more covert photos, it was a group of three he could see: the man, the woman, and a second guy who'd joined them… *What in hell's name?* They huddled together, deep in discussion about something. *Three conspirators?*

He strode towards the pub's door, wondering what he'd discover when he got inside. Ideally, he'd want to share it with Tara, but he remembered what she'd said about interfering.

He'd have to tread carefully – and to be sure of his ground before he went any further.

CHAPTER TWENTY-FIVE

Tara set off home – walking back along the Cam. The boardwalk at the town end was treacherous. The snow had become compacted and was now iced up. Next to her the river looked dark and still. She clung to the railings as she slipped along. Her gloves weren't enough to keep out the intense cold.

Verity Hipkiss's words went round in her head. Tess Curtis piqued her interest: a woman who'd once been Ralph Cairncross's lover, who'd maybe felt shut out after he'd taken up with his gang of young followers. And who'd also been on the scene the night Ralph died. It would be interesting to find out where she'd been when Christian fell to his death. And when Lucas had drowned, too. But although Tara could see that the woman had had the opportunity and potential motive to have put the snake in Ralph Cairncross's car, she couldn't imagine how she'd have engineered the other deaths.

And then what about the look that had come into Verity's eye when Tara had asked about her relationship with Ralph's family?

She needed to find out more, but from where? She couldn't see Sadie or Philippa giving her any honest information. She paused and looked across the river towards the snow-covered chimneys of Magdalene College.

She really wished she'd been in on the conversation Wilkins had had with Thom King. Something told her he might know more about Verity Hipkiss. She thought back to the way Verity had described him. 'Ah, well, Thom's a sweetie.' She'd placed him firmly in the friendzone. 'Thom would invite me out for coffee occasion-ally,' she'd said. Tara suspected he'd wanted their relationship to extend further, but that his efforts had been in vain. By the sound of it, he'd been the odd one out – keen where she wasn't. Tara had got the impression Verity's relationships with both Christian and Lucas might have been more than platonic. And she seemed to spend time trying to see more of Stephen Ross, for whatever reason. Perhaps purely because he wasn't interested and it irked her. But the artist Thom King had been left out in the cold… Stephen Ross had said he could imagine some people wanting to kill Verity. Was it Thom King he'd been thinking of? She was letting her ideas run away with her. Without speaking to him she couldn't possibly judge.

There was the matter of the near miss Thom had already had with the car, too. She'd asked if Wilkins had raised it at their interview, but of course he hadn't. He was still convinced she was obsessing over a set of coincidences that meant nothing.

She'd noted the contact details for each of the Acolytes when she'd first got permission to look into Ralph's case. Now, she opened her bag and stared at the mobile number for Thom King. He wouldn't relish two approaches from the police in one day… She paused for a moment, browsing the web for information that might help her soften him up. Then, steeling herself for hostility, she dialled.

Tara had been gushingly apologetic when Thom King picked up. She knew he must have had a terrible day, she told him, what with the death of his friend. (Though he didn't sound that broken, in fact.) She explained that a couple more queries had come up. Because of the sensitive nature of the conversation she needed to have, she wondered if she could possibly come and find him. Then she'd hesitated and mentioned his paintings and how fascinating it would be to meet him. (She was glad she'd googled them in order to sound convincing, her old journalism tactics coming into play. She felt a small twinge of guilt – Blake wouldn't approve of her less-than-honest approach. All the same, she got a buzz when it worked. His tone warmed up considerably at that point.)

Half an hour later she was sitting opposite him in the Castle.

'Thank you for seeing me.' She'd bought him a pint and they were settled by one of the windows downstairs. Outside, across the road, the houses were brightly lit, their roofs piled thick with snow. A Christmas tree in one of the windows set the scene off nicely. She smiled at her interviewee once again. 'I'm so sorry if I've dragged you out.'

He leant forward and smiled. 'It's good to have a distraction, to be honest – even if it does mean talking about the very thing that's been on my mind all day. It's still better than sitting at home visualising Christian's broken body.' Suddenly he looked down into his drink. 'I painted him so many times; he had a perfect physique.'

The scene she'd witnessed that morning filled Tara's head for the umpteenth time that day. She tried to concentrate on the man in front of her instead. It was interesting that Thom King was focusing on Beatty as an object to paint, rather than as a person.

'A very difficult time for you. And at the end of a tough six months, what with Ralph Cairncross and Lucas Everett's deaths too.'

'Absolutely. It's been appalling. Such a shock.'

He'd leapt to affirm what she'd said, but she didn't think he'd have articulated it if she hadn't prompted him. She needed to go for a more roundabout approach if she wanted to find out how they'd really got on.

'I gather you joined Ralph's group of Acolytes fourth, just after Verity Hipkiss.' She watched his eyes as she said the woman's name. 'Stephen Ross mentioned you'd been working on a commission for her parents.'

'That's right. Verity and I had arranged to meet for a drink, and she brought Ralph along with her.' He'd thought it would be just the two of them, clearly. The hurt was still there in his eyes even though it must have been months ago now.

'You hadn't expected to meet him that night?' It was the most tactful way to put it.

'No.' Thom King smiled unconvincingly. 'It was a wonderful surprise, of course. And I was very flattered when Ralph invited me to join his circle. He said he'd admired my work for some time. It's always good to meet a fan. No artist tires of it.' He seemed to realise it was time to stop talking.

'And it must have been great to be praised by such a well-known and influential figure, too.'

Thom King shrugged.

'You didn't rate him, despite being part of the group?'

The man pulled back a little in his seat. 'No, no, of course I did. He was monumentally talented.'

Tara sensed a 'but'. She waited. That usually got the best results. He didn't seem wary. She sensed he saw her as a harmless young woman who was simply there to let him offload. Professionally, that might be irritating, but it would be stupid to get cross about it. He was far more likely to give things away if he didn't see her as a threat.

'It's just that there are other writers who are every bit as talented, but haven't found fame. I suppose it's fair to say that Ralph got his rock-star status – and all the trappings – by deliberately making his work controversial. And his behaviour too.'

He might well be right, but it was interesting that he'd tried to disguise his resentment.

'Perhaps you could take me through the Acolytes now, so I can get a better idea of them. I met Stephen Ross earlier today.'

'Ah, Stephen.' Thom King shook his head as though they were talking about a troublesome child. 'With the best will in the world, he's a bit of a damp squib really. Tame.' He glanced at Tara. 'But then he *is* a poet. Ralph didn't treat him quite as he did the rest of us. I think it amused him to have someone around as an example of how not to be, if you know what I mean. Stephen was in the group from the start, along with Lucas and Letty. Letty was a treasure – we all adored her. I heard it was she who gave Ralph the idea of setting up the circle; he was enchanted with her. She was exceptional, of course: coming up to Cambridge so young. She wrote poetry, just like Stephen.'

Tara nodded. 'What about Lucas and Christian? Did you get on with them?'

'Oh yes,' Thom said. 'They were good guys.'

Tara remembered Verity's blush when she'd denied she and Christian had been more than friends, and her mention of the 'pleasant times' she'd shared with Lucas. 'Verity Hipkiss said much the same thing.' She allowed the memory of the woman's words to affect her tone.

Thom King's eyes darkened. His jaw was tight. 'Yes,' he said. 'She was a great admirer of them both. She—' But he stopped abruptly and though Tara raised her eyebrows he didn't say any more. His shoulders were hunched. Suddenly he looked larger than he had done, more aggressive.

'Do you and Verity get on?'

He took a deep breath. 'Oh, yes. We found a lot to talk about when I painted the commission for her parents.'

Tara gave him a look. 'She's very beautiful.'

'As an artist, I've noticed that. Not my type personally, but objectively she'd be a perfect subject.'

Like heck. 'She's never sat for you then?' Tara was willing to bet he'd asked.

He answered quickly. 'No. There hasn't been time. She's very busy with her writing.'

'Did Ralph mentor her?'

For a second there was disgust in Thom King's eyes, and when he spoke the emotion infiltrated his tone too. 'I believe he did something of the sort.'

It seemed like the right moment to push for more information. She remembered the way Verity had breathed out Ralph's name and her anxious expression when Tara had asked how she got on with the author's family. That and Thom King's resentment of Ralph made her increasingly sure of her ground. 'Verity seemed emotional about Ralph's death,' she said. 'I'm sorry for asking, but you know her well. Was she having an affair with him?'

Thom King blinked twice. 'How did you know?'

'I didn't,' Tara said. 'It was a guess. Just something in her tone. I can see why she wouldn't mention it openly, of course. I guess she feels Sadie Cairncross has had enough to cope with recently.'

Thom gave a hollow laugh and swigged some more of his beer, looking down again for a moment into the dark, treacle-coloured liquid. 'That's true, but it won't be what's holding Verity back.' His voice was bitter again.

'How do you mean?'

'Have you seen the quotes Ralph sent to Verity's publisher, to help publicise her book? Or the interview he gave on television, heralding her as the most influential new novelist of our generation?'

Tara sat back in her chair. 'Ah,' she said. 'I can see those wouldn't carry so much weight if everyone knew they were sleeping together.' She was glad he hadn't been able to help himself feed her that titbit. It set her thinking.

'She'll be desperate to keep the affair quiet for that reason more than any other.'

In fact, she might have had cause to want Ralph dead herself, if he'd been threatening to go public – maybe leave his wife or something. Had she really loved him? Or had he just been a pleasant distraction for a few months, and useful in terms of her career? Tara's mind ran to the dead Acolytes again for a moment, Christian and Lucas. If she'd really been stringing them all along it sounded like a dangerous game. What if Christian or Lucas had found out she'd been sleeping with Ralph earlier in the year, and had threatened to give away her secret?

But if she'd killed a series of people to silence them, surely she'd have used more certain methods…

And then Tara looked at Thom King. Wasn't he a more likely candidate for their killer? The one Acolyte who'd wanted Verity but had been rejected. His disgust at the idea of Ralph Cairncross mentoring her had created a powerful impression. But what about the near miss Thom had had himself? The close shave with the car?

'The other police officer who came to talk to you, DS Wilkins, told you to be on your guard,' Tara said.

Thom King nodded.

'It brings me to the other issue I wanted to discuss. I hear you had a close call yourself, a while back. Someone in a car almost knocked you down?' She remembered how Dr Richardson, the Cairncross expert, had speculated that Thom King might have exaggerated the incident for attention. He'd said he'd never reported it to the police.

Thom frowned, but he didn't look embarrassed. It was a moment before he spoke. 'Dear God. I hadn't thought. My incident resonates with the death in one of Ralph's books, doesn't it? Just like Christian's and Lucas's…'

He looked scared. But if he'd invented the whole near-miss thing, to make himself sound like a victim, he'd be prepared to give that sort of reaction. And after all, he'd gone around telling Dr Richardson and the Acolytes about it – yet he hadn't bothered notifying the police…

Tara took a swig of her Coke. 'We don't want to worry you. That sort of incident's not so uncommon. But it's still something we'd like to know more about.' Royal we. She was quite sure Wilkins wouldn't be in the least interested, but she certainly was. 'Could you tell me exactly what happened?'

'I'd just hired a studio to work in. It's in the middle of nowhere – great because there are no distractions and I find the countryside inspiring.'

'Is it out in the Fens?'

He shook his head. 'It's near Haslingfield, along a country lane. The parking for the studio is on the opposite side of the road, so you have to cross to reach it. A bit inconvenient when I'm carting new canvases over, and things like that, but the place is good value for money. It was as I was crossing that the car almost mowed me down.' His gaze was far away now. Was he remembering reality? Or struggling to recall a story he'd made up?

'Was it coming round a bend or something?' She wondered how he hadn't seen the car.

'Yes, but the turn in the road wasn't that close to where I crossed. I saw the car before I stepped out, but I reckoned I'd got plenty of time. People kept saying I must have misjudged the speed it was travelling at, but I'd swear the driver put their foot down. They were on me before I knew it.'

'I presume you didn't get the number plate?'

He shook his head and colour came to his cheeks. 'To be honest, I was so shocked I couldn't even remember the make of the car afterwards. I think it was blue, and a saloon maybe.' He sighed. 'I'm not even sure about that.'

'And you didn't recognise the driver, obviously.'

He drained his beer. 'I only got a glimpse. I was too busy leaping out of the way. Someone wearing a cap, maybe? And dark glasses. I wasn't even sure if it was a man or a woman. You can see why I didn't bother going to the police.'

'It's not easy. Lots of people remember very little after an incident like that.'

He nodded. 'But it worried me at the time. I mean, I know you get drivers who just put their foot down when they're irritated – think someone's crossed in front of them – not shown them sufficient respect. I've met meatheads like that. But what I did see of them made me wonder if they'd tried to hide their identity. I mentioned it to Ralph and the others, because it shook me up. But it was just after Letty died – an awful time. Ralph encouraged us to celebrate her youth, and how perfect she'd been when she was taken from us – it was a brave try, to pull us all through the upset – but of course, everyone was still affected. I soon realised it wasn't the right time to go on about my worries.' He sat back in his chair. 'And anyway, who would target me? Ralph, I could understand, to an extent – he created ripples. But I'm not sure I ever have, sadly. My paintings just happen to be en vogue at the moment. I'd better enjoy it whilst it lasts.'

At home that night, Tara debated calling Kemp to let him know the latest developments. Officially she shouldn't share, but she valued his opinion. He'd settled in at Bea's and seemed to be enjoying the cosiness and home cooking. They'd been out for a couple of drinks since he'd landed himself on her a couple of weeks ago – on one occasion with Bea too – but she'd heard nothing from him in the last few days.

But maybe she should let sleeping dogs lie. It wasn't as though she'd have much free time in the next few days if he suggested meeting up. All the same, she was slightly surprised he hadn't already come to her, wanting gossip.

She wondered what was keeping him at bay. If he went totally quiet, it tended to mean he was up to something.

Sunday 16 December

Oh, Christian, you weren't ready to embrace death either, were you? Not like the hero in Ralph's book, On High. *I seem to remember he remained serene when he jumped to his doom. Whereas I distinctly heard you scream. A sound of pure, unbridled terror. It was the same with Lucas, of course. When he finally sank beneath the waves he looked anything but calm. I think it's a lesson to us all. Ralph's books are a lie.*

And my latest achievement seems to have stirred up a hornets' nest. Not that I'm surprised.

Oh, Tara – you and your fellow officers have been rushing around with about as much direction as a group of bluebottles batting themselves against a pane of glass. It looks as though your enquiries have been ratcheted up a level, but they're not getting any more effective.

And you disappoint me. Surely you've seen by now the kind of person Ralph was – yet you carry on unabated? If anything, your sense of urgency has increased.

What do you mean by it? How can you not see that a man of his sort deserved to die?

In truth, Tara, you're trying my patience now – with your stupidity and your determination to find a 'guilty' party.

I don't feel guilty. I've done the world a service and now you know, well and truly, how evil Ralph was, you ought to feel the same and curtail your investigation. Maybe it's because you were a journalist that you can't let go. The story is more important to you than the morality.

But for me, it's all about what's right and what's wrong. The people whose fate I'm controlling are those who damage the world by their existence.

And I'm beginning to think you qualify for that list, Tara.

Maybe I'll schedule you into my plans. What shall it be: fire, suffocation... electrocution?

Choices, choices...

CHAPTER TWENTY-SIX

Instead of going straight to the station the next morning, Tara cycled to Pound Hill, where Tess Curtis had a flat. She'd had a message from Max that he'd managed to set her and Wilkins up with an appointment for nine that morning. She'd already been aware of Christian Beatty's death, apparently, having heard it on the news. It had made national programmes as well as regional, thanks to his relative fame, as well as the link with night climbing. It always captured people's imaginations.

As Tara cycled up the river, she had to focus on not skidding over. Other bikes had made ridges in the snow, which made the going bumpy – a combination of compacted flakes that had turned to ice and patches where the fall was still deeper. After crossing the river at Jesus Lock, with the sound of the rushing weir just below her, she reached Chesterton Road, where mercifully the early rush-hour traffic had melted the snow. It meant she could turn her thoughts to work again, rather than self-preservation. Her mind had been full of the Acolytes after her interviews the previous day: Stephen Ross, who was either Ralph's intellectual confidant or the runt of the group, depending on who you asked; Verity Hipkiss, desperate to keep her affair with Cairncross secret for the sake of her writing career; and Thom King, who hankered after Verity, yet remained the one group member she'd definitely friendzoned. Each of them with their own egos to protect; each fighting to stand out amongst their contemporaries.

But she needed to switch focus now and run through everything she knew about the woman she and Wilkins were about to interview. She wanted to make sure she was primed. Wilkins would either find Cairncross's PA charming, and get blinkered, or else go at her like a bull in a china shop. At least if Tara had the information she needed, fresh in her mind, she'd be able to leap in when she could.

So, Tess Curtis had dropped in at the house on the Forty Foot Bank the night Ralph Cairncross had died. It had been impromptu from what Tara could gather, but not unusual or out of character. She was very dedicated and would bring Ralph anything he might need promptly, even if he hadn't asked for it. According to the Acolyte Stephen Ross, she pretty much ran his life. But what Stephen put down to her professionalism, Verity Hipkiss attributed to jealousy and a desire to be included. She'd said Tess Curtis had a fear of missing out. And of course, if the rumours were true, and Tess and Ralph had once been lovers, she might have good cause to dislike Verity. And that might extend to the other Acolytes too. Before they turned up, perhaps she'd had a lot more of Ralph's attention. Tara tried to imagine that being a desirable thing. *Difficult.* Still, there was no accounting for taste.

She'd reached the top of Chesterton Road now – behind some queueing cars – and made to cycle straight across at the traffic lights, on to Northampton Street. The usual Monday morning jam meant the cold air was full of fumes, making clouds in front of her. Safely over, she cycled past the terrace of brick and timber-framed buildings on her left and the Museum of Cambridge on her right, through the exhaust haze, the red tail lights and orange indicators in the foreground of her view.

After a short distance, she manoeuvred right, ready to cycle up Pound Hill, between the cheerful blue and white frontage of the Punter and the imposing red-brick bulk of Westminster theological college. It was slippery again on the side road. Tara gritted her teeth. The thought of spring was very appealing.

Dr Richardson, the Cairncross expert, had mentioned Tess Curtis too. As well as bringing up the gossip about her and Ralph's personal relationship, he'd said she might be the 'T' that his final book was dedicated to – the one where the hero's death was caused by a snake…

Tara thought of the dedication again: *To T, who managed to escape unscathed. You are blessed indeed.*

What if that message, and the subject matter of the book, had got Tess Curtis thinking? What if she didn't feel she had come out of her affair with Ralph undamaged? What was her life like now? Did she feel better or worse off after her boss's death?

Tara parked her bike opposite the modern block where Tess Curtis lived and smoothed down the dress she'd chosen to wear. It hadn't been the most practical option, but she was on her bike more often than not and wearing trousers every day was boring.

Curtis had chosen a flat very close to Ralph Cairncross's home, Tara reflected. As she locked up, she wondered about the lamp that had almost killed him, sitting there, as it had been, in the unsecured family garage, just around the corner.

Two minutes later, Wilkins arrived. He nodded to her as they approached the entry phone for the block together. It was impressive that he could convey 'up yours' with such a subtle gesture. A moment later, he pressed the button for Tess Curtis's flat and announced himself when she answered.

'Second floor. Up the stairs then turn left,' the disembodied voice said. The tone was low and slightly husky. In the same moment there was a buzzing sound and the door Tara had been pushing against released, allowing them inside.

Tara guessed Tess Curtis might be in her early forties. She was smartly dressed in well-cut black trousers, matching boxy jacket and a red cowl-neck top. Her hair was a rich dark brown and currently in a French pleat. Every inch of her looked classy, but her flat was tiny. Tara had noticed three doors off the hallway they'd entered by: one must be a bedroom and one a bathroom. The third led to where they were now, an open-plan living area, with kitchen and dining spaces, an IKEA-style work station and corner sofa. It might be small, but it was a hell of a lot warmer than her own cottage. Tara was hot in her wool flannel dress and knee-length boots. She slipped off her coat and the blazer she'd worn as an added layer and put them over the back of her chair. They'd been invited to sit at the dining table and had mugs of coffee and a plate of Choco Leibniz biscuits in front of them.

Tara suddenly wondered if Ralph Cairncross had left Tess Curtis anything in his will. If the Acolytes were getting a large house – albeit in a remote area – she might feel slighted if she'd been overlooked after twenty years of hard work. She made a mental note to request a copy of the document, though given there was no confirmed murder investigation behind the enquiry, the authorities wouldn't rush to respond. She'd have to wait, just like other members of the public.

Wilkins did the job of going through their standard spiel. She was half listening to him ('Purely routine, no real reason to suppose anyone is under threat…' 'Just a precaution…' 'Warning all Ralph Cairncross's close connections…') and half scanning the room. A bookcase to one side held what looked like the entire collection of Ralph Cairncross's works, as well as numerous books about him. She noticed one by Dr Richardson – the expert she'd talked to. Tess Curtis's job for Ralph had clearly meant more to her than just a wage packet at the end of the month – and it seemed to go beyond any affair she might have had with him too. She'd studied his work. Then again, that had probably been necessary for her to perform her role. If she'd been fielding questions from journalists about his latest publications, she'd need to have read them.

Wilkins was on to alibis now. 'Again, Ms Curtis,' he said, 'this is all routine. We're asking the Acolytes and Ralph Cairncross's family exactly the same questions, as a precaution.'

Tess Curtis didn't look fazed. Tara had the impression it would take a lot more than this to ruffle her. 'In October, when Lucas Everett drowned, I was visiting my sister in Whitby,' she said. She hadn't needed to check her diary and was already scribbling the woman's number on a scrap of paper. Was she a little *too* prepared? 'And I was here at home on Saturday night. *Jean de Florette* was on television; it's a film I've always wanted to watch.'

Wilkins nodded. 'Thank you.'

Tara noted everything down. At least they could check with the sister in Whitby, though a close family member didn't hold that much weight as far as she was concerned. 'We understand you called in to the house on the Forty Foot Bank briefly on the night Ralph Cairncross died,' she said. 'Was that at his request?'

Tess Curtis laughed for a moment, but her elegant features displayed a look that spoke of irritation rather than amusement. 'Very little that I did was "at Ralph's request".' The look she gave Tara told her the woman thought she was being terribly naive. 'That would imply he was a forward planner, which he wasn't. I was the one who knew what he needed and when. He'd accuse me of fussing over the details, but without that, things tended to go awry. I went over that night to take him some papers that needed to be reviewed and returned by first thing the following day. I would have emailed them, but they required a signature and there was no printer or scanner at the house on the bank.' She gave Tara a look. 'Needless to say, it wasn't the first time I'd reminded him about them. In fact, I gave them to him, with full instructions, before I left his office that afternoon.' Her jaw was tight. 'But I knew what he was like. I went back to check later on and found they were still sitting there on his desk, unsigned. So I drove over with them. Believe you me, I almost didn't. But I knew if I left them for him to sign when he got back he'd never get round to it. He'd be as drunk as a lord on his return, and then spend most of the next day sleeping it off.' Tara was impressed she could contain her annoyance. 'He used to do it on purpose, you know,' she said, after she'd taken a deep breath. 'I mean, ignore my instructions because he didn't like to be fussed over – or so he said. But on reflection, I think it was because it amused him to keep me running around. I don't much miss the work. I'm PA to Professor Douglas Trent-Purvis now. It's a better role.'

Though Cairncross clearly hadn't set the bar very high. 'Where was Ralph's office?' Tara asked.

'At his home. If you want to check, you can ask Philippa. I came nose to nose with her on my way in that day. You can access the office space without going through the house, though. It has a separate door.'

Just as well. If Tess Curtis and Ralph had been lovers, she couldn't imagine constant interaction between her, Sadie and Philippa Cairncross would have made for a relaxed atmosphere. But had they been? It was hearsay so far.

'Your role must have been hard work,' Tara said. 'But I gather Ralph very much valued your contribution.' She watched as the woman raised her eyebrows. 'Or at least, someone suggested you were the subject of the dedication in his final book.'

'Ah.' Tess Curtis's smile was as cold as the air outside. 'I have heard people expound that theory, but no – it wasn't me.'

'How do you know?'

'I had it from the horse's mouth.'

'The T was for Thom, then?'

She shook her head. 'No. The book was for Letty. Letitia – one of the Acolytes. She died – she was only eighteen. She'd started her degree here early.'

'We'd heard about her,' Wilkins said. 'But why T?'

Tess Curtis rolled her eyes. 'Titty. That's what Ralph used to call her. It's an old-fashioned shortening for Letitia. As you can imagine, it's seldom used these days – but Ralph being Ralph…'

She let the sentence hang.

'He'd slept with her?' Wilkins said.

Tess Curtis frowned. 'Letty was an innocent; whether she fell for his tactics, I'm not sure. But I'd imagine he tried his hardest to break down her defences. When he wrote about her escaping unscathed, I'm not sure if he meant escaping him, or escaping old age – but either way he meant through death.'

Tara's disgust at the dead man manifested itself as a crawling sensation across her skin. Wilkins' lip curled. For once, she suspected they were experiencing the same emotion.

'He did dedicate a book to me once,' Tess Curtis said, her tone brittle. 'If you look through his works you can track his changing tastes. A book for Sadie, a book for me, then books for a number of others, ending in Letty. The one he was writing when he died would have been to Verity, I'd imagine.'

Tara remembered Sadie talking about her and Ralph's pact. 'We always agreed we wouldn't tie each other down,' Sadie had said, but she'd added that she'd been weak and given in to jealousy. Tara hadn't quite appreciated the background at the time. She must have had years of pain as a result of her marriage. The Acolytes had taken Ralph away from her – both the ones that he'd had as lovers, and the ones he'd simply spent all his time with. Had Sadie really been at home in bed when her husband died? If she was guilty then Tess Curtis might be on her list of prospective victims too…

'When Ralph dedicated one of his books to me, the critics worked it out,' the woman said. 'I was supposed to feel guilty, according to them, for replacing Sadie. She'd been having a rough ride.' It was as though the woman had followed her thoughts.

Tara wondered if that had been around the time Ralph Cairn-cross's wife had been forced to give up her career. 'I heard she'd been in a car crash,' she said. 'I presume the resulting injury meant she had to stop playing the flute. It sounds as though she suffered a great deal.' She was being tactless on purpose; sometimes provoking someone could reveal a lot.

'Ah, yes – the car crash,' Tess Curtis said. But there was no guilt or discomfort in her voice. 'I think they made that up.'

'I'm sorry?'

'It was the official explanation. Sadie went away – took longer than expected to return home – and came back with some kind of injury, sure. But from a car crash? She hadn't taken her own car with her, and there was nothing in Ralph's post about insurance. He dealt with all that side of things.' And then she laughed. 'Officially. In reality, of course, that meant I dealt with all that side of things. And if a car accident put a stop to her career, wouldn't that have been reported at the time, in the arts press at least, to explain her retirement?'

Now she mentioned it, Tara wondered why she hadn't thought of that before. One up to Tess Curtis. 'You think someone hurt her?'

The woman shrugged. 'If so, I don't think it was Ralph. Wherever she went, he didn't go with her. At the time I think she claimed she'd gone off to see a cousin or something.'

Wilkins was shifting in his seat. He probably regarded her current line of questioning as gossip gathering. At least he hadn't interrupted. She noticed he'd helped himself to a third biscuit.

'Could I please use your bathroom before we leave?' Tara asked, after a moment. Coffee and cold weather; a killer combination.

'Be my guest. Door on the left as you face the front door.'

She went out into the hallway and turned left as advised. After she'd been to the loo, she gave the room a once-over. She couldn't help noticing the packet of contraceptive pills on a shelf just below the bathroom cabinet as she washed her hands. She wondered who Tess Curtis's current lover was. The affair Dr Richardson had referred to hadn't lasted, she remembered. Though maybe she just kept taking them, so she was free to do what she liked, as and when.

Back in the hallway, Tara looked at the coats. Tess Curtis must like clothes. Tara did herself, but there were limits. Tess had more than enough to cover every weather condition. She scanned the winter ones and caught her breath.

There was a coat with a fur-lined hood.

Not an uncommon design, and yet… She took out her phone and looked at the stills Megan Maloney had emailed the team from the CCTV footage outside Christian Beatty's flat. It was impossible to tell for sure, but Tess Curtis's coat did look very much like the one worn by the mystery visitor to the apartment block on Saturday night.

And then she looked again at the figure in the photo. A glimpse of nose and chin. Both exactly like the features of the woman they'd just been interviewing.

And yet Tess Curtis had said she'd been at home on Saturday night, watching *Jean de Florette*. Why the heck had she lied about that – if Tara was right and she had? She'd noticed the film in the listings herself. It had been over by ten or so. It hadn't even spanned the time when Christian Beatty had died.

CHAPTER TWENTY-SEVEN

Back in Tess Curtis's living room, Wilkins was gathering his coat, ready to take his leave.

Tara sat back down again. 'What did you think of *Jean de Florette* in the end?' she asked, smiling and raising her eyebrows in a look of mock innocence.

The look reaped rewards. Tess Curtis's expression turned wary. 'Great,' she said, but she said it uncertainly, and there was a pause before she answered. Tara had been worried she might be wrong – the CCTV film was pretty grainy – but Tess Curtis's reaction told her otherwise.

Tara took out her phone and showed her the image. As soon as confusion registered on the woman's face, Tara put the phone on her lap, so Wilkins could see. She'd been able to feel his eyes on her as she'd asked her question.

'What made you lie to us about staying in to watch a film, Tess?' Tara said. 'Given we've got you on camera, you might as well tell us.'

Her eyes were ice cold. 'You tricked me.' She breathed the words out. They were all the more chilling for being uttered quietly.

Tara shook her head. 'I only realised it was you when I went out there' – she nodded over her shoulder – 'and saw your coat. It triggered a memory of the features of the woman in the picture.'

Tess Curtis had gripped part of her trouser material between her forefinger and thumb and held it tightly. There was a long pause.

'I think you'd better tell us, Ms Curtis,' Wilkins said.

She let out a sigh, short and sharp. 'For God's sake, this is just so unfair! After twenty years of nothing much going right, things were finally coming together.'

Tara waited, and thankfully Wilkins did too.

'I was there for a business meeting with Christian Beatty,' Tess Curtis said.

'On a Saturday night?' Wilkins' tone was mocking.

The woman's eyes flashed.

'It *was* an unusual time to choose,' Tara said. 'Why pick then?'

Curtis turned to face her. 'We're both busy people. Christian had been out all day and tied up the week beforehand. And he was due to go off on some job again yesterday. It was simply when we were both free – his diary being more crowded than mine.'

And of course, it had been coffee cups that had been found in Christian Beatty's flat, which fitted with a formal conversation. 'What kind of business were you discussing?' After a pause, she heard Wilkins huffing. 'It would be better to tell us.' She kept her tone gentle. 'If it's nothing to do with Christian's death then we can just keep it on record and stop bothering you.'

Tess Curtis still looked mutinous, but after another long moment, she took a deep breath and spoke. 'I don't think it's got anything to do with what happened. I don't see how it can have.'

'That's good,' Tara said. 'In that case you don't have to worry, do you?'

Tess Curtis looked at her. 'As a matter of fact, I do. Christian and I were going to collaborate on a book.'

'A book?'

'About Ralph,' she said. 'We'd just signed the paperwork. It was going to be a "warts and all" biography.' She stared at Wilkins and then at Tara. 'I know what you're thinking. Hardly the action of a loyal PA. But my God, I deserve something back after the runaround Ralph gave me over the years.' She smiled. 'And I know enough for it to make for some juicy reading. Christian promised he could give me a lot more on top of that. He'd been at all the parties – stayed when I'd had to go home. Between us we could have made a packet.'

Tara's mind was spinning with the implications. 'Did anyone else know you were planning this?'

Tess Curtis frowned. 'I don't see how they could have. Unless Christian had confided in someone.' She sighed. 'He hadn't got as far as telling me what he knew. I took what he said on trust.' She sat back in her chair.

'And why was this meeting so secret?' Wilkins said.

'Can you imagine if word had got out about what we were up to? I don't want interference from anyone that I might refer to in the book.'

Tara could see that. She knew Verity Hipkiss and Ralph had been lovers, for instance. And Thom King had told her how keen Verity was to make sure the affair stayed under wraps. She bet that was one of the juicy titbits Christian Beatty would have served up – assuming he'd got proof. It gave Verity a firm motive for getting rid of the fashion model if she'd known what he was planning. And she didn't imagine Ralph's family would be too happy at the idea of Christian and Tess washing his dirty linen in public either.

'I presume you've got a copy of the contract you can show us?' Tara said.

Tess Curtis's shoulders sagged. 'Not the version he signed. Damn.' She bit her lip. 'I wasn't sure what would happen, when I heard he'd died. The contract talked about the profits and so on. I wasn't sure if I could prove he hadn't told me anything yet. I imagined his heirs might accuse me of taking his information, then stealing his share of the book's proceeds.' Colour came to her cheeks and she looked down. 'So I burnt the contract.'

She'd be lucky if that's all his beneficiaries accused her of. 'What about an electronic copy?'

'Only of the template, and I deleted it.' She looked worried now. 'But computer forensics people can recover deleted documents, can't they?'

Tara nodded. 'Most probably. We'll need to take your machine with us. What about emails between the two of you – or texts or whatever – referring to the project?'

Tess Curtis shook her head. 'I don't think so. We had all our detailed discussions by phone.'

'Did you talk about anything else, other than the book, when you met on Saturday?' Wilkins asked.

'No,' Tess Curtis said, 'but one thing he said seems to link the project with what happened to him.'

He raised an eyebrow.

'He told me he ought to have some extra colour to add to the story we'd write, after that evening.'

What the hell did that mean? Had he simply been going to regale their readers with stories of his daredevil activities, done in Ralph Cairncross's memory? But the biography wasn't going to be about him. Had the person he'd been going to meet promised him something spectacular on Ralph? They could have proposed they drank his health first, and commemorated his devil-may-care approach to life, before they settled down to talk.

Perhaps Christian Beatty had only seen the promised prize at the end of the evening, and not the danger that lay between.

As they entered the station, Tara and Wilkins were still discussing Tess Curtis.

'It rang true to me,' Tara said. 'She's right about the interference she'll get when her project becomes public.'

Wilkins' expression was sour. 'I thought it was far-fetched – but the alternative, that she's really involved in some kind of plot to kill three men – is far more so.'

Whatever the truth, Tara was looking forward to passing on their news. She'd got a kick out of being the one to recognise Tess Curtis; it might have been luck that she'd had cause to walk past her coat rack, but that didn't dampen the buzz of achievement she felt.

Tara was about reply to Wilkins with a swift retort, but as they walked into the office, the atmosphere was oddly quiet. Her irritation with her boss was pushed from her mind. Everyone had been staring at their computer screens, but when they entered, all eyes were on her.

Something was up.

CHAPTER TWENTY-EIGHT

She saw the headline over Max Dimity's shoulder, but there was no doubt it was up on most people's screens. The byline announced it was the work of Shona Kennedy, the woman who'd turned up so quickly after Christian Beatty had fallen to his death. Tara felt her cheeks prickle with heat as she read the article.

The Serpent and the Temptress

Many people will have read with shock and sorrow about the recent death of a talented young model and Cambridge graduate, Christian Beatty. Readers may not be aware, however, that a loose connection of Christian's, Lucas Everett, a postdoctoral researcher in the English faculty, also died this year. This tragic event took place two months ago when Lucas drowned off the coast of Kellness in a swimming misadventure. Both men were part of a group that socialised with the writer, Ralph Cairncross, who died in a car accident earlier this year, in which no one else was involved. Most people would see the three deaths as a sorrowful coincidence, separated by time, geography and circumstance. But *Not Now* hears from a contact within the police that one woman – relatively junior in rank – has decided to base a far-fetched, though intriguing, conspiracy theory on the three events. It reminded the team here at *Not Now* of the works of Arthur Conan Doyle.

Sherlock Holmes. Wilkins had likened her 'obsession', as he called it, to Conan Doyle's plots. She clenched her fist and winced as her nails dug into her palm. He must be the one who'd leaked this. But then she paused. She couldn't be certain. Even she could see how elements of her theory linked in with his style. Giles, her old editor at *Not Now*, might have had the same thought independently.

According to our source, the theory puts a scheming third party in the frame for engineering all three deaths, beguiling the young men into putting their lives at risk, and planting a snake in the car of the older man to frighten him into losing control. However, *Not Now* understands there is no proof to substantiate any of these possibilities. Yet this line of enquiry – all based on what some might call fairy tales – is being actively pursued.

Readers might want to know how the young female officer who is propounding these theories comes to command such influence. *Not Now* can't say much on this.

Not without getting sued, anyway.

But we can all imagine how certain dynamics might enhance her chances of being taken seriously.

In the meantime, rest assured that the officers that serve you are working all the hours God sends on this case. *Not Now* happened to chance across this senior detective accompanying the junior officer in question to carry out a routine interview on a Sunday, nobly giving up time that might have been spent with his wife and family.

Max gave her an apologetic look and scrolled down. There was a grainy photograph which must have been taken with a long lens from somewhere on Parker's Piece. It showed her and Blake outside the station the previous afternoon, before they'd set off to interview Stephen Ross at the house on the Forty Foot Bank. How the heck had they managed that? Had Wilkins still been in the building after all, and realised they were leaving together? Could he have taken the photo and supplied it to the magazine?

Whatever the truth, it didn't alter the damage.

Her and Blake's faces were illuminated by the light that spilled out from the building. Blake was smiling, his head turned towards her and she looked – hell and damnation – she looked like a lovesick teenager. Would her pent-up feelings be that obvious to anyone else who saw the image? She hated Giles. The rage against him left her wanting to do something violent: hit a desk or scream. But if she wanted to maintain any kind of dignity she'd just have to stand there and take it, knowing everyone's eyes were on her. She hoped some of them – perhaps, with luck – were still thinking more about the Cairncross case than her possible dalliance with their DI.

And what about Blake? And his wife and their daughter? This whole situation was because Giles hated her so much. Even if she wasn't guilty of what the article implied, and even if someone *was* systematically picking off Cairncross and his Acolytes, the fact remained that she was the sort of person who had enemies. She couldn't leave that behind, and by taking a punt on her, people like Blake and Fleming had let themselves in for this sort of sniping.

Before, even when she'd worked for *Not Now*, she'd always kept herself at a distance. She could break free when she needed, so her entanglements didn't impinge on anyone else. But things were different now. Police work and being part of a team were inseparable. If she garnered the wrong sort of attention they all suffered for it.

Max Dimity turned to her. 'It's not just you. They love to latch onto anything they think will draw the readers in, no matter who gets hurt in the process.'

She knew that, of course. It wasn't the sort of article she'd ever written, but when she'd been on *Not Now*'s staff she'd seen it happen. She should never have worked for them in the first place. She'd been complicit. It was a shame eating was dependent on earning a living…

'Certain people at *Not Now* have it in for me in particular,' Tara said. 'I was stupid enough to work for them once. I resigned when I saw the error of my ways and they don't like defectors.'

At that moment, Fleming appeared in the doorway and caught Tara's eye. The DCI was white-faced with rage. Tara followed her through to her office. Blake and Wilkins were already inside. Fleming must have beckoned her boss in whilst Tara was still staring at the story on Max's computer screen. Blake looked pale – possibly hung-over, in fact – which wasn't going to help. Wilkins looked furious.

Blake glanced at Tara. She felt all the words she'd liked to say tumbling inside her head and wished she'd seen him in private before being hauled up in front of a group.

'Ma'am, I'm sorry,' Tara said. 'The article's quite obviously driven by a personal grudge. Up until now I've always been able to fight my own battles without causing other people problems.'

'Except during the Seabrook murder case,' Wilkins said.

Bloody hell, he's on dangerous ground. In their previous article, written on her return to Cambridge, *Not Now* had emphasised the 'trouble' they felt she'd caused by getting involved then. Wilkins was practically parroting their words.

'Patrick,' Fleming said, 'we don't normally accuse victims of attempted murder of causing trouble by expecting the police to help save them. We tend to put the responsibility at the would-be murderer's door.' She took a deep breath. 'Generally speaking, we wouldn't even react to something like this, but under the circumstances, and with DI Blake's family in mind too, the press office are going to put out a very brief statement to explain his decision to attend the interview with Tara.'

Tara could see by Fleming's expression that she regarded that as less than straightforward.

'In terms of the case, the article's deeply damaging to our investigation. All possibility of catching a witness out by keeping the news of the snake under wraps is gone. But it makes no difference to our actions, of course. We will work with the evidence we have and then take a view on whether we continue the investigation or not. If this does turn out to be a dead end, that will be regrettable and it's true that I have had to spend more time than usual considering your requests for resources on this, Blake. It's been a judgement call, but it's been mine, and if a mistake's been made then I take responsibility. The other priority here is to work out who *Not Now*'s source is.' She was looking at Patrick. 'I heard it mentioned, Patrick, that you'd compared the theories we're working on to a Sherlock Holmes plot.'

The DS shrugged. 'Sure – and more than once. Any of the guys here could have overheard me and passed that on. Or equally the staff at *Not Now* could have thought the same.' He looked straight at the DCI. 'Ma'am – you, DI Blake and DC Thorpe all know I've been sceptical about this investigation from the start. It's not something I've tried to hide. If I was looking for someone who's leaking to the press, I'd be eyeing up an officer who's less open about their feelings.'

Fleming looked at him for a long moment, but then nodded. 'Well, if there's any hint at all, I want to hear about it. I want that person's head on a plate. For now, you'd all better crack on.'

As they left the room, Wilkins caught Tara's eye for an infinitesimal moment and she saw the mocking amusement there – for her eyes only. *Bastard.*

Blake stopped them in the corridor and steered them into his office.

'We might have got some idiot leaking information, but we've still got a case to sort out. How was the interview with Tess Curtis?'

Wilkins relayed the results as though the detective work had all been his doing. Blake's eyes widened when he heard that she had been their mystery CCTV star. Curtis's explanation for her presence made him frown.

'I think I believe her,' Tara said. 'When I faced her with being at Beatty's flat she looked cross, not worried – as though she was coming to terms with having to tell us something that would ruin her plans. And she probably realised burning the contract Beatty had signed looked questionable too.'

'God knows why she invented watching *Jean de Florette*.' Wilkins rolled his eyes. 'Seems like a complication she didn't need.'

'Maybe it was part truth,' Tara said. 'Perhaps she'd noticed it was on and planned to watch it until she made her appointment with Beatty. That way it would have stuck in her mind and come to the fore on the spur of the moment.'

'You've got an answer for everything,' he replied, as though it was a bad thing. 'I don't see why she didn't just tell us the truth from the start.'

'I suppose she'd been waiting a long time to get her own back on Ralph Cairncross.' Tara could imagine the effect of years of pent-up frustration. 'She's not keen to let go of the opportunity now. Of course, my gut instinct might be wrong. That much resentment means she had a motive for killing him. And Beatty too. Maybe he *had* told her all he knew, and she decided she didn't want to share the book royalties. She could have arranged to meet him again later, fed his ego and encouraged him to make the jump. She's an attractive woman.'

'It'll be interesting to see whether the deleted contract for the book can be recovered,' Blake said. 'But if Tess Curtis did somehow persuade Christian Beatty to take that leap, then she must have developed the plan at the last minute. Otherwise, why risk visiting his apartment block that same evening? It's the sort of place that's bound to have CCTV.'

Wilkins pulled a face. 'Ergo, she didn't, sir. With respect, I still think this whole enquiry is a wild goose chase.'

'Thank you, Patrick. I had taken that on board. I don't happen to agree with you.'

The DS glanced at what looked like a Rolex on his wrist and sighed. 'Time to leave for the post-mortem.'

But Tara was quite sure he was delighted to be the one at the centre of things. She smiled for a moment as she remembered that Agneta Larsson didn't like him.

'You'd better go and check Sadie and Philippa Cairncross's alibis,' Wilkins added, turning to her.

'And I'll warn them too,' Tara said.

The DS laughed. 'Whatever. One thing's for certain, Philippa Cairncross can look after herself.'

CHAPTER TWENTY-NINE

Tara drove to Madingley Road, where she found Philippa Cairncross was out.

'She's broken up for the holidays,' Sadie said, showing her through to the same living room they'd sat in previously. 'But she's got her own life, of course. She's in town shopping with some friends.'

'You'll both have heard about Christian Beatty's death, I expect?'

Sadie's eyes looked frightened and she nodded. Tara sensed she was close to tears. 'I wish all this would stop.'

'You've had so much to cope with.' Tara leant forward and kept her voice gentle. 'How do you mean "all this", Sadie?'

'It's as though everyone who knew Ralph is cursed,' Sadie said, but there was something disjointed about it. It wasn't as though she was responding directly to Tara's question; her voice sounded dreamy. Tara remembered her mentioning the sleeping tablets she was in the habit of taking. But surely it couldn't be that. It was late morning now.

In terms of alibis, she was no help at all. Once Tara had reminded her of the date that Lucas Everett had drowned, she said she couldn't remember where she'd been. After a long pause, she claimed that Philippa had probably been at home with her, given that it had been just before her university term had started. And after a little more thought she said she was sure that she *had* been, but Tara wasn't. Philippa didn't strike her as the stay-at-home sort.

On Saturday, when Christian Beatty had fallen, she was more definite, again saying she and Philippa had been together. But by that stage, Tara had the impression that she'd latched on to the idea as a convenient answer. There was something strangely childlike about her responses.

When it came to warning her about the possible danger her husband's contacts might be in, Tara made even less headway. Sadie Cairncross was nodding in the right places, but her eyes were dull. It was time to give in, and she got up to leave.

The Sadie Cairncross she'd seen that day was quite different to the version she'd first encountered. What had happened? Was something frightening her? And, if so, was she relying on tranquillisers or similar to keep her panic in check?

Back at the station she texted Kemp.

How are things? Hope you're keeping out of mischief.

Then she sat down to add records of the meetings with Sadie Cairncross and Tess Curtis to the system. Wilkins wouldn't be back for a while, so at least she could rely on a spell of peace and quiet. But before she'd really got going, she caught movement out of the corner of her eye. Blake – and he was making for her desk.

'How did it go with Sadie Cairncross? Any more interesting revelations?'

She shook her head. Despite his question, the thought of *Not Now*'s article was still at the forefront of her mind, now that they were face to face again. She pushed it away. 'I'm afraid not. She seemed far more distracted this time around. And worried. I'm not sure if it's because of the build-up of pressure, following Christian Beatty's death, or if she actually knows something.' She registered the shadows under his dark eyes. He didn't look as though he was getting much sleep. Was it just the case, or something more than that? 'I'll be glad when we get the results back on the crate from the house on the bank.'

He nodded. 'You and me both. Unfortunately, it's not being treated as high priority, given there's no confirmed crime to tie it to. All the same, I've had a word in a few ears. With luck we might have something by tomorrow morning.'

Max Dimity was still working away at his desk too, a little behind Tara's.

'Anything fresh, Max?' Blake asked him.

'The alibis provided by the Acolytes check out so far,' he said. 'And Tess Curtis's sister confirms they were together back in October, when Lucas Everett died. But you couldn't call any of their stories unbreakable. I've also got a response from Beatty's old college now: they say he never got caught night climbing when he was a student. Oh, and I've got the file Tess Curtis had deleted off her laptop – the draft contract for her and Christian Beatty's collaboration on Ralph Cairncross's biography.'

'Well done. Though she could have prepared it as a prop, I suppose.' Blake turned to Tara. 'But the question remains, why risk visiting Beatty's flat on Saturday evening if she was planning to meet him later in absolute secrecy?'

He drew up a chair and placed it between her desk and Max's. 'I want to go through the planning process our conspirator would have to have followed. If someone has been influencing developments with a view to targeting a series of people, they've clearly plotted their actions carefully. We all agree they take chances – but they're chances over whether or not a potential victim will end up dead, not over the sort of details that might give them away. In that respect they've covered their tracks well. I get the impression most of what we've found, we've only discovered because the perpetrator designed it that way.'

'You mean like the Adnams vodka bottle?' Tara said.

He nodded.

'What about the crate?' Max asked.

'I think that might be the one exception,' Blake replied. 'Someone who'd taken the risk of bringing the snake to the house in the first place might reason it was safest to leave the crate where it was, behind the outhouse. If they'd tried to remove it again they'd have risked coming face to face with someone for a second time, and having to explain what they were up to. And the danger would be greater at that stage, once the drowning had already occurred. Besides, they probably assumed no one would ever suspect Cairncross's death was anything but an accident. Abandoning the crate in a garden full of junk wouldn't have seemed especially reckless.'

'I suppose it wouldn't have been quite so risky to remove the crate if the perpetrator was in and out of the house on a regular basis,' Tara said. 'They'd be in a good position then to know when they were least likely to be disturbed. But an outsider, like Sadie Cairncross or Tess Curtis, would find it harder to predict the comings and goings.'

'Makes sense,' said Max. After a moment he added: 'I still can't get my head around the note Lucas Everett left before he drowned. On the one hand, it feels like too much of a coincidence for all these deaths to be unrelated, but on the other, how the heck would a perpetrator get a victim to write such a convenient farewell letter?'

Blake nodded. 'We've got a lot more questions than answers. But I feel the pattern is too noticeable to ignore now. And I'm worried that this is a race against time. What if the people who've died so far are just a subset of the group the killer's targeting?' He ran his fingers through his already rumpled hair, then sat up straight. His jacket was creased and his tie lopsided. 'Let's take a step back. Okay, so accepting that we have one or more perpetrators: they have a couple of failed attempts at Thom and Ralph, then they manage to engineer Ralph Cairncross's death without raising any suspicions at the time. Or so they think. They're unaware that Ralph's sister is already making waves. So they decide to make their next move – somehow, maybe because of the influence they wield, they engineer Lucas Everett's drowning. Okay, so they're successful again, but we presume that, once again, they took a chance. Even if we're talking about someone Lucas looked up to, he might well have told them he'd rather go home and read a book than swim in the North Sea by night.'

'Or he might have swum strongly, and come back alive,' Tara said.

'Agreed.' Blake closed his eyes for a moment. 'The person we're talking about certainly couldn't bank on keeping their identity a secret.'

'But they had nothing to lose,' Max said. 'Because if Lucas survived, the perpetrator could have shaken his hand and congratulated him on his act of bravery. It would have put the guilty party off trying anything similar with the same aim though – either with Lucas or any of the others. Once word got around that they were involved in dangerous adventures, it wouldn't be hard to guess who'd set things up if the next instance proved fatal.'

Tara nodded. 'If Lucas had survived, presumably the perpetrator would have had to think of another way of achieving their aims – or have given up. But in the event, Lucas never came home, and the secrets of that final evening died with him.'

'So our killer was free to take what we guess was a similar approach with Christian Beatty,' Blake finished. 'And the situation was the same there, in that they couldn't be sure that Beatty would die.'

Max nodded. 'What would the conversation at the pub have been like if the guy had made the jump successfully and climbed back down again? Surely by that stage people might suspect a ringleader, encouraging people to put their lives at risk.'

'I'm not so sure,' Tara said. 'In that scenario, only one person would have died as a result of too much bravado. That might not be enough for anyone to spot a pattern. If Beatty had been successful I'm betting the others would have seen his adventure in a totally different light: probably not even have thought of it as especially life threatening. Suddenly it would have just been an act of derring-do. And I'm guessing Beatty would have revelled in it, and certainly not let our perpetrator take the credit for having made the suggestion.'

'And that brings us back to how our plotter managed to make the proposition sound appealing in the first place,' Blake said.

Tara tried to imagine what might have convinced a man like Christian Beatty: successful, admired, confident. 'Maybe our perpetrator suggested the climbing adventure to honour both Ralph and Lucas's memories,' she said. 'If they'd managed to make Beatty feel as though his reputation and status depended on him taking up the challenge, that could have worked.'

Max shook his head. 'Sure as hell wouldn't have worked on me.'

'Nor me,' said Blake.

'But in days of yore you got people fighting duels at the drop of a hat, simply to defend their honour. Maybe Beatty had a big ego and enough confidence and vodka to make him think glory was only a leap away.'

They all looked at each other. Tara wasn't sure if they bought her idea, but several people had managed to leap the gap that Beatty had misjudged. Booze was what had done for him; that and the icy conditions.

'But I assume we all agree that if Christian Beatty had survived, our conspirator would have had to change tack.' Blake looked at them in turn. Tara nodded and watched Max agree too.

'As it is, they succeeded again,' Tara said. 'But now they'll have to change method anyway, given we're systemically warning each of Ralph Cairncross's connections.' The fictional ends of the characters in the man's books came back to her. 'I wonder if they'll keep trying to echo the deaths in Cairncross's novels?' she said.

'Death by fire, and death in an airtight room?' Blake met her eye. 'And they might try electrocution or a hit-and-run again, too.'

She nodded. Not a good thought.

CHAPTER THIRTY

Blake had just returned to his office when Kemp's reply to Tara's text came through.

Mischief? Me? I'm behaving well and using my time productively. Full update as soon as I can manage. Bea sends love.

That sounded like Kemp being economical with the truth. She'd have to pummel him for information soon, but there was no time now.

She returned to recording the findings from the interviews with Tess Curtis and Sadie Cairncross. She glanced up at Wilkins' desk – still not back. He'd probably stopped off for a nice lunch somewhere after joining Agneta Larsson for Beatty's post-mortem. Though how he could stomach it under the circumstances, she didn't know. She was making do with a cereal bar and wishing it was chocolate. She hadn't had to see anyone cut open yet. She knew she'd cope with it, as she must when the time came, but it wasn't something she was looking forward to.

She began to reread everything she'd noted down from the visit to Ralph Cairncross's PA. She came to a standstill when she got to Tess Curtis's comments about the injury to Sadie Cairncross's mouth, and the supposed car accident.

It did seem odd that none of the websites she'd visited had mentioned the reason behind her retirement from her musical career. She googled again, but because the flautist had dropped out of sight years back now, the type of online articles she needed were few and far between. After a while, she found something about 'forgotten stars' which mentioned her. The article just said she'd retired. Her Wikipedia page mentioned an accident, but anyone could have edited that.

She thought back. It had been Philippa Cairncross who'd specifically told her that her mother had been forced to give up her career after a car crash. Tess Curtis had heard the same story. She put herself back in Philippa's college room and relived the conversation they'd had. She remembered probing about what had led to Sadie's early retirement. And then Wilkins had tried to interrupt her, knowing she was just being nosy. And for once he'd been right – she had been. Philippa could have knocked her back – she had no reason to pander to Tara's curiosity. And yet she'd been forthcoming. Even before Wilkins had got his protest out, Sadie Cairncross's daughter had trotted out her story of a car accident. It hadn't seemed odd at the time, but now Tara wondered. Had she put the subject to bed quickly, using the standard agreed excuse, rather than drawing attention to it by clamming up?

After another moment of googling, Tara found the name of the orchestra Sadie Cairncross had last worked for. With half an eye on the door, waiting for Wilkins to re-enter and tell her off for wasting time, she dialled.

She ended up speaking to three different people: a receptionist who'd only been at the organisation for a year, followed by an administrator who'd been there for five, and finally the PA to the artistic director, who'd been there forever.

'*You're researching a book?*' the woman said.

'That's right.' Well, she might be, if she got the sack and had to go back to journalism. 'It's about musicians who've been forced to retire in their prime. I thought Sadie Cairncross might be a good candidate. She was clearly very talented, and yet she stopped performing when she was only thirty-five. But I couldn't see anything official to say whether she'd been forced to give up through ill health, or if she'd decided to retire for other reasons.'

'I'm afraid I can't help you,' the woman said. *'What I can say is that it was very much unexpected from our point of view. She was on a contract that still had eighteen months to run. Then suddenly she was gone, and as far as I'm aware she cut herself off completely. I remember we had press wanting to interview her because she'd been such a rising star, but I was told to fob them off. The management were on her side, even though she'd let us down, so whatever it was, they must have felt sympathetic towards her. You'll have to go to the family direct if you want more.'*

'Someone mentioned she might have been involved in a car accident?'

The woman on the other end of the line sniffed. *'If that's the case, I'm sure everyone would have known about it. And why would they keep that from the press?'*

Why indeed? Tara thanked the woman and rang off.

Just as she did so, another text came in on her personal phone. She glanced at the screen. Not Kemp this time, but her mother.

Darling – Reading Not Now *between sets and saw your photograph with that extraordinary article. I take it Giles hasn't forgiven you then. I did wonder if you were storing up trouble for yourself when you left the magazine…*

The message set Tara's teeth on edge. She imagined Lydia, sitting in her chair in the Madeira sunshine whilst make-up artists ran round after her, congratulating herself on her prescience… *Thanks, Mother. I was actually aware of Giles's character myself, given that I had to work with him for three years…* In truth though, she'd never have expected something like the article that had appeared on their website that morning. Not because Giles wasn't vindictive – he certainly was – just because she'd thought he'd be too lazy. But of course, he had his vampire Shona, ready to send out into the night to do all his hard work for him.

Tara didn't bother to reply to her mother's text. Instead, she slipped her phone into her bag and turned her attention back to the case. A moment later, she was piecing together the comings and goings at the Cairncross family home, the night of the accident in the Fens. Tess Curtis said she'd bumped into Philippa when she'd visited Ralph's office to pick up the papers she wanted to take to him for signing. That would be worth cross-checking once they caught up with Cairncross junior.

Tara refocused. And of course, Tess Curtis had said that Ralph's workspace had a separate entrance – you didn't get to it through the main house. And yet she'd still managed to come face to face with Philippa. Did that mean Cairncross's daughter had been outside, near the entrance to her father's office? And if so, why? Had she been after something? Something that she'd only gone to look for when he was out of the way?

Tara flexed her shoulders. Her neck was getting stiff and she was going round in circles – every person connected with the deaths seemed to be behaving oddly. All the same, she could give Tess Curtis a call. She might as well dig a bit deeper.

She got the woman on her mobile. *'I'm at work now,'* she said. *'Can't this wait?'*

'I wanted to let you know a colleague has managed to recover the draft contract you deleted. We didn't even have to get the tech experts onto it.'

Her tone softened. *'Oh, well – that's something. Thank you for updating me.'*

Tara didn't mention Blake's thought – that she could still have invented the agreement with Christian Beatty and created the draft contract to back up her story.

'And I had a very quick question about Philippa Cairncross, too,' she said instead, waiting for curiosity to bite.

'Okay then.'

'You mentioned bumping into her when you went to Ralph's offices the night he died. I just wondered, do you think Philippa had been visiting his workspace too?'

'I don't remember saying…' There was a momentary pause, and then the mist cleared from Tess Curtis's voice. *'Oh sorry, yes, I see. No, I didn't come face to face with her in person. Our cars were nose to nose. She was manoeuvring her mother's Volvo in the driveway when I turned my car in. She went straight off, so I didn't get to speak to her.'*

Tara was in Blake's office when Wilkins finally reappeared. He made his presence known by knocking on the door.

'Just in time,' Blake said, one eyebrow raised and a look of warning in his eyes. 'Max has managed to track down Philippa Cairncross, and you and Tara need to go and see her. But before you do, you need to have a word with her boyfriend. Max says he's at the Chemistry department as we speak, and he can see you as soon as you get there.'

Wilkins frowned. 'Boyfriend?'

'You may remember she told us she was with him until late the night her father was killed, and that she went to visit him on her bike. Well, we now have a witness who says she actually left the family home by car that evening.' Blake looked at Tara. 'Perhaps you could fill Patrick in en route, Tara. And well done.'

Tara knew she deserved the praise, and she was glad to have it, but she wasn't looking forward to having to share a car with Wilkins in its immediate aftermath. Blake had clearly lost patience with her boss's bullying behaviour and given up trying not to rock the boat.

CHAPTER THIRTY-ONE

Philippa Cairncross's boyfriend, Lance Ravenscroft, was six foot three, blond and broad. Tara guessed he was normally self-assured with it. But now he had that air of someone whose equilibrium had been disturbed.

Tara knew Max Dimity had told him, over the phone, that they wanted to talk to him about the night his girlfriend's father had died. If he'd provided her with a false alibi, he ought to be stewing nicely by now. In spite of Wilkins' bad temper, they'd managed to talk enough on the way over to agree their plan of attack. Looking at the man in front of them, shifting from one foot to the other in the small office they'd been shown to, Tara was sure it would work.

'Please make yourself comfortable, Mr Ravenscroft,' Tara said, knowing it would take more than a seat to put him at his ease.

Once he was settled, she and Wilkins sat down too. They were all gathered round a small square table.

'There's no easy way to put this,' Wilkins said. 'The fact is, we know Philippa lied to us about the night her father died.'

They'd agreed to put it in its strongest terms and let him assume they knew more than they did. As it was, Philippa could claim to have simply misremembered her mode of transport that night. They wanted Lance Ravenscroft to give them more, so they had the upper hand when they went to interview her.

Lance Ravenscroft looked agitated now. Being found out for lying to the police probably wouldn't help with his career plan. He must have led a sheltered life if this was the first rock he'd hit in the road.

'We wanted to give you the chance to qualify the statement you made, back in September,' Tara said. 'I mean, if you need to rethink anything you told us, we can accommodate that. People do make mistakes sometimes, when they're recounting what happened just after a shocking incident.'

Ravenscroft nodded. There was a glimmer of hope in his eyes now. 'It's true,' he said. 'It's easy to get confused when everyone's upset. Once the dust had settled I did wonder if Philippa had got her times muddled up. But by that stage I'd already given my statement, based on hers. I mean, I'd used her recollections to jog my own memory.'

Pathetic, really. Still, he was clearly going to give them what they needed.

'So tell us again exactly what happened that night,' Wilkins said.

'I think maybe Philippa actually arrived at mine a little later than I originally said.'

'And how much later would that be?' Tara asked.

'Maybe around ten, or ten thirty.'

She and Wilkins looked at each other. Ravenscroft was trying to limit the damage, but already he was admitting she might have arrived a full two and a half hours after he'd originally claimed.

'And do you know how she reached you?' Tara said.

Lance Ravenscroft frowned. 'I didn't see her turn up, but I went out to see her off when she left.'

'At what time?'

His voice was firm now. 'At around quarter to one.'

That time hadn't changed then. Funny how he'd only been 'forgetful' about when she'd arrived.

'And how did she leave?'

'She had her bike with her. I waited whilst she unlocked it and then we said goodnight.'

*

Back in the car, Wilkins turned to shove his safety belt fastening home. He fluffed the manoeuvre and cursed.

Catching Philippa out in a lie looked pretty suspicious. He was going to come across as an idiot if he finally had to climb down and admit there was something in Tara's theory after all.

He kept his eyes ahead. 'I suppose you're going to say she went out by car, drove to the Fens, fetched the snake from the crate and did her dirty work,' he said. 'Then,' he stuck his key into the ignition, 'she drove home, dumped her mum's car and nipped out on her bike for a shag to celebrate.'

He was so poetic sometimes.

'Maybe.'

Wilkins sounded incredulous. 'Oh come on! I thought you'd be leaping on this.'

But if it had been as Wilkins suggested, where had Philippa Cairncross parked her car? She couldn't have risked pulling up on the drive of the house on the bank. It was overlooked, and the curtains might not have been drawn. But there wasn't much cover out on the main road, either. 'I guess we'd better go and ask some questions,' Tara said. 'Get her side of the story.' No doubt Lance Ravenscroft would have called ahead, to warn her of what was coming. Max had confirmed she was back home on Madingley Road now.

'I can hardly wait,' Wilkins said. 'It will be one more chance to watch you adding two and two and making five.' He was smiling again now, knowing exactly how to push her buttons.

Just you wait, Wilkins. We'll see who looks stupid at the end of this.

CHAPTER THIRTY-TWO

The main streets were clear now, but re-entering the Cairncross house on Madingley Road was like stepping back into an enchanted garden where it was permanently snow-muffled winter. The only tyre impressions on the drive were the ones they'd left earlier, but they could see footprints that must belong to Philippa Cairncross – one lot heading out, and a matching set returning to the house. Presumably they hadn't had any post that day. Tara wondered how much Sadie Cairncross went out. And how often she spoke to anyone but her daughter.

It was Philippa who came to the dark-windowed door, but just behind her in the gloomy hall Tara could see her mother, her face pale in the shadows.

'Come in then,' Philippa said, stepping back to allow them through. Her eyes weren't wary, just unfriendly, as they'd been the last time Tara had viewed them. That, and resolute. But she was sure her boyfriend would have been in touch; she'd know what was coming.

'You don't need to be with me for this,' Philippa said, glancing over her shoulder at her mother. 'They've already grilled you. You might as well go and wait in the sitting room.' Philippa turned and walked down the hallway, opening a door to the left, revealing a dresser and part of a butler sink.

But Sadie Cairncross seemed to have come out of the dream-like state she'd been in earlier. 'I'd rather be with you,' she said. 'I am your mother.' Maybe she'd sensed the tension and it had made her more alert.

'I can look after myself.' There was no doubt Philippa wanted to keep this conversation private. But once again Tara noticed her words were clipped and her tone impatient, rather than anxious.

Philippa led them into the kitchen. 'I've only just got back, so I'm going to have coffee,' she said. 'I'm freezing.' She walked over to a kettle, picked it up and took it to the sink. 'I suppose you'd like some too.'

'No thanks,' Wilkins said.

Tara could hear the haughtiness in his voice. 'But I would.' She wanted the water to take as long as possible to boil. It would give more time for Philippa to get nervous, if she was going to. And in any case, it would allow Tara a moment to size up the room, which was always useful.

Today, it was a photograph on the dresser that interested her.

'I'd like coffee too.' Sadie had followed them in.

Tara saw Philippa's shoulders tense. She'd still got her hand on the kettle's handle, having just put it back on its stand. She picked it up again and took it back to the sink to add more water.

Tara walked around the room casually and made for the dresser once Philippa had turned her back. The photograph was of Cairncross and the complete set of his Acolytes, by the look of it. The girl on the far left of the line-up must be Letty. She looked very young in the picture. Of course, she had been much younger than the rest, but the impression was accentuated because she was the only one who was relaxed and laughing. Tara remembered Tess Curtis referring to her as an 'innocent' who Ralph Cairncross would certainly have tried to bed. Thom King had called her a 'treasure' and Stephen Ross had said she'd been 'very bright and beautiful too, like the subject of a Pre-Raphaelite painting'. Letty was leaning in towards the group as though she was genuinely fond of them. She looked every inch like someone's kid sister, tagging along with the cool older siblings. Her eyes were clear and blue and her hair was that sort of red that looks sunlit, even when it's cloudy. Stephen Ross was next to her, an arm slung round her shoulders, facing the camera. His look was fierce. All the others along the line, and Cairncross himself, looked as though they'd adopted expressions especially for the pose too. Thom King had gone for an embarrassing rock-star style snarl. She was glad she'd only seen the photo after she'd interviewed him. She'd have a job to take him seriously now. But Christian Beatty was even worse: it looked as though he'd been shaking his fist. Lucas Everett and Verity Hipkiss had opted for variations on a shared theme: a sort of insolent stare. Behind the whole group, Cairncross stood, his arms outstretched. He reminded Tara of a puppet master, pulling unseen strings. Tara wondered who'd taken the shot. The long-suffering Tess Curtis, perhaps? Or someone from the press?

She was distracted from her thoughts by the sound of Philippa slapping mugs down behind her. When she turned she saw some of the coffee had spilled onto the heavy-duty oak table.

They all pulled out chairs and sat down.

'So, Mum said you wanted to warn us all that we might be in danger,' Philippa said. 'You seriously think someone's going around trying to orchestrate a series of deaths?'

'It's an outside possibility,' Wilkins said. 'Or it's seemed so up until now. But it's something we can't ignore.'

Philippa's eyes flashed. 'And I presume because so far the deaths have included my darling father and two of the Acolytes, I might look like a possible suspect, as well as a potential victim.'

'What makes you say that?' Wilkins said.

'Well, I made no secret of the fact that I despised Ralph and his idiotic band of followers last time we spoke.'

'Philippa!' There was pain in Sadie Cairncross's voice.

'You know it's true, Mum. I can't help it if you weren't able to break the spell Ralph had you under. But it was a spell.' She looked down into her drink and shook her head. 'I did tell you not to come in here and listen to all this. I don't want to hurt you. I've never wanted that.' She looked up and her cold, grey eyes met her mother's. 'If you're staying because you think your presence will hold me back, you can think again. It's too late for all that now.'

She directed her gaze at Tara and Wilkins once more. 'So, you think someone's encouraging the Acolytes to take risks, hoping their deaths will be written off as accidental? And maybe that they also encouraged my father to drink more than usual, to heighten the chances of him crashing?'

'Not just that,' Tara said.

'I saw the magazine article about the snake,' Philippa replied.

Her and everyone else.

There was a hint of wariness in her eyes now. Had she been out in the Fens that night? Was that where she'd taken her mother's car? Whatever she told them they'd check the traffic cameras to look at her possible direction of travel.

'And, of course, there was the incident with the lamp, just a week before your father's crash, too,' Tara added. 'Maybe someone with access to the garage tampered with the wiring to engineer what seemed like a mishap.'

And now there was a new look in Philippa's eye. Fear. It took a while to develop, as though her mind was working on something she hadn't considered before.

'A trap,' she said. 'But if someone did that, they might have left more. Mum or I might stumble across something that was meant for Ralph.'

Could she really fake such a convincing reaction? It was time to get to the meat of what they needed to ask. She glanced at Wilkins. It was his job – officially – though he didn't seem to relish it.

'We know you lied about your movements, the night your father died,' he said at last. 'Lance Ravenscroft has confirmed that your story about turning up at his place at eight is way off. He puts your arrival at more like ten or ten thirty that night. He thinks you must have got muddled because you were upset, but we don't agree.'

Philippa was absolutely quiet. Her mother stared at the table, and Tara could see a slight shake in her left hand. Had she known her daughter had lied?

Tara leant forward. 'Philippa, we have a witness who saw you leave this house at eight that night, in your mother's car.' Her full attention was on the young woman's face. The fear was there again now; fear for herself this time, she was sure. And to her left she heard Sadie Cairncross take a sharp intake of breath.

'You went out into the Fens, didn't you, Philippa?' Tara said.

Philippa looked at her mother, and suddenly her shoulders slumped. 'Yes,' she said. 'Yes, I did.' Her eyes flicked back to them again immediately. 'But if you think I engineered Ralph's death, you're wrong. I was angry with him and I couldn't see why he wanted to spend so much time with that gang of sycophants. I had this sort of compulsion to go and spy on them, to see the sort of stupid things they got up to. To prove myself right for despising them all, I suppose.'

There was a long pause. 'You've got to see it from our point of view, Philippa,' Wilkins said. 'You lied to us about where you were the night your dad died. You put a photograph of the site of his accident up as your Facebook cover photo. You tell us how much you hated him. What are we supposed to think?'

Sadie had started to cry, very quietly. She was still looking down at the table.

'You need to tell us exactly what happened that night,' Tara said. 'And the real reason you went over to the house on the Forty Foot Bank.' Had she been aiming to kill her father? Tara could imagine her wanting to do it – actually carrying it out even, if she'd had the means and been angry enough on the spur of the moment. But then her mind went back to the fear in the girl's eyes at the thought of any booby traps that might still be lying around the house. If she'd been responsible she wouldn't have cause to worry. 'Did you drive straight to the house on the bank, after you left Madingley Road?'

Philippa ran her fingers through her spiky hair. 'No. I saw that bitch Tess Curtis as I left, of course – I imagine she's your witness. I guessed she'd be busy finding some excuse to go and gatecrash Ralph's party too – for very different reasons.'

'So you waited, to give her a head start?'

Philippa nodded. 'I parked up and watched for her to go past. I didn't want her on my tail. After that I went straight out into the Fens.'

'And what did you do when you got there?' Wilkins asked.

'I couldn't use the house's driveway, of course. I didn't want to be seen.' She was staring into space, as though she was back in the moment she was describing. 'But there's a derelict old cottage a little way beyond it. I parked there behind an old barn. It meant there was no way Tess would see Mum's car as she left again.'

'And then what did you do?' Tara asked.

'I walked up the verge to the house on the bank. The sun was already down, but it wasn't completely dark. The curtains were still drawn back, so I could see inside the various rooms. I had to be careful where I stood, so I wouldn't be spotted, but there are hedges, and an outhouse – various bits of cover. So I watched. No one saw me and eventually I went home.'

Tara noticed her eyes flick over towards her mother at that point. Her mind was back on the here and now, clearly. Her look suggested she was holding something back.

'Did you see anyone come outside, whilst you were watching?' she asked.

She nodded. 'Tess Curtis was already on the forecourt when I arrived. She stood by her car for a bit, wiping squashed bugs off her windscreen. I reckon it was an excuse to hang around. She wanted to be part of the action – or to see what went on. But eventually she gave up and headed off.'

Tara wondered if she'd already been collecting material for her book. Writing it without interference would certainly be easier now that Ralph was out of the way. She might have put the snake in his car before Philippa Cairncross showed up. Though she – or whoever had planted it – would have to have been careful they weren't seen from the house.

'And did you see anyone else?' Tara asked.

The girl's eyes slid towards her mother again. What was this about?

'Come on, Philippa,' Wilkins said. 'You're clearly leaving something out. Without it, you're lining up a whole load of trouble for yourself.'

At last the woman took her phone out of her jeans pocket. 'I'll show you.' She opened up her camera roll and spooled back. 'There,' she said at last, not looking at her mother now, and pushing the phone to a space between Tara and Wilkins.

Tara recognised the house on the bank as the backdrop in the photograph. In the foreground, hard up against the wall of the house – between two sets of windows where they wouldn't been seen from inside – were Ralph Cairncross and Verity Hipkiss. The light was dusky, the image slightly blurred, but there was no mistaking them. They were entwined. He had one hand in her hair, the other up her skirt.

'They didn't spot me,' Philippa said, spitting the words out. 'As you can see, they were pretty engrossed.'

Before any of them could stop her, Sadie Cairncross had snatched up the phone. Philippa made a grab for it too, but she was a second too late. She stood up abruptly and went to her mother's side.

'I didn't want you to know,' she said. 'Not now. Not after he died. I'd been trying to get proof. If he'd lived, I wanted you to see him for what he was. He was still ruining your life, and you were letting him.' She gripped her mother's shoulder, her hand claw-like. 'I wanted you to wake up! How many more years would you have let him abuse you? Use you? Make you feel like nothing?' She took a huge breath. 'But when he died, then there was no point in showing you. You were free of him anyway, and I'd only be hurting you.'

She put her arm round her mother's shoulders now, but Tara could tell frustration was battling with tenderness. On the whole, she thought frustration was winning.

'Please, Mum. Take your coffee into the sitting room, let me finish up here, and then we can talk.'

At last Sadie Cairncross nodded and got up. Before she exited the room she turned one more time to face her daughter. 'You didn't need to do it, Philippa. I've known about his infidelity for years.'

With that, she walked out into the hall and Philippa closed the door behind her. Her cheeks were tinged with red, in stark contrast with the rest of her pale face.

She came back to the table and looked at Tara and Wilkins in turn.

'She might have known, in her heart of hearts, but she chose to stick her head in the sand and suffer. I thought if she saw proper evidence, it would break his hold over her. She'd be forced to face reality, and hopefully to leave Ralph.

'You've got to understand,' she went on, 'that my mother suffered for *years* because of him. It was a sort of endless, grinding humiliation and sorrow.' She looked Tara in the eye. 'You remember you asked me about what ended Mum's career as a flautist and I said it was a car crash?'

Tara nodded. 'What really happened? Did Ralph injure her?'

Philippa gave a mirthless laugh that sent the hairs on Tara's arms rising. 'In a manner of speaking.' She slumped back down into the chair she'd occupied before. 'He made it clear to Mum that he only wanted women – and indeed companions – who were in their first flush of youth. Line-free, carefree and – in his eyes – beautiful. She used to pretend she didn't mind. She called herself his anchor – but all that really meant was that she kept house for him and ensured there was a hot meal waiting if he wanted it.

'I was only a young child when I started to get the measure of what was going on. I was bright. I overheard things, and I used to hear her crying. Then she told me she had to go away for a few days. A cousin came and looked after me – it wasn't a job for Ralph, obviously. He was above that sort of thing.'

Tara remembered Tess Curtis talking about Sadie disappearing for a few weeks. 'She was gone longer than expected?'

Philippa nodded. 'Yes. And when she came back, she'd lost that mobility in her mouth. There was a scar too – I still remember it, but it's faded with time. God.' She paused for a moment and swallowed. 'I can still remember saying to her: "Mummy, your mouth's gone funny", and she cried. But I didn't know. I was only little. I found out what had really happened later. She only told me when I was fifteen.'

Tara waited.

'Plastic surgery gone wrong,' Philippa said. 'She hadn't got much money of her own. Her career was flourishing, but all her earnings went into their joint account, and she didn't want Ralph to know she'd given nature a helping hand by paying a surgeon. So she risked skimping on the cost. And that decision cost her her career.'

She looked at them steadily. 'The injury still hurts her, too. I was worried when I heard you'd been to see her this morning. She'd taken something strong earlier to numb the pain.'

It figured, though whether the hurt she suffered was still a result of her surgery, or down to other causes, was up for debate.

'She's always been ashamed of what she did,' Philippa went on. 'Ashamed – even though it was my father who was responsible. She came up with the car crash story to avoid having to admit to the truth. And all because my father had a preference for a youthful face.' Philippa put her shoulders back. 'You know, scholars spend hours of research time trying to work out why he was so obsessed with youth. They come up with all sorts of crazy theories. They actually get funded for their efforts.' Her eyes gleamed. 'But I know the truth. I overheard him talk about it once, with an old university friend of his. They were sitting in here making merry whilst my mum had yet another one of her early nights.

'I was reading in the sitting room, but it was impossible not to listen. They'd had a lot to drink.'

'What did you overhear?' Tara remembered Dr Richardson had said Sadie claimed Ralph had been scarred by seeing his grandparents suffer in old age. That had always sounded like a feeble excuse to her.

'His friend had been trying to get published too, so Ralph regaled him with his own experiences. He said he'd got nowhere when his agent first sent his work out to publishers. People loved his poetic language but his plots weren't compelling enough. So his agent suggested he should write something deliberately controversial.' She looked at them. 'And that's just what he did. Dreamt up an obsession with youth and an abhorrence of the aging process. And made a packet out of it. And as an extra bonus, it meant my mother excused his behaviour as being necessary to "feed his creativity". In reality, he just liked running after younger women and partying. Hardly a first…'

She stood up again now, her shoulders forward, her face white with anger. 'He was a prize bastard. If someone did have a hand in his accident they did us all a good turn.'

CHAPTER THIRTY-THREE

Blake had caught up with Patrick and Tara and heard the results of their interviews with Philippa and her boyfriend. As he walked through the station's corridors, he wished he'd been there. Philippa Cairncross's story might be true – and of course she'd produced the photo proving her father's infidelity – but there was no doubt she'd had a motive for killing him. He could well understand her hatred, and the way she despised Ralph's followers. What would years of resentment have done to her? He'd seen a picture of Philippa now. She really did look like her father. That could have played a part, if she'd secretly formed close relationships with Lucas Everett and Christian Beatty, ready to influence their behaviour. But could she have hidden her true feelings towards them enough to form that kind of bond?

He'd been spending his time preparing for the Hunter drugs trial. As planned, Megan Maloney and Max Dimity had been dividing their time between paperwork for that and leg work around the Cairncross investigation. Their contribution to the Hunter case was all but complete, but for Blake it had been a tense day. One of the witnesses to some associated gang violence was getting cold feet. He'd sat opposite the guy as he'd cried, and sworn he'd made false claims in his previous statement. It had taken all Blake's powers of persuasion – and some veiled threats – to talk him round.

Lesser of two evils, he told himself firmly as he opened the station door to leave for the evening. But he felt uneasy as he went to get his bike.

He was due at Agneta and Frans' for dinner. He'd stuck to his plan to make the visit alone. He'd told his wife that he needed to meet with the pathologist to talk about a case, leaving it until the last minute to mention his plans. Christian Beatty's death at the weekend made it more plausible. He felt guilty – for lying and for leaving her out, but most of all for not tackling the situation he was in head on. All the same, he couldn't help feeling relieved she wouldn't be there, brooding over Agneta and Frans' nine-month-old, ready to steer him back to the topic of expanding their own family as soon as they left.

The snow had started again: thick, slow-moving flakes drifted down, shifting at haphazard angles as the breeze took them. His route towards Milton Road took him along the river first, towards his own home in Fen Ditton and past Tara's house. He found himself pausing just after he'd crossed the cattle grid, staring ahead at her tiny cottage, hunkered down against the winter weather. He bet it was cold inside. His own house was cosy, but all at once, without being able to stop the thought, he acknowledged he'd prefer to go home to Tara's each night… were it not for Kitty. They'd have brandies, huddle round a heater and talk about whatever case they were working on. He stopped the train of thought before it strayed onto more dangerous territory.

As he sat astride his bike, looking ahead, he saw a figure. They'd stopped, just as he had, dead still, close to the Green Dragon Bridge. How long had they been there? He'd been so focused on Tara that he hadn't taken in the wider scene until that moment. He couldn't see the person clearly, but they were on a bike too. Was it a man? Hard to tell at his distance, and the snow was coming down faster, creating a filter between him and everything in his line of sight. He started to pedal towards the stationary cyclist. They only waited a moment longer, then resumed their journey as soon as it was clear he was headed in their direction.

What had they been up to? It wasn't the weather for standing around, enjoying the view. Another scandal-hungry reporter? Or someone connected to Cairncross? Then again, they might have paused for an innocent reason. After all, he'd stopped too. After a moment's hesitation, he switched direction and cycled towards Tara's place. There was a rough track where she herself must regularly cross the grass. It was all the harder to traverse now it was under a thickening layer of snow. He followed it, then propped his bike against the low wall of her garden. After a moment, he knocked.

She arrived at the front door wearing jeans and a figure-hugging emerald green jumper that echoed her eyes and contrasted with her red hair. 'Blake? Is everything all right?'

'I'm not sure.' He explained about the figure he'd seen. 'Given recent events it's probably a journalist.'

She gave him a wry look and a grimace. Some colour came to her cheeks, but that was probably just the cold. Tara was tough enough to cope; he knew that.

'All the same,' he added, 'after what Monica Cairncross said, that first time she came to see you – and the ice on your path – I wondered. I wanted to warn you. And if a photo of me outside your door appears in *Not Now* magazine tomorrow I'll go and sort them out. You might like to join me. Together I reckon we'd be invincible.'

She smiled at last. 'Count me in.' But then a frown crossed her face and there was a pause before she added: 'Do you want to come in for a drink? I've just unfrozen a bottle of red.'

The temptation to say yes was strong. Just as well he'd got a dinner appointment. 'I should probably get going,' he said. 'I'm due at Agneta Larsson and her husband's for a meal. We're old friends.'

She nodded and glanced down. 'Sure.' After a moment she added, 'I liked Agneta.'

There was an awkward pause. 'It was great work you did today,' he said at last.

'Thanks… though I feel Wilkins won't be able to let go of the idea of Philippa Cairncross as our perpetrator now.' He saw her sigh. 'It's funny: he was so set against my whole theory to start with. Now I can see he's torn between holding onto that idea and sticking the boot into Philippa. She didn't fall for his charms when they first met, and he hasn't forgiven her.'

'To be fair, she has a pretty good self-confessed motive, as well as opportunity – for her dad at least. And then there's her resemblance to Ralph Cairncross. I'm not wedded to most of Patrick's theories, but I do see that anyone who idolised her dad might transfer their admiration to her, based on looks at least.'

Tara shrugged. 'All true, but you should have seen her face when she realised there might be more undiscovered booby traps at Madingley Road. She looked scared, and sounded it too. Her reaction seemed totally spontaneous.'

'You could be right. We shouldn't discount her though, or her mother.' And, of course, Tess Curtis still had potential as a suspect too. She'd been at the house the night Cairncross died; she could have put the snake in his car. And if she'd been seen anywhere near his vehicle, the Acolytes would probably have assumed she was performing some solicitous task, like removing rubbish from his footwell. And to complete the picture, one of the Acolytes themselves could be guilty. They'd been on the spot and each had their own problematic dynamic with Ralph and the rest of the group…

Tara's eyes met his and the silence hung between them.

'I'd better be off then,' Blake said at last, turning to reach for his bike. And as he did, he caught movement out of the corner of his eye. Up by the bridge again. Someone also on a bike. The same person who'd been watching before? Had they come back? But once again, as soon as he turned to look properly the cyclist changed course, towards Chesterton, and went on their way.

'Was that them?' Tara said.

'I'm not sure.' He ought to have been keeping an eye out. His mind had been on other things. 'Take care, all right?'

She nodded. 'Will do. I had my self-defence skills put to the test recently, in fact.' She sounded awkward.

Blake raised an eyebrow.

'An old friend, Kemp, turned up out of the blue, when I came back from Kellness a couple of weeks ago. Gave me the fright of my bloody life. Still, I got him good and proper.' She grinned now. 'Without breaking any bones on this occasion, of course.'

'Of course.' He wondered where this 'old friend' had stayed for the night. Kemp. The name rang a bell. After a moment he had it. The ex-police officer who'd taught her self-defence. He must be pleased she hadn't lost her skills. The thought of him filled Blake with misgivings. The guy had been on the point of getting the sack when he'd resigned, if the gossip was true. But he bit back anything he might have said. None of his business.

'He's staying at my relative Bea's boarding house now,' Tara said, as though reading his mind.

Now. He'd stayed over before that then, Blake guessed.

Absolutely none of my business. He repeated the mantra as he turned his bike round. 'See you tomorrow, Tara,' he said.

She nodded. 'Bright and early. Or early, anyway.'

Blake bumped his way back over the rough track through the snow. He needed to cross the Green Dragon Bridge – a narrow iron construction for cyclists and pedestrians – to cut through to Milton Road. When he reached Water Street on the other side he scanned the wide lane, looking for the solitary cyclist who'd seemed to pay him and Tara such close attention. But the street was quiet, other than a couple scurrying through the cold night to the warmth of the timber-framed Green Dragon pub, with its crooked, snow-covered roof. If the watcher really had been a journalist, he didn't fancy the thought of Fleming's reaction to another photo of him and Tara together. But that possibility still beat the alternative – that whoever was doing all this had her in their sights too.

CHAPTER THIRTY-FOUR

Tara closed the door on Blake, the night, and the mysterious cyclist who'd been watching them from the Green Dragon Bridge.

What had Blake thought when she'd invited him in for a drink? Did anyone do that with their boss's boss for innocent reasons? But he'd been standing there on her doorstep in the snow, having taken the trouble to come and warn her about the person who seemed to be watching her house. She'd felt she should ask if he wanted to come in – not just leave him standing there.

She tried to push the feeling of embarrassment away, but it lingered, especially when she reflected on the awkward way in which she'd worked Kemp's recent visit into the conversation. She'd made up her mind previously that she wanted to explain in an upfront way that her old mentor had been there. She still didn't know if Blake had ever met him but, if he had, she didn't like the possibility that he might have seen Kemp exiting her house on his way to work. She could imagine what he'd assume. But in the end her mention of the former cop hadn't sounded natural at all. Just like some kind of weird confession.

This was crazy. As if she didn't have anything important to think about. After the interview with Philippa, and her and Wilkins' debrief with Blake, she'd managed to snatch a moment to bike to Heffers – the university bookshop – to buy a copy of the two poetry pamphlets Stephen Ross had had published to date, as well as a copy of Verity Hipkiss's acclaimed novel. She wanted to look at their output, and do more research on Thom King too. She didn't believe Philippa was guilty of plotting the deaths they'd seen so far. Her mother and Tess Curtis were still possibilities though, as Blake had said, and the Acolytes were of interest too. They'd have had the best opportunity to put the snake into Ralph's car.

On reflection, she ignored the bottle of red and went to make herself a hot chocolate. She guessed she'd need something sustaining if she was going to wade through their artistic output, but would probably require a clear head to go along with it.

An hour later she was wondering just how original Stephen Ross's work really was. The last poem of his that she'd looked at, 'To My Love at Evening Time', reminded her of something that could have been written centuries earlier. There was lots of imagery, with allusions to the glow of rubies in the fading sun, and the gleam of alabaster with the rising moon. Lips and skin? The metaphors were effective but not exactly groundbreaking, Tara reckoned – though she was no expert. Ross talked about his role as protector and the vulnerability of his lover. The words were tender – full of emotion and a sort of anguish – but she felt there was an unfortunate trace of Wilkins in their strong-man, weaker-woman dynamic.

She was still curious about the way Stephen had portrayed himself – as the intellectual linchpin of the group – versus the way Thom King and Philippa Cairncross had described him, as someone who was generally patronised. She tried putting Stephen and Ralph Cairncross's names into Google together. The results page gave her a lot of articles that mentioned the whole acolyte group. She carried on scanning the list of hits. On the third page she found a link to a YouTube clip of Cairncross being interviewed about his final novel, *Out of the Blue*. He was in a TV studio and had the Acolytes there with him, arranged around him like groupies. The clip dated back to two weeks before he'd died. The interviewer was trying to get some hints about the book's content. Ralph had laughed. *'My lips are sealed. Of course the Acolytes know, but you won't get anything out of them.'*

'You've shared the manuscript with them all, then?' the interviewer asked.

Cairncross nodded. *'I let you read it first, didn't I, Stephen?'* He glanced sideways at Ross and reached to pat him on the shoulder. Interestingly, *none* of the Acolytes looked pleased. It was understandable that the ones who'd had to wait to see the book should look irritated at the fact. Especially as Cairncross had implied they were inferior in some way in front of the TV cameras. But there was no smile from Stephen, either. His face was grim. *'I knew there were elements he'd appreciate in a way that no one else could,'* Ralph added, as the camera zoomed in on his face. *'But I value the opinion of the entire group, of course, beyond words. They've all read the manuscript now.'*

'I've got plenty of people to try to pump for information then,' the interviewer said with a sycophantic laugh.

Cairncross smiled. *'Now, now. No underhand tactics. You've only days to wait before you can read the book for yourself!'*

Why hadn't Stephen Ross been pleased at being singled out? Had Cairncross been secretly getting at him in some subtle way, rather than paying him the compliment that had been implied?

She'd investigated Thom King's work before, briefly, on the evening that she'd interviewed him. She could see from his website that he undertook commissions, which ranged from landscapes and grand houses to portraits. But the work he had for sale on various gallery websites – presumably what he liked to paint when left to his own devices – had a common theme. She found *Woman in Blue* (the painting did what it said on the tin), *Woman in Yellow* (ditto) and *Woman on a Chair*... he clearly hadn't felt the need to get too creative with his titles. She also found a couple of portraits on sale that featured Christian Beatty. After seeing his broken body the day before, it was shocking to come face to face with images of him looking so vibrant. *What a waste.* Staring into his painted eyes gave Tara a sense of the power and physical presence the man must have had in life.

She scrolled through more pages of Google results. On the fifth, when she'd been about to give up, she found a work in oils that caught her eye. It was called *Power*, which was unusual for a start. And when Tara enlarged the thumbnail, she realised she was looking at the face of Verity Hipkiss. He'd altered her hair – she was a brunette in this composition – but there was no mistaking her features. The smile she wore was cruel, and she'd been depicted as though she was looking down on the painter. She wore a very low-cut dress, so that much of the flesh of her breasts was visible. Goosebumps rose on Tara's arms. Thom King had said Verity had never sat for him. Presumably he'd used a photograph then, to create this portrait, without her knowledge. It was so invasive, and the way he'd overlaid his feelings about her character was clear to see. Could he be systematically arranging the deaths of every man Verity had admired? It seemed far-fetched, but that painting made her wonder. She thought back to the man's story of his near miss with a car – there was no proof the incident had really happened. If he was the guilty party he could have made it up, choosing a narrow escape that resonated with one of Ralph's books to make himself look innocent…

At eleven, another text came through from her mother. Tara still hadn't replied to the one earlier in the day.

Did Not Now *make up your affair with this senior detective? Bear his family in mind, won't you darling?*

Lydia would be at the post-cocktail stage of the evening now. She had probably worked up to sending her words of wisdom. She wished her mother would stop telling her things she already knew. There was every sign Lydia thought Tara was a witless moron with no brain cells of her own… the fact that her stepfather, Benedict, left a wife to be with her mother made the text an extra degree more irritating than it would otherwise have been.

She took Verity Hipkiss's book up to bed and plugged her phone with its unanswered text in to charge. She was so tired that the contents of the first chapter washed over her. She absorbed enough to know it was historical, and about a woman who defied the social norms. It opened with the upper-class heroine in bed with two men. *Autobiographical, perhaps?* Tara checked the dedication at the front of the book. It said: 'To you all'.

Before she went to sleep, Tara emailed her findings to Blake, knowing she should copy Wilkins in. *To hell with that…*

CHAPTER THIRTY-FIVE

Blake had a beer and a plateful of fish in front of him, with home-cooked chips. It was something Frans had cooked whilst Agneta put their baby, Elise, to bed. He wasn't sure if it was the relief of being somewhere where nothing was expected of him, or that Frans was one hell of a chef, but it tasted like the best thing he'd ever eaten.

And, to salve his conscience, they did talk about work. The take-home point about Christian Beatty was once again the sheer amount he'd drunk the night he'd died. Surely no one planning that leap would have consumed so much if they'd been alone? As with Cairncross and Everett, there'd been no drugs in his body. If Beatty had been with someone else on Saturday night, could they have pretended to get drunk too, whilst watching him, carefully calculating the moment he'd lose his sense of judgement, yet still be able to make the climb?

He and Agneta brought Frans up to speed, and then they all went to and fro, discussing the possibilities and who could have been involved: Philippa, who'd hated her father and the Acolytes, yet resembled the man they'd all loved; Tess Curtis, who felt left out of Cairncross's 'gang' and who stood to gain from any scandalous insider knowledge Christian Beatty might have passed on to her; or even Verity Hipkiss, who'd perhaps tired of her affair with Cairncross and was determined to keep it a secret, so that his high praise of her debut novel continued to look unbiased. If she'd killed three people to keep her relationship quiet it would be a particularly heartless crime, but who knew what she might be capable of, if her future success was at stake? She was charming, Blake gathered, but that happened to be a trait frequently exhibited by psychopaths. Once again, he wished he'd had more direct involvement in the case. If they could just prove for certain that there'd been foul play, Fleming wouldn't mind him muscling in…

'Sure is a weird case, Blake,' Agneta said. She'd been chipping in with questions, but behind the interest in her blue eyes he could see other things. He had a feeling she'd like to ask him about matters closer to home. He'd invited it, of course, by wanting to visit them alone.

'I'm just hoping it doesn't go any further,' Blake said, trying to make sure the conversation stayed on work. 'Until we understand what's motivating the killer – assuming Tara and I are right and there is one – we can't be sure that they've finished.' Cairncross's books came to him again. *How would the killer end their next victim's life? Electrocution, suffocation or burning…*

'Here,' Frans took up a fish slice with a black handle and red business end, 'have some more. Long hours need extra calories.' He shovelled a fresh pile onto Blake's plate with a grin.

Blake sat back in his seat and took a healthy draught of beer. 'Thanks.'

At that moment there was a high-pitched cry from the baby monitor on the sideboard. Agneta and Frans went still, and Frans rolled his eyes. After a moment of silence, there was another yelp, and then some more decided wailing.

Agneta made to get up, but Frans put a hand on her arm. 'No, I'll go,' he said. 'You did all the settling.' He left the room.

Agneta turned to Blake, the question back in her eyes again. He half wondered if she'd primed Frans to handle Elise if the situation arose, so she could pump him for information. 'So, you and Babette are having trouble again?' she said.

He stared down into his beer for a moment. When he looked up her expression was sympathetic.

'You never really got past the first split, right?'

'Has it been that obvious?'

'Probably not to everyone. But I know you, remember.' Her eyes were kind.

'I should never have agreed to give our marriage another go – but I hated being apart from Kitty.'

Agneta reached out and gave his shoulder a squeeze. 'Don't beat yourself up about that. I'd do anything for Elise. It's natural to love your child.'

He was going to tell her, he suddenly realised. The whole thing, not just the bits he'd shared before. 'Not my child, in fact,' he said.

He could see Agneta hadn't been expecting that.

'Some other guy's. Babette's never told me who.'

'I don't understand.'

Who would?

'Tell me, Blake,' she said. 'Tell me what happened. Did you always know Kitty wasn't yours?'

He gave a deliberate cough. 'Astoundingly, despite being an ace detective, I had absolutely no idea until the split, back when Kitty was a toddler.' He felt the colour come to his cheeks. 'Pretty embarrassing, huh?' He met her gaze.

'Not at all. But pretty damning on Babette if she kept it from you so completely.'

He looked down at the table. 'Apparently there was this man she saw a few times when we were first married. Usual story: I was working hard, it was as though she didn't exist as a woman, etc, etc. She kept bumping into the guy through work; he paid her lots of attention and made a dead set at her. They slept together just once – or so she says. But Kitty was the result.'

'How can she be sure?' That was Agneta – rushing in where angels feared to tread. She caught up though. 'Sorry – is it that you weren't—'

He cut her off mid-sentence. 'No, we were. Despite the difficult hours. Babette took some of Kitty's hair and her dad got a DNA test done.' He shook his head. 'And all the time, I still had no idea the guy even existed.'

'So you told her to leave when you finally found out?'

He shook his head. 'That wasn't how it worked. We'd been away for a weekend by the sea. We'd spent the whole time playing with Kitty, holding her hands, jumping the waves. It was idyllic, and I kept looking at her – a stompy little miracle – and thinking how lucky we were.' Elise had stopped crying, but even if Frans came back, he couldn't stop now. 'I drove us home, and Kitty fell asleep in her car seat, so I carried her inside and put her to bed.' He still remembered the feel of her – a solid, warm and precious bundle. 'When I got downstairs, Babette was crying. It was then that she told me Kitty wasn't mine. She'd been planning to break the news before, apparently, but she kept bottling out. As it was, it was right at the last minute.'

Agneta's eyes were huge. 'How do you mean?'

'She'd got tickets for her and Kitty – and the guy – to fly to Australia the following morning, where he was due to take up a new job.' He took a deep breath. 'She told me she'd realised she belonged with him, not me, and as Kitty was his anyway, I needed to think of her needs, not my own, and let her go.' He pressed his thumb and forefinger to the bridge of his nose. 'She said if I fought for her, it would damage her for good, but if I let her be with her natural father, she'd forget me before long, and only know stability.'

'The total bitch!' Agneta said suddenly, knocking her glass off the table and onto the floor. They both heard Elise start to cry again.

'Thank you, my darling.' Frans' wry voice was transmitted over the baby monitor.

In spite of himself, Blake laughed, and Agneta did too – it was a relief to release the tension – but they both stopped after a second.

Adrenaline was pumping round Blake's system. He still – after four whole years – couldn't think about what Babette had done without an almost uncontrollable reaction.

'So you let her go?'

He nodded. He couldn't look at Agneta again now – not without showing his emotions, anyway. And he thought Frans might lose the will if he came back downstairs and found he'd got a crying dinner guest as well as a crying daughter. 'I didn't have any time to think. I felt like killing Babette when she told me.' And that wasn't just a figure of speech. 'The following day, I hugged Kitty as though I'd never let her go and watched Babette mouth "for Kitty's sake" over her shoulder. And then she went. And they flew out to Australia.'

'Did you ask her to come back?'

He shook his head. 'I was devastated, but I didn't. The truth is, I wanted Kitty back, but not her.'

'Hell, Blake – I'm not so surprised about that.'

He swigged his beer. 'No, I guess not. But in the event, she reappeared. Only a fortnight later. God knows how she afforded her ticket home. She came back saying what a fool she'd been, and that Kitty's genes were irrelevant. She'd realised – she said – that she'd loved me all along, and the other guy – Kitty's dad – had used emotional blackmail to get her to go with him. She said he'd told her Kitty should be with her real dad, and that he'd always have time for them – unlike me.' He looked at Agneta. 'I refused to try again at first. I wanted to be there as Kitty's father, but I told Babette she should get used to the status quo of her "parents" living apart. Babs couldn't understand that. She said if I still loved Kitty and could get over the fact that she wasn't mine, then why couldn't I go that one step further and be there for her properly, in the same house, married to her mother. And of course, we *were* still married.'

'So she talked you round, eventually?'

He nodded. 'She said she wanted to put it all behind her. And because I'd been acting as Kitty's dad all that time she'd warned the other guy off. Told him no court would grant him regular access to Kitty. I thought I could get past what Babette had done. She said she still loved me, and I *had* loved her. And each time Kitty saw me when Babette and I were apart, she was in tears because she didn't understand what was going on.'

Agneta got up. 'Here.' She fetched a shot glass from their dresser and poured some Swedish vodka into it. 'You look as though you need it.'

'Thanks.' Vodka seemed to be becoming a theme. He drank it down straight. 'It's such a bloody mess. I've been a crap father to Kitty ever since. And certainly nothing like a husband to Babette. I've been wondering what to do.' He glanced sideways at Agneta. 'She wants another baby. But I can't. I can't forgive her. Not because she was unfaithful, but for her cruelty. For planning to steal Kitty away.'

'You and me both,' Agneta said, as Frans walked back into the room.

Monday 17 December

It amuses me to see that you've become a media star once again, Tara. You haven't had much good press of late, have you?

Of course, I wouldn't normally read Not Now, *but its content today was too tempting. And it confirmed that my thinking was sound when I developed this plot. I always knew people's minds would be too pedestrian to accept the evidence I put before their eyes. They'd never believe the series of events I'm engineering are part of a carefully orchestrated scheme; the whole thing would be too far-fetched.*

It's so satisfying to run rings around you all. And the staff at your old magazine really hate you, don't they? I can see why. The longer you battle with this case the more I realise the kind of person you are. You're on the side of the establishment; of the rich and the powerful. You don't care about what they've done to people who ought to have been able to trust them.

Is the rumour about you and your DI true, I wonder? Is the world full of people sleeping together when they shouldn't?

If the gossip is accurate then I suppose he'll miss you when you've gone. You see, I've made my decision about your fate now, Tara. I've added you to my list. I'm going to have fun deciding on the method...

If wiping you from the face of the earth also punishes the senior officer you're working with, then so much the better.

CHAPTER THIRTY-SIX

It was mid-morning on Tuesday and Tara was in the car with Wilkins, approaching Madingley Road. He'd got his foot down – Blake was meeting them there.

Tara was trying to digest the news and work out what to make of it.

'Still convinced we're dealing a series of coincidences?' she said.

'This latest development seems even less like part of a pattern, given the victim's still alive,' Wilkins answered.

And that was true. Great news, obviously, but it made Tara wonder as well. She knew their killer took chances, things that might or might not lead to a death, but up until now, they'd always been via methods that would look like an accident if they failed. This time there was no innocent explanation. According to the report that had come in, Sadie Cairncross had been deliberately trapped in Ralph Cairncross's archive store. Was the place airtight? Had this been an attempt at death by suffocation, to resonate with the death in *All But Over*, where the hero had allowed himself to be trapped in the storm shelter? But wouldn't old manuscripts need air conditioning or something, to keep them from being damaged?

Blake met them in the driveway. 'Tara, would you talk to the forensics guys? The store's round the back. Find out as much as you can.' His gaze moved to Wilkins. 'I want us to interview mother and daughter separately.'

Wilkins nodded, and the pair of them walked towards the front door.

Tara watched as an unfamiliar person let her boss and Blake in – a medic maybe – and then she walked around the outside of the building. She would be interested to talk to the forensics team, but she wished she could be in on the interviews too. Of course, it was Blake's territory now this extra event had moved the case up the scale.

She was looking forward to the day when she could go for promotion and take on more responsibility.

Just you wait, Wilkins. It seemed he'd let his career stagnate. Or maybe no one would let him take the next step.

She went to introduce herself and found she was talking to Tony Griggs: the same guy who'd been present when Ralph Cairncross's body had been pulled from the Forty Foot Drain. He gave her the standard protective gear and she dragged it on before ducking under their tape.

'Don't come too close,' Tony said. 'We're still photographing the footprints.'

She nodded, looking at the tracks in the snow. One lot came from smallish shoes and went straight from the back door to the store, and then back again. A second lot came at the store from round the side of the house, from a gap in the hedge. Presumably they belonged to the person who'd locked Sadie Cairncross in. Another set – which matched those – went from the store to the house and then back to the same point in the hedge. And a third came from the house to the store and back again.

The store itself was a windowless, insulated shed-like structure tacked onto the side of the house.

'All sealed up to protect what's inside,' another of the forensic team said, 'but there's an air con system.' He pointed to the footprints. 'Looks like our perpetrator went indoors to switch it off before they left. We're looking at the footprints inside and checking for fingerprints.'

Tara nodded. 'Would switching the air con off have been enough to put Mrs Cairncross at risk of suffocation?'

Tony frowned. 'Eventually, maybe – but I'd guess it would have taken a while. We'll be doing tests to check.'

It sounded as though someone had wanted to mimic the death in Ralph Cairncross's book, but they'd gone about it in an inept way. Yet there'd been nothing inept about the way their perpetrator had handled the previous deaths…

'Whether there was a threat of suffocation or not, it must have given her a hell of shock,' Tony said. 'Especially if she's even remotely claustrophobic.'

There was no denying that.

CHAPTER THIRTY-SEVEN

'We'd like to speak to you separately,' Blake said. He was standing in the sitting room.

The woman who'd been introduced to him as Philippa Cairncross looked mutinous. He wasn't entirely surprised. Her mother had still been hyperventilating when they'd turned up.

'She's none the worse, overall,' a doctor was saying. 'It's been a shock, of course, but she'll be fine.'

'How can she be fine when someone tried to kill her?' Philippa said.

The doctor looked her straight in the eye. 'You'll be in shock too.'

Tim, the constable who'd been first on the scene, was still present. 'Why don't I make you and your mum another cup of tea, whilst she talks to my colleagues?' he said. 'You show me where everything is.'

Philippa pulled a sour face, but at last she let the officer lead her from the room. The doctor followed them out too. 'I can come again if you need me,' she said, glancing at Sadie over her shoulder. Mrs Cairncross nodded absently.

Blake sat down opposite her, and Patrick took an adjacent chair.

'Tell us exactly what happened,' Blake said.

Mrs Cairncross stared into space. 'I had a phone call from Dr Richardson this morning,' she said. 'He's an academic expert on Ralph's work. He said he'd been told my husband had a manuscript by a writer I'd never heard of, filed away in the archive store. He'd agreed to write a scholarly paper about this person and asked if I would mind him borrowing the manuscript if I could find it.'

Blake remembered Tara telling him about Dr Richardson, and relaying his detailed knowledge of Cairncross's books and contacts.

'And you went to look for the manuscript straight away?' he said. 'That was why you were in the store when the intruder turned up?'

The woman nodded. 'Dr Richardson said it was urgent. Someone else had dropped out of a conference that was happening in two days' time. He said he was sorry to trouble me, but if I was able to find it, could he possibly come and pick it up later this morning? So I went straight off to search.' Her breathing was still shallow.

'And what happened then?'

'I fetched the key to the archive – it's kept hanging up in the kitchen – and then went and unlocked it. I left the door ajar, even though it's so cold. It's always struck me as airless in there when the door's closed. The storage is all on the wall that adjoins the house, opposite the entrance to the store, so my back was to the door as I began to search. It was then that I heard it slam behind me. And I found I couldn't get out. I'd left the key in the lock on the outside, and someone must have turned it.'

'That must have been terrifying.' Blake ignored Patrick's look. He thought the circumstances were odd too, but he wanted Mrs Cairncross's full cooperation. 'Were you able to call for help? Did you have your mobile on you?'

She shook her head. 'I keep it in my handbag. Most of my skirts don't have pockets.' Her eyes were far away for a moment. 'Ralph always said they ruined the line, and he was right, of course. But it's still stupidly impractical.'

But she might easily have had it with her. And any intruder would have been aware of that...

'What about your daughter?' said Patrick.

'She was out,' Sadie said. 'She'd gone into town.'

'Didn't she do that yesterday?' Wilkins snapped, hostility clear in his tone.

But it didn't seem so very odd. It wasn't far, and Blake imagined Philippa would feel cooped-up in this cavernous, shadowy house, day after day. He'd want to get out if it were him.

'She still had more Christmas shopping to do,' Sadie said. There were tears in her eyes. 'I wasn't sure when she'd be back.' She looked at Blake. 'She'd told me she might stay out for lunch. It was probably panic, but I felt breathless almost immediately. I didn't know how long I could last in there before I passed out. I thumped on the door, and shouted, but our gardens are so big, I didn't think the neighbours would hear me. I hoped Dr Richardson would come round the back when he got no reply at the door. But at the same time, I was scared he'd just think I'd forgotten and leave again.'

Blake and Patrick exchanged a glance and Sadie Cairncross picked up on it. 'It's true that I only went in there because of his call, but I don't see how he could have been the one to lock me in. And why would he, anyway?'

Indeed, and if he hadn't... 'Do you know him well, Mrs Cairncross?' Blake said.

'No, not really. We've spoken a couple of times maybe, at the odd book launch.'

'So, tell us,' Patrick said, 'what made your daughter come home early after all?' He glanced at his watch. 'It isn't even one o'clock yet. If she was going in to finish her Christmas shopping I'd have thought she'd have needed longer.'

'She called me.' Sadie took her phone from her bag and showed it to them. 'She'd seen a pair of boots she thought I might like as a present, so she sent me a photo of them. When I didn't text back she called. And when I didn't answer – either my mobile or the house phone – she got worried. She came back straight away and found me.'

'Was the key still in the door of the store?' Blake said.

Sadie shook her head. 'Philippa said not. There's a spare and she used that.'

Philippa's story tied in exactly with her mother's. She said she'd been to the shoe shop where the boots were sold and 'a few other places'. She'd wandered in and out. When they'd asked her for specifics she'd said she couldn't remember.

Back at the station, Tara, Patrick, Max and Megan were caught up in a flurry of fact checking.

A couple of hours later, Blake called everyone together.

'What's the situation now? Patrick, do you want to start?'

'As you know, sir, mother and daughter's stories match – very precisely. So much so that they come across as rehearsed.'

'Fair comment.' Blake said. 'But it might be as well to leave the theories until we've been through the facts.' He didn't want his DS colouring everyone else's judgement.

Wilkins frowned. 'Meanwhile, Dr Richardson denies making the call, claims not to know anything about the manuscript Sadie Cairncross was searching for, and insists he hasn't been invited to attend any last-minute conference.'

'Sadie Cairncross said herself that she doesn't know Dr Richardson well,' Blake added, 'so if someone rang pretending to be him, it's unlikely that she'd have noticed the voice wasn't right. What about the number of the caller?'

'It was a mobile,' Max said. 'We're trying to track down the retailer who sold the sim card and the phone. We should have that information before the day's out, but it could well be a prepaid one that's untraceable.'

'Nothing's come back yet from the team interviewing people on Madingley Road,' Patrick said. 'We're after anyone who might have witnessed a person entering the Cairncross property through the hedge. There's a footpath on the other side. It's used by dog walkers, so the snow's been trodden down there. It's hard to make out any footprints outside the garden to help us judge where the intruder came from or went to.' He looked round at them. 'If there *was* an intruder. The staff at the shoe shop Philippa claims to have visited don't remember seeing her.'

'Though they said the shop was very busy,' Tara put in, 'didn't they? And there was the photo she messaged to her mother, of the boots she wanted her to look at.'

Blake saw the look Patrick gave her. How could the team work with the two of them like this?

'Yes,' his DS said at last. 'But she could have taken that the day before. We should apply for a warrant and get the techs to look at her mobile. And on top of the shop staff not remembering her, she had no receipts for any purchases today. Only those from yesterday. I'll be interested to see the shop's CCTV footage.'

'You're thinking this is all staged?' Blake said. 'Because one or other of them – most likely Philippa – is guilty of being involved in the other deaths, and they want to make themselves look like victims?'

'Easy enough to buy a disposable mobile, make the fake call, and stomp around the garden in boots that aren't yours. If there was a genuine would-be murderer at work today they were pretty useless. Mrs Cairncross might easily have taken her mobile with her into the archive store, enabling her to call for help and be out of there again in five minutes.'

Blake hated it when Wilkins had thoughts that independently echoed his own. It worried him.

'But those mistakes are almost too much, wouldn't you say?' asked Tara. 'Surely Philippa would have noticed the same holes you're picking up on, and have made the arrangements more believable? She's no fool.' She paused, and Blake watched a frown trace itself across her brow. 'It's certainly true, though, that this plan seemed far more likely to fail than the others our perpetrator has tried. It's like a crude copy, still with a reference to one of Ralph

Cairncross's books. There was no attempt to hide the involvement of a third party. But maybe that's deliberate.' They all looked at her, but she seemed unfazed. 'So far, Philippa Cairncross has looked guilty, and this latest development accentuates that impression. We're all sitting here wondering if today's drama was a set-up. But maybe that was the real killer's intention all along. Perhaps we're drawing just the conclusions they want us to, and this latest development wasn't so clumsily engineered after all.'

'Nice try,' Patrick said. 'But if so, how could the killer be sure Philippa would come home in time to save her mother? Without that intervention Sadie Cairncross might really have died.'

Tara's pause was longer this time, but eventually her expression cleared. 'We've always said the person's a gambler. Maybe for them it was a win-win situation after all. Either Sadie Cairncross lives, and it looks like a put-up job between her and her daughter, or she dies, and another person they have cause to resent – for whatever reason – is wiped out.'

That was all possible too, but Blake knew how much Tara wanted Patrick to be wrong. Did she really think her version of events was the most likely one, or was her animosity influencing her judgement?

'Another interesting theory.' Patrick's tone was mocking. 'Personally, I still doubt that anyone else was involved in the other deaths. But I think we've got Sadie and Philippa Cairncross convinced that someone was. And that's been enough. They're frightened that we think they're responsible, so they've cooked up this plan to make themselves look innocent.'

'Not Sadie, surely?' Tara said. 'Her shock looked genuine to me.'

'We should talk to her doctor again,' Blake said. 'Do that, would you, Max? See if she thinks Sadie Cairncross could have faked her reaction.'

'If they didn't cook up the incident together, then I'm betting Philippa acted alone,' Wilkins said. 'She's very hard-nosed.'

'Though she'd have known she was frightening her mother half to death,' Tara said. 'Would she have done that willingly? She seems to mind about her.'

'Philippa might have felt that was better than the alternative,' Wilkins said. 'If she ends up in jail she'll leave her mother shamed and alone.'

Blake held up a hand. 'But with reference to your idea of the other deaths being innocent and coincidental, Patrick, I have an update too. Forensics have come back on the crate Tara and I found behind the house on the Forty Foot Bank. It gives us proof that someone kept a grass snake in there, and there are traces of what they gave it to eat, too: crickets, apparently. So they clearly kept it for a little while. There's a plot all right. How far it goes is still up for debate.' He looked at his DS. 'The Cairncross mother and daughter might yet have staged this morning's attack. I could believe that. But the story on *Not Now*'s website – with its allusions to fairy tales – was way off the mark. And pretty soon, everyone's going to know that.'

He glanced at Tara, knowing it would be the first time she'd heard the news too. He watched the relief flood over her face; he was right with her. Fleming had looked pretty chirpy about it as well. He was guessing they'd all be having a celebratory drink tonight.

Except Patrick…

CHAPTER THIRTY-EIGHT

Like everyone else, Tara was chasing facts. Had Philippa been seen in town? Who had sold the phone used to contact Sadie Cairncross, when, and to whom? Had it been used to call any other numbers? What had the neighbours on Madingley Road seen? The more holes they could pick in Sadie and Philippa Cairncross's story, the better the case became against Philippa.

But Tara still wasn't convinced. When the coast was clear she slipped outside to call Dr Richardson. She was after insight and opinion rather than hard facts – but she reckoned it would be time well spent.

Of course, she knew he could have been lying when he'd denied ringing Sadie Cairncross that morning. He could have used a new phone, made the call from just outside the house on Madingley Road, crouched behind the garden's perimeter hedge and watched as Sadie had entered the store. He might have been the one to cross the garden, leaving those footprints in the snow, and lock her in. Someone had, whether they'd been for real or staging the whole incident. But Tara couldn't think why he would. Yes, he'd mocked Ralph Cairncross's ideas – hadn't liked him much perhaps – but there'd been no animosity in his voice when Tara had interviewed him. He seemed to view Cairncross and his Acolytes as a collective curiosity, nothing more. And he was far less likely to be responsible for the series of deaths. He wouldn't have influence over Lucas Everett and Christian Beatty, or have had an obvious opportunity to put the snake in Ralph's car.

So, satisfied that he wasn't involved, she called him, and knew she'd give weight to what he said. She stood outside, looking over Parker's Piece, crowded with young children and dogs playing in the snow. Her breath clouded the air and her hands felt numb as she dialled Richardson's number.

'*Good to speak to you again,*' he said, when she got through. '*This is a bit of a business, isn't it?*'

'That's one way of putting it. I just wanted to get your take on our mystery caller. I realise it'll be speculation, but is there anything that struck you about what Sadie Cairncross claims she was asked to find from the store? Sadie never got as far as actually searching for the manuscript, for obvious reasons. Do you know if it's something that really exists?'

'*My mind's been running along similar lines,*' Dr Richardson said. '*And I've been trying to check. It's not something I've heard of, and I can't find any record of it existing in the standard databases and academic reviews, so it's possible your caller made it up.*'

'But they didn't invent the writer?' Tara had read the interview transcript. Sadie Cairncross had said it was someone she'd never heard of.

'*Oh no,*' Richardson said. '*The writer's real all right. But he's very obscure. And that's interesting in itself. Whoever dreamt up the mission they sent Sadie Cairncross on wouldn't have stumbled across Maurice Fox-Thompson's name very easily. But he is the kind of writer Ralph would have collected – he had a thing about youth too – and he only published a very few poetry pamphlets and essays. It looks as though whoever placed the call had also studied the literature Ralph was interested in. To the same obsessive degree as he did, it seems.*'

As Tara walked back into the station, she realised Richardson's news didn't help Philippa's case. She was studying literature at university and had ready access to all of her father's papers. She could have researched his academic interests. And if her father really possessed any of Maurice Fox-Thompson's works she might even have seen them. But that applied to Tess Curtis too. She'd clearly been very involved in her employer's work. If he'd ever corresponded with Fox-Thompson she'd probably know about it – and more than likely have been the one to file his works in the archive store if Cairncross had ever acquired any. She'd have needed an accomplice though, to make the call to Sadie Cairncross. She'd been a constant presence in the household until six months ago. Even if she'd been able to convincingly mimic a man, Tara was sure she wouldn't have risked her voice being recognised. But it could have been she who locked Sadie Cairncross in. She wondered where Tess Curtis had been that morning. Someone needed to check – it was no use going after Philippa to the exclusion of all others.

She knocked on Blake's door, knowing she wouldn't get any kind of hearing from Wilkins, and relayed her call with Richardson and her thoughts about Ralph's former PA. Blake's dark eyes looked thoughtful. 'Yes,' he said. 'We need to interview her again. But I've just had Max in here too. He's checked Philippa Cairncross's record on the Police National Computer. Three years ago, Ralph Cairncross reported criminal damage to his car.'

'What kind of damage?'

'Someone had been piercing his tyres.'

'Piercing?' She'd come across people getting their tyres slashed.

Blake nodded. 'Cairncross didn't even know what was happening at first, they just kept going flat. The garage checked it out and found holes caused by a tough, needle-like object. It was too much of a coincidence when precisely the same type of puncture mark was inflicted on the replacement tyre as well as the original. There was nothing in the family garage that could have caused the damage accidentally, and Cairncross hadn't visited the same locations twice on the two tyres either.'

'And they found Philippa was responsible?'

'Ralph caught her at it, brought her into the station and made her explain to the officer in charge what she'd done.'

'Sounds like an annoying prank, undertaken by a rebellious teen,' Tara said.

'Sounds like, yes. But piercing the tyres that way causes them to deflate slowly, so that a driver might head off thinking their vehicle's perfectly roadworthy, only to realise later that they've got a problem. And damage like that causes an outside possibility of a blowout. On top of that, each time the tyres were sabotaged, Cairncross was due to head off on an extended motorway journey. So, you see that this new evidence is very damaging for Philippa.'

She did. And it was the same modus operandi she'd noted herself in their perpetrator – that willingness to take a gamble; to do something that might or might not kill the victim. 'How rare would a blow-out be, under those circumstances?' she asked.

'Pretty rare,' Blake said. 'It was far less dangerous than putting a snake into a drunk man's car late at night. And Philippa might not even have known the possibilities. She was only fifteen at the time, and not yet a driver herself. But' – he met Tara's eyes – 'on the other hand, maybe she was just getting warmed up.' He moved closer to her, coming round from behind his desk. 'I think you're right, and we should check Tess Curtis out too. This isn't case closed. But I can also imagine that you're royally pissed off with Patrick. I know he's rubbished your every move on this case, and if he's right about Philippa now, after letting you do all the work, it's going to be galling. But we have to go into this completely neutral.'

As if she couldn't rise above what she thought of Wilkins. She wanted him to lose, but she wanted justice and the truth more.

Blake must have read the look in her eye. 'I know what you're thinking,' he said. 'And I trust you. But right now, Philippa Cairncross deserves the attention she's getting. We've got no reason to suppose our perpetrator's working with an accomplice. And would

Tess Curtis have had enough influence over Lucas and Christian to get them to do what they did?'

But Tess Curtis was a good-looking and intelligent woman, and she'd have had time to build relationships in the group. Her planned writing venture with Christian Beatty proved that.

Tara's mobile rang. Blake nodded and she picked up. Verity Hipkiss. She sounded slurred and emotional. Tara guessed she'd been drinking, although it was only five o'clock. 'What can I do for you?' Tara said.

'I saw the report in Not Now,*'* she answered. *'I mean, I knew the ideas you were working on already, of course.'* There was a long pause. *'But seeing it all laid out like that, in black and white – the snake and all the deaths being linked…'*

Described in the most sensational way possible by Shona bloody Kennedy…

'It just made me think about what's happened afresh, in a more clear-headed way.'

She sounded anything but.

'I've been having a think, and I'd like to talk to you again. I've got some ideas.'

'Couldn't you tell me over the phone?'

Another long pause. *'I'm worried. I'd really like a proper chat. I need to get my thoughts in order. Can you come? I don't think I should drive.'*

Tara didn't think so either. 'Where are you?'

'I'm at the house on the bank. I just stopped by to relive old times. It's peaceful here.'

Tara sighed. 'I'll be there as soon as I can.'

Blake raised an eyebrow and she told him. 'It's bad timing. I'd rather go to Tess Curtis,' she said.

'I can see why. And someone definitely does need to go to her. But maybe Verity's more likely to open up to you than anyone else from the team – after all, it's you she rang.' He paused. 'I've told Patrick I'll go back with him to interview Philippa and Sadie Cairncross again. Why don't you take Max and go to Verity via Tess Curtis, so you can check her alibi for this morning en route?'

She nodded. 'All right.'

Tess Curtis was still at work when they rang her, finishing up an afternoon on duty for Professor Trent-Purvis. He'd had a soirée for other academics that day, and she insisted she couldn't see them until they'd gone home.

'The professor can't possibly talk to them all at once,' she'd said. 'I'm circulating too, and handing out the drinks.'

When Tara had tried to ask about her movements that morning over the phone she'd immediately got cross and told her she'd have to wait. She sounded rattled.

So Tara and Max sat in the car, outside the professor's grand house in Newnham – with its tall windows and wide entrance – for the optimistic ten minutes Tess Curtis had reckoned it would take to wind things up. There were still four cars on the drive: a Jaguar, a Mercedes, an Audi and a Volvo. Presumably at least one of the cars was owned by the professor, but the rest must belong to stragglers, unless Tess herself had driven the short distance across town.

After five more minutes, Tara was getting fidgety. Verity Hipkiss had sounded very drunk. She might have just wanted company, and not have useful information at all. But she'd been the most closely involved with Ralph – his lover. Out of all the people who might know more or remember something significant, she was one of the most promising.

Then again, Tess Curtis was in the thick of it too. Could she have an accomplice who'd made the phone call that morning? Tara remembered the contraceptives in her bathroom cabinet. A lover?

Either way, she didn't want to leave without checking her alibi. At last she turned to Max. 'How would you feel about staying here, in the freezing cold, to wait for Tess Curtis, whilst I carry on to the house on the bank?'

He grinned. 'I've got gloves. She is taking her time, isn't she?' He opened up the passenger door and clambered out.

'Thanks, Max. Let me know what happens.'

He nodded. 'You'll know as soon as I do.'

CHAPTER THIRTY-NINE

Philippa Cairncross's story of what had happened earlier that day didn't waver. Her steady look met Blake's as she repeated what she'd told them that morning.

'Take us back to when you vandalised your dad's car tyres,' Blake said, without warning.

Philippa flushed, but it was anger, not shame, that much he could see. 'That was years ago. I was just a kid.'

'What made you do it?'

'I was angry with him.' Her voice had dropped to a whisper now. 'It was just after I found out that mum's facial injuries were down to botched plastic surgery. His fake ideals had skewed her views on life and cost her her career and her happiness.'

'What did you think would happen, as a result of puncturing his tyres?'

There was a pause, and she shrugged. 'I hated him,' she said. 'And I mean really hated. I didn't think through what might happen. I just wanted to hurt him the way he'd hurt mum.' Her fierce stare met his. 'I'm not sorry he's dead. Not for an instant. But whatever I feel now, and whatever I did back then, I'm not involved in what happened to him in September.'

'And what are your feelings towards the Acolytes?' Blake asked.

'He knows.' Philippa tossed her head in Patrick's direction. 'He was there when I said what I thought of them all. A waste of space. But there are lots of people in this world who are just that. I'd spend the rest of my life trying to wipe them all out, if that was my aim.'

'You lumped them all together, then,' Blake said. 'You didn't feel any of them were less worthy of your contempt than others?' He wondered just how well she'd known them. Did she really understand their individual personalities? If she was the perpetrator, she must surely have studied them closely enough to see the way their minds worked. The killer had obviously been confident that they could persuade Lucas to swim out to sea, and Christian to show off and take that leap.

'I could tell they were all as bad as each other,' she said. 'And I don't believe they really cared about Ralph. Last laugh's on him for leaving them that vast house "to carry on living by his ideals" or whatever it was. It was almost as though he'd started to believe his own tosh. If he meant the fake ideals he peddled in his books, then no way will they do that. But perhaps he was alluding to his true guiding principles, in which case I think he's in luck. Just like him they'll carry on working for their own ends, using their association with my father to further their careers. They strike me as a self-serving bunch.'

She seemed to be generalising – perhaps based on things she'd overheard – rather than displaying a more intimate knowledge of members of the group. But he could be wrong. 'Didn't one of them try to stop your dad from setting off, the night he died? It's in the police report. That must mean they were looking out for his safety.'

Philippa looked scornful. 'Snooty Stephen? Yes, I remember hearing that. Fat lot of good it did. My father didn't like fussing.'

'And what about Verity Hipkiss?'

'I'm sure she just slept with my dad so he'd big up her work. He'd done that job, so I imagine she was planning to move on pretty quickly – if she hadn't already. I don't suppose she was exclusive. He really was a fool if he thought she actually liked him.'

'But there was Letty too.' And she'd been younger, less cynical perhaps.

'She was a pale-faced, mock-innocent drip,' Philippa said. 'I met her at a party once, exchanged two words and reached my conclusion.'

All the hate and motivation were there, Blake reflected, but something didn't ring true. Philippa Cairncross was full of bluster. She was letting her feelings out. But Blake had the notion that the person they wanted was someone who'd bottled things up; who plotted and planned in isolation, standing by quietly, ready to wreak havoc.

CHAPTER FORTY

Once Tara left the main road the feeling of fenland isolation set in. The evening was clear and the more minor byways needed careful handling. Snow and ice melt had left the surfaces damp during the day, and now everything had frozen hard again. At first the road had taken her through a deserted residential area, but she'd left that behind now. Through the darkness she was aware of flat, lonely fields to the left and right. There seemed to be no one else on the roads. It was after six now. People had probably come home from work early, to avoid the hazardous conditions they knew would take hold as the cold intensified.

As she drove she tried to keep her focus on the road, but part of her mind was always spooling through what they knew so far. She tried again to justify her gut feeling that Philippa was innocent. Or, at least, not guilty of this series of crimes. No one could call her innocent, per se. Was Blake right? Was she simply baulking at the idea because Wilkins was so keen to prove Philippa guilty? There was plenty of evidence against her.

But there were multiple small things, on top of gut instinct, that made Tara hesitate. What about finding the grass snake, for instance? It wasn't as though the Cairncross's place had a stream running through its garden. If Tara had wanted to find such a creature, she'd have come to the Fens to do it. Had Philippa really travelled out here, day after day in the early autumn, to try to catch the creature she wanted? And then contained it in a crate that matched the others that had been abandoned to rot at the house on the bank?

And then, of course, Philippa would have to have fed it until it was time to put it in her father's car. That would have involved quite a lot of creeping around the place, trying not to be seen by regulars at the house. Tess, or any of the Acolytes, would have had less difficulty with both those tasks. And that included Verity Hipkiss, the woman she was on her way to see… Tara was glad Verity was drunk; and that her own self defence-skills were sound. Unless the woman was a secret martial arts expert, Tara ought to be safe enough.

At that moment her phone rang. She touched the control to answer handsfree.

'Tara Thorpe.'

'It's Max.' The line wasn't great. Coverage in the Fens was patchy.

'Go ahead, Max. How'd it go with Tess Curtis?'

'She was "in and out" all morning, so she says, fetching groceries and the like for her employer's do. She'd got the receipts, but there's nothing to say she didn't nip round to Madingley Road and lock Sadie Cairncross into the archive store between errands. All the same, the times on the bills mean she'd have to have been quick.'

And someone would have had to make the call for her… 'Hmm. That's interesting. Thanks. I'm nearly at the Forty Foot Bank now, so I'll be able to update you on Verity Hipkiss soon, too.'

'Great,' Max said. *'I'll follow on now I've finished with Curtis; I just need to pick up a car from the station. I've got one more bit of news, too. The number used to call Sadie Cairncross this morning was also found on Lucas Everett and Christian Beatty's phones. Neither of them had bothered adding it to their contact lists, so we still don't know who was using it.'*

'Wow. Thanks, Max.'

That was evidence that one person was linked to all three incidents at least. It made the theory that Wilkins was still clinging to – of the two men's deaths being unrelated acts of misadventure –

look pathetic. But Tess Curtis's involvement also looked less likely now. *You win some, you lose some.*

She was deep in thought, but still conscious of the bridge she was crossing and the dark waters of the Forty Foot Drain below. Immediately afterwards, she made the turn onto the bank.

She crawled along the icy road, wishing she wasn't so close to the water-filled drain to her left. She could feel the changes in traction under her wheels. One minute things felt reasonably sure, the next she was gripping the steering wheel and slowing down still further to ensure she had control. She knew you were meant to steer into a skid, but if she slipped towards the water, it would be nigh-on impossible to override her instincts and follow that advice.

She tried to focus on the remaining suspects. What about Thom King's near miss? It matched a death in one of Cairncross's books, but in other respects it seemed different from the 'accidents' that had befallen Ralph, Christian and Lucas. It was an act of direct violence, where the perpetrator would have risked injuring themselves too. With the other incidents, the plotter could have remained relatively detached, but knocking someone down in a car was a whole different ball game. So why the variation? Had the near miss been a coincidence? Or had Thom made it up? Or if not, had the killer had a different mindset back then? Maybe they'd made that one, rash attempt in advance of the others for some reason, but then taken a step back, cooled down and rethought their approach? If so, what had made them lose control that day when they'd tried to mow Thom King down? And crucially, who had known where to find him? It must have been someone who knew the whereabouts of the studio he'd only just rented.

She tried to think of the timelines. If the near miss had really happened it must have been back in late summer. Thom had mentioned it had been just after Letty had died. It was the reason he'd given for not making a fuss – that and the fact that he couldn't remember much about the car or the driver. But would he really have left the matter unreported if he'd believed it had been a deliberate attempt to knock him down?

At last, she saw the sign for the house on the bank, swinging in the icy breeze. She made the turn, relieved to be away from the water.

How the hell would she make the journey back again, when conditions would be even worse?

CHAPTER FORTY-ONE

Blake was talking to a security manager at a boutique just off the market square in the centre of Cambridge. Before they'd left Philippa Cairncross, he'd had one more go at impressing upon her the importance of proving she'd been into town that morning. It wouldn't necessarily put her in the clear, depending on the times involved, but they had to start somewhere. She was leading them a merry dance. He got the impression she didn't give a damn what they thought or how much of their time she wasted.

But Blake had spotted her Achilles heel: she cared about her mother. When he'd threatened to take her in, charge her and keep her overnight, Sadie had collapsed into a chair, and Philippa had finally got the message. And then it turned out that she could remember the other shops she'd visited. Either that, or she'd done some hasty inventing under pressure. With a sour expression on her lips, she'd reeled off the names of three outlets, including the one he was now standing in.

'Be my guest,' the security guard said, and Blake scanned the shop's CCTV for the times when Philippa said she might have been there. The place had been far less crowded than the shoe shop and the cameras better sited.

At last he saw a familiar figure on the footage. Bloody hell. She really had been there. He checked the time. Fifteen minutes after Sadie Cairncross had received the mystery call. That was it. There was no way she could have got home in time to lock her mother in the archive store and then get back to the shop. She could still have done it if her mother had been in on the whole thing too, of course. If that were the case, she could have locked her in any time – it might have been a while later than they claimed – or indeed not at all. They could simply have made all the right footprints and left it at that. But that didn't work. Her mother's shock had been genuine, from what the medics said. They'd had to treat her for a full-blown panic attack. She wouldn't have had that reaction if she'd known she was never in danger.

No. Blake reckoned Philippa Cairncross was out of it. And Tess Curtis was sounding unlikely, from Max's latest update.

They needed to think again. Patrick wasn't going to be pleased. Tara had been right about him latching onto Philippa too quickly, though wrong about Tess Curtis's possible guilt as far as he could see.

He called Patrick and was pleased when he was forced to leave a message. He didn't feel like dealing with him right now. He was still one of Blake's top suspects for leaking that story to *Not Now* magazine. He only wished he could prove it.

As he stepped out of the shop's doorway, onto the pedestrian walkway next to the university church, Great St Mary's, he wondered how Tara was doing. Max had explained how he'd had to let her make the visit to Verity Hipkiss alone. The going would be unpleasant out in the Fens. And if Philippa Cairncross wasn't their killer, nor Tess Curtis, then who was?

He thought afresh about putting the snake into Ralph Cairncross's car. Now he knew Philippa was out of it, the possibility of someone who'd been at the party doing the job seemed most likely.

He made up his mind to follow Tara and find out first-hand what Verity Hipkiss had to say.

CHAPTER FORTY-TWO

Tara pulled up on the wide, rough driveway outside the house on the bank. It was still rutted with ice-hardened snow. Very little light spilled out from the house onto the forecourt. Verity had the curtains closed.

Tara pulled her coat tightly around her and went up to knock on the door. Whilst she waited for Verity to appear she heard something crash inside. When at last the door opened, the woman leant against the frame. Tara wondered if she'd drunk more since she'd called earlier. Behind her, she could see a vase that had smashed on the floor. The table it had presumably sat on was tipped up on one leg and rested precariously against the wall. Tara guessed Verity had cannoned into it on her way to open up.

'Are you okay?'

Verity's eyes were red and puffy. She nodded and put out a hand, clutching at Tara's coat sleeve. 'I'm so glad you're here. I thought you might have decided not to come and I need to talk to someone. I think I might know who's behind all this.' She stepped back into the hall. 'Because it's not just a coincidence, is it?'

Tara followed her in and closed the door on the night behind her. Once again, she noticed that the place hadn't been well maintained. There were damp patches on the wall of the hallway.

'I mean,' Verity went on, 'when you and DS Wilkins came to see me, you said you were just being cautious, going round interviewing us all, and warning us to be on our guard. But that was so we didn't get scared, wasn't it? You knew something was up. You took that crate away, didn't you? That means you were looking for proper evidence of some kind.' Her eyes were glassy. 'The article in *Not Now* mentioned a snake. Was that where it was kept? In the crate?'

She turned on her heel and led Tara along a corridor. 'There's an upstairs sitting room,' she said, one hand on the polished newel post at the bottom of the stairs. 'It's warmer up there.'

Tara followed her. 'It's true that we're increasingly sure someone else was involved in the deaths of Ralph, Lucas and Christian,' she said carefully. The release of the information in *Not Now* had been a disaster. Up until then they could have interviewed each of Ralph Cairncross's contacts until one of them slipped up and mentioned a detail they shouldn't know. But thanks to Shona Kennedy the whole of Cambridge and beyond now had access to details that ought to have been under wraps. Was that really how Verity knew about the snake, or had she been more intimately involved in the drama? She could have had an accomplice – a new lover, keen to replace Ralph, who'd put the snake in his car whilst Verity kept him busy. That same man could have called Sadie Cairncross. It was still possible she'd wanted Lucas and Christian dead because of what they could reveal about her: her affair with Ralph.

Ahead of Tara, Verity stumbled. She was wearing a long, floaty dress, insubstantial for the weather. She had a soft woollen cardigan – *cashmere?* – slung round her shoulders. After a second, she caught her elbow on the wall and paused again. Even if she was guilty, Tara didn't think she was much of a threat. If she was acting, she was doing a bloody good job. And if there was anyone else in the house – an accomplice perhaps – then Tara was primed and ready. It was good to know Max was on his way, though.

At the top of the stairs, everything was in near darkness.

'Where's the light switch, Verity?' Tara said.

'Bulb's gone.'

But something was shedding low levels of light onto the landing. The effect was flickering and guttering, a warm glow.

'Verity, stop.'

The woman looked at her dazedly over her shoulder. 'What's wrong?'

Fire. That was Tara's immediate thought. The final method of death in Ralph Cairncross's books. Her heart beat faster. Tara was great at self-defence – quick in the face of danger – but fire was something else. But even as she had the thought she realised this was something on a smaller scale. 'You've lit candles?'

Verity nodded. 'It's three months to the day since Ralph died. That's one of the reasons I came over here. To feel close to him.' She shrugged her elegant shoulders. 'I come from a Catholic family, so I lit a candle.'

Several, by the look of the light spilling onto the landing.

Verity was stumbling ahead again, through a door and into a room that was indeed full of candles. Her long dress swept past one she'd set on the floor, on a white saucer. The flame danced and weakened in the draught created by her movement, but then sprang up again.

'Careful, Verity,' Tara said sharply, wetting her finger and thumb and putting the flame out. 'It's not safe to leave them burning on the floor.' But there were more. Everywhere she looked. Night lights, large pillar-shaped ones of the sort you saw in cathedrals, old ones, already half burnt down. Verity had lined them along a window seat, next to aged velvet curtains that moved slightly in a draught from the sash.

'God, Verity, you'll have the whole place up in flames,' Tara said, going to put out the candles near the window.

'Please leave the rest,' Verity said. 'I'll sit down, and you sit too. We won't disturb them then. I wanted to mark the occasion.'

Tara sat on a slouchy blue corduroy sofa, her heart thumping in her chest, her palms clammy. On the wall next to her was a montage of photographs in frames. They were of Ralph and his Acolytes. They weren't all group shots. Some were of the individual members on their own. There was one of Verity wearing only a towel, her hair tousled, lips pouting. Someone – Ralph presumably – had scrawled 'My voluptuous Verity' across her shoulder in marker pen, and added a kiss. It made Tara's skin crawl. Somehow, it was as though he'd marked her as his.

'Ralph took that one,' Verity said. She must have followed the direction of Tara's gaze. 'He took all of them – except the ones where he's present, of course.'

'Who took those?'

'Letty took the one of him there.' Verity pointed at a head and shoulders shot, where Ralph had raised his hand and blown a kiss in the direction of the lens.

Tara reacted to her tone and looked at her face. There was jealousy there. 'Letty was very young, wasn't she?'

'Very. Far too young for Ralph.' She gave an elaborate roll of her eyes. 'It was unsuitable.' The final word came out loudly – she still seemed very drunk.

Tara scanned the wall of photos again. There were a couple of gaps, she noticed, and no photos of Letty on her own. 'Did you take the portraits of Letty down?' she said.

But Verity shook her head. 'Stephen did.' She squinted at Tara. 'They're still here though.' She twisted where she sat and reached towards a bookcase to her right. She reached in amongst the volumes on the top shelf and pulled out three photographs, handing them to Tara. 'Far too young,' she said again as she sat back on the sofa and closed her eyes.

The first photo Tara looked at showed the same girl she'd seen in the group shot in the Cairncross family kitchen. But something had happened between when the two photographs were taken, Tara guessed. The carefree kid-sister look, full of easy laughter, had gone.

In this portrait, Letty looked uncertain, her lips parted. The strappy dress she wore was coming down off one shoulder. The shot was taken outside, in the grounds of the house they were sitting in, by the look of it. Behind Letty, the sun shone, lighting up her red hair. Her pale skin was striking by contrast and Tara remembered Stephen Ross comparing her to a pre-Raphaelite painting. And then suddenly, Tara felt the hairs on her arms lift. She remembered Ross's poem 'To My Love at Evening Time'. Rubies and alabaster… Letty's *hair* and her skin? Evening time… because Letty had been dying? She remembered how weak Stephen had made the subject of the poem sound – and she'd thought the words must reflect his views on women in general. But if it had been about Letty, laid low by her illness…

Scrawled across the bottom of the photograph, in what was probably the same pen used to annotate Verity's picture, was 'My pretty Titty'.

Verity had her eyes open again. 'He always used that old-fashioned shortening of Letitia,' she said. 'Stephen hated it. That's why he took the pictures down.'

Small bits of information started to coalesce in Tara's head. Hadn't Stephen said he and Letty were the first people Ralph scooped up as his Acolytes? They'd been together at a party – something to do with the English department. She searched her memory. He'd said they'd shared the same tutor. But what else…? She took out her notebook, flicking back through the pages. He'd mentioned in passing that they'd known each other before they came to Cambridge. She'd forgotten that. And he'd said she was 'very bright and beautiful too'.

Memories shifted in Tara's head, like cogs in a machine that hadn't quite interlocked, but suddenly slipped into place. Again she thought of the photograph of the Acolytes and Ralph in the kitchen at Madingley Road. Stephen had had his arm around Letty's shoulders and he'd looked fierce. Had he felt he'd been defending Letty against something… the group she'd got sucked into?

'So, were Stephen and Letty an item, then, when they joined the Acolytes?' Tara said, watching Verity's face in the flickering light.

'He was in love with her,' Verity said, a note of irritation in her voice. 'But she was very young. I think she looked up to him as an adoring kid sister might hero-worship an older brother. He was so protective of her; even after she died he was more interested in her than anyone else.'

And this girl was the subject of Ralph Cairncross's final dedication, according to Tess Curtis.

To T, who managed to escape unscathed. You are blessed indeed.

Had Stephen guessed that his Letty was the T in the dedication? If Ralph had called her Titty all the time, then surely it was likely. And then she remembered how Ralph had shared the manuscript of his final book with Stephen first. 'I knew there were elements he'd appreciate in a way that no one else could,' Ralph had said. He'd looked amused, but Stephen Ross had looked angry. Had Ralph been talking about the dedication? Had he known how it would make Stephen feel? He'd been a cruel man – you only had to talk to Philippa to understand that.

He'd been publicly celebrating the early death of the woman Stephen Ross had loved. All at once she remembered Bea's horror at the writer's thoughts on old age. His views on dying young wounded her, having just lost Greg. How must Stephen – dealing with Ralph first-hand – have felt? The interview would have been conducted a few short weeks after Letty's death.

'Stephen only really tagged along with the group to keep an eye on Letty,' Verity said, reaching to a side table to pour herself more brandy from a bottle she had next to her. 'I think he felt she was too young to hold her own if he left her to the rest of us. And yet she'd got Ralph wrapped round her little finger. It was such a shame when she got ill, but it was only then that Ralph started to pay attention to me.'

Had Stephen seen that? Had he noticed that Verity was a tiny bit glad that the girl he'd loved was out of the way?

'You said Stephen only stayed with the group to keep an eye on Letty,' Tara said, 'and yet he carried on as a member after she'd died.'

Verity sipped her brandy and frowned. 'That's true,' she said. 'I hadn't thought about it. I suppose by that stage he'd integrated himself. Though Lucas and Christian always thought of him as lesser, somehow. He wasn't such a strong physical specimen as them. But everyone indulged him.' She blinked. 'He can be a bit snooty at times – and taciturn too.'

She knocked back the rest of her drink and the candlelight flickered on her glass. 'Sorry,' she said after a moment, 'would you like one?'

Tara shook her head. If ever she'd felt the need to keep her wits about her it was now.

'I shouldn't be talking Stephen down though,' Verity said, leaning forward now, her expression becoming more focused. 'He's the reason I wanted to talk to you. We were speaking earlier today, and I told him what I think: that there's only one person who could be carrying out such an audacious plan. Who hates us all and who would have the power and the guts to do this.'

'And who's that?'

'Philippa, Ralph's daughter.'

Bloody hell, what was the obsession with her? 'What makes you say that?'

'I reckon she must have got round Lucas and Christian – and Stephen agrees. And she hated Ralph. And me for that matter,' Verity said. 'But what's most compelling is that she knew Ralph was afraid of snakes.'

'Wait a moment. He was? I hadn't heard that before.'

'Well, nor had I. Not until Stephen told me Philippa knew about his phobia.'

'So obviously Stephen knew too.'

Verity was losing focus again. 'He must have.'

'Verity!' Tara grabbed her arm and shook her. She opened her eyes once more. 'You said you and Stephen were talking. When? Where was this? Where is he now?'

She shrugged. 'He was here before. He helped me to light the candles. We talked, and when I said what I thought about Philippa he said I should call you, so I could tell you all about it.' She paused and blinked. 'And then he went off somewhere.'

Suddenly Tara thought of Thom King, and the person who'd tried to run him down. He'd said he hadn't gone on about it to Ralph and the Acolytes because it had been just after Letty had died, and they'd all been so low.

'Can you remember, Verity, how the other Acolytes reacted when Letty died?'

'Hum?' She licked her lips. 'Well, they followed Ralph's lead, of course. We had a ritual out here in the grounds to celebrate the fact that she'd still been in her prime and never withered. I'm not sure they all bought it really. They missed her. But they wanted to keep in with the group.'

Was that when Stephen had decided he wanted to get rid of the lot of them? When he saw them all celebrating the death of the woman he'd loved, who could have gone on to have had a long and happy life, if only she hadn't been so unlucky?

Had he heard Thom King banging on about this new studio, when all Stephen could think of was the dead girl he'd wanted to be with? Maybe he'd gone and waited for the artist, full of pent-up rage and sorrow, and driven straight at him. Perhaps the raw emotion he'd experienced had caused him to misjudge his approach. It hadn't worked out, but he hadn't let go of his plans to make them all pay. No wonder he'd stayed on in the group. He'd got unfinished business…

But – if all that were true – how the hell had he managed to persuade Lucas and Christian to take the actions that led to their deaths?

She reached for her phone. Whatever the answer, they needed to pick Stephen up. He'd been in the right place to find the snake, in between writing his poems at the house on the bank. He could have been the man who rang Sadie Cairncross to ask her to look for the Maurice Fox-Thompson poetry pamphlet.

Poetry. Another cog slotted into place. It was Stephen's field. And of course, if he'd become incensed about Ralph's attitude to dying young, he might well have obsessively read up on other writers with the same views. He'd said he'd been away camping when Lucas Everett had died – but camping alone. That now sounded like something arranged to muddy the waters. The campsite owner remembered him turning up and leaving, but it was a pretty anonymous way of spending a holiday. He could have come and gone at any stage in between without people noticing.

Max was on his way. He'd said he'd catch her up; he might want to divert now, to see if he could pick Stephen up at his home…

She called him and started to make her points. She spoke as quickly as she could, but she felt panicky, her chest tight, her breath short. Verity had roused herself and was at the window. Every time she moved, she was perilously close to the candles.

'Verity, careful,' she broke off from Max to say.

'Oh,' the woman said suddenly. She sounded puzzled.

'What is it?'

'He's out there…'

Tara was at her side in a second.

'What's going on?' Max asked.

But for just a moment, she couldn't speak. Down below, she could see Stephen. In the moonlight, it was hard to make out the detail. There seemed to be stuff piled up round the perimeter of the house. And he had something in his hand. She put her phone down to wrench the window open.

She was about to call to him when the smell hit her. And then she realised what he was holding.

She grabbed her phone again. *Shit. Shit.* 'Max, we need a fire engine and an ambulance to the house on the bank now. Stephen Ross is outside. He's piled up stuff that will burn round the edge of the house – he must already have been at it when I arrived.' She wished to God she'd had cause to look round outside before she'd come in. He must have pretty much cleared the outbuilding of the junk that had been dumped there. She recognised odds and bits below: tyres, beaten-up soft furnishings, crates and pallets… 'Max – he's holding a petrol can.'

Down below, Ross looked up at her. He lit a match and she saw his eyes glint in the flame.

CHAPTER FORTY-THREE

Blake was still ten miles from the Forty Foot Bank when he got Max's call. After the DC had explained the immediate danger he'd started to talk about Stephen Ross, but Blake hardly heard. He put on lights and sirens and slammed his foot to the floor. *Shit.* Ramsey and Chatteris were the two closest fire stations, but neither of them were staffed 24/7. The firefighters would be on call. And in weather like this, they might well be out on the road already, dealing with traffic accidents. Thank God the A142 he was travelling was a main route and reasonably ice-free.

The thought of the situation almost made him lose control. If Stephen Ross had already doused the entire perimeter of the house with petrol before Tara had phoned, and he'd added extra fuel to keep the fire going... It was all Blake could do to hold it together. The whole place would be up in flames.

'We've got backup at the scene,' Max was saying, *'but they can't get inside – the fire's too intense. And they haven't picked Ross up yet. They're going to get the helicopter in. I'm on my way too. I'm not that far.'*

'What's the situation on the ground?' Blake asked.

Max's voice had a wobble to it. *'Not great. They say the flames had already taken hold when our lot got there. The heat's cracked the downstairs windows and the curtains have gone up. They're doing what they can, but one of them...'* There was pause.

'What, Max?'

'One of the guys said they could see flames on the upper floor too, where Tara was.'

CHAPTER FORTY-FOUR

Fear had made Verity more alert, but her moves had become quick and panicky.

'Careful! Stay calm, Verity,' Tara said, shoving her phone inside her pocket.

But the woman was close to hysteria. She stepped backwards suddenly, away from the window, and Tara watched in horror as the edge of her dress caught one of the candles, knocking it onto the carpet.

Within seconds the hem of Verity's skirt was on fire, and she was screaming. Tara hadn't yet managed to close the sash window. There was no way they could escape via that route – the flames below were high and fierce – and the draught was now accelerating the progress of the fire inside, where the carpet had caught.

Tara grabbed a thick rug and flung it over Verity's dress, pressing it and her to the floor, as far away from the carpet fire as possible. Verity was still screaming and didn't seem to realise what Tara was trying to do. She struggled and tried to wriggle free.

'We can't run until the fire on your dress is out!' Tara shouted, trying to make herself heard above the woman's shouts and the sound of the fire. Who would have thought it would make so much noise? A loud roaring accompanied the wall of heat. There was a lot of smoke now too.

At last she managed to get Verity sorted. They needed to get out of there fast.

'Come on,' she said, dragging the woman by the arm. She touched the sitting room door handle but it didn't feel hot, so she yanked it open. For a second the fire in the room leapt even higher as the through draught intensified, before she slammed the door shut behind them.

She knew they didn't have long, and fire cut off their every escape route.

She swallowed down rising panic. *Think. You have to think.*

CHAPTER FORTY-FIVE

Blake had narrowly missed an oncoming car as he sped past the turning to Chatteris. There was no sign or sound of a fire engine. He could only hope they had one coming from Ramsey. He didn't want to take his attention off driving for one moment to call Max for an update.

At last, he turned onto the Forty Foot Bank. He slowed, but only by a fraction, concentrating furiously. If he went into the water now he'd be no help to anyone.

But then up ahead he saw the flames. The whole of the fenland sky was lit up, a wide, golden canopy, clouded with smoke. His mouth went dry, and he felt sick to the stomach.

And he'd sent Tara off whilst he and Patrick followed a wild goose chase. She ought to have brought Max with her at least. But would he have been able to help? Most likely he'd have lost two officers, not one.

The idea of losing Tara made pain shoot through him, hitting him at his core.

CHAPTER FORTY-SIX

Out on the landing, Tara had to make a split-second decision. Downstairs, the fire had already taken hold at the front door. And probably elsewhere, too. She might have less than a minute before the stairs went up in flames. If she went down there and that happened they'd be trapped, and death would be certain.

She steered Verity towards a back bedroom instead. She remembered from her and Blake's previous visit that there was a sloping roof at the rear of the building, where the ground floor jutted out beyond the upper one. It had looked like a slightly more modern extension. If that roof had an up-to-date fire-resistant ceiling underneath, it might be several minutes before it went up in smoke. But they'd still have to leap clear of the flames beyond it to escape.

She pushed the bedroom door shut behind them and rolled up the duvet from the bed, jamming it round the cracks underneath the door to slow the smoke that was seeping through. Only then did she shove the window open.

She took a sharp breath. Beyond the sloping roof she could see flames, fierce and intense. But as she'd hoped, the roof itself was still intact. For now.

She took the under sheet from the bed, plus another one she found in a cupboard, and knotted them together. Then she pushed the bed against the wall by the window and tied one end of the sheet chain to one of the bed's legs.

'Come on, Verity,' she said. 'We can hold onto this as we climb. It'll stop us slipping off the edge of the roof, into the flames.'

'I don't want to,' she said.

'We've got no choice.' Tara dragged at her arm until she gave in. At last she helped Verity clamber out, over the sill. She had to push the woman's hands round the bed sheets and into position before she'd grip them for herself. Shock seemed to have sent her back into a dreamlike state.

The snow and ice that must have been on the roof had turned to water. The tiles felt warm to the touch. Tara was glad of the sheets; the slope of the roof was steep and long, and without them they'd have been sure to slip in the wet.

Suddenly, through the thick flames and choking black smoke, she spotted Max down below. There was another officer too, but neither of them could get near the house because of the fire. The combustible material Stephen had banked up had worked horribly well. He'd made good use of all the discarded crates and other flammable junk that had been left at the house. There were flames everywhere and they weren't dying down. He must have been working on it ever since he'd left Verity earlier, only adding the finishing touches at the front of the house once Tara was safely inside, before dousing the whole lot with petrol. She'd definitely have smelt it if he'd performed that stage any earlier.

Beyond the end of the roof, not so very far off, was the outbuilding she and Blake had explored that day they'd come to interview Stephen Ross. The vision of her would-be killer flashed through her mind. He'd downed a lot of booze that day, but he'd come across as stone-cold sober. Slight though he was, she was starting to see how he must have been able to drink Lucas and Christian under the table. They hadn't known what they were dealing with.

If only they could make the leap to the outbuilding. It was a hell of a lot less high than the one Christian had attempted, but the gap was far too wide. And falling meant landing in a fire so hot they'd have no chance. She glanced for a second at Verity in her long dress, coughing and then gasping for air. Tara's own chest tightened as she breathed in the noxious smoke.

Help was so near, but utterly out of reach.

CHAPTER FORTY-SEVEN

Blake slewed his car to the side of the driveway. He had just enough presence of mind to leave room for the fire engine. Yet still there were no sirens. He knew they'd do their damnedest to reach them, but they might already be out dealing with some multi-casualty pile-up.

He couldn't take his eyes off the house as he threw himself from the car. His legs felt weak underneath him. Ross must have built the fire with care. Everywhere he looked, flames licked at the broken downstairs windows.

He was running full pelt, yelling as he went. 'Any sign? Has there been any sign? Where are they trapped?' The acrid, smoke-filled air caught at his lungs.

Max was waving and pointing. Blake's heart lurched as he saw Tara out on the roof with the woman who must be Verity Hipkiss by her side. How long had they got? How long before that bloody roof gave way and they fell into an abyss of flames? The entire lower floor was raging.

But suddenly he realised Tara was gesticulating. Not just for help in general, but at him. She was pointing. Pointing at the outbuilding. She couldn't be thinking of jumping it, surely? The gap was way too wide. And Ross had seen to it that the ring of fire round the house was several feet deep. If only they had a ladder to bridge the gap.

A ladder. *Hell.* Suddenly he got it. Inside the outbuilding, that day they'd looked round. There'd been something in there. A weird metal rack – for crop spraying maybe? It had been long.

Long enough? He waved back and ran to the concrete structure, shouting to Max and two other officers who were with him for help.

The light for the outbuilding wasn't working. Max pulled a torch from his coat pocket, switched it on and shone it round the interior, illuminating the object Blake was after.

'There!' he said. 'Help me. We need to get this up on the roof, and then see if it'll stretch far enough to reach Tara.' He hoped to God that it would. And that it would hold. It looked knackered, as though it had taken a knock in the middle at some stage in its long history.

They tugged and pulled, finally freeing it from the other junk around it. The area was less congested than it had been. All of the combustible stuff they'd seen previously had no doubt been used as fuel for the fire…

'Give me a leg up onto the roof and then shove it up for me to grab,' Blake shouted.

'Got it.' Max meshed his hands together and Blake was up in one go, onto the outbuilding's flat roof.

It took Max and both the other officers down below to manhandle the old bit of machinery and get it to the point where Blake could grab it. Then the other two gave Max a leg up as well, so he could help Blake drag it up onto the roof.

Blake looked across to Tara as he and Max hauled it into position. He could see flames reflected in her wide eyes. Below, the fire was all consuming, both inside and out. They couldn't have more than a minute before the roof gave. Nothing could withstand flames that strong.

'Ready?' he said to Max.

He nodded.

They pushed down on their end of the rack with all their might as they slid it over the gap. They had to keep it from sloping down into the fire. Behind them, he could hear that another of the officers had made it up onto the roof.

The rack stretched. It reached about a foot beyond the edge of the roof where Tara crouched. It rested there precariously, balanced on the sloping surface.

Tara had made Verity knot her long skirt up round her waist. Now, as the fourth officer joined Blake and Max, adding his weight to their end of the rack, Tara got Verity to start the crossing.

Blake held his breath. If she fell… or if the roof collapsed when she was halfway across, with Tara still stranded…

Suddenly, Verity swayed. Blake, Max and the others felt the strain on the rack. Their weight kept it from sliding to one side. Blake felt sweat drop from his forehead and held his breath. At last Hipkiss regained control. The fright seemed to have made her more determined, but it had cost precious seconds too.

Blake was desperate for Tara to start her journey as well, but he knew the rusty rack might not hold their combined weight at once.

At last Verity was with them, and they edged round so they could pull her onto the roof.

'Come on, Tara,' Blake shouted.

She'd crouched down and had one hand on the rack. What if Verity's journey had been as much as the structure could stand? What if it gave way now? He tried not to look at the flames below and willed Tara not to either.

She was edging her way forwards at last, but like Verity, she was struggling. The rack hadn't been designed for scrambling. She kept her eyes on them, but the way she moved told him the metal of the rack was uncomfortably hot.

At last she was within arm's reach.

And then the roof of the house collapsed.

The other end of the rack crashed down, but Tara must have felt it going. She scrambled fast, like a lithe animal acting on instinct, and in the same moment they were all grabbing her and dragging her up, releasing the rack.

Blake held her. He couldn't help himself. If anyone leaked this to *Not Now*, they'd have a field day. 'Good thinking, Batman,' he said at last, and heard her laugh in response. It turned to a cough halfway through.

It took Max, tapping him on the arm, to make him notice the medics that had arrived and wanted to take a look at her. To his shame, he hadn't registered that Verity Hipkiss had already been helped down.

In the distance, he was conscious of a fire engine's siren. He hadn't even heard the ambulance arrive.

CHAPTER FORTY-EIGHT

Stephen Ross had been picked up overnight. He'd made off on foot, once he realised Tara had spotted him and was still in a position to pass the information on to her colleagues. The thermal imaging camera in the helicopter had helped the team on the ground to track him down. It was clear that framing Philippa Cairncross had been part of the plan. Ross had used petrol cans from the Cairncross family garage when he was setting the fire at the house on the bank.

'Where's Detective Constable Thorpe?' he asked. He was in an interview room. Blake sat opposite him, with Wilkins at his side.

Blake didn't answer; didn't want the man to know anything about Tara. In fact, she was still in hospital. They'd kept both her and Verity Hipkiss in overnight to be on the safe side, but they were doing well – under the circumstances. He imagined nightmares might be a problem for a while to come.

The interview had already run for an hour. They had plenty of evidence of Ross's guilt, as far as the arson and attempted murder went, and, presented with a fait accompli, the man had started to talk. It was clear the anger and desire for revenge had built up to such an extent that now the dam was breached, he was going to give them what they needed. The recorder was going, and Fleming was watching from the observation suite.

'Tell us about Thom King,' Blake said. 'You drove at him, didn't you, hoping to collide with him and kill him?'

Anger flashed across Ross's features. 'It was a clumsy attempt. I let myself down because I was out of control. Letty had only just died, and Thom had joined in with the rest of them, *celebrating* her being taken from us whilst she was still in her prime!' The man paused for a moment and Blake could see he was fighting to contain his emotions. 'That hateful pagan ritual Ralph performed,' he went on at last, 'it was so false. And the moment we came back indoors, Thom started going on about his work again, and how excited he was to have got the keys to his new studio. Any emotion he'd displayed minutes earlier was only for show – that was crystal clear. I pretended to be interested in his new workspace so I could find out where it was.'

'Then you went out there and waited for him to drive by?' Blake said.

Ross nodded. 'I can hardly think of how stupid I was now. I even used my own car. It shows how weak Thom is; he was so scared that he didn't take it in.' The man's eyes focused on the middle distance for a moment. 'Though Thom was mainly drunk or stoned when we met anyway. Perhaps he'd never noticed what car I drove. Either way, I was lucky not to have been identified or reported by someone.

'I spent a week or two feeling shocked at what I'd almost done, and questioning my actions. But at the same time, the incident had made me conscious of what I might be capable of. I'd been planning to leave the Acolytes once Letty died. I'd only stayed as long as I did to try to protect her. But the attempt I'd made on Thom's life opened up the possibility in my head of getting my revenge on all of them. Wanting to bring them down made me stick around.

'And then – not long afterwards – Ralph showed me the manuscript of his last novel, *Out of the Blue*. He made a big thing about sharing it with me first.' He shook his head. 'I couldn't work out what was going on. I knew from the moment we met that he didn't think much of me. I was an amusement as far as he was concerned; it was fun to have me around as someone who had talent but who was eminently mockable. And yet there he was, singling me out for what he considered to be a great honour. I went with him to one of the downstairs back rooms at the house on the bank and he took out the manuscript. "I'm going to give this to the others to read too," he said, "but I wanted you to see it first." He gave me that lazy smile of his. "I know how much you'll appreciate the dedication. *To T, who managed to escape unscathed. You are blessed indeed.*" As soon as he said the words I knew the T must be Letty. The bastard always called her Titty and he was aware of how much I hated it. He watched my reaction and I could see the laughter in his eyes. Then he said, "When I say she escaped unscathed, I mean she was never tainted by age, of course. She didn't escape me. I managed to bed her before she lost her bloom.'"

Ross's eyes were lit with fury. Blake could understand why, even if he could never condone his actions.

'And then Ralph added: "Don't look so crestfallen. I'm sure you wouldn't have wanted her taken from us before she'd experienced life. And it wasn't as though she was ever interested in *you*, was it?" Then he patted me on the arm. "My poor Stephen," he said. "The entire gang have been prowling round her. Had you not noticed? I had her first, but I doubt I was the last.'"

'You believed him?' Wilkins said.

Ross had his head in his hands. 'About the others? No! No. Well, I don't know.' His voice was muffled. 'I didn't believe Letty would willingly sleep with *any* of them, but I believed they'd have taken advantage; coerced her into it. It must have been before she got really ill – months earlier – and yet I hadn't known.' He took a great shuddering breath. 'When I left the house on the bank that day I knew I had to make them pay; the whole lot of them, starting with Ralph. When I went after Thom in my car the resonance with Ralph's book – where the hero is mown down on Route 66 – was a coincidence. But as I sat there that evening, planning, I realised how fitting it would be to copy the causes of death he'd used in his novels.

'He'd treated the subject so lightly, showing it in such a glorious light. I wanted him and the other Acolytes to realise that there's nothing pleasing or romantic about dying. What better way to drive home my message than to make each of them share the fate of one of Ralph's heroes in turn? To see how they liked it when fiction became reality?

'Tampering with Ralph's garage lamp was my first, more sophisticated attempt to take action.'

He described in detail how he'd gone to the house when he knew the family were away, walked straight into the garage, just as Tara had, and got to work. He claimed it was the only booby trap he'd left, but Blake had a team giving every accessible place at Madingley Road a thorough once-over.

After that, Ross told them how he'd found, caught and kept the grass snake. He'd gone out to the put the snake in the car after dark on the night Ralph died, when the house's curtains had been closed. It explained why no one had seen what went on.

'Why didn't you try to get rid of the crate, once you'd finished using it?' Blake asked. He didn't need the information, but he was curious.

Ross looked irritated suddenly and Blake was reminded of the man when he and Tara had first been to interview him. 'Initially, it was because I never thought anyone would find out about the snake. Once Tara Thorpe got so inquisitive about Ralph's death, I started to wonder if some kind of evidence had been found. But at that point, I realised leaving the crate where it was might be safest. If it was found and recognised for what it was, it would point to someone from outside our group being responsible. After all, one of us could easily have removed it – broken it up, perhaps, or taken it to the dump. It would have been a much bigger risk for someone like Philippa Cairncross to start marching around the place, disposing of the evidence. I guessed you'd assume that she, or maybe Tess Curtis, must be responsible – and that they'd felt too conspicuous to come and get rid of it again.'

Blake glanced at Wilkins, who looked sour.

'Why were you so keen to frame Philippa Cairncross?' Blake said. 'Seems as though she hated her father just as much as you did.'

Stephen Ross's lips went white. 'That may be, but she's just as full of spite as Ralph was. We came across her at a party once. She made comments about us that were clearly meant to be overheard. She called Letty a pale-faced drip. It was just after she'd been diagnosed with cancer. She wasn't usually pale. She was in shock. My one regret is that I haven't managed to pay Philippa back. Maybe I will one day.' He smiled. 'I haven't given up. It was my main aim when I locked her mother in the archive store. I thought it was highly likely she'd be rescued – or even call for help herself. I didn't know if she'd got a mobile on her. But if she had died, it would have served her right too. She bought into Ralph's ideals and went along with them.'

'What makes you say that?' Wilkins asked.

'Any right-minded person would have divorced him. She was complicit. It's unforgiveable.'

Blake felt his head start to ache. He could understand Ross's pain, but his way of looking at things was totally skewed. He'd been surrounded by a group of self-serving and in some cases amoral individuals, but in response he'd turned to murder, a far worse crime than any they'd committed, however abhorrent they were.

'How did you know Mrs Cairncross would be alone, when you went to lock her in the archive store?' It was one more detail that had been bugging him.

'I'd been keeping an eye on the house.' The man smiled. 'I live on Grange Road, don't forget. I can see comings and goings just by looking out of my flat's attic window.'

It all figured. His street led straight onto Madingley Road. 'Tell us what happened the night Lucas Everett died,' Blake said.

Ross laughed. 'You were so obsessed, weren't you, with the idea of someone he admired egging him on? I remember you asking me who I thought would have had enough influence. But you don't have to be the one everyone looks up to, to wield power.'

Suddenly, the man slumped in his chair. He adopted an eager, innocent and slightly rueful expression. It was frightening to see what a different proposition he seemed to be, when he put on that guise.

'I was always the underdog,' he said, smiling again. 'The timid one. And that was perfect. I set the whole adventure with Lucas up as a tribute to Ralph. I'd arranged to stay at that campsite I told you about, but it was easy enough to travel to Suffolk for the event.

'I told Lucas I wanted to do something crazy in Ralph's memory, but that I was scared. Then I wondered aloud about swimming out to sea, as far as I could go, daring myself to go that bit further. But then I said I'd never have the guts; I wasn't like the rest of the gang.' His blue eyes seemed to come alive with the memory of his success.

'It was at that point that Lucas started to encourage me. "Come on," he said, "it's about time we got you involved with some of our little exploits." He was so pleased to have the chance to take me under his wing and show me just what a brave guy he was. So much more capable, and so much more daring than me. I protested and said we should write notes to leave on the beach in case we didn't make it back. He laughed at that, but he wrote one, all the same. I wrote one too and left it with his – only of course I removed it again when I swam back to shore.'

'How could you be sure you'd make it back?' Wilkins said.

The smile was there again – in Ross's eyes as much as anything. 'We started to swim out,' he said. 'And I just kept going. On and on. After establishing so firmly how weak and pathetic I was in comparison to Lucas, he couldn't very well stop before I did. Imagine how he'd lose face. Then, when I reckoned I'd pushed him beyond his limit, I said I thought I might have to give in and swim back.

'And even then, he couldn't immediately follow me. He had to go further, to keep up the pretence that he was Mr Tough Guy. So he laughed – he sounded pretty breathless by then – and went that bit further.'

'You took a risk yourself, with your own safety,' Wilkins said.

'Not much. You see, I've always been a good swimmer. Then, when Letty got ill, I did sponsored swims to raise money for cancer charities. The rest of the Acolytes didn't take any notice of course – they were too busy with their own concerns – so my ability to swim a long way in tough conditions wasn't something Lucas had banked on.' He put his head on one side. 'And I suggested we have a few drinks before the swim, to keep out the cold and build up courage. Only I pretended not to like the vodka he'd chosen. I brought my own bottle instead – gin on the label, but water inside.'

'You bought the same vodka Lucas chose, to give to Christian Beatty, the night he died,' Blake said.

Ross pulled a face. 'Yes. So sorry about that. I was playing with you. And I still thought you'd suspect Philippa Cairncross over me. And I was right. You did.'

He seemed to have forgotten he was now sitting in a police station with a watertight case against him for attempted murder.

'My reputation as tame also meant it was perfectly natural for me to discourage Ralph from driving after he'd drunk too much the night he died.' Ross raised an eyebrow. 'But of course, I knew the more I protested, the more determined he'd be to set off home. By the time I'd finished fussing over him, he'd had several for the road, just to make sure I knew he was ignoring my every word.'

Blake thought back and cursed himself for not picking up on that. Talk about the perfect cover.

He could see why Stephen Ross had hated Ralph Cairncross. He could only imagine the intense hurt and fury the older man had caused when he'd celebrated the death of the young woman Ross had loved – not to mention when he'd bragged about sleeping with her – but this wasn't a case of a single crime of passion, committed by someone who'd been pushed to the brink. The man in front of him had had all the humanity drained out of him – if he'd had it in the first place. His love for Letty and his anger at Ralph Cairncross's repugnant views didn't mean he wasn't cruel and calculating himself.

'You really blew it last night, didn't you?' Blake was sick of seeing the man's satisfied expression. 'Letting two people see you setting a fire that was intended to kill them ranks as pretty stupid.'

Ross's eyes flashed. 'I was within a hair's breadth of succeeding. Your colleague happened on the truth just a moment too soon. But it took her long enough, and I believe it was down to chance rather than detection.'

'Then you believe wrong,' Blake said. 'The evidence she'd gathered slotted into place the moment she realised you'd taken down the photos in the house labelled "Titty".' He could feel Patrick's eyes on him, but the evidence had mainly been Tara's. And she was the one who'd taken it seriously. 'But if you were so confident she didn't suspect you, why try to kill her?'

Ross shrugged. 'The fire was only meant for Verity at first. To pay her back. She was glad when Letty died; I could see it in her eyes. It meant there was no more competition for Ralph's affection – and his patronage. But when she came up with the very theory I'd been promoting to the police – that Philippa was guilty – I saw how easy it would be for her to get Tara Thorpe over to the house on the bank, ready to pass on her worries and accusations. And then the idea of getting rid of both of them was just too tempting.' His eyes were wild now. 'The more time went on, the more I hated your detective constable. I'd been wondering whether to add her to my list of targets. She was interviewing all Ralph's contacts – she must have known just how poisonous he was. But instead of letting his death go, she kept digging – preferring to victimise whoever had sought to harm him, rather than let the matter lie. What kind of person would do that?'

'Someone who's paid to uphold the law.' Blake's voice rose so suddenly that he had the pleasure of seeing Ross jump. It was the first time during the interview his words had had any effect. The breakthrough didn't stop him from wanting to thump something.

But Ross was already back to justifying his views. 'Ralph Cairncross deserved to die,' he said. 'You'd have hated him too, if he'd treated someone you loved that way.'

'I would,' Blake said, 'to my very core. But I would never have schemed to murder him and those who apparently shared his views.'

By the end of the interview, Stephen Ross had also given an account of his evening with Christian Beatty. As with Lucas, Ross had kidded Beatty into thinking he was getting as drunk as his companion was. And once again, he'd played the scared friend, who'd always wished he had the guts to do something brave. They'd hatched the plan to try to leap the gap, and Ross had begun to scale the building with Beatty, choosing a route that wasn't overlooked. But when they were nearly at the top, he'd told Beatty he'd had a change of heart. It was a crazy thing to do. Why didn't they go back down again, sober up and get some coffee? If Beatty had agreed, that would have been that, but of course, he hadn't. He was fuelled by vodka and bravado. He'd laughed at Ross for losing his bottle. By the time he leapt, Ross had climbed quietly down and was well out of sight.

CHAPTER FORTY-NINE

Blake was writing up notes and trying to get Stephen Ross's features out of his head. He kept thinking of small things he'd missed – like the fact that the man had recognised Tara when they'd first shown up to interview him at the house on the bank. He'd said it was because he'd seen her in *Not Now* magazine, but there was no way a man like Ross would normally read that sort of publication. He'd made some disparaging remark about it in the same breath. No, the fact was he'd followed her, and deliberately researched her. And then, when she'd turned up, he realised Blake had clocked the look of recognition on his face, so he'd made an excuse to explain himself. Blake should have seen through that from the start. Tara hadn't had the chance, she'd been looking at her phone…

He was glad when Gail on reception interrupted his thoughts. She said Paul Kemp was in the front entrance, asking to see him. Tara's renegade police officer? What the hell did he want? Blake was curious to meet him face to face. He was still wondering if he and Tara were more than just friends.

The man he went to collect was taller than him – around six foot two – and looked as though he'd been around the block. His nose had been broken more than once, he guessed, and he was a good ten years older than Blake. But he had a ready, roguish grin he imagined Tara would appreciate. She liked people who were straightforward; not pretending to be something they weren't.

'What can I do for you?' Blake said, after he'd introduced himself and shown Kemp to an interview room.

The man grinned again. 'I've got something for you,' he said, and handed Blake two USB sticks. 'You can copy the files off. No viruses, I promise.'

'What's on them?'

'I'd rather talk you through the contents once we can look at it together,' he said.

Blake was too intrigued – and exhausted – to argue. He'd been up all night and Paul Kemp didn't have the air of someone who was trying to put one over on him. Besides, Tara trusted him, and that counted for something – even if he did wonder about their relationship. He went to fetch his laptop.

'This one first,' Kemp said, pushing the silver USB stick forward.

'Okay.' Blake shoved it into the port on his machine and a folder of jpeg files popped up. What the hell was going on? He double-clicked on the first one and was presented with a picture of Patrick Wilkins, getting out of his Ford in what appeared to be the car park of a country pub called the Dog and Gun, according to the lit sign outside. It was evening time, and recent; there was snow on the ground. He right clicked and checked the image's properties. It had been taken at 9 p.m. on Sunday.

The next image showed a view through the pub window. It must have been taken with a long lens. Patrick again, with a woman by his side. He recognised her as Shona Kennedy, Tara's ex-colleague from *Not Now* magazine and author of what everyone at the station was now referring to as 'that article'.

Next came one of the pair of them standing together. Patrick's arm was round Shona's shoulders, and opposite him was Giles Troy, *Not Now*'s editor – a foul man with no conscience, as Blake knew to his cost. It looked as though introductions were being made. The men were shaking hands, both looking remarkably pleased to see each other.

Blake felt his blood pressure rise, anger flooding through his system like electricity.

Later photos in the series showed Shona Kennedy and Patrick outside the pub again, kissing good night. They were making a thorough job of it, too.

Blake looked across at Kemp, trying to keep his voice steady. 'How come you've got these?'

He shrugged. 'I do PI and security work. When I'm investigating, I specialise in errant partners, but I decided to use my skills for other purposes whilst I'm here in Cambridge. Tara Thorpe on your team's an old mate. She mentioned Patrick Wilkins. I could tell he was a thorn in her side, and she doesn't need another one of those.'

Blake couldn't help but agree.

'When I turned up at her house a couple of weeks back I was mighty curious to know more about the case she's been working on.' He laughed. 'She warned me off, of course, but I needed something to occupy me. In the end, I figured I'd set myself the challenge of finding out more about this Wilkins. In my experience, his sort always have skeletons in their cupboards. Even so, I ended up with more than I bargained for. Talk about hitting the jackpot.'

'You know who his companions are then?' Blake said, indicating Shona Kennedy and Giles Troy.

'I do now,' Kemp said. 'I followed them into the pub, once I'd taken the photos outside.' Then his grin broadened. 'The other USB stick's got the recording I made of their conversation. It's a bit muffled in places, I had to put the microphone on the seat behind me, half under my coat. But I think you'll get the gist. Makes it quite clear where the magazine got its recent scoop.'

Blake had still been reeling over the information on Wilkins – torn between fury and satisfaction at the fact that he'd finally got something on his DS – when he got his second visitor of the day. It took him over an hour to hear Dr Monica Cairncross's grievances.

Tara had kept her partially up to date with the investigation into her brother's death, and of course she'd seen the latest highlights on the news. Now she wanted to make a formal complaint about the way Wilkins had handled the case back in the autumn. After she'd left, Blake added it to the list of matters to discuss with DCI Fleming the following day.

But Dr Cairncross's complaint was the least of Patrick's worries. As Blake left the station he enjoyed wishing the man a good evening, knowing that in less than twelve hours they'd be hauling him over the coals.

As he made his journey back to Fen Ditton, Blake finally had enough headspace to think properly about his personal life. It seemed like an eternity since he'd had dinner with Agneta and Frans, just two nights earlier. He'd told Agneta that he didn't know what to do, but in that moment he'd realised that he'd have to take action of some kind. He and Babette couldn't go on as they were. For the four years since they'd got back together he'd refused to even think about the possibility of ending the marriage. If it crossed his consciousness, the image of Kitty immediately filled his head: the thought of her crying as her parents once again broke apart. She wouldn't understand. How could he do that to her?

But as he cycled back towards Fen Ditton, past Tara's empty house (he'd heard they were keeping her in an extra night), he knew in his heart of hearts that he wasn't doing Kitty much good as a father in the current set-up. So long as he could retain the right to spend time with her, it might be better for all of them if he and Babette called it a day.

The thought of the upset he'd cause still weighed heavy in his mind, but he also felt a lightening inside. It was the answer. It was a mess, but one he hadn't made, and if the status quo wasn't working, it was better to make a decisive move. It would be the quickest way towards a new settled future for Kitty. Years of rows and prevarication were hardly going to help.

He'd wait until after Christmas and then he'd have a heart-to-heart with Babette. The new year would be tough, but the decision felt right.

He felt different as he entered his house. The constant tension he'd dealt with had lifted and he could breathe more easily. After he'd been to hug Kitty – who was doing some colouring before bed – and greet Babette, who was reading a book, he went upstairs. He wanted to have a shower, to wash away the previous thirty-six hours, and then just to sleep.

But inside the bathroom he realised the day hadn't finished with him yet.

There was a used pregnancy test on the side of bath. And there, in the window, was a strong, blue line. Positive. He picked it up and looked at it more closely, as though it might suddenly disappear. He turned back towards the door and realised Babette was standing there.

'When?' It was all he could say. They hadn't had sex since she'd mentioned wanting to have another child. He managed to refrain from asking her if it was his.

She bit her lip. 'Sorry, Garstin. We conceived about three months ago.' She sighed. 'I had a feeling it wasn't what you wanted, so instead of telling you straight away, I thought I'd sort of pave the way by raising the subject, suggesting we go for it, you know? And then you really backed off, so I know you're not going to be pleased. But I thought I'd better tell you before I started to show.'

He felt an immediate heavy sinking in his chest. It was a minute before he could take it in. And that was the thing about Babette. She was never straightforward. Never one hundred per cent honest.

She was always managing information – and whether she meant to or not, manipulating him.

'But you were taking the pill, weren't you?' he said at last. 'I mean, I offered to be the one to take responsibility for contraception way back, but you said it was all covered.'

She was looking at the floor now. 'Guess I must have missed a dose,' she said. And now her eyes met his. They were slightly damp. 'I made a mistake, Garstin.'

A mistake. It wasn't the first time she'd looked at him with sad eyes and told him she'd messed up.

'Say you're pleased now?' she said, walking towards him slowly. 'It's Christmas in a few days. By next year we can be a proper family of four.'

At that moment, Kitty appeared just behind her, her eyes dancing. Blake had a feeling he wasn't the first person to hear Babette's news – or to have that seemingly perfect vision of the future held up before them.

CHAPTER FIFTY

After the year Bea had had, Tara had never expected Christmas day to be so much fun.

'Blimey, Bea,' Kemp said. 'I don't know how you do this on a regular basis.'

Tara's mother's cousin threw a tea towel at him and laughed. 'Wimp. Look at you, all muscle and cunning, but you struggle with serving eight guests a Christmas lunch!'

'Come on, you two,' Tara said. 'No fighting in here. I've just put out the flutes. It's our turn now they're all sorted. And against the odds, there are no lumps in Kemp's gravy, so I think we're all set.' She glanced from one of them to the other. They were both rosy cheeked and grinning. Not unusual for Kemp but nothing short of a miracle for Bea, on today of all days. He'd worked wonders since he'd shown up and thrown her routine out of kilter.

Earlier in the day Tara had wondered what would happen when he moved on again, but Kemp tended to have a lasting effect. There was a new look of purposefulness in Bea's eye, and she'd seen her drawing up plans to streamline her operation.

It was after they'd eaten, and were sitting round sharing cracker jokes, that a text came in on her phone. She'd already exchanged messages with her mum, and Matt from *Not Now*. She glanced at the screen.

Blake.

Thought I'd save this news for Christmas day, unless Kemp's already stolen my thunder. Patrick's suspended, pending an investigation.

She'd just turned to Kemp, ready to insist he fill her in, when a second text came through.

Blake again. It was shorter than the last.

Happy Christmas

And suddenly, in her mind's eye, she was back on the outbuilding roof, just after she'd escaped the fire. She remembered dimly the feeling of Blake's arms around her, holding her tight.

She fumbled over her reply, trying to work out what to say. How could it take so long to settle on *You too*?

In the end, it was a good five minutes before she remembered to ask Kemp what he'd done to scupper her DS.

A LETTER FROM CLARE

Thank you so much for reading *Death on the River*. I do hope you enjoyed it – it was great fun to write. If you'd like to keep up to date with all of my latest releases, you can sign up at the following link. Your email address will never be shared, and you can unsubscribe at any time.

www.bookouture.com/clare-chase

My idea for this book came to me after rereading *Murder is Easy* by Agatha Christie. If you haven't read it, I don't want to spoil the plot. However, it's not giving too much away to say it got me wondering how a perpetrator in a modern-day setting could get away with orchestrating a series of deaths without making people suspicious. As ever, I've used Cambridge and the surrounding area as the backdrop. The Fens provide the perfect remote, atmospheric location for a murder mystery, and Cambridge's mix of artists, writers and academics was useful for this story too. (Though the ones I've met in real life aren't a bit like the ones in this book, thank goodness!)

If you have time, I'd love it if you were able to **write a review of** *Death on the River*. Feedback is incredibly useful, and it also makes a huge difference in helping new readers discover my books for the first time.

Alternatively, if you'd like to contact me personally, you can reach me via my website, Facebook page, Twitter or Instagram. I love hearing from readers.

Again, thank you so much for deciding to spend some time reading *Death on the River*. I'm looking forward to sharing my next book with you very soon.

With all best wishes,
Clare x

www.clarechase.com

@ClareChaseAuthor

@ClareChase_

ACKNOWLEDGEMENTS

As always, very much love and huge thanks to my wonderful family, Charlie, George and Ros, for their good humour, encouragement, patience and understanding. Love and thanks also to my parents, Penny and Mike, and to Phil and Jenny, David and Pat, Helen, the Westfield gang, Andrea, Shelly, Mark, my lovely colleagues at the RSC, as well as my wider family and friends. Special gratitude to Margaret for taking the time to show me round areas of the Fens I hadn't visited before, and also to Nigel Adams, fire forensic consultant, for sharing his expertise so generously. His input was fascinating and any mistakes I've made are my own.

In addition, I'd like to say how much I appreciate the writer friends I've made, including the truly wonderful Bookouture gang – I really enjoy being part of such a friendly and supportive group. Thanks as well to the wonderful book bloggers I've got to know, whose generosity, kindness and enthusiasm has been amazing. I'm also hugely grateful to my readers. Getting messages via my website, Twitter and Facebook page is truly special.

Lastly, but very importantly, massive thanks to my inspiring and insightful editor Kathryn Taussig, whose ideas, advice and encouragement have been second to none, as well as to Maisie Lawrence, whose thoughts and ideas have been so valuable. I'd also like to relay heartfelt thanks to Peta Nightingale, as well as to Alexandra Holmes, Fraser, Liz, and everyone involved in the book production and marketing process. And massive thanks as ever to Noelle Holten and Kim Nash, who do the most incredible amount to publicise our books and support us. I feel so lucky to be published and promoted by such a wonderful team.

Made in the USA
Columbia, SC
12 October 2020

22685281R00205